"From the minute I showed up here I've rubbed you the wrong way."

Harper stared at him in helpless fascination. This was the Ashton Croft she'd been dying to get to know. The dashing adventurer who'd gamely hiked into dangerous surroundings to share a meal with locals and educate his viewers about what was unique to the area. It was always fascinating and often stuck with her long after the credits rolled.

"If you knew that, why didn't you try rubbing me the right way?" Harper regretted the words the instant they left her lips. They sounded like flirtatious banter. "What I meant was…"

Ashton shook his head, stopping her flow of words. A low chuckle vibrated in his chest. "Please don't try to explain it," he said. "I think it's the first honest thing you've ever said to me."

* * *

A Taste of Temptation
is part of the Las Vegas Nights trilogy:
Where love is the riskiest gamble of all!

al Hotline

A TASTE OF TEMPTATION

BY
CAT SCHIELD

Published in Great Britain 2014
by Mills & Boon, an imprint of Harlequin (UK) Limited,
Eton House, 18-24 Paradise Road, Richmond, Surrey, TW9 1SR

© 2014 Catherine Schield

ISBN: 978-0-263-91473-3

51-0714

Harlequin (UK) Limited's policy is to use papers that are natural, renewable and recyclable products and made from wood grown in sustainable forests. The logging and manufacturing processes conform to the legal environmental regulations of the country of origin.

Printed and bound in Spain
by Blackprint CPI, Barcelona

Cat Schield has been reading and writing romance since high school. Although she graduated from college with a BA in business, her idea of a perfect career was writing books for Mils & Boon. And now, after winning the Romance Writers of America 2010 Golden Heart Award for series contemporary romance, that dream has come true. Cat lives in Minnesota with her daughter, Emily, and their Burmese cat. When she's not writing sexy, romantic stories for Mills & Boon® Desire™, she can be found sailing with friends on the St. Croix River, or in more exotic locales, like the Caribbean and Europe. She loves to hear from readers. Find her at www.catschield.com. Follow her on Twitter, @catschield.

To my MFW-BIAW Golden Girls: Nan Dixon,
Lizbeth Selvig and Nancy Holland.
Thanks for keeping me motivated and inspired.
You ladies rock.

One

As soon as Harper Fontaine stepped from her lively casino into her stylish new restaurant, she checked near the door for a rolling black leather duffel. Ashton Croft's *go* bag. She loathed the thing. It represented everything that drove her crazy about the celebrity chef. His tendency to show up without warning. The way he thrived on excitement, and when none could be found, his knack for either stirring it up or heading out of town on some adventure or another.

But she needed the bag to be there because it would mean that Ashton had shown up for today's head chef interview. Batouri's grand opening was two weeks away. When the original deadline for the opening of the restaurant had come and gone without it being ready, Harper had questioned the wisdom of asking an unreliable television personality to start a restaurant in her hotel.

True, the buzz about the grand opening had drawn all eyes and scads of publicity to her hotel, Fontaine Ciel, but was the attention worth the stress Ashton had heaped on those in charge of making the restaurant a success? Carlo Perrault, the restaurant's manager, wasn't sleeping and had grown irritable these past two months. Harper was grinding her teeth at night. The headaches induced by this behavior had forced to her seek medical help. She now wore a mouth guard when she went to bed. Slipping the awkward plastic device into her mouth, she would lie on the mattress and wish she had some idea what happened to Ashton's initial enthusiasm about the restaurant.

The longer the filming of *The Culinary Wanderer* had gone in Indonesia, the more difficult she'd found working with him to be. They'd had to postpone Batouri's launch date twice because of scheduling conflicts with his travels for his wildly popular television series.

Which was why Harper refused to delay again. The restaurant's black floors were polished. The chandeliers had been hung from the high cove ceiling. Their light illuminated the white napkins and crystal wine goblets on the black tables. Ten days earlier the painters had completed the metallic gold treatment on the three wide pillars down the center of the room. Near the fully stocked bar, the assistant manager was putting the waitstaff through their paces.

But for two things, Batouri was ready to open. Two key things. It lacked a head chef and a menu.

And seeing that Ashton's *go* bag wasn't in its usual place, it looked as if that menu was going to have to wait. Harper glanced at her watch. It was exactly four in the afternoon. She'd told Ashton the interview would happen at three to make certain he arrived on time. Playing these sorts of games wasn't in her nature, but she was at her wits' end in dealing with the celebrity chef.

She dialed her assistant. Mary picked up on the second ring.

Harper got straight to business. "Did Ashton Croft call to say he'd be delayed?"

"No."

"And his plane was supposed to land in Las Vegas at one?"

"Yes, I confirmed his itinerary this morning."

Damn the man. Two weeks ago Ashton had promised Harper his full attention starting today. She should have known better. "Thank you, Mary. Let me know if you hear from him."

"Sure thing." Harper was on the verge of disconnecting the call when something Mary said caught her attention. "…in your office."

Carlo Perrault emerged from the kitchen, a scowl on his handsome face. The forty-six-year-old restaurant manager was known for his composure, but even he was showing signs of stress at all the things that still needed to be done. "We have a problem."

"I'm sorry, Mary. Who did you say was in my office?"

"Your mother."

"My mother?" Surprise kept her from guarding her tone. Aware of Carlo's scrutiny, Harper turned her back on him and stepped away to give herself some semblance of privacy. "Did she say what she was doing in Vegas?"

"No, but she seems upset."

"Just upset?" Harper mused.

Penelope Fontaine wouldn't have left her elegant condo in Boca Raton to fly two thousand miles to visit Harper unless something was seriously wrong. And if it was, why had Penelope come to Harper? Usually Penelope took her problems to her father-in-law, Henry Fontaine.

"You once mentioned she smokes when she's agitated," Mary said. "She's starting her second cigarette."

"She's smoking in my office?" Harper pinched the bridge of her nose. She wanted to insist Mary tell her mother to put out the cigarette, but knew that would be asking too much of her assistant. "I'll be there in five minutes."

"You can't leave," Carlo protested. "Croft has started the interview without you."

"Great," she muttered. "How long has he been here?"

"Long enough to taste everything Chef Cole has prepared." Carlo's dour expression was enough to tell Harper that this interview was going the way the other seven had.

"Mary, looks like I am going to be a while. Get my mother settled in a suite and I'll visit her as soon as I'm done here." Harper hung up and turned to Carlo. "If he messes this interview up, I'm going to kill him."

Carlo offered her a tight nod of understanding.

The hostility in the two male voices hit her before she'd reached the food pass area.

"There's nothing wrong with the sear on these scallops," one of the men protested, his tone both arrogant and simmering with hostility. "And the sauce is not under seasoned."

"It's obvious the only thing worse than your culinary skills is your wretched palate."

Pain stabbed Harper's temple as she recognized the voice of the second speaker. Ashton Croft had been interviewing head chefs for two months, rejecting one after another for failing to live up to his exacting standards.

Harper snapped her vertebrae into a stiff line and stepped into the meticulously organized, stainless-steel kitchen. As was her habit, her gaze swung immediately to Ashton. He dominated the room with his presence. Tall and imposing in his chef whites, he stood glaring at Chef Cole, muscular arms crossed over his broad chest.

He hadn't yet noticed her, hadn't turned his Persian-blue eyes her way, hadn't noted her slight breathlessness. His passion for food sent his innate charisma soaring. She cursed the hero worship that she couldn't completely squash despite her professionalism. She was unequal parts frustrated with the restaurateur and enamored of the dashing adventurer.

His travels fascinated her. Some of the things Ashton had eaten made Harper shudder, but he boldly consumed whatever he was offered. She'd spend her entire life knowing exactly where she was going, and the way he allowed random opportunities to push him into unexpected and sometimes startling discoveries both unnerved and captivated her. Watching his television shows had made her realize just how safe her world was. And a seed of restlessness had sprouted inside her.

With effort Harper ripped her gaze from Ashton and turned her attention to the other chef. Taking in the interviewee's blazing eyes and clenched fists, she donned her most diplomatic expression and entered the war zone.

"Good afternoon, gentlemen." She stepped into the middle of the clash with calm authority. She wanted Chef Dillon Cole to run Batouri's kitchen. He was an excellent chef as well as a strong, organized leader. Harper restrained a weary sigh. Of all the candidates, he'd been Harper's first choice for head chef. It was why she'd saved his interview until the last. This close to the restaurant's already delayed grand opening, she had the leverage she needed to force Ashton's hand. "I stopped by to see how things are going."

"Taste this," Ashton commanded, pushing the plate in her direction without ever taking his eyes off Cole. "Tell me if you think it's up to Batouri standards."

The first time he'd done this she'd been flattered that he wanted her opinion. After the third candidate had been rejected, she'd realized he was merely using her to drive home a point. If someone with no culinary experience could taste the inferior quality of the entrées, the chef who'd prepared the dish had failed.

Harper made no move to do as he'd asked. "May I speak to you privately for a moment?"

"Can it wait?" Ashton never took his eyes off Chef Cole.

She fought to keep her frustration on a tight leash. How would it play out on social media if the general manager of Fontaine Ciel was recorded shrieking empty threats at the famous Chef Croft?

"No."

Her conviction came through loud and clear, snagging Ashton's complete attention. His laser-sharp blue eyes scanned her expression. Sexual interest flared low in her belly. It traveled upward, leaving every nerve it touched sizzling with anticipation. She cursed silently. Her body's tendency to overreact to the man's rakish good looks and raw masculinity had distracted her all too often. She was not her professional best around him.

Once again Harper reminded herself that the flesh and blood man standing before her was unreliable and unconcerned with how his priorities impacted those around her. The dashing adventurer he portrayed on television was entertaining to watch as he charmed locals by listening attentively to their stories and sampling the regional specialties. But when it came to the routine matters necessary to start a restaurant, he easily became distracted.

Lips tightening, Ashton nodded. "Excuse us," he said to Chef Cole, and gestured for Harper to return to the dining room. "What's so important?" he demanded as soon as they'd exited the kitchen.

"The restaurant opens in two weeks."

"I'm aware of that."

"The press releases have gone out. There will be no further postponement."

"Understood."

She tamped down her irritation. "We need a head chef."

"I will take charge of the kitchen."

If only that were true. "I need someone I can rely on to be here every day."

His nod indicated he saw where she was going. "You want me to hire Cole."

"The last time I was in Chicago I ate at his restaurant. It was excellent. I was looking forward to tasting what he'd created today."

"You didn't miss much."

Harper spent a minute studying Ashton. There was something different about him today. Usually he breezed in, found something wrong with the construction or the fixtures and then stirred up everyone associated with the project before coming up with a fix for whatever he perceived wrong. Working with him had been stressful and invigorating, but in the end the restaurant was far better for his interference.

Today he seemed to be creating trouble for the sake of drama rather than because he had real issues with Chef Cole.

"Is there something going on with you?"

Her abrupt change in topic startled him into a moment of uncertainty. "Not a thing. Why?"

"Because you were on time for a change."

"I believe I was an hour early."

She gestured toward the door, making no effort to correct him. "And there's no *go* bag."

"*Go* bag?" he echoed.

"The black leather bag that you bring with you everywhere."

"You mean my rolling duffel?" He pointed toward a far corner of the restaurant where the bag sat beside a semicircular corner booth. "Why do you call it a *go* bag?"

"Because it's your crutch."

Amusement narrowed his eyes. "My crutch."

"When things get too tedious you make some excuse, grab the bag and head off in search of greater excitement."

"Leaving you behind to clean up after me?"

She let a brief silence answer his question. "You've interviewed and rejected seven head chef candidates."

He cocked an eyebrow. "What's your point?"

"I need you to hire someone. Chef Cole is that person."

"You didn't taste his entrées." When it came to food, Ashton was a creative genius. She wasn't surprised he couldn't find someone who was capable of living up to his demanding criteria. "I found them lacking."

"He has the experience and the organization to run this kitchen the way I expect it to be run—"

Ashton interrupted. "When you came to me about opening a restaurant in your hotel, I thought you understood that I had the last and final word on all creative."

"Creative, yes, but this is about the management of the kitchen." Which was why she was determined to get her way. She'd been able to control costs and manage the construction schedule, working hard to manifest Ashton's vision for the restaurant without exceeding budget.

In that respect their working relationship meshed.

"But the kitchen is where the magic happens."

"Except there's no magic happening because we don't have a menu or a head chef to work with the kitchen staff." Pain shot through her head. She winced.

"We will be ready for the opening." His absolute confidence should have shut down all her worries.

"But—"

"Trust me." His deep voice broke into her protest, his soothing cadence catching her off guard.

"I do." That's not what she'd meant to say.

But she knew it was true. They might have had completely different philosophies on how to accomplish something, but he had proven time and again he was as capable of getting things done as she. Deep down she knew he'd plan a fantastic menu and win the love of customers and critics alike.

That it would happen in the frantic last hours before the door opened was what made her crazy.

Famous dimples flashing, he countered, "No, you don't. From the minute I showed up here I've rubbed you the wrong way."

Harper stared at him in helpless fascination. This was the Ashton Croft she'd been dying to get to know. The man who charmed smiles from people who'd seen nothing but hardship and violence. The dashing adventurer who'd on occasion gamely hiked into dangerous surroundings to share a meal with locals and educate his viewers about what was unique to the area. It was always intriguing and often stuck with her long after the credits rolled.

"If you knew that, why didn't you try rubbing me the right way?" Harper regretted the words the instant they left her lips. They sounded like flirtatious banter. "What I meant was…"

Ashton shook his head, stopping her flow of words.

Not once since they'd first met nine months ago had she given him any hint that her interest in him went beyond his skills in the kitchen. Plagued by unruly flashes of lust for the überprofessional businesswoman and not wanting anything to interfere with the negotiations for the Las Vegas restaurant, he'd ignored his disobedient hormones and kept things strictly business.

But as they neared the date for the restaurant opening, he found it harder and harder to stop seeing her as an attractive—if too serious—woman.

It made him crazy that he couldn't accept that she wasn't interested and move on. This was Vegas. There were thousands of women arriving every day looking to have a good time. Perfect for a frequent flier like him. He rarely stayed in the same location for more than a few days. The time he'd spent in Vegas these past few months was the most settled he'd been since leaving New York City ten years earlier.

A low chuckle vibrated his chest. "Please don't try to explain it," he said. "I think it's the first honest thing you've ever said to me."

"That's not true." But she went no further.

"I think it is."

Ashton had watched her walking the line between frustration and diplomacy with finesse and grace these many months. He wasn't completely oblivious to how hard he'd made her life.

At the beginning of the project he'd been excited to put his creative stamp on Las Vegas. He hadn't understood until it was too late how difficult his ideas would be to communicate. He'd demanded changes that irritated the designers and caused forward progress to halt. Forced by his filming timeline to oversee the restaurant from thousands of miles away, he'd found few things that met with his approval. The layout of the kitchen wasn't to his satisfaction. Numerous shipments of lighting and furniture samples didn't meet his expectations.

Then there were the filming delays caused by the Indonesian weather. Days of rain threw off their schedule. The crew joked that their ratings would skyrocket if they captured him soaked through, his clothes plastered to his body, but no one wanted to venture out into the mud and damp.

"Why don't I tell Cole he blew the interview and then fix something delicious. You can tell me what's bothering you while we eat."

"The lack of a head chef is what's bothering me."

"There has to be something else. You're not usually so testy."

"I'm not testy. I simply don't have time to eat with you."

"Five minutes ago you were ready to sit down and taste everything Cole had prepared." He crossed his arms and regarded her solemnly. "So I have to ask, what is it about my food you don't like?"

"It's not your food. I ate at Turinos while you were executive chef and the food was brilliant. You don't seriously think I'd invite you to open a restaurant here if I didn't love your cooking."

"Then is it me you don't like?" He held up his hand to forestall her denial. "I've been told I can be difficult to work with."

She took a deep breath and let it out, releasing some of the tension. "You've been murder to work with, but I think the restaurant's going to be worth every name I've called you."

Her bluntness made the corners of his mouth twitch. "You've called me names?"

"Never where anyone could hear me."

"Of course."

"Meaning?"

"Just that you're too much of a lady to ever let loose."

"And there's something wrong with being a lady?"

In the back of his mind a rational voice warned that he was baiting her. At the beginning of their association he'd often lobbed provocative statements her way. But she'd been far too professional to react and eventually he'd stopped aggravating her. This conversation felt different. As if she'd let the mask slide and was giving him a taste of her true self.

"Only that you never seem to have any fun."

She wasn't the only one who'd done her homework. He knew about the contest she was waging against her half sisters to one day take over as CEO of the family business. She'd had a phenomenal amount of success in her career, but Harper wasn't one to rest on her past achievements. In that way, they were alike. No one could put as much pressure on Harper as she put on herself.

"I have a great deal riding on the success of my hotel." She wouldn't stop until she had everything exactly the way she wanted it. "And you aren't one to talk. You barely take any time off between filming *The Culinary Wanderer,* promoting the series and managing your other restaurants."

"I won't deny that I'm busy, but I also take time to enjoy what I'm doing." He cocked his head. "Do you?"

"I enjoy my work. I wouldn't be doing it if I didn't." But beneath her vehemence was a grain of doubt.

She'd tried to hide her weariness with a careful application of concealer and blush, but he'd watched her long hours bite deeper into her energy each time he came to check on the restaurant's progress.

"But there must be something for you besides work," he said. "What's something you've always wanted to do but haven't gotten around to yet?"

"You make it sound like I'm sacrificing everything for my career."

In fact, he hadn't been saying that at all, but that she chose to interpret his question this way told him more than she'd intended.

"Everyone has dreams of something carefree and fun they'd like to do someday."

"I agree."

"Tell me one of yours."

"I don't get the point."

Was she stalling? Trying to come up with something safe? "Humor me. What's the first thing that pops into your mind?"

With her brows drawn together in exasperation, she blurted out, "I'd like to ride a camel across the desert and sleep in a tent."

Ashton wasn't sure which of them was more surprised by her outburst. "Seriously?" He laughed. "That's not at all what I expected you to say. I thought you'd tell me you wanted to…" He trailed off. They'd worked together for nine months and he knew so little about her.

"Wanted to what?" she prompted, wary curiosity in her warm brown eyes.

"I'm not sure. You aren't the sort of woman I imagine wanting to run off to Paris on a shopping spree or lounge on a yacht." She was too driven by timetables to enjoy such frivolous pursuits. "Maybe something more serious-minded. A visit to a museum, perhaps?"

His suggestion didn't meet with her approval. "You

know, I'm a little tired of everyone criticizing me for being too serious."

Whoa, he'd definitely touched a nerve there. "Who is everyone?"

"My family. My classmates when I was in school. Friends. Life isn't all about play, you know." She glanced down at her smartphone and frowned.

"It's also not all about work."

Sharp irritation sliced through her voice. "Says the man who rarely does any."

"Well, well, well." He flashed her a big grin. "That's some hellcat you keep bottled up."

She stared at him in consternation before sputtering, "That's ridiculous. There's no hellcat here."

"You didn't see the bloodlust in your eyes just now."

Her jaw worked as if she was grinding something particularly nasty between her teeth. "I'll admit to being a little on edge. You are not the easiest man to work with."

"Maybe not work with," he agreed. "But when you're ready to have some fun, give me a call."

In the quiet of the restaurant, Harper stared at Ashton with raised brows and lips softly parted. His offer wasn't sexual in nature, but when he spied the hope that flickered in her melted-chocolate eyes, his perception of her shifted dramatically.

"I don't have time—"

"For fun." He scrutinized her expression. "Yes, so you've said."

As a teenager, he'd fallen in with some dangerous criminals. Learning to read micro expressions had helped him survive. That he'd not picked up on the passionate woman concealed beneath Harper's professional exterior pointed out just how complacent he'd become.

Time to wake up and start paying attention.

She cleared her throat. "Getting back to Chef Cole…"

"I'll hire him if you spend an evening with me." This time he was deliberately hitting on her.

She set her hands on her hips and scowled at him. "Five minutes ago you were ready to pass on him."

"Five minutes ago I didn't realize just how starved for adventure you were."

"I'm very happy right where I am."

"When the first thing on your bucket list is riding a camel in the desert and sleeping in a tent, forgive me if I don't believe your life is as satisfying as you'd have people believe."

"I don't have a bucket list," she retorted. "And if I did, that wouldn't be the first thing on it. It was just something that popped into my head. I remember you doing that in an episode of *The Culinary Wanderer*."

"You're a fan?"

"Before I get into business with someone I do my research."

Sensible. But he hoped that hadn't been her only motivation. Swept by the urge to see her let her hair down, literally and figuratively, he decided to ignore her verbal cues and concentrate on what she was saying with her body.

"And your research involved watching my shows? I would have thought you'd be more interested in hard facts such as the financials of my four other restaurants and the uptick in advertising revenue my show brings to the network."

"All those things paint a very positive picture of you. I also spoke with a number of your employees and several of the crew who worked with you on your shows. As I said, I do my research."

Obviously she knew much more about him than he knew about her. The imbalance bothered him. "Then you know the sort of businessman I am, and when I say I'm willing to hire a chef you favor, it's not done lightly."

With her gaze firmly attached to his left shoulder, she murmured, "In exchange for a night with me."

"I proposed an evening." He couldn't help but laugh at the conclusion she'd jumped to. "You have a naughty mind if you think I'd barter hiring Cole for sex."

Hot color flared in her cheeks. "That's not what I was thinking."

"Oh, I think it was. I told you that hellcat was going to get you into trouble."

"I misspoke."

"I don't think so." Now that she was off balance, he decided to keep her that way. "I think it was a Freudian slip. You want me. You just can't admit it."

"What I want is for you to hire a chef and get him trained to your exacting standards so I don't have to worry about what happens after you leave."

She'd taken refuge in exasperation, but it wasn't fooling him.

"My offer still stands. Give me one evening and I'll hire Cole."

"Why would you want to spend an evening with me?" She looked as frazzled as he'd ever seen her.

"I thought you'd be interested in tasting the dishes I'm considering for the restaurant."

Her eyes narrowed. "And that's all there is to it?"

"Of course."

She regarded him in silence for several heartbeats before replying. "Hire Cole. You need someone accomplished to run your kitchen while you're off playing celebrity." With that, she pivoted on her conservative black pumps and strode across to his bag. Snagging the handle, she pulled it after her. "I'm taking this as collateral," she called over her shoulder.

It was a silly gesture—taking his clothes hostage wouldn't prevent him from getting on a plane—and so unlike Harper, the consummate professional. Ashton's gaze followed her, appreciating the pronounced sway of her hips. Thinking she'd put one over on him had injected a trace of strut into her stride.

"I will hire him," Ashton promised her. "And you will spend the evening with me."

"Sampling your menu." Her words floated back to him.

He'd been right about the hellcat lurking beneath her skin. It had been asleep far too long and he was the perfect guy to rouse it.

His final shot chased her out of the restaurant. "I'm going to make it a night you'll never forget."

Two

Smugness from her encounter with Ashton lasted about a second as she strode out of the restaurant and headed toward her office. What had she been thinking to walk off with his luggage? He must think she'd gone mad.

Well, hadn't she?

She'd agreed to an evening with him. Harper had no doubt she'd signed on for more than a private tasting of his menu. Which meant she was in big trouble. Already her mouth watered at the prospect of being the beneficiary of his culinary prowess. As long as that was the only prowess he plied her with, she might survive the evening without making a fool of herself. If he decided to test her level of resistance to his manly charms she wasn't going to maintain her professionalism very long.

Her skin burned as she thought of how he'd called her on her assumption that he wanted sex in exchange for hiring the chef she preferred. Not once had she suspected Ashton was the sort of man to make such a sordid offer. So why had she jumped to that conclusion? Even worse, why had she lobbed the accusation at him? Naturally, he'd presumed her misunderstanding represented her deepest desires.

And he was probably right. For the past nine months she'd been complaining that the real Ashton Croft wasn't as wonderful as the one on television. But that wasn't exactly true. His persona on TV was charismatic and amusing. He was the cool guy everyone wanted to hang out with. The flesh and blood Ashton Croft was no less appealing. It was just that the travel series didn't fully convey the masculine energy of the man. The rawness of his sex appeal.

Most of the time she focused on how frustrating he was. She was terrified of being bamboozled by his dimples and rakish grin. If he had any idea how easily he could knock her socks off, he'd probably go after a few other items of clothing, as well.

Harper shook her head at the thought. She was not going to sleep with Ashton Croft. It would be different if they'd met in some exotic locale; she could see herself being one of his random hook ups. The next morning, she would chalk up the evening as an adventure worth having. Hadn't she spent tedious hours on the treadmill imagining all sorts of spicy scenarios where she bumped into Ashton at a vineyard in Tuscany or on a walk around Dubrovnik's ancient city walls? There they would share a sunset and he'd persuade her to join him for dinner. On a private terrace overlooking the Adriatic Sea and surrounded by candles, he'd take her into his arms and…

The faint smell of cigarette smoke ripped Harper from her daydream.

Parking Ashton's *go* bag just inside the door of her office, Harper surveyed her formerly pristine sanctuary. Her mother's ostrich leather Burberry holdall sat on the sky-blue sofa, half the contents scattered around it. An empty pack of cigarettes lay crushed on the coffee table beside a crystal tumbler with a pale pink lipstick stain. The elegant lines of a cream trench coat were draped over Harper's executive chair. Her mother had definitely moved in.

Penelope Fontaine stood by the window overlooking the Las Vegas strip, her right hand resting at her throat, as if protecting the string of large black pearls she wore. A thin tendril of smoke rose from the cigarette pinched between the fingers of her other hand. In a black-and-white Chanel dress, with her long blond hair pulled away from her face in a classic chignon, she looked elegant and untouchable.

The sight stirred up memories of the day her parents had sat her down and explained that they were splitting up. Her mother needed to move to Florida for her health. Harper would remain in New York City with her father. Which basically meant she'd be alone with the staff because Ross Fontaine had spent most of his time avoiding the company's New York headquarters and his father's expectations. With Fontaine Hotels and Resorts' extensive holdings in the U.S. and abroad, Harper's father could be as irresponsible as he wanted without Henry Fontaine being the wiser.

"Mother, I would appreciate it if you didn't smoke in my office." Harper advanced toward Penelope, ready to pluck the cigarette from her mother if she didn't comply.

"I'm sorry, Harper." Crossing to the coffee table, she dropped the cigarette into the empty glass. "You know how I revert when I'm upset."

The lingering smell of smoke made Harper's nose tingle unpleasantly. "What's bothering you?" She fetched a can of air freshener from one of the cabinets that lined the east wall and sprayed the room with ocean breezes.

"I need your help." Penelope's voice warbled as she spoke the last word.

Unsure whether her mother was being theatrical or if she was truly in trouble, Harper took a quick inventory. Penelope's eyes looked like a forest after a downpour, the green enhanced by the redness that rimmed them.

"You've been crying." This was no bid for her daughter's attention. "What's wrong?"

"Something terrible has happened." Harper heard the weight of the world in Penelope's voice. "Why else do you think I came to this godforsaken city? It's not as if you'd come visit me in Florida."

"The hotel is taking all my energy right now." Harper knew better than to book passage on her mother's guilt trip, but her encounter with Ashton had stirred up her emotions. "Why didn't you go to Grandfather?"

Penelope fiddled with the ten-carat diamond she wore on her left hand despite her husband's death five years earlier. Why would she take if off now when she'd worn the ring through eighteen years of being separated from Ross Fontaine?

"Henry can't help me with this."

"But I can?" Harper struggled to get her head around this shift in her world's axis.

Never once had her mother reached out like this. Penelope was of the mindset that only men could solve the world's problems. Women were supposed to adorn their husbands' arms, looking beautiful and displaying graceful manners. They weren't supposed to run billion-dollar corporations at the expense of attracting lovers, much less suitable husbands.

"You're the only one who can."

All her life Harper had been waiting for her mother to acknowledge her as powerful and capable. That Penelope had turned to her daughter for help was as thrilling a victory as Harper had ever known. "What do you need?"

"Money."

Her mother received a sizeable allowance each month from the Fontaine family trust. What could she possibly need to buy that she couldn't turn to Harper's grandfather? "Why?"

"I'm being blackmailed."

Blackmailed? This was the last thing Harper expected to hear.

"Have you spoken to the police?" To Harper's mind, paying a blackmailer was never a good idea.

Penelope stared at Harper as if she'd suggested her mother get a job. "This is private business."

"Blackmail is illegal."

"I will not have my personal affairs become public knowledge."

Until her mother had retreated to Florida, Harper had been conditioned daily to believe that image was everything. And even though she'd subsequently found her true strength lay in being resourceful and focused, that earlier rhetoric wasn't easily ignored.

"I understand your reputation means everything to you, but what's to say the blackmailer won't leak the information even though you pay him?"

"He's promised not to." Penelope said this as if stunned that her daughter could be that stupid. "I came here thinking you'd help me."

Harper chewed on a sigh before saying, "How much do you need?"

"Three hundred and fifty thousand dollars."

The sum rendered Harper speechless for a long moment. "What did you do?"

Treating her mother with such bluntness wasn't going to win Harper any points, but the amount had caught her off guard.

Penelope gathered outrage around her like a shawl. "That's none of your concern."

"Excuse me for interrupting." Ashton strode into the room, looking far from remorseful that he'd barged in.

Too stunned by the bomb her mother had dropped to react to his intrusion, Harper sat motionless and watched him approach. His gaze shifted from her to Penelope, and Harper wondered if he was comparing mother and daughter.

Was he making the assumption that Harper and her mother were the same? Wealthy women, confident in their identity, knowing exactly how their lives were going to play out and content with the direction. Most days that's how Harper felt. Not today.

"Harper?" her mother's low warning tone prodded Harper to her feet.

"Mother, this is Chef Ashton Croft. He is the creative genius behind Batouri. Ashton, this is my mother, Penelope Fontaine."

She ignored the flash of humor in Ashton's eyes as she introduced him as a creative genius. It was true. No matter how big a pain in the ass he'd been, there was no denying the man was brilliant in the kitchen.

"Delighted to meet you," Penelope murmured, extending her hand like a queen to her subject.

Harper mentally rolled her eyes as Ashton clasped her mother's hand and flashed his charismatic celebrity grin.

"I've enjoyed working with your daughter."

Liar.

He'd tolerated her at best.

Seeing the effect his dazzling persona was having on her mother, Harper momentarily surrendered to amusement. Not normally one to be charmed by a handsome face or flirtation, Penelope appeared as if she'd forgotten all about the blackmail that had driven her more than two thousand miles to seek her daughter's help.

As much as she hated interrupting their mutual love fest, Harper wanted to return to her mother's blackmail problem and get the issue solved. "Is there something you needed from me?" she asked Ashton.

His attention swung to her. "Just my laptop. I have a video conference in ten minutes."

"It's over there." She gestured toward the black bag.

He bent to a side pocket in the duffel and took out a thin silver computer. Harper followed the smooth bunch and flex of his muscles, and her breath hissed out in appreciation. Strong and athletic in his cargo pants, denim shirt and hiking boots, sun-streaked shaggy hair falling into his bright blue eyes, he represented everything that Harper was not. Physical, unpredictable, exciting. The yang to her yin, she realized, and felt heat rise in her cheeks.

"Leave the bag," she commanded, her voice a husky blur. "I'm not done with you yet."

The corner of his mouth kicked up. "Of course."

She caught his smug gaze and stared him down in silence, refusing to backpedal or stumble through an explanation of what she'd actually meant. And maybe just a little afraid to ask herself about the subtext he'd picked up on.

"Check with Mary to see which conference room is available."

"I appreciate the accommodation."

"Come see me when you're done. I'm interested to hear how your conversation with Chef Cole went."

"I look forward to telling you. Will you be here?"

Harper glanced at her mother. "I'm not certain where I'll be. Ask Mary. She has a knack for finding me."

He nodded and exited her office. With his departure, the energy level in the room plummeted. Harper's heart pounded in her chest as if she'd done a two-minute sprint on her treadmill.

"You're letting that scruffy man open a restaurant in your hotel?"

Penelope's criticism would've stung if Harper hadn't witnessed her mother batting her eyelash extensions at *that scruffy man* only moments before. "He only recently returned from four months in Indonesia."

"I thought you said he was a chef. What was he doing there?"

"Filming his television series, *The Culinary Wanderer*." Harper waited for her mother to recognize the name. "He travels all over the world, eating local cuisine and bringing attention to the history or current troubles of the places where he films."

"I don't watch much television. It's too depressing."

Harper didn't bother arguing. Penelope lived in a snug bubble. She played golf in the morning and then lunched with friends. After a few hours spent shopping, the remainder of her day was taken up by something cultural or philanthropic. The only interruption to her schedule happened when she traveled to the Hamptons to visit her mother or decided a room of her condo needed updating.

"His show is very popular."

"I'm sure you know what you're doing," Penelope replied, her tone indicating that she'd dismissed a subject that no longer interested her. "How soon can you get me the money I need?"

"I'll call the bank and have them wire the funds as soon as you tell me who is blackmailing you and why."

"I'm your mother," Penelope huffed. "Don't you dare barter with me."

Before Harper could argue, Mary appeared in the doorway. "Your grandfather is on line one and Carlo called to say Chef Cole wants to talk to you as soon as you're available." Mary placed a wealth of emphasis on that last part.

She needed to do some damage control. "Tell him I'll be down as soon as I'm done talking to Grandfather. Maybe ten or fifteen minutes."

Penelope clutched her daughter's arm as Harper began to rise. "You can't say anything to Henry."

"Why don't we sort this business out over dinner later," she suggested, attempting to pacify her mother. "I need to know more details before we proceed."

"But you are going to help me," Penelope stated, anxiety shadowing her determined tone.

"Of course." Harper's gaze skittered away from the relief in her mother's eyes and fell on her assistant.

Mary had been waiting patiently through their exchange.

Seeing she'd regained Harper's attention, she switched on her headset and spoke to the caller. "She's on her way to the phone now. Okay, I'll let her know. Your grandfather has had to take another call. He'll catch up with you at four our time."

"Thank you, Mary." Harper turned to her mother. "I have some business to take care of. It shouldn't take more than twenty minutes."

Penelope glanced at her watch. "I have a manicure appointment in half an hour."

It made perfect sense to Harper that her mother would schedule a beauty treatment in the midst of a personal crisis. No matter how bad things got, she never neglected her appearance.

"Mary will get you settled in a suite. I'll order dinner to be served there at seven. We can talk then."

Ashton lounged in the Fontaine Ciel's executive conference room, tapping his fingers against the tabletop in a rhythm that called to him from the past. He had his back to the large monitor set on the wall opposite the door that led to the hall. The network suits in New York had not yet figured out the connection was live and he was gaining some useful insights into their thought processes.

He'd been in negotiations for a brand-new television series for almost five months now. The Lifestyle Network wanted him to star in a culinary show that "showcased his talent." Or at least that was the way his manager, Vince, had pitched it. Ashton agreed that it was a solid career move. Something he'd been working toward these past eight years.

It would allow him to live permanently in New York City. He'd never again have to travel under the most uncomfortable conditions to places that no one in their right mind wanted to live.

Too bad he loved all those miserable out-of-the-way places he visited. Nor was Lifestyle Network's demand that he quit *The Culinary Wanderer* if they gave him his new show sitting well with Ashton. With the sort of taping schedule he had with the travel show, there was no reason why he couldn't do both. He'd given six years to Phillips Consolidated Networks and *The Culinary Wanderer.* The show remained vital and continued to do well in the ratings. Giving it up made no sense. And then there was all the aid that the places he visited received as a result of the show.

He hadn't set out to do a culinary series that highlighted socioeconomic and political issues around the world. He'd started out romping around the globe doing a six-part series featuring out of the way culinary adventures for the network's travel channel. At some point toward the end of the first season, he'd started to see the potential of shining the light of television on some of the places regular travelers would never go. But it wasn't until the first segments aired that he realized he was raising social awareness.

The series' high ratings caught the network executives' attention. They liked what they saw and wanted to work with him again so Ashton pitched them a show focused as much on the problems faced by the locals as it was about the regional cuisine. Six months later, *The Culinary Wanderer* was born.

By the end of the first season, his viewership had increased threefold. Inspired by the flood of emails from viewers asking how they could help, the network partnered with a world help organization to bring aid to the areas hit hardest by war and poverty. It was somewhat surreal to discover he did more good with his half-hour television series than his parents did in a year with their missionary work. And it was sad to realize no matter how much he did, they would never approve of his methods.

Still, money had been raised. People had been fed and given medicine. Sources of fresh water had been brought to villages that needed it. But no matter how much Ashton accomplished there was always another town ravaged by unrest or burdened by poverty. His gut told him he shouldn't walk away from all those who still needed help. Yet wasn't it this exact sort of arrogance—that he was somehow special and necessary for others' salvation—that made him so angry with his father?

"Chef Croft, are you ready to begin?"

Ashton swiveled around and gave the assembled group an easy smile. "Whenever you are, gentlemen."

He could see that his manager was on the call from his L.A. office. Vince's expression gave away none of the concern he'd voiced to Ashton late last night, but he wasn't looking as relaxed as usual. This show would take Ashton from celebrity chef to household name. From there the possibilities were endless.

"Chef Croft," began Steven Bell, a midlevel executive who'd been acting as the group's mouthpiece these past several months. He was the third in a line of conservatively dressed, middle-aged men with a talent for pointing out problems and little else. "We have slotted the new show to begin the end of February and would like to start taping in three weeks. Is that a problem?"

"Not at all."

Several of the men exchanged glances, and Ashton picked up on it. If he'd learned anything in the past several months, he'd discovered the path to superstardom wasn't a smooth one.

"We've been told your restaurant in the Fontaine hotel is behind schedule," said the man Ashton thought of as Executive Orange because whatever spray tan he used gave his skin a sunset glow.

"Untrue. It's set to open in two weeks."

"And your expectation is that you'll have it running smoothly immediately?"

Ashton knew what was going on. Vince had warned him that since Ashton was unwilling to give in on the matter of quitting *The Culinary Wanderer* they were looking at other chefs in an effort to force his hand.

"I will be leaving my kitchen in good hands. I offered Chef Dillon Cole the head chef position." He left out the fact that Cole hadn't agreed to take the job.

"He's out of Chicago, correct?"

Unsure which of the six executives had spoken, Ashton nodded. "A talented chef." Which was perfectly true, despite his earlier criticism. Ashton just wasn't sure he was the right man for Batouri, but he was running out of time and options. If he wanted to host the new show, he needed to be available.

"We'd like you to come to New York next week and spend a couple days working with our producers. We feel you should be on the set and run through a couple versions of the show to get some film that we could run past a couple of our current hosts for their input."

"What days did you have in mind?"

"Wednesday and Thursday. We could schedule something in the afternoon, say around two?"

Harper was going to filet him when she caught wind of this impromptu trip. "I'll be there."

"We're looking forward to seeing you."

After a few more niceties and good luck wishes for his restaurant opening, the New York executives signed off. When it was just Ashton and Vince still on the call, the manager let his true feelings show.

"Those bastards are not making this easy, are they?"

"Did you really expect them to?" Ashton countered. "This isn't a travel network with a couple hundred thousand viewers. This channel draws over a million viewers for some of its least popular primetime shows."

"What I expected is for them to be falling all over themselves to bring you in. They're looking to give their lineup more sex appeal. While the numbers have been slipping for cooking shows lately, home improvement segments are on the rise."

"Any idea why?"

"If you listen to my wife and daughter, it's all due to the hunky carpenters they've been hiring."

Ashton grinned. "So you're saying they aren't as interested in my culinary expertise as my impressive physique?"

"How does that make you feel?"

"Like we should be negotiating for more money."

"Maybe I should suggest you do the episodes shirtless."

"Don't give them any ideas." Ashton grimaced. "They'll probably turn it into a bit. Stay tuned for the next segment when Chef Croft will burn off his shirt."

"Well, you'd better get that restaurant of yours open in Vegas or you won't have to worry about what they want you to wear."

"Have you heard from the guys over at Phillips about the proposals I made regarding next season's location?"

In addition to negotiating with the Lifestyle Network, he was in talks with Phillips Consolidated Networks for his seventh season of *The Culinary Wanderer.* They were pushing him to film next season in Africa. They'd reasoned that since he was South African, he would enjoy returning to the land of his birth. The exact opposite was true, but since he'd created an elaborate backstory that had nothing to do with his true history, he couldn't provide an excuse strong enough to dissuade them.

"They rejected England immediately. Apparently your best ratings come when you are off the beaten track. The Indonesian stuff has been a huge hit with everyone who's seen it."

"What about South America? I could get six or seven episodes out of Brazil alone."

"They said they'd consider it for next year." Vince rolled a pen between his palms. "I think if you want to keep doing the show, it's going to have to be Africa. Of course, that's dependent on whether Lifestyle Network gives up on getting an exclusive on you."

Frustration with the producers of *The Culinary Wanderer* had led him to talk to Lifestyle Network. He wanted to grow his career in a big way and the new show could do that. Becoming a household name would open a lot of doors. But it wasn't where his heart lay. He'd never stop craving new adventures in exotic locations. It's why he intended to find a way to do both. Being forced to choose between his passion and his ambition wasn't an option.

"I really don't want to go to Africa."

"Come on. How bad can it be? You still have family there, don't you?"

"Sure." In fact, he had no idea if his parents were still alive. He hadn't spoken to them since he left home at fifteen. A lot of bad things could happen in twenty years, especially in the sort of places his parents took their missionary work.

He heard the door open behind him and noticed the change in Vince's demeanor. His manager sat forward in his desk chair and ran his fingers through his short sandy-blond hair. Glancing over his shoulder, Ashton noticed Harper had entered the room. She didn't look happy.

"Gotta go, Vince. Keep in touch." He ended the network connection and the monitor in the room went blank. "Thanks for letting me borrow your equipment. This is some nice stuff."

"Chef Cole tells me he's not going to be our head chef."

"I offered him the job just like you wanted."

"I wanted you to hire him."

"He turned me down." Ashton pushed his chair back from the conference table and stood up.

"So, now what?"

"You have me."

"I need someone permanent. How long before you take off again?"

Next week, but in her current state of displeasure, he wasn't going to mention that.

"Not to worry. I have someone I trust who I've been training. He arrives tomorrow."

"Who is it?"

"I met Dae Tan a few months ago. Helped him out of a jam."

"What sort of a jam?" Her skepticism came through loud and clear.

"He was arrested for something he didn't do."

"You're sure he was innocent."

"Absolutely. After that, things got a little hot for him. He's been traveling with me and I've been training him."

"Why didn't he come with you today?"

"He wanted to see L.A. He has this thing about movie stars."

Harper regarded him with suspicion. "Where has he worked? Is he capable of handling the pressure of a restaurant like Batouri?"

"It'll be fine. The kid's got talent."

"Kid?" She echoed his description and her irritation grew. "How old is he?"

"Twenty-five. Twenty-six."

"You can't be serious." Harper advanced on him. "You've passed on chefs with twenty-five *years* of experience and now you're telling me you want to hire someone who's been in the field a couple years."

"Months," Ashton corrected. "He only had the most rudimentary skills when I met him."

Harper's eyes closed while she sucked in a deep breath and let it out. When she opened them again, she looked no calmer. "You're crazy if you think I'll go for this."

"You really don't have a choice."

"We'll see about that." Harper folded her arms across her chest. "You forget we have a contract." Her tone indicated he'd stretched her goodwill as far as it would go.

"I have a great deal riding on this restaurant, as well," he reminded her.

"Then act like it."

The trouble was, he had a great deal riding on every iron he had in the fire. He was determined to leave his mark on the world and that meant going big. Would it have been smarter to not stick his neck out? Sure. He could have played it safe, kept going with the same shows he'd had success with these past eight years, but Ashton liked the rush of conquering new territory, seeing what lay beyond the horizon.

Harper continued, "Go convince Cole to take the job at Batouri."

"I thought you said he'd gone to the airport."

"I caught him before he left the hotel and convinced him to fly to Chicago tomorrow. You have reservations next door at Fontaine Chic's award-winning steakhouse at seven. You might as well sample the competition. Perhaps you will both dislike the food and find some common ground to build a relationship on."

"And our evening together?"

She shot him a cool smile. "When Cole takes the job, I'll block out two hours for you."

"Make it three and you have a deal."

Three

With the Chef Cole problem handled for the time being and her mother safely ensconced in the day spa, Harper was able to steal a few minutes to herself to take stock of the day. Thank heavens they weren't all like this.

Unable to imagine what her mother had done to open herself up to blackmail, Harper paced her hotel, trying to find comfort in achievement. The ceilings throughout had been painted to represent different aspects of the sky her hotel was named for. In the lobby, it was a pale midday blue dotted with clouds. Lighting changed from dawn to dusk to match what was happening outside. The casino ceiling was a midnight indigo sparkling with thousands of pinpoint lights configured like the star patterns above Las Vegas.

It was a simple concept, beautifully rendered. She was proud of all she'd accomplished. But today, there was no joy to be found in surveying her domain. Harper glanced at her watch. Two hours to kill. With her ability to concentrate shot and no meetings or crisis pending, she considered returning to her suite and running on her treadmill. Or she could go talk to Scarlett.

Five years ago when her grandfather had come to her with news that she had two half sisters, she'd been angry, miserable and excited. She'd been eleven when she'd first learned her father regularly cheated on his wife, but until five years ago, she'd had no idea his extramarital wandering had messed up more lives than just hers and her mother's.

A quick walk through the skyways that connected the three Fontaine hotels brought Harper to Fontaine Richesse, Scarlett's hotel. She sought out her sister in the casino. Spotting Scarlett was easy. She radiated sex appeal and charisma in her emerald-green flapper costume, her long brown hair tucked beneath a twenties-style, shingle bob wig with bangs.

The rest of the casino staff was dressed like something out of a movie from the forties and fifties: men in elegant tuxedos and suits or military uniforms from the Second World War, women in evening gowns or stylish dresses.

Harper had thought the whole idea of a Golden Age of Hollywood night was crazy. But she'd underestimated her sister's brilliance. The casino was packed. Many of those playing the machines or lining the tables were also dressed in costume. There were prizes awarded for best outfit, and casino cash was given to anyone who guessed what particular movie the dealers or waitresses were dressed from.

Scarlett wore a delighted grin as the man who'd approached her guessed her costume.

"Cyd Charrise, *Singin' In The Rain?*"

"That's right." She handed him a card he could trade in for money to gamble with. As he walked off, she spotted Harper. "What a surprise."

"You look amazing," Harper said, admiring the dress and matching green satin pumps. "Is it new?"

"First time I've worn it." She struck a pose. "I think Laurie outdid herself." Scarlett had been friends with the

Hollywood costume designer for years and used her for every costume in the casino.

"I would agree."

When she'd first met Scarlett, Harper hadn't given the former child actress much credit. She couldn't imagine what her grandfather had been thinking when he'd concocted the contest between his three granddaughters. What could someone with Scarlett's background know about running a multibillion-dollar hotel much less a corporation the size of Fontaine Hotels and Resorts? Five years later, Harper was a huge fan of Scarlett's creativity and authenticity. She knew exactly who she was and had played directly to her strengths.

"Do you have time for a drink?" Harper asked, instantly seeing her request had startled Scarlett.

Harper was the family workaholic. Rarely did she sit down in the evenings when the casino was busiest, much less take time out to eat or drink.

"For you, always." They found a table in a quiet corner of the lobby bar. Scarlett ordered two glasses of cabernet and made small talk until the drinks arrived. "What's wrong?" she asked as soon as Harper had taken a sip of wine.

"What makes you think…?" She could see Scarlett wasn't fooled. "I don't want you to assume that I'm only here because I needed help."

"I don't care why you're here." Scarlett gave her a lopsided smile. "And I'm glad Violet is out of town with JT. Otherwise, I know you'd have gone to her first."

"That's unfair." But probably true. As much as Harper loved her half sister, she wasn't always comfortable with Scarlett.

In so many ways, they were opposites. Scarlett was gorgeous, flamboyant and utterly fearless when it came to her relationships. Hadn't she tackled Logan Wolfe and turned the tetchy security expert into a big purring lion?

She'd managed to do the same thing with Harper. Wariness had become loyalty, something Harper gave rarely and not without reservation. But Scarlett had won her over for the most part.

"Okay, there is something wrong." Harper paused, knowing Scarlett deserved more. "But you aren't right about how I'd go to Violet instead of you. If she was here, I'd have come to both of you with this."

"Must be serious." Scarlett's lips curved into a wicked smile. "Do you need some advice about Ashton Croft? I heard he's back in town."

"Nothing like that."

"I suggest you sleep with him."

"What?" Harper cursed the sudden heat in her cheeks. "I'm not going to sleep with him. Our relationship is strictly professional."

"You should reconsider that. I know you have a thing for him. And he looks like he'd be a riot in bed."

Harper needed Scarlett to get off that particular subject. "My mother is being blackmailed."

All mischief went out of Scarlett. She paled. "Blackmailed? Why?"

"I don't know. She won't tell me."

"Does she know who is doing it?"

Harper shook her head. "It's all so crazy. My mother. The perfect Penelope Fontaine. I can't imagine her doing anything wrong much less anything scandalous enough to invite blackmail."

"How did you find out?"

"She came here needing to borrow money."

"How much?"

"Three hundred and fifty thousand."

Scarlett gasped. "That's a lot."

"I keep wondering what she's done. It must be something truly awful for them to be asking that much."

"From what you've told me," Scarlett began, "your

mother isn't great at considering the value of something before she spends. Is she sure what happened is worth that much money?"

"It's hard to say with my mother. She's so big on keeping her reputation unsullied, it might be something as simple as a bump and run." But Harper couldn't picture her mother having a minor accident much less fleeing the scene of one.

"Could she have cheated on her taxes?"

"Impossible. Grandfather handles all her finances." Penelope's lack of financial smarts was what had caused Grandfather to put her on an allowance and hire a money manager to pay the bills.

"I don't suppose she wants to call the police." Scarlett framed the question as if she already knew the answer.

"She won't do that," Harper said. "The blackmailer will make her secret public."

"Do you need help coming up with the cash? I have some money set aside."

Her sister's offer came so fast Harper doubted Scarlett considered the magnitude of the gesture. She was humbled by her sister's affection. "Thanks, but I didn't come here for that."

"Then why?"

"I thought talking with you would put me in a calmer frame of mind before I have dinner with my mother."

"She's here?"

"Showed up this afternoon out of the blue."

Harper had never spoken directly about how she and Penelope got along, but both her sisters knew that Harper's mother had left her daughter behind in New York City and moved to Florida. It wasn't a stretch to deduce that things between mother and daughter weren't good. But if anyone understood that family could produce the most complicated relationships, it would be Harper and Scarlett.

"Why don't I talk with Logan," Scarlett suggested. "Maybe there's something he or Lucas can do."

"I don't know if anyone can help at this point."

"Are you kidding? Logan and his brother are security experts. They should be able to figure out who's blackmailing your mom without breaking a sweat. If not before the blackmail is paid, then I know they can track where the money goes."

Harper was suddenly feeling a whole lot better. Impulsively, she hugged Scarlett. "I don't know what I would do without you and Violet."

"I'm glad to hear you say that. I wasn't always sure you liked having us in your life."

Scarlett's admission twisted Harper's stomach into knots of regret. "I'm sorry I've made you feel that way. In the beginning it wasn't easy embracing you as sisters. I'd been alone my whole life and hadn't exactly been smothered with love by my parents. I didn't really understand what it meant to be family."

"I hope that's changed."

"It has. You and Violet are the most important people in my life along with Grandfather." Seeing the tears that filled Scarlett's beautiful green eyes, Harper wished she'd made this confession long ago. "I'm sorry if I made it seem otherwise. I've been so focused on getting Fontaine Ciel built and running that I haven't been a very good sister."

Scarlett waved the apology away and dabbed at her eyes with a napkin. Delight filled her voice as she said, "You didn't need to say anything. We knew how you felt."

Harper made a resolution to be more open with her sisters going forward. It wouldn't be easy. She'd spent her whole life bottling up her feelings. Her mother wasn't demonstrative and her father's rare appearances in her life hadn't been filled with warm moments. In school she'd been a leader and her habit of ruling by persuasion and occasional ruthlessness hadn't won her the love of the majority of her classmates. But it hadn't mattered as long as they followed her. Or so she'd told herself.

"Let me call Logan and see what he suggests we do."

"I'm sure he's not going to want you to do anything," Harper said with a faint smile.

"Since when has that stopped me?"

Scarlett had given her fiancé a lot to worry about after inheriting some files from Tiberius Stone, Violet's surrogate father. The casino owner had been murdered by a local councilman who'd been embezzling campaign contributions. Tiberius had accumulated a storage unit full of people's secrets including his brother-in-law, a man who'd stolen the identity of Preston Rhodes, a wealthy orphan from California. Violet had gone to Miami intent on bringing him to justice in order to help her husband take back his family's company.

"It's rolling to voice mail," Scarlett said. After leaving Logan a brief summary of the situation, she hung up. "It won't take him long to call me back. Do you want to wait?"

About to say yes, Harper suddenly remembered she still had Ashton's *go* bag. "Can't. I have to see a man about a bag."

Scarlett cocked her head in puzzlement, but nodded. "As soon as I hear from Logan, I'll call you. In the meantime, can you stall your mother?"

"I can try."

Leaving Scarlett, Harper made her way back to the Fontaine Ciel's executive floor. Mary had gone for the day, locking Harper's office before she left. Harper half expected Ashton to have persuaded the personal assistant to give him his bag, but to her surprise, either Mary had resisted the celebrity chef's charm or Ashton had stuck to his part of the bargain.

Either way, she grabbed the bag and shot a quick text to let him know the luggage would be waiting for him at Batouri. But when she got there, she was surprised to find Ashton sitting at the corner table where his bag had sat earlier.

* * *

When the door to the restaurant opened, Ashton was nursing a tumbler of ten-year-old Scotch. It was his third. The first two had gone down fast and smooth. He didn't think he should continue at that pace or his dinner with Cole might not go the way Harper wanted.

That she spotted him so fast made him smile. She felt it, too. This irresistible pull between them. How had he ignored it until now? Oh, she was good at hiding it. And he hadn't exactly given her any reason to feel more than irritation toward him. He wanted to strip her layers of professionalism away and get to the firecracker below. How hot would the fire burn? And for how long? With fireworks, the thrill was in those seconds of exhilarating danger. The breathtaking waterfall of light. The big boom that lingered in the chest even after the sound faded.

Still, it might be worth sacrificing her goodwill to experience the rush.

"What brings you here?" He sipped the Scotch, felt the burn in his chest.

"I'm returning your *go* bag."

He'd been so focused on Harper he hadn't even noticed that she was towing his bag along.

You're slipping.

In the places he traveled, being distracted for even a moment could be trouble.

"The deal isn't done with Cole yet," he reminded her. "Are you sure you don't want to keep it hostage for a bit longer?" Maybe take it back to her suite. "I could pick it up later."

She parked the bag beside the booth. "I've lost my taste for blackmail in the past few hours." Her gaze flicked to the glass and then to his mouth.

His heart tapped unsteadily against his ribs. "Anything you'd like to talk about?"

"No."

"Are you sure?"

Was it the alcohol that was making him light-headed or the way she was staring at him as if she wondered what he'd taste like? She reached for his glass, and he figured she was going to chastise him for drinking up the restaurant's stock. Instead, she lifted the tumbler to her lips and tossed back the last ounce of Scotch. He expected her to come up coughing as the strong liquor hit her throat. Instead, she licked her lips and smiled, her eyes thoughtful and distant.

"My grandfather loves Scotch." She set the glass back on the table and turned to go.

"I'm a very good listener." Ashton claimed few virtues. Giving a speaker his full attention was one. But would she trust him to share what was going on?

Harper hesitated before facing him once more. "My mother came into town unexpectedly."

Ashton relaxed, unaware until his lungs started working again that he'd been holding his breath. "I noticed the air between you two wasn't particularly cheerful."

"Do you have a good relationship with your parents?"

He shook his head, the twinge in his gut barely noticeable. "I left home at fifteen and never looked back."

"I've read everything ever written about you and I'm pretty sure that wasn't part of your history."

He knew better than to be flattered. "It's a story for another day. We're talking about you."

Her gaze was steady on his for several seconds. "My mother moved to Florida when I was eleven, leaving me in New York with my father who was rarely home. At the time I hated her for not being around, but as I grew up, I realized that being away from her criticism gave me the freedom to make mistakes and learn from them without being afraid she'd make me feel worse."

"I'm not sure many people would be as unaffected by their mother's abandonment as you are."

Harper gave him a wry smile. "Don't for a second think

I'm unaffected. I'm just realistic. My mother didn't abandon me. She fled a situation she'd didn't like. Penelope isn't someone who stands and fights when she can run away and go shopping." Harper shrugged, but she was far from sounding nonchalant. "Okay, so maybe I'm a little more bothered than I let on."

"It's nice to hear you admit that."

"Why?"

"Because I like you and I haven't been able to figure out why."

"You like me?" Her breathless laugh wasn't the reaction he'd expected.

"Very much," he admitted, more than a little disturbed by the way her delighted smile transformed her into a stunning, vivacious woman.

"After the way I've hounded you these past nine months?" She shook her head, and the career woman took over once more. "I think you're just trying to charm me. If this is your way of changing my mind about Chef Cole, you've got it all wrong."

"So suspicious," he taunted. "That's not it at all. I'm starting to come around to your opinion about Cole. As for the way you've acted these past few months, I get it. This hotel is important to you. Batouri will make a statement and depending on how it does, that statement will be good or bad. I'd be a hypocrite to criticize you for doing whatever it took to make sure Batouri is a complete success."

"That's awfully accommodating of you."

Rub me the right way and I can be very accommodating.

But that's the sort of comeback she'd expect. "Does your mother visit you in Las Vegas often?"

"Never. She hates it here."

"Must be important for her to show up then."

"She needs my help. Which is different. She usually

takes her problems to my grandfather because he's a man and taking care of women is what men do."

"That sounds very traditional minded."

"It goes against everything I believe in. I'm a modern career girl." A trace of self-mockery put a lilt in her voice. "She disapproves of my choices. Thinks I should have married a tycoon like my grandfather and dazzled New York society on his arm."

"That seems like a waste of your intelligence and drive."

"It's hard being a disappointment."

"I agree." This they shared. No matter how much either of them accomplished, they weren't living up to their parents' perception of success. "It spoils what you've achieved, doesn't it."

She looked surprised by his insight. Her gaze became keen as it rested on him. "It does."

He lifted the bottle of Scotch. "Do you want another drink?" He was dying to watch her swallow another glass. And then lick her lips again. There'd been something so decadent, so wickedly un-Harper-like about the deed.

"I should get back to work."

"See you tomorrow night."

"Text me when Chef Cole agrees to come work for you." She started to leave, but then paused. "Thanks for listening."

He suspected voicing her gratitude hadn't come easily. "Anytime. You know where to find me."

Shaking her head in exasperation, Harper spun away and headed toward the exit, her stride purposeful. Whatever sharing she'd done, it was now over. Ashton was left with an increased appreciation for Harper Fontaine.

These past few months he'd assumed her arrogance was a natural byproduct of her family's money and connections, that life was a breeze for her. He'd been as guilty of stereotyping as his critics often were. To be fair, her confidence had always been dent-free.

Now he realized there were a few pinholes in her armor.

And they had more in common than he'd have ever guessed.

Harper pushed lettuce around on her plate, her appetite deadened by the smell of cigarette smoke. The suite would have to be deep cleaned before any guests could be booked in here. Over dinner, her mother had refused to speak about the blackmail. Harper's impatience was growing with each minute that ticked by. She set down her fork. It clattered on the china. The discordant sound startled her mother.

"We have to talk about why you're here."

"I don't want to."

"If you expect me to give you three hundred and fifty thousand dollars, I'm going to need to know why you're being blackmailed."

"I can't tell you."

"Did you kill someone?"

"Don't be an idiot."

"That's a relief," Harper muttered. She left the table, needing activity to think. As she crossed the room, a dozen ideas sprang into her mind. She picked the most likely one and turned to confront her mother. "You stole something."

"I'm not a thief." Penelope stubbed out her cigarette and reached for another, but Harper beat her to the package.

"No more smoking."

Her mother glared at her. "You are trying to provoke me into telling you something you're not ready to hear."

Why not? Harper mused. Her mother had been aggravating her for years. "I'm trying to figure out what could be worth three hundred and fifty thousand dollars."

"Actually it's a million."

"A mill...?" Harper crushed the cigarette package in her fist.

Penelope pouted. "It's a small price to pay compared to the consequences."

"What sort of consequences?"

"Life or death."

Now her mother had gone too far. "This is serious, Mother. You need to talk to Grandfather."

"I can't. He'd demand to know why I was being black-mailed. I can't tell him."

"Give me some idea what the blackmail is or I'm going to call him."

Penelope shot her daughter a wounded look. "There are some indelicate photos that if they got out would be very damaging."

Unsure how her conservative mother defined indelicate, Harper sought clarification. "Surely it can't be that bad."

"It could ruin us."

Us?

For a second Harper wasn't sure whom her mother was referring to. Penelope certainly hadn't worried about her daughter's welfare when she ran off to Florida.

"Who is 'us'?" she questioned, her voice scarcely audible.

Her mother looked startled. "Why you and I, of course."

Harper knelt beside Penelope. Taking her mother's hands, surprised by the icy chill in her fingers, Harper squeezed just hard enough to capture Penelope's full attention.

"If this involves me, you need to tell me what is going on."

"I had an affair," Penelope whispered, unable to maintain eye contact with Harper. Her mother was something other than mortified. She was afraid. "If that came out—" She broke off and shook her head.

Was something besides her mother's reputation at stake? "Who was it?"

"I met him at an exhibition of wildlife photography in London. His work was being honored." She released an impassioned sigh. "His photos were amazing."

"You had an affair with a photographer." Harper didn't know what to think. She had little trouble imaging her mother dallying with a duke or an Italian prince while in London, but a wildlife photographer?

"He was exciting and handsome and I couldn't get enough of his stories of Africa. He actually lived in the bush for ten months to get one particular shot of a group of lions."

Harper couldn't stop herself from drawing a parallel between her fascination with Ashton's adventures and her mother having an affair with someone who lived dangerously. Harper winced away from the comparison, dismayed to think she was more like her mother than she'd ever imagined.

"When did you have this affair?"

"Your father was out of the country a great deal."

"Before you split." Is that what had caused her mother to go to Florida? Had she been banished for being unfaithful? That seemed awfully unfair considering her husband's rampant infidelities. "Did Daddy know?"

"Not at first. I was very discreet. But in the end he figured it out."

"Why did you and father stay married when that's obviously not what either of you wanted?"

"What makes you think either of us wanted a divorce? Your father married me to cement a deal for Henry to buy my family's hotels. It was never a love match. I received security in exchange for ignoring all his affairs. It wasn't as if he intended to marry any of those women he slept with." Penelope sipped at her wine. "As for my brief indiscretion—" her mother offered an indifferent shrug "—I was out of the country and I knew I'd never see him again."

Yet thirty years later keeping the affair from being revealed was worth a million dollars. Was it just her mother's overdeveloped sense of propriety at work or was there something more going on?

"How brief an indiscretion was it?" Curiosity overpowered Harper as she tried to imagine her mother as young, impulsive and happy. All three were a stretch.

Penelope shot her a repressive frown. "What does it matter?"

How could her mother not understand how fascinating Harper found all this? Harper's whole life she'd had this image of her mother as the victim of Ross Fontaine's adulterous wandering. Suffering because her pride or a sense of honor kept her from divorcing the man who made her miserable.

"I'm just having a hard time picturing you..." Harper couldn't think of a way to say what was on her mind without it sounding like an insult.

"Engaging in a torrid affair?" Penelope spat out the words as if they tasted bad.

"I was going to say happy."

The diamond on Penelope's left hand sent out spikes of color as she waved away Harper's explanation. "Happy is overrated."

Was it? Harper considered her own life. Was she happy? Content maybe. Unless she compared herself to Violet and Scarlett and then she looked positively miserable. Being in love had certainly given her sisters a glow.

But it wasn't just being in love, for often love didn't last in a relationship. It was the fact that they'd found the other half of themselves. It wasn't something Harper had imagined for herself. Her ideal life involved a large executive office in Fontaine's New York City headquarters, rising profits, a cover article in *Forbes*. She didn't think in terms of a private life. She couldn't imagine having the energy to navigate the unpredictable waters of a serious relationship.

Once again her thoughts drifted to Ashton Croft and the awareness that spiked through her every time they occupied the same room. Regret rubbed at her. As much as he irritated her as a businessman, she was wildly attracted to the adventurous chef. If her responsibilities didn't weigh her down, she wouldn't hesitate to take those dimples of his for a spin.

"I don't see anything about this situation worth smiling over," Harper's mother stated, her voice sharp and impatient.

Harper pushed Ashton out of her mind and resumed her mask of professionalism. "You're right. There isn't."

"How soon can I get the money?"

"First thing tomorrow. What are we supposed to do? Gather the cash in a briefcase and drop it off at the bus station?"

Harper was struck with untimely amusement by the idea of her mother setting one Manolo-clad toe in such a place. But the urge to laugh vanished abruptly as she recalled Ashton's assessing gaze earlier. In all likelihood he had the same opinion about her. Worse, he'd be right. She'd never been to a bus station or ridden a bus. She'd spent her whole childhood in New York City and had only used the subway once.

"Don't be ridiculous," her mother said. "The money is to be wired. I've been given an account."

"That's safer." And she'd bet Scarlett's fiancé had a team of computer experts that could track the money to its final destination. "Give me the account number and I'll take care of everything."

Four

"Wow, boss." Dae's white grin split his tanned face as he toured Batouri's kitchen. "Nice place you got here."

The former Bali surfing instructor gazed around in admiration, taking in the pristine appliances and immaculate counters. Ashton had picked Dae up at the airport half an hour earlier and had intended to take him straight to the apartment he'd rented, but Dae had wanted to see the kitchen first. Ashton understood. He'd been discussing the project with the young Balinese man for the past four months. Naturally, he was curious.

"Glad you like it. You sure this is where you want to be? You have no idea what Chef Cole is going to be like to work with." Ashton had smoothed things over with the Chicago chef and persuaded him to accept the job at Batouri.

"Can't be worse than you."

Ashton ignored the taunt. "He'll probably start you at the bottom. I'm not sure that's the best use of your talents. I could find you something in one of my New York or London restaurants."

Dae shook his head. "I like Vegas. It's happening."

After marking the first twenty-five years of his life by island time, Dae was looking for a little excitement. Ashton understood. Hadn't he gotten out of Africa at twenty for the exact same reason?

"Just don't lose your shirt gambling."

"No worries." Dae tugged at the tails of his bright tropical shirt. "No one would give me a nickel for this thing."

"That's not what I meant," Ashton began, before seeing that his protégé was pulling his leg. "That dumb island boy stuff isn't going to get you too far."

Dae winked. "It got me here and that's pretty far."

With a rueful grin, Ashton stopped playing wise old guy. The role didn't suit him. Usually he was the one on the receiving end of advice, not the other way around. It was just that most of the time in Dae's company, the ten-year age difference seemed more like twenty.

Ever since he'd brought the young Indonesian kid under his wing, Ashton had felt responsible for him. Owner of four restaurants with over a hundred staff, he had a lot of people depending on him. But that was business. With Dae it was personal.

A chance to pay forward against a debt he could never repay.

"I found you a place to stay not far from here. It's on the bus line."

"You know I appreciate all you've done for me."

"Someone helped me out once. It changed my life." Saved it was more like it. And Dae was far more deserving of help than Ashton had ever been. "The best way to repay me is to succeed."

"You know I will."

That was the great thing about Dae. He had a limitless reserve of optimism. Even when his situation had been truly bad in Bali, he'd just grinned and said that things would get better. And they had because Ashton had traded cooking lessons for surfing lessons and discovered the kid had a natural aptitude and a fantastic palate.

"Shall we go check out your new apartment?" Ashton gestured toward the exit.

"Lead the way. How are things going with the new show?" Dae asked as Ashton got behind the wheel of the SUV he'd rented and started the engine.

"I'm not sure. They're still demanding I give up *The Culinary Wanderer*."

"You gonna?"

"The producers haven't stopped pushing Africa for next year and you know how I feel about it."

"Maybe you should forget about them. Do the show in New York."

Sound advice. Vince had been urging him in the same direction. Even his own brain was telling him to dump the travel show and move on to bigger and better things. And with the Phillips producers digging in their heels about doing next year's show in Africa, there didn't seem to be any good reason to sign a new contract.

So why was he having trouble letting go?

"That's probably what's going to end up happening," Ashton said. "I'll know more next week when I go meet with them. They want me to make a pilot for some people to look at."

"What are you going to do?"

"I have a few ideas."

None of which felt quite right. When they'd first approached him, Ashton had known exactly what he wanted to do. But as the negotiations lengthened, the more he learned about their concept for the show, the less confident he was that it was the sort of thing he wanted to do. And yet, the opportunity to take his career to the next level was a temptation he couldn't reject out of hand.

Once he'd settled Dae in his new apartment, Ashton

returned to the hotel. Dae's questions had prodded him into action.

He was beginning to wonder if they would ever see eye to eye on this project and what would happen if they didn't. After his last round of recipes had been rejected by the producers as too exotic, Ashton was finding it hard to come up with anything that excited him. Was it supposed to be this hard? Ashton didn't remember ever having to struggle like this to make anything happen in his career. Sure, he'd worked hard. Pushed himself to the limits of his energy and beyond. During his years filming *The Culinary Wanderer,* he'd been chilled to the bone, taken shelter from a tropical storm in a shallow cave, broken his arm, sprained his knee and been grazed by a ricocheting bullet. In the days before he'd landed his first television show, he'd worked for arrogant chefs who'd made his life hell but hadn't cared because it had been all about the food.

This was different. The executives of Lifestyle Network weren't thinking about good food or interesting stories— they wanted big numbers, and to them that meant doing something everyone could relate to. Ashton didn't think that would ever play to his strengths. Unless Vince was right and they were just hiring him to up their beefcake quotient.

The thought both amused and horrified him.

Ashton pushed aside the notes he'd been scribbling for the show and went to work on the more immediate problem. Figuring out Batouri's menu. Harper would expect culinary perfection and a cohesive plan for how that would happen. Impressing her should have been secondary in his thoughts. But he liked what happened when she dropped her guard and that only happened when he surprised her.

Unfortunately, an hour after sitting down with his thick notebook filled with recipes he'd gathered over the years, inspiration still eluded him. He was on the verge of picking ten at random when he heard the clink of china and looked up as Harper slid into the booth opposite him.

When Harper first entered the restaurant and spotted Ashton at the corner table he seemed to prefer, she realized they were both stuck in a rut. Him, sitting in the dim restaurant brooding. Her, tracking him down like some infatuated groupie. Which she was. But her reasons for coming here were a little more complicated than simple hero worship.

Last night, she'd left the restaurant feeling calmer and more grounded than when she'd arrived. Perhaps he wasn't the most reliable or altruistic man she'd ever met, but his brand of roguish charm had provided a much-needed distraction.

Today he was bent over a notebook, a cup of coffee at his elbow. It was the first time she'd ever seen him this utterly focused on his work. Usually he was a whirling dervish of energy. Flamboyant and passionate while interviewing chefs, directing staff in the bright stainless-steel kitchen or conveying his vision for the decor, gesturing broadly to emphasize whatever point he was trying to make.

As she studied him, some of her anxiety faded. Even sitting still, his body hummed with energy. Yet last night, he'd been an oasis of peace in her otherwise chaotic day. The experience had surprised her. She'd stayed to chat with him, looking to be distracted for a little while. With Scarlett's teasing still occupying her thoughts, was it any wonder she'd been contemplating what being with him would be like?

She'd assumed all he could offer her would be mind-blowing sex with no strings. Her perception had changed when he shared that he'd left home at fifteen and never looked back. She was certain this was something few knew. Why had he given her a glimpse of the man behind the celebrity? He was more complicated than she'd imagined and that spurred her fascination with him to new heights.

It also made tumbling into bed with him a lot riskier than she'd first thought.

Her head told her to turn around and walk out the door. Life had become complicated enough without falling for Ashton Croft. But curiosity drove her forward. She simply had to know what he was working on.

Grabbing a cup from the wait station as she passed, she slid into the booth beside Ashton. He'd been lost in thought, but looked up as the cushion shifted with her weight. Without questioning her reason for joining him, he took her cup and filled it with coffee from the stainless-steel airpot.

"Checking up on me?"

"Do I need to?"

"Probably." He flipped through the notebook, displaying pages filled with his bold handwriting. "I'm going a dozen different directions."

"I never expected you to second-guess yourself." She pulled his notebook toward her. "I always picture you jumping off the cliff without checking to see if there's a safer way down."

"Maybe you're rubbing off on me a little."

His claim made her grin. "Then my work here is done."

"Not even close. You need to help me finalize my menu."

"Me?"

"For someone who doesn't eat, you have one of the best palates I've ever known."

"I eat," she protested. "I just make sure it's healthy. And I exercise a lot. Running helps me think."

"If you ask me, you need to spend less time in your head."

"I don't remember asking you." Her mild tone kept harshness out of the retort. "But that hasn't stopped you from offering your opinion in the past."

"Stop trying to provoke me and pick a dish that appeals to you."

Resisting a grin, Harper focused on Ashton's notebook.

She'd never had a relationship where she felt comfortable being playful. In New York the men she dated were serious types whose pedigrees would satisfy her mother. Ashton didn't fit that mold. And her grandfather's opinion of him was what mattered to her. Henry Fontaine appreciated Ashton's rise from humble beginnings. Her grandfather had built his hotel empire through hard work, too.

After a while, Harper found herself unable to choose a single dish from the recipes he'd jotted down, which only caused her admiration for Ashton to grow. Each dish sounded better than the last. The man was nothing short of brilliant. She saw why he was having trouble settling on his menu. He had enough here for ten restaurants.

"Any one of these would be perfect. It's too bad you can't make them all." She slid the notebook back toward him. "You should do a cookbook. One of the things your television show didn't do was spotlight your talent."

His eyes narrowed as he studied her. "I've missed cooking. It's part of why I'm looking at doing a kitchen-based show for Lifestyle Network."

Harper sighed. Because his other restaurants were critically well received and extremely profitable, she hadn't been able to understand his lack of focus when it came to Batouri. Now she was beginning to realize it was a timing issue. He'd put his television career ahead of the restaurant at every turn. And now he was entertaining the idea of a new project. No wonder he was finding it too difficult to settle down and focus on the mundane details required to make the restaurant successful.

"We've come too far to change things now," Harper began, determined to voice her concerns. "But I have to ask if you're truly committed to making Batouri successful."

"Of course."

When she'd first approached him about the restaurant, she'd hoped they'd form a partnership. Blinded by her admiration for his talent, she hadn't realized that Ashton liked to fly solo.

"It just seems as if your attention isn't one hundred percent focused on this project."

"I'm in negotiations for the next season of my show, but most of that is being handled by my manager. I'm committed to getting the restaurant up and running."

She hoped that was true, but what was going to happen when this new show took off? He already had four other restaurants and *The Culinary Wanderer*. Now a new show?

"Will you have time to do both shows plus manage all your restaurants?"

"I'm not sure I'm going to be doing *The Culinary Wanderer* much longer."

Disappointment raced through her. "You can't stop." What could possibly provide him the same thrill as filming in a country where travel was risky due to political upheaval or in remote locations that few outsiders bothered to visit? Playing it safe wasn't Ashton's first priority. "That show is wonderful."

"I don't want to stop," he told her. "But it's a sticking point in the negotiations for the new show. They want me to be exclusive to the Lifestyle Network."

"Why exclusive?"

"They're planning on promoting the hell out of the new show and the exposure will lead to bigger things."

"And that's what's important to you?" Part of her recognized it was none of her business, but she couldn't get enough of his travel show. She'd seen every episode at least three times. "I thought you loved traveling to out-of-the-way places and meeting new people."

"I do." He rubbed his temple with his palm. "It's just that I'm looking for new challenges and this new show fits the bill."

"You're sure you can't do both?"

"You were just asking me if I was going to have time."

"That was before I realized you were going to stop doing *The Culinary Wanderer*."

"Sorry to disappoint you."

She wished she'd kept quiet. Badgering him with her concerns wasn't constructive. He wasn't a man she could control. In the past nine months she'd learned that lesson all too well.

"It's none of my business. I just love your show."

"Thank you." Ashton put his hand over hers and squeezed gently. "I'll make several dishes I'm on the fence about including on the menu. You offer your opinion and we'll get everything finalized tonight."

Harper knew it was an unnecessary exercise. No matter what she suggested, he would select his menu based on his preferences. But she appreciated his effort to put her mind at ease.

"Sure."

"Come back at eight?"

She slid from the booth. "See you then."

As she exited the restaurant she glanced at her phone. She'd muted it before starting her conversation with Ashton, and now saw that she'd missed six calls and ten emails. Heaving a sigh, she lengthened her stride and headed for her office.

The interlude with Ashton had increased her anxiety rather than calmed her. She caught herself scowling as she rode the elevator to the administrative floor. It was just a television show, she reminded herself, unsure if that was all there was to it. For a half an hour once a week she got to escape the constant pressure of the hotel and travel with Ashton as he learned about elephant conservation in Sri Lanka or braved the Fairy Meadow Road in Pakistan.

The vicarious thrill was a secret she preferred to keep hidden because it didn't sync with the levelheaded, hardworking hotel executive she was 99 percent of the time. Her compulsive desire to protect the secret left her questioning many of the choices she'd made. And she knew nothing good would come of doubting herself.

Ashton crossed his arms over his chest, the white executive chef's jacket pulling tight against his shoulders. He had outdone himself. After Harper had left him that afternoon, he'd benefited from a creative surge that resulted in eight brand new entrées. Each one was something he thought she'd enjoy based on what had caught her attention in his notebook of recipes.

He'd gladly let her preferences define his menu. Batouri wouldn't exist without her. In the past twenty-four hours, as he'd immersed himself in planning, he'd discovered a sense of purpose he hadn't expected. It wasn't in his nature to stop and reflect. Like a shark, he needed to keep swimming in order to stay alive. Or was it to feel alive?

At precisely eight o'clock, Harper entered the kitchen. His pulse jabbed against his throat as he surveyed her. She'd changed into a sleeveless wrap dress made with layers of ethereal blue-gray material.

"What you're wearing reminds me of a fog bank I saw on a motorcycle ride in the highlands of Vietnam last year." He paused, unaccustomed to sharing his thoughts when he wasn't in front of the camera.

She tilted her head, signaling interest. "Tell me about it."

"We had a couple days off from filming so I rented a bike and headed up into the mountains. As you can imagine, the road was narrow and poorly maintained. I'd meet cars and trucks careening around hairpin turns with no guardrails between the road and the sheer cliffs."

"Sounds terrifying."

"It should have been. I'd pass villages where kids ran out into the road. I was chased by dogs." Amid all the craziness he'd felt both exhilarated and completely at peace. "At one point I glanced over my shoulder and down into the valley. A fog hung over the lush green far below."

In those hours he'd not known where he was headed and hadn't cared. The journey was everything. His time in Harper's company was the same. He wanted to live in the present, but she was a woman who needed to know what lay ahead. How far could their relationship develop before she grew frustrated with his act-first, worry-later attitude?

"You got all that from my dress?" Her brow creased. "You should write those experiences down."

"To what end?" It was one thing to put on a show for his television series; it was another to reflect on his personal experiences. "It was just a motorcycle trip."

"One that few people will have the opportunity to experience. You have a knack for drawing in your audience. It will make your cookbook that much more appealing."

"I'm not doing a cookbook."

"Why not?"

"You know why not."

"Because it would require you to sit still too long. Why don't you collaborate with someone?"

"How about I collaborate with you?"

"Me?"

"Why not? It was your idea."

"I don't know the first thing about creating a cookbook."

"But you could figure out what needed to be done."

"I'm too busy." But after a pause, she added, "We can talk about this after the restaurant opens."

He could see that she was on her way to becoming his partner. Why he'd proposed the idea to her was immediately obvious. She possessed the organization and dedication to detail he lacked. Plus, he trusted her opinion. He could count on one hand how many people fell into that category.

"Fair enough," he said, snagging her fingers with his and drawing her deeper into the kitchen. "Let's get down to why you're here."

"Your menu."

"I thought we'd start with a sea bass." He went on to explain the other seven dishes he planned to make for her.

"They all sound wonderful. Good thing I brought my appetite."

He'd prepared his sauces and assembled his ingredients through the afternoon so now it was just a matter of cooking the proteins and assembling the plates. Harper's gaze followed his every move as he shifted between burners and oven. He worked in silence, concentrating on his process, but occasionally felt the pull of her rapt attention.

"Would you mind taking these out to the dining room?" He indicated two of the plates. "I'll follow with the others in a minute."

By the time he had the last of his dishes plated, she'd returned and grabbed three more entrées, leaving the rest for him. He left the kitchen and crossed the dining room to the same table they'd sat at earlier in the day. It was his favorite in the whole restaurant. Quiet, out of the way, but with the vantage of being able to see the whole room.

Candles in crystal holders sent light flickering through the medium-bodied, golden 2006 Chenin Blanc he'd chosen to pair with the sea bass and the truffle risotto. Harper's eyes were bright with wonder as she surveyed their laden table and the assortment of wines he'd opened.

"I'm not sure how we're supposed to eat and drink all this," she said, sounding overwhelmed but delighted.

"It's a buffet. Taste a little of each. Sample the wines. I chose a selection of African vintages for tonight. We'll offer these as well as domestic and foreign."

"I love that your heritage is the backbone of Batouri. When you first told me the name, you explained that the restaurant is named after a town in Africa, but I can't remember where it was located. "

"It's in the East Province of Cameroon."

"Why did you choose it?"

He didn't think she'd like hearing the raw truth, but respected her enough to give her a doctored-up version. "I lived there for three years when I was a teenager."

"It was your home, then."

He poured her a glass of Pinotage. "Try the lamb. It's marinated in yogurt, garlic, coriander seeds, ground cumin and onion."

"Delicious," she murmured, her eyes half closing as she savored the bite.

Ashton couldn't tear his gaze from her face. Her open expression of pure sensual delight shot through him like a laser. Something came undone in his chest. He ached with the unraveling. The temptation to capture her lips with his, to share in her pleasure, swept through him. He reminded himself that a great deal of work had been involved in putting these dishes together. Work that would be for nothing if he acted on his impulse to make love to her right here and now.

He cleared his throat. "I'm glad you like it." His voice had a rough edge as if he'd been cheering on his team in a World Cup final.

"*Love* would be a better word." She sipped the wine and nodded. "This pairs very well with the lamb. What's next?"

Her eagerness made him smile. "Try the duck confit with the Chardonnay."

By the time she'd tasted the final dish, she wore a dreamy, satiated smile. He'd eaten little, preferring to watch her relish every bite. His gut took a hit every time she sighed in appreciation. It was foreplay unlike anything he'd ever known, and he was grateful for the experience.

"Everything was fantastic," she said. "Put it all on the menu. Batouri will be the most sought after reservation in Las Vegas."

He hoped she was right.

"I only have one dessert," he said, watching her take another bite of the scallop crudo with blood orange, watercress and fennel. "I hope you've left room."

"I'll make room."

He left her to fetch the dessert, bringing out only one plate since he doubted she had room for more than a bite or two. "It's a spiced chestnut cake with orange confit."

She accepted the dessert fork he handed her and dug in. "Oh, this is amazing. Are you tired of me telling you how wonderful you are?"

"That could never happen." In fact, he hadn't enjoyed her praise half as much as he'd been happy that his food had moved her to smile and laugh and groan in delight.

She shifted on the seat, turning her torso fully toward him. Taking his face between her hands, she compelled his gaze to hers. The candlelight picked out the amber flecks in her brown eyes, intensifying their compelling power. Slowly, deliberately, she leaned forward until their lips grazed in a dragonfly whisper of a kiss.

"You have an incredible gift. Thank you for sharing it with me tonight."

There was only so much a man could take. Ashton tunneled his fingers into her hair and caught her mouth with a fervent moan of surrender. Greedy for the taste of her, he licked past her lips and was greeted by no resistance, no hesitation, only the delicious slide of her tongue against his.

The layered fruitiness of Chenin Blanc and spiced chestnut danced across his taste buds as Harper tilted her head and gave him deeper access to her mouth. He hadn't realized just how ravenous he was until her arms went around his neck, and she pressed her breasts hard against his chest. Their breath combined in great heaving gasps as one kiss followed another. Drinking his fill of her soft lips seemed impossible. Each second that ticked by he wanted her more.

Dishes rattled on the table as they bumped against it. Distantly, Ashton considered the impracticality of their current location. He'd never be able to get her naked in such a confined space. And that's how he intended she be when he made love to her. Not one inch of her slender frame was going to go unexplored by him. He'd lain awake too many nights imagining her flawless skin and how it would feel to slide his palms against its softness.

He nipped lightly at her throat. Her body jerked reflexively, startling a laugh out of her. When he shifted his grip from her nape to her spine, his elbow banged the table hard. A wineglass tipped over.

"Damn it," he muttered.

"It's empty." She leaned back and surveyed the damage they'd done. "This really isn't the opportune place to get carried away like that."

"No." Desire shrieked through him, fierce and unquenched. He set his spine against the back of the booth and raked his fingers through his hair. "Damn."

"Let's clean all this up."

"There'll be a cleaning crew coming by at midnight." He didn't want to leave the intimacy of the candlelit booth for the harsh fluorescent starkness of the stainless-steel kitchen.

"Then they'll have less to do." Already she was shifting out of the booth and piling up the plates.

He paused a second before moving, taking a moment to survey her high color, mussed hair and the extra bit of skin bared by their sensual tussling. Damn but she was glorious. Graceful and romantic, confident and feminine. If her employees could see her now, would they take her seriously as a businesswoman? They would if they noticed the determination in her stare.

"Come on," she said, her tone a stern nudge.

"I suppose the faster we put everything away the sooner we can get back to the getting acquainted portion of tonight's schedule."

She gave him a *we'll see* smile and headed toward the kitchen. Ashton quickly bussed the table and followed her, unconcerned that Harper appeared to be in full retreat. He had a restaurant to open. That meant he wasn't going anywhere for now. There would be plenty of time to get better acquainted.

Once Harper had deemed the kitchen was organized enough to leave to the cleaners, they shut off the lights and exited the restaurant.

"This has been a nice night," he told her, lacing his fingers through hers. "I don't want it to end."

"If you have in mind a nightcap in your room…" She let the sentence trail off and shook her head.

He couldn't resist a wicked grin. "So, sex is a no." He tugged her close and slipped his fingers into her silky hair, captured her gaze with his and let suspense build. The way her breath hitched, she obviously expected him to push his agenda on her. "How about a walk instead?"

Five

The persistent rattle of her smartphone on the nightstand yanked Harper out of a delicious dream. She had been riding behind Ashton on a motorcycle that was speeding along a coastal highway. Each curve had offered different views of the treacherous terrain ahead, and the exhilarating danger had stolen her breath. Heart still pounding in reaction to the dream, Harper threw her arms wide and stretched, enjoying the slide of cool sheets against her bare skin. Glancing at the clock she saw it was almost nine. She should have been in the office an hour ago. No doubt Mary was frantically looking for her.

With a sigh, Harper slid out of bed and headed straight for the shower. No time to work out this morning. Breaking her routine gave Harper a guilty thrill. So did the reason why she'd turned off the alarm before falling into bed the night before. The walk that Ashton had proposed had lasted two hours. They'd meandered all over the three Fontaine hotels, taking time to tour the gardens at Richesse and have a drink at Chic's chandelier bar.

At first Harper hadn't said much. Mostly she'd asked for the stories that hadn't made it onto the show. Apparently there were hundreds of hours of footage that had gone unseen. Harper would have given a lot to view all of it. She imagined hilarious outtakes and unrehearsed moments of awkwardness. But there would also be bittersweet interviews and breathtaking scenery.

After the walk, they'd ended up at a table in Fontaine Ciel's coffee shop that overlooked the pool area. Ashton had turned the conversation away from him and gleaned a great deal of Harper's history, including her parents' difficult marriage and how she'd coped with finding out about her two half sisters. He'd known she was ambitious, but now he knew the life experiences that had molded her dreams and goals.

It was the most time she'd ever spent with him and by far the least adversarial. Ashton had proven to be an accomplished interviewer and a charming companion. Funny, perceptive and insightful, he'd turned out to be more interesting than she'd expected. And that was saying a lot.

Now a decidedly infatuated woman stared back at Harper when she cleared the steam from the bathroom mirror. Her reflection told her all she needed to know about how much trouble she was in. The last thing she should do was fall for Ashton Croft. Given his track record, he was almost guaranteed to disappoint her in the very near future.

Putting the celebrity chef out of her mind, Harper dressed and picked up her phone. She winced as she read through her emails and texts. A lot of issues needed her attention before noon when she was meeting her sisters. Because Violet hadn't returned home until late yesterday, they'd decided their weekly breakfast should change to lunch this one time.

Harper had taken advantage of this change in her schedule to spend more time with Ashton the night before. One cup of coffee had become two and then three. By the time she tumbled into bed at four in the morning, she'd been far too wired to sleep despite the fact that she'd been drinking decaf the whole time.

But the reduced amount of sleep she'd gotten didn't seem to be affecting her energy level, just her mental capacity. Harper was having a hard time concentrating on all the details competing for her attention.

Lost in daydreams featuring the lush scenery of Indonesia where Ashton had most recently been, she exited her hotel suite and headed to the executive floor. What incredible adventures he'd had. And she hadn't needed to wait another three months to learn about them on his show.

"Harper, are you okay?"

"Hmmm?" She blinked and noticed her assistant was frowning at her. Harper was standing by Mary's desk, but her mind was thousands of miles away. "Sorry. I was thinking about…" Stumped for an excuse, Harper trailed off. She couldn't admit she'd been fantasizing about Ashton Croft and the romantic beaches of Bali. "You were saying?"

"It can wait until this afternoon. Are you planning on coming back here after lunch with your sisters?"

"I think so. Unless something comes up." Rarely was she this indecisive. "I'll call you and let you know."

The walk to Scarlett's office at Fontaine Richesse through the connecting skyways took longer than her usual ten minutes of brisk walking. To maximize the all-inclusive feel of the three hotels, a variety of high-end stores lined the second floor route. The only reason Harper normally paid attention to the boutiques was to eyeball the number of customers and gauge what worked and what didn't. Today, she found herself window-shopping.

A particularly sexy black dress in a front display caught her eye, causing Harper to stop. She didn't need to glance at her watch to know she was running behind schedule, but the need to try on the dress drew her into the store. It wasn't her usual style, but Harper imagined Ashton's eyes lighting up on Batouri's opening night and knew she had to have it. She directed the sales clerk to send it to her office at Fontaine Ciel and made arrangements for payment. She'd need a sexy pair of black stilettos to complete the look, but those would have to wait until later. She was really late for lunch.

Her sisters wore matching expressions of concern as Harper entered Scarlett's organized, roomy office.

"Sorry I'm late."

"It's fine," Violet said. "I love your hair down. You should wear it that way more often."

Harper self-consciously brushed the fine strands away from her face. "I was in a hurry this morning." That wasn't exactly true. She'd been reliving the pleasure of Ashton's fingers playing in her hair. Her skin had tingled as the ends had swept her shoulder and caressed her cheek.

"So it has nothing to do with your canoodling with Ashton last night?" Scarlett queried, her expression knowing and smug.

Violet's eyes went wide. "Canoodling?"

"Hardly," Harper said. "We simply went for a walk."

"Sweetie, after my night manager mentioned he'd caught sight of you with a man last night, I watched video of that walk," Scarlett teased. "You might not have been touching, but that was big-time canoodling for you."

The delight fluttering in Harper's stomach was messing with her head. She tried to shoot her sister a repressive glare, but felt the corner of her mouth tilted upward. "We talked until almost four this morning."

"Talked?"

Harper stared Scarlett down. "Talked."

"You mean to tell me Ashton Croft didn't put the moves on you?"

"He tried." Harper was both relieved and disappointed that he hadn't put more effort into persuading her to have that drink in his suite. "I'm not going to hop into bed with him that fast."

Scarlett made a disgusted noise. "That fast? You two have been flirting for nine months."

"Flirting? No. We've been politely fighting."

"For you that's flirting."

Harper threw up her hand to block any more of her sister's crazy notions. "Is there a particular reason there's a bottle of champagne chilling over there?"

"We have a lot to celebrate, starting with Violet," Scarlett explained. She poured the sparkling liquid into three flutes and motioned her sisters over.

"You were able to help JT get his company back, weren't you," Harper guessed, delighted.

The smirk on Violet's face was priceless. "And Preston has been arrested. He was dragged out of Cobalt in handcuffs."

"I would have loved to see the look on his face as he was escorted out of his hotel by the FBI," said Harper.

Violet nodded. "It was pretty satisfying."

"And things between you and JT?" Scarlett prompted.

"Perfect."

Harper's heart lifted at the joy on her sister's face. "You're not separating then."

"Not a chance." Fierce and romantic, Violet beamed. "He loves me."

"I'm happy for you," Harper said, but already she was worrying about how this would change things between the three of them. "Have you figured out what's going to happen when JT takes over Stone Properties?"

"He's not. Once his father was out of the way I thought for sure that JT would step in as CEO." The sole reason Violet had married JT was to help him take over his family's company. "Instead, he sold his shares to his cousin in order to buy Titanium." Titanium was the Stone Properties hotel and casino JT ran in Las Vegas. It was the largest and most profitable of all the company's properties, thanks to JT's excellent management.

Harper couldn't see the sense in his decision. "I'm surprised he would do that when he could have all of Stone Properties to run."

"He wanted to stay in Las Vegas." Violet looked as blissful as a woman in love should. "He knew my heart was here."

"What about Grandfather's contest?" Harper asked. The corporate offices for Fontaine Hotels and Resorts were in New York City.

"Last week I told Grandfather I wasn't interested in being CEO." Violet looked at Scarlett.

Before Harper grasped what Violet's decision meant for the future, Scarlett held her glass high and proclaimed, "All hail the future CEO of Fontaine Hotels and Resorts."

Harper's heart twisted in her chest. Had Grandfather made his decision? Was Scarlett his choice for a successor?

"Congratulations," Harper said to Scarlett, proud that her voice was so bright when her heart was lost in shadow. She'd wanted Grandfather to pick her, had spent her entire life working toward that goal. More than that, she needed his acceptance. To think that she wasn't good enough was a blow she hadn't prepared herself for.

Scarlett rolled her eyes. "Not me, silly. You."

"Me?" Harper looked from Scarlett to Violet. "I don't understand. Grandfather hasn't said anything about the contest being over."

Scarlett piped up. "I called Grandfather this morning and told him that the network executives loved the pilot for my new series and picked up the show." Her starlet smile flashed bold and brilliant. "That means you are going to be Fontaine's next CEO."

The news should have thrilled Harper. It was why she'd worked hard and sacrificed a social life in high school to ensure she got into Cornell University's School of Hotel

Administration. After graduating with top honors she'd gone to work at a Fontaine property in Chicago, starting at the bottom to learn every aspect of the business. All her energy had gone into proving to her grandfather that she was not her father's daughter. She would give Fontaine Hotels and Resorts her complete attention.

But to get the job because her competition had dropped out. That wasn't her idea of winning.

"Grandfather still has the final word," she reminded her sisters, not ready to celebrate. "He might just decide that I wasn't going to be his first choice."

"Don't be ridiculous," Scarlett scoffed, clinking her crystal flute with Harper's. "You are and always have been the front-runner." She glanced at Violet. "No offense, Violet. I think if you'd hung in there you might have given Harper a run for her money."

"I'm not insulted," Violet said, a fond look in her eyes. "I love Las Vegas. And I love running my hotel. I'm not really cut out to sit in endless meetings and read reports all day." But Harper knew Violet was downplaying how serious her decision had been.

At Scarlett's urging, Harper sipped at the sparkling wine, but the effervescent liquid didn't ignite joy or even relief. As soon as Ashton's restaurant opened, she would head to New York and have a face-to-face chat with her grandfather. Until she knew his thoughts on her future with the company, she wouldn't let herself hope her dreams were coming true.

In a state of conflicting emotions, Harper ate her salad in silence and listened to Violet and Scarlett with half her attention. Both of them were madly in love with wonderful men. It was hard for Harper to contribute to the conversation. Listening to them discuss Violet's upcoming belated honeymoon and Scarlett's wedding arrangements demonstrated just how two-dimensional Harper's life was. She had her work and her sisters. Both meant everything to her, but after spending the evening with Ashton, she couldn't help feeling as if she was missing out on something important.

"I got an update from Logan a little before you showed up today," Scarlett said, catching Harper's eye. "He said his people have tracked the million your mother wired to the blackmailer." Scarlett didn't explain how this had been done and Harper refrained from asking, expecting that the methods were not official. "It went through several banks before it landed in an account belonging to some guy named Saul Eddings. The strange part is he doesn't seem to exist."

So, the blackmailer was clever. Harper had been racking her brains for days trying to figure out who could have dug up a thirty-year-old affair. Why wait until now to trade the information for money?

"What's going on?" Violet asked.

"My mother is being blackmailed."

"Your mother?" Violet shot Scarlett a worried look. "Blackmailed about what?"

"Ancient history," Harper explained, wondering what was causing Violet's escalating tension. "Apparently she had an affair thirty years ago."

Violet whirled on Scarlett. "You didn't tell her, did you?"

"No." Scarlett eyes grew hard as she stared at Violet.

"She needs to know."

"I need to know what?" Harper demanded, alarmed by the sudden animosity between her sisters.

"It won't help," Scarlett said. "Logan will find out who's doing this and he and Lucas will take care of it. So, you need to just let it go."

"Have you thought of what's best for Harper?"

"Repeatedly." Scarlett could be a force of nature when she sank her teeth into something. "Drop it."

Harper couldn't take it anymore. "Stop it, both of you.

I need to know what's going on. Who's blackmailing my mother?"

"I don't know," Scarlett admitted, as somber as Harper had ever seen her.

Harper persisted. "But you know something about it."

"I think so."

"And you weren't planning on telling me?" The room suddenly felt cold, as if the air conditioners were working at twice their normal capacity. Harper rubbed her arms. "Why?"

"Because no good will come of it," Scarlett said.

All the more reason for her to know. "It's about my mother and the affair?"

"Yes." Violet reached out and took Harper's icy fingers, rubbing them to bring back some warmth. "Tiberius had files on all of us."

"I already knew that."

"Including your mother."

"When I was attacked and the files were stolen," Scarlett explained, her voice quiet and reluctant, "the one on your mother was taken."

"That explains where the photos came from and why the blackmail began now." One question answered. But was that all there was to the sharp looks and tense exchange between Violet and Scarlett? "Is there more to it?"

"If you don't tell her, I will," Violet declared.

"It's about the timing of the affair," Scarlett said. "It happened nine months before you were born."

"That doesn't mean…" Harper wasn't sure she wanted to make the connections Scarlett was hinting at. "The affair only lasted two weeks."

"And from what we've determined about your father's travels, he was gone for almost six weeks around that same time."

Bile rose in Harper's throat. It couldn't be possible. It certainly wasn't fair.

She wasn't a Fontaine.

These two wonderful women weren't her sisters.

She had no right to run Fontaine Ciel, much less become CEO of the company.

Suddenly, Harper couldn't breathe. She put her hand to her chest. "I have to go."

She pushed back from the table so abruptly her chair crashed to the ground. Scarlett's office spun as Harper struggled to figure out where the door had gone.

"Harper, are you okay?"

Okay? Would she ever be okay again?

"Fine. I just remembered that I was going to…" She never finished the sentence. The door had come into view and Harper made for it.

"Are you sure you're all right?" Violet had pursued her from Scarlett's office into the hallway. "I know this must be a huge shock. But it doesn't matter. You know that."

"Of course it matters." Harper didn't know how to make Violet understand. Everything she'd worked for. Every sacrifice she'd made. Was it all for nothing? "I'll talk to you and Scarlett later. Right now I just need to grab some air."

Scarlett appeared on Harper's other side, her fingers biting hard into Harper's arm. "You are our sister. You will be Fontaine's next CEO. It's what you've always wanted."

"Of course." Harper patted Scarlett's hand. "I get it. This is our secret."

Violet relaxed. "Exactly."

"I love you both, but I need to get back to work. I'll check in with you later."

And before they could protest further, she briskly walked away.

Instead of retracing her steps through the skyways, she wound through the casino and emerged onto the Vegas Strip. The heat, noise and press of the crowd hit her like a rogue wave. How long had it been since she'd ventured beyond the insulation of Fontaine walls? She slept, ate and worked within a square city block, finding little need to explore the world outside. There was a drugstore attached to the hotel if she needed sundries. When she traveled, it was in a hired car that swept her to the airport and a private plane that carried her to her destination.

Always there was someone around to guide her to meetings and keep her on schedule. She'd never detoured because the mood hadn't struck her. Her activities were planned and organized. It was the way she liked it. What had made her successful.

With more vigor than necessary, Harper pushed through the ground floor door that led into Fontaine Ciel's casino. Nothing looked familiar. The persistent noise from the slot machines and the dazzling lights battered her senses. She had no idea how to get to her office. Disoriented, Harper turned in a slow circle. Confusion overwhelmed her. Harper put her arms out for balance as the edges of her vision began to darken.

"Harper, are you okay?"

She couldn't remember the name of the man who spoke. Distantly she knew she should. That she dealt with him on a daily basis. Tom something. Tim maybe.

"I'm a little dizzy all of a sudden." She shook her head, hoping to clear her vision. To her right was an open slot machine. "I just need to sit down for a second." She took a step and swayed.

"Let me help," Tom or Tim said, reaching for her arm.

She flinched away from his touch. Her skin felt as if it was on fire. "No." She reached the chair and dropped into it. "Sorry. I'll be fine in a couple seconds. Perhaps you could get me a glass of water."

"Sure."

While he headed off to intercept a waitress, Harper closed her eyes and rubbed at her temples. Her brain was coming back online, allowing her to think more clearly. What the hell had just happened? From her symptoms she guessed it had been a panic attack. Made sense. Her whole world was spinning out of control.

By the time Tim Hoffman—she'd finally recalled the name of her facilities manager—returned with her water, Harper was on her feet and feeling much steadier. But her need to run hadn't abated. For someone who always met problems head-on, she wasn't sure what to make of the impulse to flee. Work wasn't the remedy for her troubles. It was the cause of her angst. Better that she spend some time alone. To think. To sort out her emotions.

"I should have taken the skyway back from Richesse. Must have been the heat outside that made me dizzy."

The short, dark-haired man looked relieved. "It's warmer than usual, that's for sure."

"Thanks for the water." Without another word, Harper headed for the elevators. Maybe an hour on her treadmill would enable her to reach some clarity.

Six

Ashton stretched out on the couch in his suite and stared at the ceiling. Beyond the wall of windows the day was fading and the Las Vegas Strip was lighting up. As much as he loved the fascinating sights he'd seen in some of the most remote spots on the planet, enjoying the luxury of a first-class hotel was an indulgence he appreciated most of all.

Unfortunately, his current career issues weren't allowing him to put aside his worries and savor the lavender scented sheets, decadent bathroom or spectacular view. Vince had called this morning with bad news. Unless the producers of *The Culinary Wanderer* received his decision about filming in Africa three days from now they were cancelling the show.

As much as Ashton hated having anyone force his hand, he should be relieved that he would soon be free to sign with the Lifestyle Network. He and Phillips could part without bad feelings. But if everything was so great, why did he feel numb?

A knock sounded on his door. Shoving to a sitting position, Ashton ran his fingers through his hair and got to his feet. Dae had said he'd call later and see if Ashton wanted to check out the Strip. He hadn't expected the kid to show up.

But it wasn't Dae. The visitor at his door was so unexpected, he stood staring at her in dumfounded silence.

"Hi." Harper stood in the hallway wearing stretchy gray pants that highlighted her long, lean legs and an oversized pale pink sweater that she wrapped tight around her body. "I probably should have called before stopping by." Her casual attire and indecisive posture meant she hadn't come here to talk business.

"No need. I was just thinking that I could use a little company." He gestured her inside.

"That's how I felt, too." She shuffled in and gazed around the suite as if she hadn't been instrumental in overseeing every aspect of the design and decor. Sounding dreamy and vague, she continued. "I enjoyed our conversation last night."

"So did I." Catching her hand, he drew her toward the couch. "Do you want some wine?"

"Sure."

He poured glasses for both of them and sat close beside her. Content to enjoy her company, Ashton sipped his wine and watched her. She wore no makeup and that added to the aura of vulnerability that surrounded her at the moment. The scent of jasmine clung to her skin. A trace of damp lingered in the thick wave of brown hair cascading around her delicate shoulders. He guessed she'd been working out recently for a healthy glow suffused her skin.

"Did you always want to be a chef?" With her feet tucked beneath her, she took up very little space, but vibrancy had returned to her voice.

"I sort of stumbled into it."

The truth wanted to spill out of him. Last night she'd shared a great deal about her childhood and school years.

Her openness had tempted him to talk about his own past. But most of the people who knew what he'd done had either been dumped in the African jungle or buried in a shallow grave. An elegant, cultured woman like Harper would be horrified by what it had cost him to survive.

"When I was fifteen," he began, abandoning the press release version of his past, "I left home and fell in with some bad guys."

Describing Chapman's ruthless gang of smugglers as bad guys was woefully inadequate. They'd been a mean bunch of criminals brought together by the most loathsome man Ashton had ever met.

"How bad?"

He pushed back his left sleeve and showed her a pair of long, faint scars on his forearm. "They liked to play with knives."

"They did this to you? That doesn't look much like playing. Why did you stick around?"

"Because I was cocky and stubborn. I thought I could take care of myself." And he'd had nowhere else to go. Ashton brushed his sleeve down. "One of the guys did all the cooking for the gang. He took me under his wing. Kept me away from the worst of the lot. Turns out I had a knack for combining flavors." Not the whole truth, just a sterilized version of what had really happened.

"Had you planned to do anything else?"

Ashton shrugged. He'd been a stupid, rebellious teenager who'd rarely thought beyond the moment. "I only knew I wasn't going to follow in my father's footsteps."

Her lips twisted into an unhappy grimace. "What did he do?"

"He was a missionary." He hadn't planned to disclose that fact. Usually, he told people his father was a salesman. Which was pretty close to the truth. His parents spent their whole lives selling salvation to people who had no idea they were damned.

For the first time since she'd arrived on his doorstep, her eyes brightened. "A missionary? Forgive me if I say that you don't strike me as the son of a religious man."

She made no attempt to hide her curiosity. Nor did she curb the trace of laughter in her tone. This wasn't the withdrawn, mentally drained woman who'd shown up at his door. The cloud that had followed her into his suite had retreated for the moment.

"I could say I'm not and explain that there are all sorts of missionaries in Africa, but my father and mother spent a great deal of my childhood visiting villages and spreading Christian values."

His muscles grew more taut with each syllable that passed his lips. He began to notice an ache in his shoulders. The pain reminded him that he'd never set down the burden of unfinished business created by his choice to leave home and never look back.

"Wow, that was not a happy memory for you at all." She set her fingertips on his forearm, her touch light and friendly.

Too bad his heart didn't recognize the contact as casual. It gave a giant lurch like a racehorse surging from a starting gate. In seconds his breath came more quickly. Usually when desire hit him, he rolled with the blow. Why resist? Beautiful women were their own type of adventure.

But Harper Fontaine wasn't just a beautiful woman. She was intelligent and ambitious, dynamic and resourceful. When he'd first started working with her, he'd been annoyed by her bluntness and impressed by her sincerity. Last night he'd discovered she was also a warm, passionate woman and the chemistry between them was electrifying.

"What about you?" he asked, turning the topic away from himself. "Did you always want to be a hotel executive?"

"From the time I was five years old." She smiled fondly. "My father took me to the Waldorf Astoria and I fell in love. It was everything a grand hotel should be. We went at Christmas and the lobby was filled with these enormous evergreen trees covered in white lights and big red and gold balls. The railings were decorated with swags of ribbon and lights. It was magical. I knew I wanted to be a part of that someday."

He had little trouble imagining her as a wide-eyed child, holding tight to her father's hand while she soaked up the magnificence of that fine old hotel. For her, it had probably been as exciting a place to visit as FAO Schwarz would be for most other children.

"I suppose being a Fontaine, hotels are in your blood."

Her expression changed—the glow in her eyes dimmed, her mouth flattening into a somber line. "What's it like traveling all over the world like you do?"

"Exciting. Exhausting." Sometimes he longed to go home. Or at least that's what he assumed he wanted. He never really felt as if he belonged anywhere. "I crave an ever-changing landscape."

"That's so different from what I'm used to." Setting her elbow on the back of the couch, she propped her head on her hand and sipped her wine. "I've never traveled anywhere."

"I find that hard to believe. There are Fontaine hotels all over the world."

"Yes, but when I've visited the hotels I've never had time to sightsee. You said you couldn't see me shopping in Paris. You were right. I've been there three times and never once toured the city."

"That's a shame. It's a wonderful city. I spent two years there attending culinary school and working in various restaurants." It had been the first place he'd gone after leaving South Africa. At the time, it had seemed the perfect place to re-create himself.

"I spent the first eighteen years of my life in New York City and the next four in Ithaca attending Cornell University."

"You didn't want to travel?"

"My parents were separated from the time I was eleven. My mother lived in Florida, and I visited her during the holidays. My father..." She stumbled over the word and appeared distressed for a moment. "He was gone a lot, overseeing various hotels. The company expanded a great deal in the nineties."

Her childhood sounded as lonely as his had been. "Who did you stay with when your father was away?"

"Servants. Once in a while my grandfather." Her sweater had slipped off one shoulder, baring the thin strap of her gray camisole. "Is there any place you want to visit but haven't?"

The smooth line of her shoulder captivated him. Could her skin be as soft as it looked? "Niagara Falls."

She stared at him in stunned silence for a few moments and then began to laugh. "Niagara Falls? Even I've been there."

Her deep, throaty laugh made him want to kiss her. The mischief dancing in her eyes captivated him. Strong. Soft. Smart. Sexy. Was she as oblivious to her appeal as she appeared or was it all a ruse to catch him off guard?

"Then you'd be a good tour guide."

"I don't know about that. I was seven at the time." Her good mood faded. "My father took me." She blinked rapidly and pushed off the couch. "Damn it. I swore I wasn't going to cry."

Curiosity induced him to follow her. At least that's what he told himself until she was wrapped in his arms, her face pressed against his chest. Her body shuddered as she gulped in air and released an unsteady sigh.

"What's wrong?" He nuzzled the top of her head with his chin while a part of his mind wondered where this urge to comfort had come from. Selfish. Self-involved. Those were the words that described him. It balanced out the fifteen years of selflessness his parents had shoved down his throat.

"Why Niagara Falls?"

"I have a thing for waterfalls." He paused a beat. "What do you have a thing for?"

"You…" she shifted as far away from him as his arms snaked around her waist would allow "…r show."

"Nice save."

"Okay, I'll admit I'm a fan."

He leaned back and peered down at her. "That explains why you've been so nice to me."

"I've been nothing but professional to you."

"Your lips say civilized things," he taunted. "But your eyes tell me how much you'd like to lock me in the walk-in freezer."

"Be honest. Have you been easy to work with?"

"Of course not, but I'm a genius and everyone knows that geniuses are notoriously difficult to get along with."

His candor gave her pause. Head cocked, she regarded him. "Even your arrogance is charming."

"I don't get you."

She avoided his gaze. "What's there to get?"

"You have money and family connections. Anything you want could be yours."

"Is that how you see me?" She asked the question calmly enough, but below the surface he sensed tension.

"That's who you are."

"And if I lacked money and family connections, what am I then?"

The intensity with which she awaited his answer kept Ashton from spouting some flippant remark. "A beautiful, intelligent woman who is ambitious and focused enough to do anything she sets her mind to."

"What if I don't know what I want to do?"

"I don't understand. I thought you were going to take over as CEO of Fontaine Hotels and Resorts."

"I'm no longer sure that's where I belong." She pushed out of his arms and headed toward the door to the hallway. "Thanks for the wine and the shoulder to cry on. I should turn in for the night. I've got a lot to do tomorrow."

Ashton followed her to the door and caught her arm as she reached for the handle, stopping her from leaving. She turned at his touch and swayed into him. Pushing onto her toes, she kissed his cheek.

The warmth of her lips against his skin set his blood alight. His fingers slid into the small of her back and held her against him as he cupped her cheek in his palm and angled her face so he could reach her mouth.

Pliant and slightly salty from her earlier tears, her lips moved beneath his, responding to his searching kiss. It wasn't passion that consumed him. Her somber mood connected him to an emotion he believed he'd lost long ago: compassion. Something radical had happened to her today. Something related to the visit from her mother. The encounter had knocked her off her game.

Just like this kiss was throwing him.

He lifted his lips from hers, shocked by his lightheadedness. One simple kiss shouldn't have affected him so strongly. But then again, he couldn't remember wanting to kiss away someone's unhappiness, either.

"Stay," he urged, brushing his lips across her cheek.

Her muscles tensed. A flight response?

"That's not a good idea."

"You're wrong," he assured her. "It's a great idea."

"I've never jumped into bed with a man I scarcely know."

He'd divulged the truth about his parents with her. That was a huge secret from his past he hadn't shared with anyone else in his present. "Consider it an adventure into the unfamiliar territory."

"I guess I'm not ready to leave behind everything I know."

Yet another enigmatic statement. Ashton was starting to think that Harper had more weighing on her mind than she wanted to confront.

"Why would you think you have to?"

"I don't need to ask you what you'd do if you couldn't be a chef. You've already made a name for yourself as a TV personality and a restaurateur."

This would have been an excellent moment to tell her his project was taking him to New York for a few days, but he was reluctant to shatter the rapport between them.

"Have you been considering a career change?"

A faint smile found its way to her lips. "I was thinking of a television series that featured exotic hotels around the world."

"Want me to talk to my manager about pitching your idea to the network?"

Her eyes widened. "You're serious."

"You seem as if you're grappling with the status quo. Maybe you need to take some risks, challenge yourself. Do something that terrifies you."

"I've already done that." Her expression grew wry. "I came here, didn't I?"

"I terrify you?"

"Not you. Just what you represent."

"And that is?"

"Everything that I grew up avoiding."

He didn't respond to her jab. Better to give her space to assemble her thoughts, let the silence expand to an uncomfortable level until she gave up more than she intended. It was an interview technique he'd often used with great results.

"I didn't mean that as an insult," she said at last. "It's just that I like everything organized and predictable. You thrive on the unexpected."

"It's what makes life interesting. Some of my best recipes have come from putting together flavors that I've never tried before." Hell, his entire career had been framed by a combination of happenstance and his ability to capitalize on all things unconventional. "And I never would've made a career out of cooking if I hadn't run away from home at fifteen and needed to survive."

She didn't look at all surprised by what he'd told her. "I've never wanted to be in a desperate situation, so I never have been." The rest of her admission remained unspoken, but her expression was easy to read.

"And now you're wondering what you've missed?"

"I'm fully aware of what I've missed. I've made sacrifices to keep on track with my goal."

"To run the company someday."

"It was my job to win or lose."

"Has that changed?"

"You must have guessed that it has or I wouldn't have come here tonight and cried all over you." She stepped back and gathered her soft sweater tight about her slim body. "I found out something today that I'm not ready to talk about."

"Use me as a sounding board or keep everything bottled up. It's no matter to me."

"I guess I should say thank you."

"There's no need. As you probably already figured out, I'm a selfish bastard. If a beautiful woman comes to me for comfort, I'm going to enjoy every second of the time she spends in my arms."

"And if she decides to let you comfort her through the night?"

"All the better."

"How do women manage to resist you?"

"Usually they don't."

"So I'm an anomaly?"

"In a class all of your own."

She put her hand on the door handle once again, and this time Ashton didn't stop her. He'd learned to coax the flavor out of food. Forcing something to happen often led to an inferior outcome and above all else, he wanted the first time he made love to Harper to be a moment she'd never forget.

Harper couldn't make herself open the door. Her body ached for his touch. Last night when they'd kissed she'd been able to resist him—just barely. But she'd been nervous about being discovered and had no intention of being seen accompanying Ashton to his suite.

Would it be any better if she was seen exiting his suite in the morning? No, but she was on the verge of not caring.

He must have picked up on her ambivalence because he gently pried her fingers from the handle and dropped a sizzling kiss in her palm. She melted beneath the heat of his gaze and didn't protest when his fingers sought the small of her back. Nor did she resist when with a soft groan he pulled her torso up and firmly into his body.

"Ask me again to stay," she whispered, exhilarated by the leashed passion vibrating in Ashton's muscles.

She dug her fingers into his biceps as he set his open mouth on her neck. The sweep of his tongue against her skin made her moan. Her breasts felt heavy as his arm tightened around her, his chest pushing into her as his breath deepened. The burn beneath her skin made the touch of her clothes unbearable. She needed them gone. Needed to feel his naked flesh against her.

She was half out of her mind with hunger by the time he murmured, "Stay."

"Okay."

He swept her off her feet before the word faded. The air around her cooled as his long, rapid strides brought them to the bedroom. With gentleness she never imagined he possessed, he laid her on the mattress and braced his hands on either side of her head. Wondering what he was up to, she peered at his looming form from beneath her lashes. The intensity of his stare ramped up her desire to be utterly devoured by him.

Raising one hand, she traced the faint hollow of his dimple with her fingertips. The corner of his mouth lifted in response to her touch, deepening the sexy indent. He leaned over her to rub his lips over hers in a tantalizing caress. With an encouraging murmur, she slid her fingers into his hair and brought him closer, deepening the kiss.

Tongues dancing, mouths fused as the heat between them increased, Harper decided the reality of Ashton Croft's kisses was so much better than any fantasy. She wanted to savor the feel of his lips on hers forever, but already her body needed more. Working blindly, she slipped all his shirt buttons free and stroked the fabric off his shoulders. A purr of satisfaction rumbled from her as her palms coasted over the hills and valleys of muscle from his collarbone to his belt.

He seized her lip between his teeth and bit lightly before licking the tender spot. Standing up, he stripped off his shirt, shed his pants and shoes. She scrambled to her knees and peeled off her sweater, but in her haste got her arms caught. Turning the soft knit inside out, she freed herself in time to meet the rush of Ashton's lips as he rejoined her on the bed.

In a jumble of limbs, they rolled across the mattress. Somehow Harper ended up on top. Breathless and laughing, she pressed her lips against Ashton's throat. His hands coasted over her butt and down the backs of her thighs, urging her against the erection straining his boxer briefs. Her head spun as she waited to see where his fingers would explore next.

When they dipped below the waistband of her yoga pants and followed the seam between her butt cheeks to the molten core of her, she gasped. As fleeting as his touch was, it seared her through. She whimpered a protest as he retreated, palms gliding back over the same path. This time he caressed upward, riding the hem of her camisole up over her rib cage.

Almost too shaken to move, but dying to feel his hands on her breasts, Harper placed her palms on the mattress and shoved herself upward. As she'd hoped, he claimed her breasts in his large hands, sending wave after wave of acute pleasure surging through her with his firm touch. She ducked her head as he finished removing her top and emerged from the folds of fabric with a jubilant cry. The sound was cut short as Ashton rolled her beneath him and pulled her nipple into his mouth.

First he sucked, and then swirled his tongue around her nipple, the sensation heightening the lust rampaging through her. She combed her fingers into his hair and held him close. From her throat, mindless, encouraging sounds erupted. She was beyond words. Completely at his command. Whatever he wanted from her she'd give him.

Why had she denied herself this amazing experience for so long? She should have slept with him the first day they met and every time after that. Obviously she wasn't thinking straight because she'd completely forgiven him for all those months of frustration.

Ashton shifted his attention to her second breast and devoted a considerable amount of time driving her desire to alarming heights. His fingers were as busy as his mouth, tracing the skin across her belly, making her stomach muscles pitch and roll. At last he hooked her waistband and applied pressure downward. Harper lifted her hips off the bed to make his job easier. He peeled her pants down her legs, and she finished removing them with three frantic kicks.

His tongue dipped into her navel. Sensation lanced downward. He shifted his broad shoulders between her thighs and used his thumbs to part her folds. Harper clutched the sheets just as his mouth settled over her. Her body jolted, the movement wringing a murmur from her. That's all she had strength for. The rest of her energy was focused on the amazing thing he was doing with his tongue.

Sex wasn't usually on her weekly agenda. She found it

difficult to make time to indulge in a decadent spa treatment or take an afternoon and go shopping. Finding a man she was attracted to seemed far too challenging a prospect, so she went long periods of time without being intimate with anyone.

When first Scarlett and then Violet had fallen in love, Harper might never admit it out loud, but she had envied their glow, the satisfied glint in their eye. Nor had it helped that she'd just begun working with the roguishly handsome Ashton Croft. Hormones long asleep had begun to stir with ever-increasing agitation.

She'd put his ability to exasperate her down to their differing approaches, but with Ashton's mouth sending her into orbit she realized it had just been sexual chemistry and she'd been too long absorbed in her work to recognize the signs.

As pleasure rose, she planted her feet against the mattress and hung on for dear life. His fingers flexed into the soft flesh of her butt, his firm grasp the perfect catalyst to send her spinning out of control. She cried his name as her body exploded. For a second there was a burst of light behind her eyes, and then it slowly faded and she drifted in darkness.

Dimly she felt Ashton shift away from her, but she couldn't move, couldn't protest his leaving. Dimly, she heard the rustle of a condom wrapper and was glad that he'd thought to protect them both. Very few seconds passed before the mattress dipped again. Her lashes fluttered upward as he moved over her once more. His mouth stroked across her lips, tongue dipping between them to tease and arouse all over. Harper put her arms around his shoulders as he shifted his hips between her thighs.

She felt him nudge against her entrance and raised up to meet his thrust as he pushed inside her in one fluid movement. Her inner muscles shuddered in delight, and Ashton buried his face in her neck with a ragged sigh. He was not a small man, and she was a little shocked that her body was able to take him fully. But the rightness of their joining was not to be denied.

Slowly, he started to move. Finding his rhythm took her barely any time at all. Soon it was as if they'd made love a hundred times. She ran her hands over him, finding spots that excited him. He adjusted the angle of her hips and drove into her a little more forcefully. The evocative twist he gave as he plunged into her over and over quickly brought Harper back to the brink of release. As it swept up to claim her once again, she clutched Ashton's forearms and welcomed the frenzied pounding of his body into her as he, too, closed in on his orgasm.

They didn't quite climax together, but it was awfully close. Harper felt the first spasm hit her and dug her nails into Ashton's skin. He kissed her long and hard and with two deep thrusts emptied himself into her with a powerful shudder.

Stunned by the power of what had just happened between them, Harper buried her nose in Ashton's neck and held on while his body trembled. Her sparse personal life hadn't given her a lot of experience in these sorts of matters, but Harper was pretty sure Ashton was as moved as she was.

So what came next?

As if in answer to her question, Ashton shifted his lax muscles and collapsed onto the mattress beside her. They lay side by side, staring up at the ceiling. Harper listened as his breath returned to normal. Her skin was cooling fast. She needed to decide whether to put on her clothes and get out of here or to snuggle against Ashton. Before she'd made up her mind, his fingers closed over hers.

"Don't run off just yet."

Harper turned her head and realized he was watching her. "You don't know that's what I was thinking."

"Don't I?" He rolled onto his side and caught her around

the waist, pulling her beneath him. "Tell me you weren't going to make the excuse that you had to get back to work."

With his warm skin pressing against hers, she knew her opportunity to make a clean getaway had just vanished. Surrendering to the pleasure of his large body overwhelming her, she slid her hands along his muscular arms and marveled at the beauty of his broad shoulders. Already her body craved to be possessed by his once more. He was going to be a hard man to get over.

"I wasn't."

"That doesn't sound much like the Harper I know." He drew back so he could look into her face. "What's happened?"

"I'm pretty sure I'm not the Harper anyone knows."

"I don't understand."

"I found out something today." She pressed her lips together, knowing she shouldn't talk about her secret. If the truth about her paternity got out, she'd never become the CEO of Fontaine Hotels and Resorts. "Something that has changed everything I thought I ever knew about myself."

"That sounds troubling." He stroked her cheek with the tips of his fingers. "What are you going to do?"

Most people would have asked what she'd discovered. With what she'd learned about him in these past few days, Harper understood why he didn't pry. He had a past he wanted to keep private. Things he wasn't proud of.

"I don't know," she told him. "I haven't been thinking too clearly these past few hours." She gave him a wry grin. "I mean, look at me. Twenty-four hours earlier, would I have slept with you?"

"I like to think you were heading down that road."

And she probably had been. "Maybe I'm just making excuses for doing something I've wanted all along."

"Why do you have to make excuses?"

"I don't take sex lightly. For me it's something that comes out of a relationship that has the chance of lasting."

"And you don't think ours will?"

"I think our business relationship will be a lasting one."

He kissed her lightly on the mouth. "I hope so. As for the other, I think we are good for each other. Let's hold on to that for the time being."

As promises went, it wasn't much, but Harper reasoned that for Ashton it was major. She snuggled against his body and let the rhythmic thump of his heart mesmerize her into complete relaxation. The shock of earlier revelations faded as did her ambivalence about what the future held. In Ashton's arms she knew exactly who she was. More than that could wait until the next day.

Seven

Ashton was on his second cup of coffee when the sound of a knock at the door of his suite made him smile. So, after sneaking off while he slept at some point during the wee hours, she'd decided to come back for round four. Smirking, Ashton went to let her in. Only, it wasn't Harper standing in the hall, but Vince.

"What's going on?" he asked his manager, not liking the grim expression Vince wore. "How come you're here?"

"The Lifestyle people have moved up the taping date on your pilot. They want you to come to New York and do it tomorrow."

Ashton cursed, disliking that they were making him jump through hoops. "What's going on?"

"I don't know. We might have dug our heels in a little too hard. I heard they may be looking at other chefs."

And he was going to lose this fantastic opportunity if he didn't move quickly. "What can we do?"

"I'd suggest that we show them how committed we are to Lifestyle Network."

"You want me to quit *The Culinary Wanderer.*"

"You're not happy with the direction they intend to take the show next year. I think it's a good time to cut ties."

His gut told him this was the wrong thing to do, but he'd hired Vince because his gut wasn't right 100 percent of the time. Nor was Ashton convinced he could make decisions about the show he'd worked on for so many years without letting his emotions get the better of him.

"Call Phillips and tell them I'm not going to continue with *The Culinary Wanderer.*" Harper's face flashed before his eyes as he said this. She would be disappointed. And that bothered him more than it should. But this was business. In the end she'd accept that.

"I have things to do before I can head to New York." Chef Cole had not yet arrived from Chicago to take up his duties. Ashton would brief Dae on all the things that needed to be done in the next few days. The kid was smart and resourceful. "How did you get here?"

"Commercial. The network is sending their plane to pick us up tonight."

Well, at least that was one thing he didn't have to worry about. The biggest challenge was going to be telling Harper that he was leaving ten days before Batouri was due to open. That was a conversation he'd better have sooner than later.

After leaving Ashton slumbering peacefully in his bed, Harper had spent the rest of the night on her couch, burrowed beneath a cotton throw, watching one episode after another of *The Culinary Wanderer.* She'd stared at Ashton's image on the screen, unable to believe she'd fulfilled the only sexual fantasy she'd ever had.

Reality had far exceeded anything she could have dreamed up. She'd expected Ashton would be a skilled and masterful lover, but he'd demonstrated a level of caring and consideration of her pleasure that had far surpassed any intimacy she'd ever known. Even now, after several rounds of lovemaking, her body throbbed with desire for him.

But would she have made love with him last night if her defenses hadn't been crushed by the knowledge that she wasn't a Fontaine? The answer wasn't clear enough for Harper's liking. She felt lost and adrift. It's why she couldn't sleep, couldn't make her mind function the way it normally did. No patterns emerged out of the chaos of her thoughts. Her ability to plan and make things happen had left her. She was a shell, waiting to be filled with purpose.

Harper passed her hand over her dry, tired eyes before levering herself off the cushions and heading to make coffee. Her cell phone chirped. A text message. Probably Mary wondering why she hadn't picked up the report on last night's numbers.

Harper picked up the phone, intending to shut it off. For the first time in her life, she didn't feel like being responsible. But she really should call Mary. Unless Harper explicitly stated her unavailability, her assistant expected her to answer, and if she didn't, Mary would probably send security to check on her.

Heaving a sigh, Harper dialed. With Fontaine Ciel open and running smoothly, she could hand over the reins to her general manager for a while. When her assistant picked up, Harper said, "I'm going to take some time off. If anything comes up have Bob handle it."

As simple as that, she was free. She'd expected to feel lighter with the concerns of the hotel off her shoulders, but it was only a matter of time before her hours of playing hooky would end and she'd take up the reins once more.

Mug in hand, she headed off to shower. In the past ten hours she'd watched the entire season Ashton had spent in Europe. She'd chosen these particular episodes to watch because she'd visited several of the same countries. The contrast between her experiences and his could not have been more dramatic. He loved what he did. The people he

met fascinated him. His culinary encounters often astonished him. Not everything was to his taste, but he was always game to try.

She'd visited and left countries without ever getting to
know their cultures. Most of the time she was on a tight
deadline that left little room to go exploring. She'd been
proud of how hard she worked, had wallowed in her arrogance that she knew best in almost every situation.

In her own way, she was as committed to her path as
Ashton was to his. She'd grown impatient with his lack of
focus on the restaurant. How many people had she frustrated with her inability to relax? She drove herself hard and
expected her employees to follow in her footsteps. Being a
woman, she'd known she'd have to work hard to prove to
her grandfather that she was executive material, worthy of
someday taking her place as head of the family business.

All that work only to find out she'd wasted the past
twenty-nine years of her life chasing a goal that wasn't
hers to pursue. The futility of it all infuriated her. Leaving
her suite, Harper headed to the parking garage where she
retrieved her car and headed to the mall for a little shopping therapy.

Harper cruised store after store without buying anything
while she pondered how profoundly her life had changed.
She had to tell her grandfather the truth, didn't she? Neither Scarlett nor Violet thought it was a good idea. But what
toll would living a lie take on her psyche?

Sick of questions that had no easy answers, Harper
ducked into a bookstore, deciding what she needed was a
few hours of getting lost in someone else's problems. It had
been too long since she'd taken time to read something besides reports. She picked up a copy of her favorite author's
latest novel and headed to the front to pay.

While she waited behind a mother with two children
under the age of five, her attention drifted toward a display of coffee table books. The leopard on the cover of one

caught her attention. As a child she'd spent hours flipping through a book of African wildlife photos at her grandmother's home in the Hamptons. She'd found the images riveting and realized now that it was probably what had planted the seeds of longing to travel.

The hair on Harper's arms lifted as she was struck by a sudden realization. Penelope had engaged in an affair with a wildlife photographer. Was it just a coincidence that she'd given Harper's grandmother a book of wildlife photos? Deep in her soul, Harper knew it wasn't.

She stepped out of the checkout line and headed toward the display that had caught her attention. This book wasn't the same as the one in her grandmother's library. Gripped by sudden urgency, she dialed her grandmother's Hamptons house. As expected, Tilly, her grandmother's housekeeper, answered.

"Hi, Tilly, it's Harper."

"Hello, Harper. I'm afraid your grandmother isn't here at the moment."

"Oh, that's right. She mentioned her plans to go shopping when I spoke with her last Sunday." Which was why Harper knew she could call at this time and accomplish her goal without explaining why she was so interested in a book of photographs. "Could you do me a favor?"

"Of course."

"There's a book of African wildlife photos in the library that my mother gave Grandma for her birthday a long time ago. I used to look at it when I visited, but I don't think I've see it since I was thirteen or fourteen. Could you find it for me?"

"Give me a second." If Tilly thought the request was odd, coming out of the blue like this, she gave no sign. The Hamptons house had a five-thousand-square-foot first floor so it took a few minutes before Tilly came back on the line. "I have it here."

Harper exhaled in relief. She'd been half afraid that

the book would have been lost in the past fifteen years. Her grandmother wasn't the most sentimental woman and might not have kept a birthday present from her daughter that long.

"Can you tell me who the photographer was?"

"Greg LeDay."

"Perfect. Thank you, Tilly. And don't mention to anyone that I called. I'll check in with Grandma on Sunday as usual."

"She always loves to hear from you."

Harper ended the call and felt a bit light-headed. Was Greg LeDay her father? With shaking fingers, she tapped his name into the internet browser on her phone and waited impatiently for the search results to come up. To her immense delight he had a website. She went straight to his bio page and spent a long moment staring at the black-and-white photo of a handsome, rugged man in his mid-fifties standing beside a battered jeep, a camera with an enormous lens in his hands. Five giraffes loped across the landscape behind him.

His easy posture and half grin reminded her so much of Ashton that she couldn't breathe for a second. The two men were obviously cut from the same cloth. No wonder she was so drawn to the man who starred in *The Culinary Wanderer*. She had an adventurer's blood running through her veins.

After several minutes of staring at the photo, she began exploring LeDay's website. In addition to being a photographer, he also acted as a guide for others who were interested in taking pictures of wildlife. In fact, he had several tours lined up in the coming months. One left in two days.

An idea bloomed. She emailed LeDay about joining the safari. Abandoning the book she'd come to purchase for a travel guide to South Africa, Harper headed for her car and the nearest sporting goods store. Within ten minutes, she stood before a display of travel bags and finally understood the importance of Ashton's *go* bag. Pack light and be ready to take off for the next exotic location at a moment's notice.

Isn't that what fascinated her about his television show? His lack of baggage, both physical and spiritual? He took what he could comfortably carry. Lightweight clothes that would travel well. His notebooks for when inspiration struck. Some toiletries. And most important? A camera.

Seized by a vision of what she would take on her own adventure, Harper picked out a rolling backpack system and gathered whatever accessories she would need for the next few weeks.

It wasn't until she'd paid for her purchases and lugged them out to her car that she began to question the sanity of what she intended to do. What made her think that this man who might be her father would appreciate her showing up out of the blue? She had no idea if he knew she existed. But if she didn't take the chance and meet him, she might never stop questioning who she was. Her identity secure, she would know whether or not she could stay quiet about her true parentage and spend the rest of her life living a lie. Scarlett and Violet had already promised to support whatever decision she made. She was lucky to have them in her life.

Anticipation filled her with a wild sort of joy as she returned to her hotel suite and sifted through all she'd bought. It was a ridiculous amount, she realized, staring at it scattered over her bed. Never before had she needed to mull over every ounce of what she was packing. Her trips had involved porters, bellhops and hired cars.

Harper abandoned her packing conundrum and went online to check flights to Johannesburg, South Africa. To her surprise she had several choices all leaving that evening. Why wait? Now that she'd made the decision to go, every minute that went by increased her craving to be off.

Unable to believe how easy the whole thing was, she assembled her own *go* bag. Small enough to fit in an over-head bin, it weighed thirty pounds completely loaded. By the time she'd dressed in jeans, a white T-shirt and a brown leather bomber jacket she'd found in the back of her closet, her nerves were humming with excitement.

As she turned off the lights and pulled the door of her suite shut behind her, Harper was struck by a profound sense of stepping across the threshold into a whole new state of being. It was thrilling to be rushing off into the night with no idea what to anticipate next and no way of controlling the outcome.

She was halfway down the hall when the elevator door opened and Ashton emerged pulling his own *go* bag behind him. When he spotted her, he stopped dead. His position in the doorway kept the elevator open.

"Where are you going?" he demanded as she stepped onto the elevator beside him.

"I could ask you the same thing." Disappointment hit her. She needed him in Las Vegas, focused on the soon-to-open restaurant.

"I was coming to see you."

She glanced pointedly at his luggage. "And after that?"

"I'm flying to New York for a few days. The negotiations for the new show have reached a critical point."

"How critical?"

"I may be on the verge of losing the deal."

Hope flared. If he didn't do the new show he could stay on with *The Culinary Wanderer.* She was careful to keep her voice neutral as she said, "Maybe that's not the worst that could happen."

"But doing the new show means I'll get to spend most of the year in New York City."

Where she would be if she stopped asking questions about her biological father and accepted that she belonged in charge of Fontaine Hotels and Resorts. Would her relationship with Ashton develop into something serious if they were both in New York?

"It sounds like an amazing opportunity," she told him. "I just wish you could do both the new show and *The Culinary Wanderer*."

"Sounds like you don't want me around." He said it with a wry kick of his lips, but his eyes were serious as he awaited her response.

She'd felt connected to him these past few days. He'd filled her head with his stories and inspired her to go in search of a few of her own.

"It isn't that." She paused, unsure if she should voice how much she craved his company. The man had one foot out the door on the best of days. "Are you sure you're going to be happy if you're stuck in one place for a long time? Won't you get bored?"

"If you're worried about my ability to control my need for change, don't be. Once I find something I love, I have no trouble sticking with it."

"And yet here you are leaving town a week and a half before Batouri is set to open."

His lips tightened momentarily. "Everything is handled. I've given Dae my recipes and instructions and he knows how I work. He can keep things on track until Cole gets here. And I'll be back in a few days."

"It's your restaurant. Your reputation on the line." From his expression she could tell he hadn't expected her to pass complete control of the project to him. "I'm sure you know what you're doing."

"Which brings us to you. If you're heading to New York, I can give you a ride in the network's corporate jet."

"Thank you, but I've already booked my flight."

"Wouldn't you rather travel in style? I can promise the pantry is well stocked."

"It's kind of you to offer, but we are destined for different locations."

He scrutinized her clothes and her bag. "Where are you going?"

"South Africa."

Ashton didn't know what to make of her answer. Two nights earlier they'd enjoyed a playful evening of food and wine. Last night they'd made love. She'd never once made mention of an upcoming trip much less one to Africa. Maybe he wasn't the only one keeping secrets.

The elevator doors opened, and Harper stepped forward with purpose and energy. Ashton followed. Since they were both heading to the airport, he'd have a good twenty minutes to get to the core of what was going on.

He eyed her suitcase. It was the size he'd expect a woman to take for a long weekend. "How long are you planning to be gone?"

"I don't know. A week. Maybe two. It depends." She trailed off.

Not normally one to pick up on the nuances of other people's emotional states, Ashton found that when it came to Harper, he'd become hyperaware of her moods. Something was up and he wasn't going to let her go until he knew what it was.

"I didn't realize Fontaine had expanded into Africa."

"It hasn't."

"Then you're scouting locations?"

"No."

Her short answers were creating more confusion than understanding. Harper was many things. Goal oriented, resourceful, outspoken. Never evasive.

Ashton used his height and weight advantage to herd her away from the line of taxis. She was not escaping from him until he was satisfied he knew the whole story. "I have a car waiting."

"I can take a cab."

"You can also accept a ride."

"Thank you." But there was very little gratitude in her tone. She wanted to go her own way. It made him all that much more determined to not let her.

After giving instructions to the driver where to drop Harper off, he waited until their luggage was stowed in the trunk and the town car was navigating East Flamingo Road before he continued his interrogation. "Is this trip business or pleasure?"

"Why are you so curious?"

"Because I would think with Batouri set to open in less than two weeks you might have mentioned an impending trip out of the country."

"It came up rather fast."

"How fast?"

"This afternoon."

The traffic was flowing more smoothly than usual down Paradise Road. The short ride to the airport, which usually took twenty minutes, was going to take closer to ten. Ashton was running out of time to get the answers he wanted.

"What the hell is going on with you, Harper? This isn't like you at all."

Her brown eyes were fierce as she met his gaze. "I'm not sure that's true."

"You've lost me."

"Since I was eleven I've had a plan for how my life was going to go. I set goals and achieved them, all with one target in mind."

"Running Fontaine Hotels and Resorts."

She nodded. "But what no one knows is how often I've wondered what it would be like to give it all up and run away. To pack a bag and see the world, not from the back of a taxi, but on the back of a motorcycle or in an open jeep or even on a camel."

Passion drenched her tone. Her longing made his heart contract. He recognized what it felt like to yearn, even though he'd long ago come to terms with the futility of craving what could never be. He'd promised himself to never be that weak again, but his developing connection with Harper sparked a long-buried emotion. Hope.

"What does all this have to do with your trip to South Africa?"

"I realize it's all been in vain."

Harper's hand had been hovering near the door handle since the car had entered the airport limits. As soon as the vehicle came to a complete stop, she was out the door. The driver popped the trunk, and Harper had her bag on the curb before Ashton even exited the car. Despite her haste, he moved quickly enough to block her path into the terminal.

"My flight leaves in ninety minutes. I have to get through security."

"Then you don't have a lot of time to waste. Why are you going to Africa?"

"I have something I need to take care of."

"Such as?" He crossed his arms over his chest and regarded her as if he had all the time in the world to wait for her answer.

She blew out a breath. "Some complicated family business."

"Hotel business?"

"Personal business."

"And you don't feel like sharing?"

"Maybe when I get back."

"Talk to me, Harper." Ashton was more than a little disturbed to feel her slipping away from him. "I told you things no one else knows."

Her gaze pleaded with him to let her go, but he held firm and at last she caved. "Fine. I'm going to find a man who might be my father."

"I thought your father was dead."

She paused a beat before answering. "The man I thought was my father is dead. I think my real father is a wildlife photographer who leads photography safaris throughout Africa." She sounded completely composed as if this was old news, but the tension around her mouth betrayed that all was not well.

It all came together in a heartbeat. "So you're not a Fontaine?"

"It appears I'm not."

"And finding this out has led to the questions you've been having about the decisions you've made in your career?"

"I'm not a Fontaine." Agony fractured her voice. "I have no right to be CEO."

"You have worked toward this all your life."

"My grandfather wants one of his granddaughters to take over the company."

"And you think he will reject you after twenty-nine years because you're not biologically related? Could anyone be that heartless?"

"You don't understand how important family is to my grandfather. After my father..." She grimaced. "After my father died and Grandfather discovered he had other granddaughters, he came up with his contest to determine who was best qualified to run the company." She dashed away a tear from the corner of her eye and rushed on. "It was my birthright. My dream. I'd dedicated my life to proving I deserved to be CEO one day, and he expected me to prove it all over again."

Horns honked behind him as cars jockeyed for space at the curb. Departing passengers hurried past. A police officer, directing traffic, blew his whistle. The chaos pressed against Ashton's back, but he braced himself and focused completely on Harper.

Four words summed up everything he felt for her. "How can I help?"

He put out a hand, offering comfort and support, but she backed away.

"You can't." She gave her head a vehement shake.

Despite being stung by her rejection, he persisted. "Where in South Africa are you heading?"

"Pretoria."

"Where are you staying?"

"I haven't decided." It wasn't like her to be so unprepared.

"I have a friend at the Pretoria Capital Hotel. Ask for Giles Dumas. He's the executive chef for their restaurant."

"Thank you." Gratitude softened her lips into a smile for a second. "I have to go. I can't miss my flight."

Staying put and letting her walk away from him was the hardest thing he'd done in a long time. When she disappeared through the sliding glass doors of the terminal, Ashton slid into the back of the town car and focused his attention on the traffic visible through the windshield.

She had her path to follow. He had his. If only he could shake his thoughts free of her. He had his own problems to worry about. The network folks would expect him to make a strong showing during his taping. He needed to be completely focused to impress them.

Eight

With the first and shortest leg of her long journey behind her, Harper fastened her seat belt and stared out the window with dry, scratchy eyes. By flying business class, she'd saved eight thousand dollars on her ticket, but she'd found herself incapable of sleeping sitting up during the nearly ten-hour flight to London. Nor had she been able to nod off during her five-hour layover. Pair that with her sleepless night the previous evening and Harper estimated she'd been awake around forty-eight hours.

At least on the leg between London and Johannesburg she wasn't stuck in a middle seat. She propped a pillow between her head and the wall of the cabin and let out a huge breath as a wave of exhaustion flowed over her. She fell asleep not long after the plane stopped climbing.

The popping of her ears woke her as the plane reduced altitude. She checked the seat back monitor that kept track of the distance traveled and saw that they were a little over an hour from touching down in South Africa. Her pulse jumped. She was about to land in a foreign country and go in search of a man she hadn't known existed two days earlier. The town where he lived was a forty-five minute drive from Johannesburg and she had yet to receive a response to her email requesting information on the seven-day safari he was leading the day after she arrived.

She thought it might be a good idea to get to know him a little before announcing that she'd traveled halfway around the world to see if she was his daughter.

From his bio she knew that he'd never been married. Dedicating his life to his passion for Africa, he'd won several prestigious awards and had his work published in more than two dozen magazines. For the past day and a half she'd tried to find herself in this man she shared genes with. They shared a focus on their work and a determination to achieve greatness, but when it came to their careers, Greg LeDay had more in common with Ashton than her.

Both men were creative geniuses. LeDay's photography was brilliant in the same way Ashton's culinary masterpieces won him notoriety.

By comparison, what had she done? She'd worked hard and had nothing she was proud to display as her body of work. Her passion involved planning, organizing and making things happen. She was good at telling people what to do, being ruthless. How many of her employees called her a bitch behind her back?

Harper wasn't feeling all that organized or ruthless at the moment. She was drifting on a sea of uncertainty. Impatient with herself, she pulled out her phone and logged on to the plane's Wi-Fi network. It was time to reconnect with her organized self. She hadn't yet planned her trip beyond booking her flight to Johannesburg. She needed to figure out how she was going to get to Pretoria and where she was going to stay once she got there.

To her delight, the two cities were linked by a high-speed train line that she could pick up at the airport. She would have to change trains, but after doing so she would arrive in Pretoria in less than half an hour. Harper then turned her attention to finding the hotel Ashton had suggested and booked a room for two nights. By the time the plane's doors opened to allow the passengers to disembark, she was feeling completely in charge once more.

Finding the train was easy. She'd exchanged dollars for rand along the way and arrived at the platform just as the train was pulling in. As adventures went, this trip was feeling awfully mundane. She stepped onto the train, secured her bag and settled into a clean, comfortable seat by the window. Despite getting sleep on the plane, the train's rocking motion made it difficult to keep her eyes open. She fought the pull. The distance between the stations wasn't great and she could miss her exchange if she wasn't careful.

As it was, she wasn't fully awake when the train pulled into Marlboro station. Yawning wearily, she got to her feet and waited for an opening in the crowd of exiting passengers so she could step into the aisle and collect her bag. Something hard clipped her temple, knocking her sideways. Stunned by the blow, on the verge of losing consciousness, she didn't fight the hands that shoved her into the seat and stripped away the bag that held her cash and passport.

Before her head cleared, her assailant was long gone and the last of the passengers had disembarked. Harper staggered to her feet, but before she could reach her luggage, the door closed and the train moved forward. The pain in her head made Harper's thoughts thick and sluggish. She dropped into the closest empty seat and closed her eyes. What was she supposed to do now?

Ashton stepped out of a cab on the corner of Ninth Avenue and Twenty-eighth Street in Chelsea and saw his old friend Craig Turner waiting for him by the curb. Since the Lifestyle people weren't expecting him until two that afternoon, Ashton had decided to check in with his old mentor and wasn't surprised to learn that Craig was still volunteering at Holy Apostles Soup Kitchen.

"Ashton, good to see you." The sixty-five-year-old restaurateur wrapped Ashton in a tight bear hug. "You're looking wonderful. Television suits you."

"It has its moments."

When Ashton had first come to New York before landing his first television series, he'd spent two years in Craig's kitchen learning everything there was to know about what it took to run a successful restaurant. He'd gleaned a lot. And yet, with four restaurants under his belt, Ashton knew he still had plenty of Craig's wisdom left to absorb.

"And now you're stepping into the big time with a show here in New York."

It shouldn't have astonished him that Craig knew this; little happened in New York having to do with food that Craig missed. "We'll see. Nothing's finalized yet."

"And your restaurant in Las Vegas. That's set to open next week. Things going okay?"

"I'll tell you in a couple weeks."

Craig laughed heartily. "I'm glad you could meet me here."

"No problem."

"Once a week I come down to volunteer. For two hours every day they serve a hot meal to over a thousand people. Makes me feel good to give back."

"Of course." Ashton smiled, but as soon as he entered the busy church, he felt his muscles tense as long-forgotten memories of the dinners his parents had organized for the locals resurfaced.

As a kid he'd resented the hours of free time he'd lost helping his mother fix and serve the meals while his father practiced his ministry on the captive audience. Now, as he put on an apron and rolled up his sleeves, he recalled the day when his outlook had changed—when a loathsome chore had become an opportunity to create something amazing in the kitchen. But for a long time after he'd left home and joined up with Chapman's gang, he'd equated his love for cooking with surrendering to his parents' insistence that he become more like them.

He fell into the rhythm of serving as if twenty years hadn't passed. Looking back on those days, he could recall his resentment and frustration, but lacked empathy for his younger self. Seeing the gratitude in the eyes of those who moved past him now, Ashton recalled how many people his parents had been able to help.

So maybe he'd been too hard on his mother and father all these years. But he still wasn't able to excuse his father's insistence that everyone should believe the same things he did. His disregard for any opinion that wasn't his had put father and son at odds too many times. If his father had listened to him once or twice, maybe Ashton would have felt valued and wouldn't have left. He'd never know.

Several hours later, Ashton waved off the thanks from the volunteer leaders and followed Craig outside. It might not have been how he'd chosen to spend the morning, but it had given him some fodder for thought.

"Thanks for the help. Can I drop you somewhere?"

Ashton shook his head. "I'm going to walk a bit."

"It was good seeing you. Perhaps when your new series gets rolling you can come have dinner with me."

"I'd like that."

The two men parted ways and Ashton strode down the street as if he had someplace to be, when in truth, he was just trying to escape the pressure inside himself.

He'd not yet heard anything from Giles. Given that Harper's flight time was a little over twenty-six hours and the time difference between New York and Johannesburg was seven hours, he imagined she should be arriving in Pretoria around one in the morning New York time, depending on her stops and layovers. Being out of touch with her bothered him. He craved the sound of her voice and longed to share with her his revelations while serving at the soup kitchen.

Something about her invited him to confide his secrets. He wasn't sure why he'd told her about his parents or how he'd left home. Disclosing his past wasn't something he did. He wasn't sure why he didn't want anyone to know that he was the son of missionaries or that he'd left home at an early age. Maybe it was the mess he'd been involved in when he left home that he was ashamed of. What he'd been forced to do. The darkness he'd faced in his soul.

He reflected on his decision to keep those things hidden. Who was he really protecting? If Harper had an inkling of what he held back, she would dig until she unearthed the truth. Would she turn away in disgust or understand? She'd grown up in a cocoon of wealth and polite society. Instinct told him she'd be appalled to learn what he'd done while living with Chapman's gang.

They were so different. She, all bossy businesswoman, planning every little thing to death. He, the go-getter, leaping before looking because what fun was life without a little danger? She conquered. He explored. Very different philosophies.

That they'd been able to work together these past nine months without driving each other mad continued to baffle him. Maybe it worked because they were good for each other. He needed her planning capabilities to keep him in check. And he knew his adventurous side had rubbed off on her. Why else would she have hopped on a plane to South Africa?

Harper gripped the armrest as the train sped through the flat landscape dotted with buildings. She was traveling in the wrong direction. How far out of her way had she gone? Almost as soon as the question surfaced, the train began to slow down. She was on her feet, her luggage in her hand by the time the doors opened.

No longer able to assume the people around her were innocuous fellow travelers, Harper regarded everyone who drew near her as a potential threat. When no one in her vicinity seemed at all interested in her, she took a seat on a nearby bench and took stock of her situation.

Her cash and passport were gone. She still had her rail pass and the credit card she'd used to purchase it tucked in her back pocket. Her phone had been in her hand at the time of the attack and she'd managed to keep ahold of it. And she had her luggage. All was not lost. She would get on the train to Pretoria and catch a cab to the American Embassy there.

All she needed was her birth certificate and the extra photo…which she kept in the luggage she'd left behind in Las Vegas. Anxiety swelled once more. Without identification how was she supposed to prove who she was?

Frozen and unable to function, Harper stared at her hands. She was far from home and quite alone. Not to mention her head ached and panic was jumbling her thoughts. The ebb and flow of train passengers caused her suspicion to spike.

By fits and starts her brain began to function again. She needed to figure out which train traveled north so she could get back on track. The Gautrain's schedule was still in her internet browser. She located the route map and discovered she wasn't in as bad a shape as she thought. The train to Pretoria passed through this station, as well. She just needed to find the correct track.

Fifteen minutes later, Harper collapsed into her seat on the Pretoria-bound train and patted herself on the back. With the shock of being robbed fading, she was better able to function. During the journey north she pinned the American Embassy on her map app and located the hotel, as well.

Her stomach growled, reminding her she hadn't eaten anything since her stopover in London. She would worry about that later. She had to secure a home base where Mary could send her documents. Once she had those in hand, she could go to the embassy. Ashton had told her to ask for his friend. Perhaps that would be enough to enable her to check in without her passport. She crossed her fingers and hoped.

An hour after stepping onto the platform in Pretoria station and taking a taxi to the hotel, Harper launched into her story of being mugged for the third time. Hunger and frustration were draining what few reserves she had left.

"No, I didn't file a report with the police. I didn't know where to find a police station. I just wanted to get here and register."

"But we can't do that without you having documentation," the manager in charge of the front desk explained. "Don't you have a copy of your passport page to show us?"

"As I've already told your staff, the decision to visit Pretoria was a last-minute thing and I left all my backup documentation behind. My assistant is going to overnight it to me, but I need to have a place she can send it."

"She can't send it here unless you're registered."

Harper closed her eyes and sucked in a huge breath. "Giles." She'd forgotten about him. "I was supposed to ask for Giles…" His last name eluded her. "I believe he's the executive chef here?"

The manager regarded her solemnly. "He is our executive chef."

"Would he be around? I was told to come here and to say that Ashton Croft sent me."

"We'll call the kitchen. Perhaps you should take a seat over there and we'll see if he has time to speak to you."

It wasn't the most promising offer, but at this point Harper was ready to take what she could get. "I'm quite hungry. Tell him I'll be in the restaurant."

She followed the hostess toward a table on the patio and sank into the plastic chair with a grateful sigh. A smiling waitress came almost immediately to take her order. The dinner menu had so many delicious items on it she had trouble choosing. In the end she settled on game picatta because the description made her mouth water. Tender slices of game pan fried with button mushrooms, mixed peppercorns, doused with sweet Marsala and bound with cream, served on fettuccine dusted with Parmesan cheese.

It arrived at her table, delivered by a tall, handsome man with salt-and-pepper hair and a dashing goatee. She glanced from his face to his chef whites without comprehension as he set the plate before her.

"You're Harper Fontaine?"

At his recognition tears began streaming down her face. She nodded, too overcome by relief to speak.

"My name is Giles Dumas. I understand you ran into a little trouble getting here." He smiled gently as she nodded a second time. "Our mutual friend will be very glad to hear you've arrived. Now, what can I do to help?"

Nine

Gut tight with foreboding, Ashton stood with his back to the conference table and stared out over the Manhattan skyline. Behind him two of the network guys were speaking with Vince. The taping hadn't gone as well as he would have liked. Since dropping Harper off at the airport he'd been edgy and distracted. Nor could he be certain that she'd taken his advice and booked a room at the Pretoria Capital Hotel until he heard from his buddy Giles.

He told himself just because he enjoyed venturing off the beaten track didn't mean she would be foolish enough to go somewhere she could get into trouble. But until he knew she was safe, Ashton wouldn't be able to shake the sensation that he'd made a mistake letting her go by herself halfway around the world to find a father she'd never met. Even after she shoved his offer of help back at him he couldn't get her out of his head. He was worried about her emotional state and the fact that she was a woman un-used to traveling alone.

Vince came to stand beside him. His manager's lack of chatter felt as ominous as the clouds above the city.

Ashton broke the silence. "They weren't wowed by my audition tape."

"It wasn't quite what they were expecting," Vince agreed. "Some aspects of it went over great, others they'd like to work on with you."

"And?" Ashton prompted, hearing the low note in Vince's voice and guessing there was more bad news.

"It's just this little thing about your image. You've been the bad boy of travel adventures, eating exotic cuisine, meeting the natives."

The description was a little off-putting, but Ashton figured Vince was offering his own spin on what the producers had said.

"How do they want my image to change?"

"They're thinking lose the jeans and leather jacket and put you into chef whites. But mostly..." Vince hesitated. "They want you to cut your hair so that you'll look more... polished."

It wasn't an outrageous demand, but Ashton wasn't sure he wanted to look like something he wasn't. And yet, wasn't the whole point of doing this cooking show so he could change things up in his career? "Anything else?"

Vince looked relieved that Ashton's temper hadn't blown up. "They're wondering if you can stay in New York a few more days."

He needed to get back to Las Vegas and Batouri. Even though Dae was sending him frequent updates that things were running smoothly, it was a week and a half before the restaurant opened. And as Harper had repeatedly pointed out, Batouri was his responsibility.

"Ash?" Vince prompted. "What should I tell them?"

Harper had accused him of putting his television career before Batouri, but hadn't he also put it before her? So what if they barely knew each other? Ashton couldn't shake the notion that she needed him and he'd let her down.

"Tell them no."

"Have you lost your mind? You can't say no after quitting *The Culinary Wanderer.* What if they find someone else? What are you going to do then?"

Vince seemed to have forgotten that with several restaurants in various countries, Ashton wasn't dependent on the money he made doing television shows. He just enjoyed the celebrity and the experiences he'd had over the years.

"Write a cookbook." With the help of a very special woman who was at a crossroads of her own.

"A cookbook? Have you lost your mind? Lifestyle Network is going to make you famous."

"They've left me hanging for four months. Now they're demanding I drop everything at a moment's notice?" Ashton's frustration spilled over. "They're going to have to wait."

"I'm not sure they'll like that answer." Vince's eyes shifted toward the group of executives. "They could go with someone else."

Ashton mentally cursed. This was his project. They'd strung him along and now they were threatening to replace him?

"Let them," he snarled. "Whatever they do with the show, it's not going to be a success without me." His gaze collided with Vince's.

"Okay." But his manager didn't look happy. "You're the star. We walk away from this deal." Vince assessed Ashton's expression and shed his doubts with a nod. "Once word gets out you'll be hit with a dozen offers before the week's out."

Ashton wasn't sure his manager was right, but he was confident something bigger and better was just around the next curve. In the meantime he would see to Batouri's grand opening and spend some time getting to know more about Harper Fontaine.

As his thoughts returned to her, all optimism drained away. Why couldn't he shake the notion that he should travel to Africa to be with her? The thought was ridiculous. She'd insisted he focus his full attention on Batouri. He'd incur her fury if he did anything as idiotic as leave the country mere days before its opening.

"I need to get to the airport," Ashton announced. "Let me know what the outcome of the meeting is."

"Are you heading back to Las Vegas now?"

"Not yet."

"Where then?"

"Pretoria."

Vince looked utterly baffled. "Where?"

"South Africa."

Harper's second day in South Africa had gone much more smoothly than her first. Before going to bed the night before, she'd contacted Mary and arranged to have her backup documentation shipped to the hotel. Then, with nothing to do but wait, she took the opportunity to sleep late and get her bearings.

Now, bathed in early afternoon sunshine, Harper was enjoying a glass of wine in a corner of the patio. A shadow fell across her South African tour book. Thinking it was her waitress she looked up. Ashton stood beside her chair looking every inch a dashing world traveler in jeans and a pale blue button-down shirt with the sleeves rolled up to expose the long faint scars on his forearms. With one hand he held a black leather jacket over his shoulder and the other rested on the handle of his *go* bag.

Heart jumping wildly, Harper was too stunned to answer the come-and-get-me call of his lopsided grin. "What are you doing here?"

"I decided someone needed to chronicle your first adventure, so here I am." He pulled out the chair beside hers and settled into it.

"I thought you had a meeting in New York."

"It was over sooner than I expected so I hopped on a plane and here I am."

He didn't elaborate, and she wondered how things had gone.

"My trip took over twenty-six hours. How did you get here so fast?"

"Direct flights from JFK only take fifteen hours." He settled into the chair across from hers. "What are you drinking?"

"Something local. It's quite good." Her brain still wasn't functioning properly. She continued to stare at him in amazement. With his arrival, being in South Africa had taken on a whole new joy. "Shouldn't you be in Las Vegas preparing for Batouri's opening?"

"I spoke with Cole an hour ago. He arrived in Vegas and has everything running smoothly. Tell me about your visit so far."

Concern for what might be going wrong with the opening buzzed in the back of her mind, but she'd made the decision to abandon her post at this critical time and had to trust that Ashton knew what he was doing, too. "You called Giles to tell him I was coming. How did you know I would?"

"Since you usually have everything planned to the second and hadn't yet booked a hotel, I knew you'd be open to my recommendation." He paused a beat. "And you trust me."

The knowing glint in his gaze made her cross. Harper picked up her wine and took a sip. "Your meeting in New York must have gone your way for you to be here right now."

"Actually, it went rather poorly." He signaled the waitress. "They want me to cut my hair. I told them to go to hell."

While he ordered wine for himself and a melted cheese bowl appetizer, Harper narrowed her eyes and tried to picture him without his wayward, sun-streaked locks. With his dimples and sparkling blue eyes it didn't really matter what the producers did to try and make him look more civilized. In his heart, he was always going to be a reckless adventurer. That they were trying to change him was idiotic. Didn't they understand that was the basis of his charm?

"And instead of returning to Las Vegas where your restaurant is opening in a week you decided to come here?" Did he expect her to be glad to see him? Which she was.

"I didn't think you were ready to fly solo."

"You think I need a babysitter."

He radiated innocence. "Did I say that?"

"You've spoken with Giles."

"He called me before my flight left."

"He told you, didn't he?"

"Told me what?"

She didn't believe his casualness for a second. "That I was mugged on the train." When he didn't react with shock and concern, she knew her suspicions had been right. "I suppose you think I was foolish for coming here alone."

"Not at all. This is a very safe country for tourists. The same thing could have happened to you in New York or Las Vegas. I'm sorry you were attacked and I'm angry with myself for not coming with you."

His words stirred up the emotional tornado she'd been caught in all week. A tear formed in the corner of her eye. She dashed it away. "You had important things to do."

"None of them are more important than you."

It was a huge admission for her to hear, and she wondered how he'd react if she told him that she was falling in love with him. Better not. She was feeling too vulnerable and he'd already confessed that he didn't want her depending on him. If she harnessed him with the burden of her growing attachment, he might turn right around and get back on a plane. And she very badly needed him. She'd just have to keep letting him think she didn't.

"Because you aren't free to pursue another project until Batouri is opened and I'm satisfied that your end of our arrangement is complete?" It hurt to see shadows overcome the bright blue of his gaze.

His wine arrived at the same time as the food, interrupting the silence that hung between them. Harper focused on putting the goat cheese and roasted tomato bruschetta mixture on a slice of toasted baguette.

"When are you planning on going to the embassy about getting a new passport?"

"My assistant overnighted my documents. I'll go when they get here."

"And in the meantime? Have you had any luck locating the man you believe is your father?"

"His name is Greg LeDay. He left this morning for Kruger National Park. The safari he's leading was booked and I couldn't get in. He won't be back in town for ten days. I can't wait around that long." She gave him a sheepish smile. "Seems my first impulsive adventure is a complete disaster."

"Adventure is immune to disaster." Ashton pointed at her with the knife he'd been using to smooth cheese on his bread. "There may be setbacks and detours, but often those are what send you in a new and exciting direction."

His optimism was contagious. "See, this is why I'm such a fan." She couldn't help but be drawn in by his enthusiasm. "You have a knack for transforming the challenges into opportunities."

"Words to put on my tombstone."

"It's a lot better than what they'd inscribe on mine. 'She planned every second of her life to death.'"

Ashton coughed long and hard until tears ran from his eyes.

"Are you okay?" she asked him as the fit slowly abated.

"I inhaled some of my wine. That was some pretty dark humor just now," he said. "It caught me by surprise."

"Did it?" She considered what she'd said. "I guess I think that way fairly often, but it rarely comes out. It's not the sort of thing my mother appreciated hearing so I learned to bottle it up."

"There are more layers to you than anyone realizes, aren't there?"

Harper shrugged. The admiration in his gaze was both thrilling and a touch uncomfortable. She'd concentrated on doing and saying the right thing her whole life. It was liberating to let loose, but it worried her a little how unmanageable her impulses might become.

It wasn't until after a second round of wine, when Ashton glanced at his watch, that Harper realized the shadows had lengthened. Once again she noticed how in his entertaining company time seemed to fly.

"I'm going to shower and then take you out for a terrific dinner."

"Have you registered?"

"Not yet." He rose and went to where he'd stashed his *go* bag by a large planter.

"Why don't you use my shower then?"

He turned and looked at her, his eyes searching her face.

"We both know how tonight will end up. Why pay for two rooms?"

"That's rather presumptuous of you."

Despite the cooling air, her skin heated. She got to her feet, hoping to appear more confident than she felt. "I'm just being realistic."

Ashton wrapped his arm around her waist and kissed

her, his lips warm and sweetly persuasive. "Have I mentioned how much I appreciate your practical nature?"

Relaxing against his solid body, Harper gave in to a satisfied smile. "You can after dinner."

"How about a little before and a lot after?"

"That sounds quite acceptable."

A sliver of sunlight lanced through a narrow gap between the closed curtains, waking Ashton. From the angle, he surmised it was early afternoon. Jumping multiple time zones had always been a part of his life and from an early age he'd adapted to functioning on less sleep than the average person, but combine his long trip with an insatiable Harper Fontaine and it was amazing he hadn't slept until dusk.

He rolled onto his back and stretched his arm across the empty mattress. It was cool to the touch. She'd been gone some time. He couldn't blame her. From the heaviness of his limbs he'd probably been sleeping like the dead. Some fun traveling companion he was.

A tented piece of paper sat on her pillow. He read her note and grimaced. She'd gone to the embassy to see about her passport. That meant she wouldn't return anytime soon.

Ashton pushed upright and ran his fingers through his hair. He'd use the time to make some arrangements. Last night as they'd talked over dinner, it came to him that no matter how short her trip was, she really shouldn't leave South Africa without seeing a little of its natural beauty.

It took him an hour's worth of phone calls to get everything in place. When she arrived half an hour later, looking jubilant and proud of herself, he wrapped her in a warm embrace.

"How'd it go at the embassy?"

"They scolded me for not filing a police report, but I should have a temporary passport early afternoon tomorrow."

"That's good news. And I have some, as well." He drew her toward the hotel room door. "Let's get something to eat and I'll tell you all about it."

This time he took her to a restaurant with unassuming furnishings and mouthwatering aromas emanating from the long buffet. They filled their plates with authentic South African dishes and returned to their table. As they ate, Ashton did his best to explain all the things they'd chosen. It had been over ten years since he'd last visited South Africa and some of the more exotic fare wasn't familiar.

As he chewed a bite of crocodile, he wondered if maybe the producers of *The Culinary Wanderer* had been right about coming to Africa for this next season. He'd blocked out just how diverse and delicious the cuisine was.

"Tell me your news."

"I found your father."

"But I'd already done that."

"Yes, but I know where he is right now."

"How?"

"You forget how well-connected I am." He saluted himself with his wineglass before continuing. "A guy I knew knew another guy who has used your father to gather wildlife footage in the past and had his phone number. Turns out he's not far from here. I wasn't able to get us into the camp where he's staying, but there's a lodge about an hour away that a friend of mine owns."

Harper had stopped eating and was looking a little shell-shocked. "When?"

"Late tomorrow after you get your passport. I chartered a plane to take us into Nelspruit where we'll pick up a car and drive to Kruger National Park. It shouldn't take more than a couple hours. We can catch up with him before he heads out the following day."

What he really needed to do was get on a plane and go back to Las Vegas, but she couldn't bring herself to remind him that his first priority should be Batouri.

"I don't know what to say." Her voice wavered. "I'd pre-pared myself to leave without even meeting him. Thank you."

"No thanks required."

Her gaze locked on his face. "Well, I won't take it back."

Warmth spread from his chest through his whole body. He reached for her hand and smiled as she slipped her fingers through his. The couple sitting at the table beside them smiled. Ashton imagined the romantic picture he and Harper made. In the past while he'd never kept his personal life hidden, he hadn't indulged in public displays of affection, either. With Harper he wanted the whole world to notice that she belonged with him.

He'd even started thinking in terms of guiding her to all the places he'd visited and loved. Her ambivalence about her future was a perfect opening to present all the possibilities they could explore together.

By two the next day, Harper's temporary passport was ready to pick up. They headed straight for the airport where they were met by their flight's copilot and escorted onto a well-maintained eight-passenger plane.

As the sun was approaching the horizon almost three hours later, Ashton was braking to a halt alongside a Range Rover of similar age to their own at the Grant Tented Camp. Scattered along the river were six luxurious tents with king-size beds, en suite bathrooms and private terraces. Tucked among thick stands of mature trees and connected by a raised wooden walkway, each tent enjoyed a great deal of privacy.

"Why don't you have a look around while I get us checked in."

Harper opened her door and stepped out, a look of awe on her face. "This isn't exactly what I pictured when you told me we were going to spend a couple nights in a tent camp."

He patted the roof of the Range Rover. "It's not exactly a

camel." He gestured around them. "And it's not exactly the desert, although we are close to the end of the dry season. But at least there are tents. I hope you enjoy it."

She was touched that he'd gone to so much trouble to make her quest to South Africa such a marvelous experience. "Of course I will. How could I not?"

She accompanied him into the tented, open-air lounge and wandered toward the small pool nestled against the deck that overlooked the river. Built of local rock and surrounded by lush plants, it seemed like a completely natural addition to the landscape. Ashton went to see about their accommodations, and Harper wandered until she found the small dining room, also tented, with tables set with white cloth, china and crystal, mahogany chairs and candelabras awaiting the touch of a match.

Such elegance tucked into a wild, untamed landscape charmed Harper. Had Ashton guessed the place was so romantic? She was almost dizzy in anticipation of seeing where they would sleep as she went back to the lounge to await Ashton's return.

The dozen or so guests she noticed scattered about spoke in low voices as if not wanting to disturb the peacefulness of such a tranquil spot. Harper hadn't been here more than ten minutes and she was as relaxed as if she'd been hypnotized by a master.

"Ready?" Ashton's low voice rumbled behind her.

She turned and willingly accepted the hand he held out to her. "I love it here."

"I'm glad."

They walked down a path bordered by hanging lanterns that wound through the vegetation behind the cottages. When they reached the last one, Ashton unlocked the door and pushed it open. Harper took a few steps inside and hesitated in the dimness until Ashton located a light switch.

She gasped in delight.

The tent fabric was held up by a pole in the middle of

the large space, forming a fifteen-foot-high ceiling. There was a king-size bed with white bedding, a walnut wardrobe with glass doors and a chandelier suspended overhead, and a sitting area that held a couch flanked by two chairs and a fireplace. Golden light spilled from an assortment of lamps both attached to the olive-green walls and scattered on the various small tables. A bottle of champagne was cooling in a wine bucket on the colonial-style coffee table.

Kicking off her sandals, she curled her toes into the thick area rug that covered the tent's wood floor. After a slow spin to catalog their accommodations, she pulled Ashton toward her and dazzled him with a long, sexy kiss. "I've been in five-star hotels that weren't as nice as this," she murmured, leaning her cheek against his heaving chest. "It's the most perfect place I've ever seen."

"I'm glad you approve."

A knock sounded on the screen door. Ashton's arms tightened around her briefly before he went to answer. It was a porter. He deposited their luggage inside the door and showed them the canvas flaps they could roll down over the wall of screen windows if the night grew too chilly. When he left, Harper turned to Ashton with a predatory smile and backed him up to the couch.

He ripped his navy Henley shirt over his head while her fingers plucked his belt loose and released the button that held his waistband closed. As she unzipped his pants, she used her free hand to shove him onto the couch. He landed with a soft bounce, and she climbed onto his lap, her knees sinking into the pale gold cushions on either side of his thighs.

With her fingers tangled in his hair, she sought his mouth with hers in an open, wet kiss that left no doubt about her intentions. He gave her all the passion she demanded, groaning deep in his chest as she rocked against his swollen erection, the brief contact satisfying neither of them. Her fingers stroked over his skin in hot, frantic movements. The feel of him brushing against where she needed him the most shot a bolt of the purest frustration through her.

Her hunger communicated itself to Ashton. He stripped off her T-shirt and popped the clasp of her bra, tossing both aside with a ragged exhale. Then his fingers cupped her bare breasts, kneading evocatively until her nipples pebbled against his palms. The thrumming in her blood grew more urgent.

She sucked on his lip and let his breath fill her. A growl greeted her ears as she eased her hand between their bodies and lifted him free of his confining clothes. Smiling, she nipped his neck and at the same time grasped his erection firmly and stroked from base to tip before putting her mouth down over him. His hips bucked. He let out a startled curse, and she chuckled.

"Damn." He had no more words.

His head fell back against the cushion as she continued her slow, steady strokes. When she felt she had him completely beneath her spell, she slid his pants down his muscular thighs and tossed them aside. Naked, he lay half sprawled before her, a gorgeous powerful male who was all hers.

Quick as she could, Harper shimmied out of her pants and returned to her earlier position on the couch. Without opening his eyes, Ashton ran his hands over the curve of her hips and butt and down the back of her thighs. She gasped when his fingers dipped into the heat of her and stroked deep. Shuddering, she braced her hands against his shoulders and surrendered to the pleasure he gave.

He lifted her so he could fill his mouth with her breast. Harper wrapped her arms around his neck and gave a soft cry as he sucked hard. Pummeled by desire, she rode the waves of pleasure, each one a little stronger than the last.

"Ashton, I can't wait any longer."

He eased her down until she was poised over him. She

was so wet that he slid inside her an inch without meaning to. He intended to savor the anticipation, let the hunger build, but he underestimated Harper's passion. With a smile of sheer bliss she lowered herself onto his shaft, taking him deep. The perfection of her snug fit cradled him in a way that he'd never known before. Almost immediately, she began to move, her hips dancing in a seductive rhythm that slammed into his willpower and sent his lust into overdrive.

Digging his fingers into the soft flesh of her backside, he began to thrust in time with her movements. Her breasts swayed, hypnotically close to his face as she arched her back and surrendered to the pressure building inside her.

A soft keening escaped her parted lips as her skin flushed red. Ashton slowed his movements and deepened each thrust, watching her come apart. Her body bowed, muscles tensing as she climaxed. In this magical place he felt humbled by her vulnerability and her strength. She'd given him her all, held nothing back. She opened her eyes and locked gazes at him.

"That was incredible." She licked her lips and puffed out a breath, then murmured, "Come for me."

At her command, he renewed his drive toward orgasm. He pumped into her, distantly hearing her encouraging words. It was over faster than he would have liked. Her hands on his body, her inner muscles clenching to increase that amazing friction and her teeth on his earlobe sent him spiraling into one hell of a climax. He came for what seemed like forever. The pleasure of his release was almost painful in its intensity.

While the last spasms were fading he wrapped his arms around her slim form and buried his face in her neck. He drifted his fingertips over the bumps of her spine and waited for the hammering in his chest to slow. It hurt to breathe.

"You are amazing," he said.

"You're not so bad yourself." She kissed his neck. "How long do we have until dinner?"

"A couple hours, I think." Sucking in a lungful of her spicy scent, he closed his eyes and imprinted this moment forever on his soul. "But if I don't eat until morning, I'll be fine."

"Won't Franco wonder what happened to us?"

"Oh, he'll know. He got a look at you while you stood beside the pool. And he'll understand if my appetite this evening won't be sated by food."

She poked him in the ribs and made him grunt. "Is there a bathroom in this lovely tent or do we bathe in the river?"

"Only if you wish to meet a crocodile face-to-face." He pushed aside damp strands of her hair and drifted his lips across her cheek, tasting the saltiness of her sweat. "There's an outdoor shower."

"I'm not sure I'm ready for that much adventure."

"Then I won't recommend the fried caterpillars Franco might have on the menu."

Harper shuddered. "I'm sure you'll tell me they're delicious but I'm just going to have to take your word on that."

"There should be a bathroom behind there with a slipper tub." He pointed to the wall behind the wardrobe.

Ashton accepted the perfunctory kiss she dropped onto his lips and watched with appreciation as she padded naked to collect her bag and then head to the bathroom. The last of the afternoon sunlight played over her soft skin, highlighting the different textures of bone, sinew and muscle. She had an athletic body that she pushed hard. In fact, she had it all. Resilient body. Strong mind. Romantic heart. Idealist soul.

Was the last going to survive the meeting with her father? Ashton had a bad feeling about what was to come tomorrow. A man didn't dedicate himself completely to a lifestyle that involved being gone for several months or even a year at a time without understanding it would be difficult to maintain close relationships. A wife and family wouldn't be a top priority.

More than anything Ashton wanted to spare Harper any disappointment Greg LeDay might heap upon her, but she'd come too far to turn back now. The best he could do was be a shoulder to cry on.

Not wishing his solemn mood to put a damper on their evening, Ashton chose to use the shower outside before dressing for dinner. Slipping on a pair of khaki pants and a beige knit shirt, he toyed with his Saint Christopher medal while he waited for Harper to appear. His mother had given the medal to him on a trip back to South Africa. They were traveling by plane. He'd been six. They'd encountered a storm halfway and been tossed around. While lightning darted around the wings, his mother had removed the medal from her neck and fastened it around his, telling him that Saint Christopher, the patron saint of travelers, would protect him.

When he'd left home at fifteen, he'd taken the medal with him and had worn it every day since. Ashton wasn't sure why, whether it was superstition or faith. Whichever it was, it had kept him safe.

He'd spent more time thinking about his parents in the past week than he had in the past twenty years. Being on the front lines of Harper's identity struggle had opened doors he'd thought long locked and barred. What awaited him hadn't been as painful as he'd expected. Having someone he cared about accept him unconditionally had made the difference.

Now all he had to do was offer Harper the same unequivocal support, no matter how misguided he thought her decision to confront her biological father was. He would be there to comfort her if things went awry.

Ten

Harper's fingers bit into the passenger door armrest as the Range Rover neared the camp that Greg LeDay was using as the base for the safari he was leading. The sun was lowering toward the horizon, casting a warm glow over the landscape. This morning they'd overslept and arrived too late to catch LeDay before he took out his clients.

For the past six hours she and Ashton had been driving around Kruger National Park, hoping for a glimpse of wildlife. The roads they'd taken had been paved, and the truck had decent springs, but her stomach wasn't feeling particularly settled. She blamed it on nerves. Soon she would get to meet the man who might be her father.

How it went would determine the rest of her life. There was a great deal riding on the outcome of this meeting.

"Hang in there." Ashton's hand covered hers in a reassuring squeeze. As he'd been doing these past few days, he'd picked up on her mood and knew just what to say.

"I wish I knew how he was going to react."

"Looks like the trucks are back. You should know pretty quick."

Before Ashton threw the Range Rover into Park, she spotted Greg LeDay. He wore khaki-colored cotton pants, a short-sleeved beige shirt and a tan vest with six pockets. A wide-brimmed hat in some drab color between gray and brown shielded his face from the sun. But even with that protection, he looked older than the photo on his webpage. Years of living in the bush had etched lines around his eyes and given his skin a look of worn leather.

Heart thumping erratically, Harper approached the group he was addressing. She'd asked Ashton to hang back and give her time to introduce herself. He wasn't happy about her request, but he'd agreed.

LeDay's gaze found her lingering on the fringes of the crowd and dwelled on her for a moment before he returned his attention to his charges. "This was a great day. Tomorrow we'll go out and see if we can't find some cats."

The crowd dispersed, sidestepping Harper, who stood tongue-tied and uncertain. She'd practiced a hundred different openings and none of them seemed right.

"Can I help you?"

"My name is Harper Fontaine." She stumbled over her surname, wondering at the last second if he'd recognize it.

"Nice to meet you." No recognition flared in his eyes.

"I believe you met my mother several years ago. Penelope Fontaine?"

"Was she on one of my safaris?"

Things had just gotten awkward. "You met her in London. At an exhibition of your work."

"I'm sorry. The name just doesn't ring a bell."

"Perhaps a picture would help." Harper pulled out her smartphone and showed him an image of her mother, knowing Penelope would be quite put out that a lover—even one she'd had a brief affair with thirty years prior—could forget her so easily.

LeDay didn't look at the photo; he stared at Harper. "Why don't you tell me what this is about."

"You had an affair with my mother." Now that the words were out, Harper was struck with an awful thought. What if she'd flown halfway around the world to meet the wrong man?

"And if I did?"

"Then I'm your daughter."

Other than a brief tightening of his mouth, LeDay didn't react to her announcement. He regarded Harper in silence for a long time and she started to understand how he'd captured all those incredible moments in his photographs. He had the ability to stay very still for long periods of time. Meanwhile her heart rate was escalating and her breath had gone unsteady.

At last LeDay moved. He crossed his arms over his chest. "What do you want?"

"Nothing." Obviously that wasn't true, but Harper hadn't defined for herself what chasing him halfway around the globe was supposed to accomplish. "I only recently found out. I simply wanted to meet you." Her voice trailed off. His expression hadn't changed. He looked as welcoming as a rock pile.

"Where are you from?"

"I live in Las Vegas at the moment."

"That's a long way to come for nothing."

"I guess I was hoping that getting to know you would help answer some questions I have."

"Are you staying here?"

"No, we drove over from Grant's."

His eyebrows rose. "We?"

Harper turned in Ashton's direction and he left the car and headed toward them. "This is Ashton Croft," she said, catching his hand and drawing him to her side.

The two men shook hands, sizing each other up, like a

pair of competing alpha males. Harper sensed they came to some sort of understanding.

"I've seen your show. You've traveled extensively."

"Experiencing new cultures and cuisine is a passion of mine."

LeDay shifted his attention to Harper, but he continued to speak to Ashton. "It's hard having a career where you're gone all the time and maintaining a relationship."

"I know."

They were two of a kind, Harper realized. Adventure-loving men who didn't want to be tied down. She'd known that going in and didn't want to domesticate Ashton. He'd never be happy staying put for long. He would go wherever the wind blew next. Two questions remained. Would he ever invite her to travel with him? Would she say yes if he did?

LeDay gestured toward the cluster of buildings. "The restaurant has opened for dinner. If you'd like to eat before returning to your camp."

"Would you join us?" Harper asked, barely able to hope he'd agree.

He hesitated and then nodded. Still hand in hand, she and Ashton followed him toward the outdoor dining area. Trembling slightly in reaction to the stress of meeting the man she believed to be her father, Harper leaned her head against Ashton's shoulder.

"You okay?" he asked, his fingers brushing her cheek.

"Just a little overwhelmed."

"That's to be expected."

"I'm glad you're here," she whispered.

He squeezed her hand in response as they followed a waiter to their table. Once they sat down and Harper had a chance to survey the menu, she wasn't sure she'd be able to eat anything. She glanced to Ashton for help.

"Will you order something for me? I can't make up my mind."

"Of course."

The waiter brought beer for the men and a glass of red wine for Harper, wrote down their dinner selections and left.

Harper gathered a breath, surprised by how unsteady she felt, and plunged in. "I know you must be annoyed with me for showing up here like this, and I'm sorry that I didn't give you some warning. But I wasn't sure if you'd see me."

"I'm still not sure I'm the person you're looking for."

"Frankly, neither am I, but my mother said she met a wildlife photographer at an exhibition of his work in London and then she bought a book of your photographs for my grandmother." Hearing herself, Harper broke off. She caught Ashton's gaze and saw reassurance there. "It sounds a bit crazy when I say it out loud."

"Let me see that photo of your mother."

Harper pulled out her phone and handed it to him.

LeDay looked at the photo for a long time before speaking. "Penny."

Penny?

"A beautiful girl."

Harper clapped a hand over her mouth to smother a wild bubble of laughter. It was weird to hear someone call her formal, inflexible mother a girl. Even weirder to hear a man use a nickname in such fond tones. Penelope hated nicknames. And then Harper remembered.

"Her father used to call her that. He died when she was nine."

"We spent almost two weeks together. She was quite the mystery. Had never tasted beer before. Couldn't comprehend how to navigate the Tube. And yet she spoke effortlessly about art, history and politics."

"My mother is fascinated with current events and the background that shaped them. Sometimes I think she knows more about what's going on in Washington, D.C., than the journalists."

"Is she a politician?"

"It's just her hobby."

"What do you do in Las Vegas?"

"My family… I manage a hotel. Fontaine Ciel."

"Fontaine. That's your mother's last name?"

Harper nodded. "Did you know she was married when you were together?"

"She didn't say and wasn't wearing a ring, but I sensed that might have been the case." He paused and stared out over the valley. "What gives you the idea that I'm your father?"

"My father… I recently found out the man I believed was my father was out of town in Macao when I was conceived. My mother isn't the sort of woman to have an affair." Harper glimpsed LeDay's doubt and rushed on. "She was married to a man who cheated on her every chance he got, but I know you were the only time she broke her vows."

"You said you had questions you needed answers to. I don't know what I can tell you."

She hesitated. What had happened to the woman who had all the answers? She never entered a negotiation without a strategy for how to get what she wanted. Beneath the table, Ashton's hand closed over hers, offering support and strength.

"I don't know what to ask. I thought everything would be clear if I met you."

Harper had no choice but to fall silent. Meeting this man hadn't made her confusion disappear. If anything, she was even more lost. As Ashton drew the man out, asking questions about his life in Africa and the magnificent photos he'd taken over the years, Harper listened in fascination and growing dismay. What had she been thinking to come here and expect he would gladly welcome her into his life?

His passion for the country of his birth was all-consuming. The wildlife. The ecosystem. He devoted himself to sharing his experiences and by doing so hoped to increase people's appreciation for the animals and support for his conservation efforts.

A noble cause and one he was ideally suited for. Harper pushed food around on her plate, her appetite nonexistent, and listened with only half her attention until he said something that pulled her out of her thoughts.

"You have two sisters?"

It shocked Harper to think she had aunts she'd never known.

"And a half-dozen nieces and nephews."

"That sounds lovely."

She stopped herself from asking for further details. As much as she longed to hear about this family she'd never known, she remembered what it had been like when her grandfather had told her she had two half sisters. She'd initially viewed them as trespassers in her neatly planned life. This must be how LeDay was feeling. She'd descended into his life without warning and how he must resent her intrusion.

Never mind that Violet and Scarlett had gone from being strangers to family at their first meeting.

"Ashton," she finally said, deciding it was time to stop waiting for some sign that she and LeDay had a connection. The man had enjoyed a brief encounter with a beautiful woman. End of story. That the affair had produced a daughter wasn't going to touch his life. "We should be getting back to camp." She gave LeDay a bright smile. "Thank you for having dinner with us. I enjoyed meeting you."

"Nice meeting you, as well," he replied.

"Ready?" Ashton gave her a searching look.

"Absolutely."

There were no halfhearted offers to stay in touch. Just a simple wave goodbye and a sinking feeling in Harper's stomach that she should have stayed home.

Overwhelmed by futility, Harper trudged back to the car. Her boots felt as if they weighed ten pounds each.

She'd been uncharacteristically naive to expect that she and LeDay would have some sort of immediate connection.

"That didn't go as you'd hoped," Ashton said, stating the obvious. "I suspected he wasn't going to welcome you with open arms."

That he was right didn't make Harper feel any better about how meeting her father had gone. She was angry with herself for wondering if the reason Ross Fontaine hadn't been a loving father was because they weren't biologically related.

"A man like that isn't interested in family," Ashton continued, and Harper wasn't sure if he was trying to make her feel better or just pointing out the obvious. "He has his photography and the safaris. They're his passion. He doesn't seem to need anyone."

Weighed down by disappointment, Harper's temper got the better of her. "Like someone else I know?"

"Criticize me all you want, but I'm here for you."

As she threw herself into the Range Rover and waited for him to get behind the wheel, she wondered what he did feel about her. The way he'd made love to her left her emotions jumbled and her confidence rocky. Could a man kiss with such gut-wrenching passion and feel nothing more than uncomplicated lust? Ashton wasn't exactly the easiest person to read and she couldn't expect him to start spouting poetry.

Who was Ashton Croft? Selfish adventurer? Celebrity hound? Romantic lover?

Seeing that Ashton continued to stand where she'd left him, Harper got out of the vehicle and crossed to stand before him. Hands bracketing his hips, he was staring at the distant horizon, a scowl of absolute frustration drawing his brows together. If he'd noticed she'd reappeared, he gave no sign.

"How do I make you feel?" she asked softly, scarcely

able to believe she had the nerve to have her heart stomped all over for a second time that day.

"Dependable." He made the word sound like a curse.

It wasn't at all what she expected him to say, and the giddy relief that struck her made little sense. "You don't like being dependable?"

"I don't like living up to anyone's expectations but my own."

"I wish you could teach me your trick of living that way."

He cupped her face in his hands and kissed her hard. She met the bold thrust of his tongue with matching hunger and let herself be swept up in the rising passion of their embrace. This was easy. Surrendering to his mastery. Letting his insistent kisses and eager hands sweep away all her worries.

Breathing unevenly, Ashton placed his forehead against hers. They stayed that way for several minutes as the sun sank below the horizon and the night sounds swelled. At long last he stirred.

"We'd better get going. It's an hour back to camp."

She nodded and let him draw her back to the truck. As the ancient shocks struggled to absorb the road's dips and bumps, Harper reflected over the past few hours.

"You know it doesn't matter that LeDay disappointed me," she said, determination in her voice. "In fact, I'm glad. I can stop second-guessing who I am. I can go back to my life and my career and never look back again. It's better for everyone this way."

Ashton's features could have been carved from stone. "You're not going to tell your grandfather the truth about who your father really is."

"Why should I?"

"Because maybe if you know you'll never be Fontaine's CEO you might look around and see there's something you'd rather be doing."

"Being CEO is what I want."

"Then why did you hop on a plane at the last second and fly all this way to meet your father? You could have saved time and money by staying home and making the same decision."

He was right. "I became a businesswoman because that's what my father and grandfather did. It defined me. Then I find out I'm not a businessman's daughter, but the offspring of a brilliant photographer. I know I should take something away from that, but I don't know what."

"Who your parents are doesn't define you any more than your environment does. You are the sum of your choices."

"You're a fool to believe your parents didn't define you. You've spent your whole life rejecting their selflessness and believing you're out for no one but yourself."

"At least I admit that I'm selfish. It's my parents who are hypocrites. They were so obsessed with their mission to save every person they met that they couldn't take two minutes to recognize the person closest to them needed their help, as well."

Ashton made the accusation without heat or bitterness, as if he'd made peace with his parents' flaws long ago. By proclaiming his own selfishness he warned the world what they could expect from him.

Harper's heart constricted in sympathy.

"So you ran away and got caught up with a bad group."

"I was fifteen and my parents never tried to find me." And there was the crux of all his pain. Abandoned. Left to fend for himself. Terrorized for three years. Of course he'd developed a protective shell.

"How do you know that? The criminals you fell in with needed to stay way below the radar. They couldn't have been easy for the police to find."

"My parents never filed a report that I was missing. No one was looking for me." He took one hand off the wheel and pinched the bridge of his nose. "When I first joined the gang, Franco checked. Couldn't find anyone looking for a fifteen-year-old white kid. He told me to go home, offered to help me get out."

"Why didn't you?"

"Go home to what? I'd left because my parents didn't give a damn about me. Nothing had changed. They went on with their work. That's what was important to them."

The unfairness of it burned like acid in Harper's stomach. She knew loneliness. Hadn't she been an afterthought in her parents' lives? Ross Fontaine had taken to fatherhood with less enthusiasm than he'd put into being a husband. But her situation hadn't been unique among her classmates. Many of them had successful, driven parents who worked eighty hours a week and traveled extensively.

But she couldn't imagine any of them losing a child and going on as if nothing had happened.

"Do you ever wonder what happened to them?"

For a moment Ashton regretted sharing his past with Harper. She wasn't good at leaving things alone. That her journey to self-discovery hadn't ended well wasn't going to diminish her confidence for long. He was certain by the time they got on the plane tomorrow that she would have the plan for her future all documented with bullet points and colorful graphs.

"I don't wonder." Or he hadn't until she'd raised the question. Franco had offered to track down his parents on several occasions, but Ashton had turned him down each time. If they hadn't looked for him, why should he make sure they were doing all right? "They were committed to their ministry. Whatever happened to them, they will not regret the sacrifices they made."

And for that he couldn't condemn them. They'd chosen a path that gave them satisfaction. He'd done the same. He accepted that they wouldn't be proud that he'd made a great deal of money and become famous. Nothing about what he did fell into their value system.

"I envy your ability to put your past behind you like that."

He wasn't completely sure he'd attained the sort of peace of mind she believed he had. Returning to Africa had raised too many old ghosts. He might have left his life here behind fifteen years ago, but it had shaped him into the man he was. That wasn't something he could completely escape.

They were silent for the rest of the drive back to the camp, the barrier between them created by his stubbornness and her disappointment. Ashton was aware of a sharp ache in his chest. It was a sensation he hadn't felt in a long time. Harper's questions about his parents had unlocked the door on regret. Wanting to know if his mother and father were all right meant he cared. By caring about them he betrayed himself, and the choice he'd made to put his needs first because they never had.

Being selfish at thirty-five wasn't the same as acting out when he was fifteen. In the years since he'd left home, he'd learned to feel compassion for others the way his parents hoped he would. Even if he hated to admit it and seemed to live his life as if it wasn't the case, they'd had a powerful influence on him. Maybe it was past time he surrendered to it.

The walkways and outdoor areas of the tent camp were lit with softly glowing oil lamps by the time the Range Rover rolled into a parking space. Ashton glanced at Harper and saw her gaze was fixed on the fanciful beauty of the camp nestled among thousands of acres of wild African countryside.

He took her hand as they traversed the raised walkway to their tent. Although she neither looked his way, nor offered any inkling of her thoughts, she spread her fingers and welcomed the connection.

To Ashton's great surprise, she began stripping out of her clothes as soon as they entered the tent. Given her difficult day, he expected her to want distance and space. But as she came to stand naked before him and attacked his buttons with single-minded intensity, he decided not to question her motivation.

They tumbled into the big soft bed in a tangle of tongues and limbs. Ashton made love to her with demanding passion, offering no tenderness. She seemed to need none. Her movements beneath him were feverish. Fingernails bit into his skin. Teeth found sensitive areas and left marks.

At last he settled between her thighs, spreading them wide so she would feel a tiny spark of helplessness. Her head thrashed on the pillow as his size and weight pinned her to the mattress, but he hesitated before joining their bodies. He wanted her to recognize his strength, wanted to demonstrate what it felt like to be at his mercy. His power, his determination would protect her from anything, but she had to let him.

As she reached out to touch him, he grasped her wrists and pinned them above her head. She fought his hold, glaring at him the whole time. It wasn't until her lashes fell and her muscles relaxed that he shifted his hips forward and slid his entire length into her.

Almost immediately her body began to shake with release. He pushed deeper, and she began to cry out. He released her wrists and meshed their fingers, withdrawing so he could drive into her a second time. The strength and swiftness of her climax stirred an uproar in his own body and he followed her over the edge in a matter of seconds.

They lay panting in the aftermath. Ashton shifted to lie on his back and drew her snugly against his side. She fit against him with such blissful perfection that he closed his eyes to savor the moment. For a long time the only sound in the room was their breathing and the muted tick of the clock on the nightstand. Before long, however, as their bodies settled into normal rhythms, he realized the buzzing in his ears wasn't the pounding of his blood through his veins, but the nighttime chorus of cicadas and frogs.

"Hear that?" Ashton whispered.

Beside him, Harper held her breath and listened. From far off came the sound of someone trying to get a chain-saw going with short quick pulls of the start cord. "Yes."

"That's a leopard call."

A thrill of excitement raced down her arms. "It sounds close."

"Probably a half mile away."

Safe in Ashton's embrace, she snuggled her face into the crook of his neck and smiled. No one could be in better hands than her right now. Absently she traced the scar crisscrossing his abdomen. When she'd touched it before, he'd seemed to withdraw from her. Despite her curiosity, she hadn't asked him to expand on his days with the gang. This time, he might be more open to her inquisitiveness.

"More knife play?"

His answer took a long time coming. "Yes."

Hearing the tightness in his voice, she held silent. They were old scars. From a lifetime ago. Long healed, but permanent reminders of what…?

Beneath her hand his torso rose and fell on a deep breath. The force of it ruffled the hair scattered across her shoulder and tickled her skin.

"Chapman didn't hire weaklings." His voice sounded ghostly in the dim room. "Everyone had to prove they could fight. Even a fifteen-year-old boy whose only knife experience had come from slicing vegetables." His short laugh held no amusement. "He was a sadistic bastard. Once a week he pitted one of his crew against another in sporting matches. Some sport. Whoever drew first blood won. Three losses and you were out." Ashton threw his forearm over his eyes. "Throat slit, dumped in the jungle for the scavengers to feast on."

Harper couldn't imagine what this had been like for a teenager. "Why'd anyone stay working for him?"

"He made them rich. How do you think Franco could open this place?"

"Why did you stay?"

"I was proving a point to my parents."

"At the risk of your life?"

"Who doesn't think they're invincible at fifteen? I was big for my age. I'd gotten into a lot of trouble fighting the neighborhood kids. What I lacked was the technique to fight with a knife. Franco took me under his wing right away, but I didn't learn fast enough and lost two weeks in a row."

"So Chapman wanted you dead?"

Ashton shook his head. "I don't think so. The pairings were random. It was bad luck is all. My second bout I almost took the guy out. His reach was longer, but he was bulky and I was fast." He caught her fingers and drew them to a spot on his left side just below the ribs. "A wild swing caught me here. It took twenty stitches to sew me up."

"You're lucky you didn't die from infection."

"My luck turned when Chapman didn't pull my name for two months. I spent a lot of time with Franco after that. Never lost again."

The strain in Ashton's voice betrayed the toll that had taken on him. He might not have killed anyone directly, but he had to know that by saving himself he was signing someone else's death warrant. From missionaries' son to criminal to world-renowned chef.

"You can't forgive yourself."

"Should I?"

"What happened wasn't your fault. Chapman's game went on whether you were there or not. Those men made a choice just as you did. And you got out."

"But I never turned him in. When the opportunity presented itself I ran."

And pursued by guilt he'd been running ever since.

"Do you really want the cooking show in New York?"

she asked. "I can't help but feel you'll be turning your back on what made you successful."

"And what is that?"

"You thrived in situations that would terrify most people. Every episode contained an edge of danger that kept me glued to the TV."

"As much as I enjoyed doing the show, I'm looking to change my image. Go more mainstream." He rolled away from her and sat with his legs hanging off the side of the bed, his back toward her. "The network is going to push it hard. My popularity will skyrocket. It's what I've been working for."

"And all this time I thought it was the joy of food that motivated you." If he hoped to find legitimacy in success, how high did his star have to rise before he could be at peace with what he'd done to survive?

"More viewers means my culinary point of view reaches more people."

With their earlier rapport slipping away, Harper left the bed and slipped into a pair of leggings and a sweater. She handed Ashton his clothes and waited in silence while he put them on. Then she drew him out onto the deck and stood beside him near the rail, looking out over the river.

Surrounded by the night sounds it was easy to feel one with the bush. For several minutes they listened without speaking. One call was repeated several times, causing Harper to break the quiet.

"What is that?"

"A baboon sounding an alarm. Probably because of the leopard we heard earlier."

"You were right when you said we're the sum of our experiences. The things that you've been through had a profound effect on the man you've become. If you'd stayed with your parents you wouldn't resent them any less, but your strength of will might never have been tested and you might never have discovered the heights of your courage."

Harper paused to let her words sink in. "But I'm right, too. You inherited their generosity of spirit and desire to help those less fortunate. How many thousands of people have been helped through the foundations you promote?"

"I'm nothing more than a spokesman. I don't tangibly help anyone."

"What about Dae? You saved him from going to prison for something he didn't do and taught him how to cook. Someday he'll run one of your restaurants. How far is that from where he started?"

Ashton bumped his shoulder against her, forcing her to step to the side in order to maintain her balance. His fingers snaked around her waist and pulled her against his side. "This was supposed to be your journey to self-discovery, not mine."

"Ironic, isn't it?" Suddenly she felt a weight lift off her shoulders. "You know what? I don't care about the man who impregnated my mother. He doesn't want to be anyone's father. Why should I take that personally and cry about it?" She gripped the railing hard. "I need to worry about me."

"So, you've decided what to do when you get home?"

"I'm going to do what everyone expects of me and keep my mother's secret. I came to South Africa in search of who I am. Now I know. I'm Harper Fontaine. Future CEO of Fontaine Hotels and Resorts. I've worked my whole life to run the company. I don't know who else to be."

"And that's all you need to make you happy in the long run?"

"It's been my goal since I was five, so, achieving it will bring me great satisfaction."

"I hope you're right."

Eleven

Harper woke to an empty bed and a heavy heart. From the light outside she gathered it was a few hours after sunrise. She sat up and glanced around the tent, but from the room's low energy level, she could tell Ashton wasn't nearby. Flopping back onto the pillows, she closed her eyes and willed herself to stop feeling so vulnerable and out of sorts. It wasn't as if she hadn't endured setbacks in her life before. Failure was a necessary part of growing. But one emotional blow after the other had weakened her ability to recover swiftly.

Still, she did recover and an hour after waking, she was showered, dressed, packed and on her way to breakfast. That Ashton still hadn't made an appearance didn't bother her. He and Franco hadn't spent much time together since they'd arrived. Ashton was probably with his old friend. Or maybe taking a walk along the river. There were several trails around the camp.

Harper was accustomed to spending a great deal of time

alone. Being surrounded by staff wasn't like sharing a bath-room and a bed with someone. The intimacy she'd enjoyed with Ashton these past few days had been pretty all-consuming. She wouldn't blame him if he needed a break.

And she needed to get used to being without him. She had no illusions about their relationship. It was an inter-lude, similar to what her mother had enjoyed with LeDay. A break from routine. A wonderful adventure. Harper rec-ognized that she couldn't hold on to Ashton. His career took him all over the world. Hers kept her grounded in one place.

Except he was on the verge of doing a show that would keep him in New York for an extended period of time. They could be together if she accepted the job of Fontaine's CEO. Unfortunately, he'd made her question if that was the best choice for her.

As she was finishing up her breakfast, Ashton found her. She didn't ask him where he'd been and he didn't vol-unteer the information. His mouth was set in a grim line as he sat down across from her and poured himself a cup of coffee from the silver pot on the table.

"Are you okay?" she asked, unable to shake the feeling that their magical trip was over.

"Fine."

"Have you eaten?"

"I had a little something earlier." He sipped his coffee and stared past her. "I saw that you're packed."

"I wasn't sure what time the plane would be return-ing us to Johannesburg so I thought I'd be ready to leave."

"I told them noon."

Harper checked her watch. If they left in the next fifteen minutes, they would be right on time. She reached out her hand and placed it over his, calling his attention back to her.

"Thank you for coming to Africa to help me. I've really appreciated having you here."

"No need to thank me."

His short replies were starting to irritate her. She needed

to get to the bottom of it before they started the long journey home.

"So this is it then?"

"What do you mean?"

"The end of the road for us. It was a fun week, but now it's over."

"Is that what you want?"

"No." Her throat tightened, but she'd taken too many emotional risks to let fear dominate her now. "I want for us to be together." For the first time she understood Violet's decision to put her marriage before her ambition. "It would be nice to hear that you feel the same."

"Are you sure you really know what you want? A few days ago you couldn't wait to run off to Africa to meet your biological father. What would you have done if he'd wanted to have a relationship with you? Would you have stayed in Africa? Made a new life here?"

"I don't know. I hadn't thought that far ahead."

"Then last night you decided you weren't going to let anything stand in the way of your becoming CEO. You claim you want to know who you are, yet instead of pushing forward and doing what you want for a change, you fall back into old patterns."

Was Ashton asking her to quit the hotel business and spend the rest of her life…doing what?

She still didn't know her true passion. Damn him for being right. And for being the practical one for a change. She needed the old Ashton, the impulsive one, to sweep her into adventure. She was sick of planning her future. She'd come to Africa because she wanted to be bold and daring. But obviously that wasn't her nature. It had taken less than a week before she regressed to comfortable patterns. What she needed to do was take a risk and keep taking them until she felt completely free.

"I love you," she said, captured by a yearning that grew

stronger the more time she spent with Ashton. "I can't imagine my days without you. I'm ready to give up everything and be with you. Just tell me you want me."

Ashton closed his eyes. "I don't want you to give up anything."

"Then what do you want?"

"Don't use me as an excuse to avoid admitting who you are and what you truly want."

"I already told you, I want you."

"Because it's easier to explain to your grandfather that you want to be with the man you love than disappoint him by revealing you're not actually his granddaughter?"

"That's unfair."

"Is it?"

She couldn't answer him truthfully so she traded him question for question. "What about you?"

"What about me?"

"Would you give up the new show and go back to doing *The Culinary Wanderer* again?" It wasn't fair to ask him to set aside his goals. So what if she didn't think he would be happy. They'd been lovers for little more than a week. Who was she to judge what was best for him?

"I already quit and I don't want to go backward."

Her heart sank. "Then you're going to do whatever it takes to make the new network want you."

"That's the plan."

"Then I guess we're destined to disappoint each other, aren't we?"

"I don't believe that's true."

Was his faith so much greater than hers? She wished she could do as he asked and start over, but she'd tried that when she'd come here to meet her father and look how poorly that had turned out.

Her phone chimed. A text message from Violet had come in.

Grandfather has had a mild stroke. He's going to be okay.
Wants to see you.

A sound in her ears swelled as if every insect in the entire bush had chosen that moment to sing. Disoriented, she
shook her head to clear it. Ashton grabbed her hand and
said something that she couldn't catch, but she guessed he
was asking her what was wrong.

With her voice unable to escape her tight throat, she
showed him the message.

"You should call and let them know we're coming."

"We?" she whispered. "You're coming with me?"

"Whatever you need from me. I'll be there."

Ashton didn't expect to be heading to Las Vegas mere
hours after completing the transatlantic flight from Johannesburg. While the charter jet he'd hired cruised over
the heartland of the U.S., he fidgeted with his phone, rest-
lessly checking for updated emails and new texts, knowing if anything came in he would be notified with a tone.

That he'd left Harper behind wasn't sitting well, but
she'd insisted. An hour before they'd touched down at JFK,
she'd sat straighter in her seat and gathered herself. He'd
gotten used to taking care of her these past few days. Discovered he liked that she needed him. But with their return
to the States, her independent nature had reasserted itself.

And she'd been right when she'd insisted the restaurant
was days away from opening. He needed to be at Batouri
overseeing the last-minute details. He should have been
there these past five days instead of traveling to South
Africa. But Dae's updates had reassured him that the staff
was working well together. Chef Cole had proven to be a
good choice. He was organized and a good leader. Harper
had been right about that.

When his phone chimed, it wasn't the person he'd been
hoping to hear from. Vince had sent him a terse text.

Call me.

The brevity of the message could only mean the network had decided to take the cooking show in a different direction and not use him. Ashton had been expecting this ever since he'd walked out and was surprised how little he cared. In the past few days he'd had a lot of time to think. Conversations with Harper regarding her ambivalence toward her career left him debating what he wanted to do versus what he thought he should do.

"Vince," he said as soon as his manager picked up. "What's the word?"

"Lifestyle Network wants you."

Ashton didn't feel the rush of satisfaction he'd expected. "That's not the impression I got from the last meeting."

"They took another look at the tape and saw what I see. You're a star. Soon every household in America is going to know it. They sent me a contract. I've looked it over and everything we asked for is in there."

"I need a few days to think about it."

Silence greeted his response. Ashton imagined his manager was pretty pissed at him right now.

"I've put in a lot of time on this deal," Vince said. "They're giving us everything we want except for the whole *Culinary Wanderer* thing, but you've already quit, so that's a nonfactor."

"Frankly, Vince, when I left the conference room last Monday I was under the impression they wanted to go a different way."

"But they don't."

With nothing standing in the way of signing onto the new show, Ashton had to tackle the doubts raised by his conversation with Harper. "I'm questioning whether staying put in New York is the best thing for me."

Vince's disappointment came through the phone seconds before he spoke. "I wish I'd known that three days ago."

"Why don't we table this for a while. I need to focus on the restaurant right now. Send me the contract and give me a few days to sort through everything."

"Sending it now. Don't leave them hanging too long about this."

"I won't."

When he received Vince's email a minute later, Ashton scanned through the contract with only half his mind on the words. He could really use Harper's input on this. But the last thing he wanted to do right now was disturb her. She had enough on her plate.

Maybe he could talk to her when she returned to Las Vegas for the opening. If she returned. It occurred to him with her grandfather out of commission, it was a perfect time for her to step into the role she'd been training for. She'd decided to follow her head not her heart. He wasn't convinced that was the right decision. And now he had the project that would allow him to be with her. If only it all felt right.

Harper entered her grandfather's New York apartment and was immediately embraced by Violet. The warmth of her greeting was a delightful contrast to the indifference Harper had felt from LeDay. Biology didn't make a family. Caring did.

"How's grandfather?"

"Much better," Violet said, reaching her hand back to her husband for support. JT Stone put his arm around his wife and hugged gently. "He's already protesting the doctor's order to rest."

"Did the stroke cause any permanent damage?"

"From what Dr. Amhull told us, it was a very minor stroke so there shouldn't be any lasting effects. It was a warning that worse could come. He prescribed medication and wants Grandfather to slow down."

"Can I go see him?"

"Of course. And afterward, I think we should talk. Scarlett and Logan went for a walk. They should be back shortly. The six of us should sit down before dinner. There are some things we think you should know."

"The six of us?"

"Isn't Ashton in New York with you?"

"The restaurant is opening in a few days." Harper's stomach turned over as she pictured his tight expression when she told him to go on to Las Vegas without her. "He needs to be in Vegas for that."

Violet stared at her a long moment before nodding. "Of course."

Further explanations would have to wait until later. The most important thing was seeing her grandfather. "Is Grandfather in his room?"

"No. He's in his study. We confiscated his cell phone to keep him from working, but nothing can convince him to stay in bed."

Harper shook her head as she walked down the hallway toward her grandfather's favorite room in the apartment. His work ethic had inspired her own. They were so much alike. Maybe that's why it had been such a shock to discover they weren't related.

She found him sitting in one of a pair of leather chairs that flanked the fireplace. He had a stack of magazines on the table beside him eight inches high. Pausing in the doorway, she scrutinized him. His color was better than she'd expected, and he was scowling at the article he was perusing. Temper was a positive sign.

"Grandfather?"

He looked up from his reading and waved her over. "This is nothing but a fluff piece." The page he showed her had a photo of Gil Kurtz, one of her grandfather's classmates from Harvard and a Connecticut state senator. They'd been rivals since they were twenty years old, and

Henry rarely had anything but disparaging things to say about Gil's political career.

"How are you feeling?"

"I'm fine. Your sisters won't let me leave the house. Don't they understand I have a business to run?"

"They're just concerned about you."

"Violet said you were in Africa. Feel like telling me what you were doing there?"

"I just needed a little break."

Her grandfather grunted. "Bob tried not to give me the impression you'd cracked up, but wasn't able to mask his concern."

"Cracked up?" She laughed a little at the thought. "Why?"

"Because you dropped the entire running of the hotel on him and disappeared."

"I took a vacation."

"When was the last time you took any substantial time off?"

"I don't know." She thought back over the past few years and couldn't recall a span of more than three days where she'd been unavailable to her staff. "Which should make it even more evident I needed a vacation."

"The last time was when I told you about Scarlett and Violet."

"Was it?" She had a vague recollection of going to her grandmother's Hamptons house for a few days.

"You were gone almost two weeks."

"Sorry, but I don't recall that. And I'm sure I had the time coming."

"You did. And much more besides. You're more like me than your father." He was staring out the window at the park across the street. "But occasionally you remind me that you're also your mother's daughter. She's an emotional woman who has difficulty handling any sort of turmoil in her life. Which leads me to wonder what is going on with you. Is that Croft fellow causing problems?"

"Ashton?" Harper was more than a little stunned by her grandfather's analysis of her. He never appeared to notice anything that didn't pertain to his business, but now she wondered if he saw everything and just kept it to himself. "No, he and I have reached a place where we're working well together."

"How about your personal relationship? Everything okay there, too?"

"Ah…" What was he asking? "We work well together."

Her grandfather blew out an impatient breath. "I'm not dense. I know you went to Africa with him."

"Technically, I went to Africa and he followed."

"Why?"

What was her grandfather asking? "Why did he follow me to Africa?"

"Yes. And why did you go in the first place?"

"I wanted an adventure, and Ashton thought I was acting recklessly by traveling alone. Turns out he was a little right."

"More than a little. You were mugged on the train. Had your passport stolen."

How was she going to keep the truth about her biological father hidden when her grandfather was so good at keeping tabs on her?

"Who told you?"

"When I heard you were traveling to South Africa I called a buddy of mine in the State Department and had him keep an eye out for you."

Harper was both touched and annoyed. Didn't anyone think she could take care of herself? "Is that why I was able to get a temporary passport so fast?"

"Partially." Her grandfather's eyes narrowed. "Anything else you'd like to tell me about your time in South Africa?"

"Ashton took me on safari where I was fortunate enough

to see three of the big five. Elephants, cape buffalo and lions." She paused. "Although one night we heard a leopard, as well."

"And that's all?"

"It's a beautiful country. We should consider putting a hotel there."

"Maybe when you become CEO of Fontaine Hotels and Resorts you can do that."

The walls of her grandfather's study seemed to close in. Ashton's warning sounded in her mind. She wanted to silence it, but couldn't. He was right. Becoming CEO under false pretenses would never make her happy. "When that happens, I'll definitely look into it."

They chatted about her impression of Africa until Scarlett appeared in the doorway.

"Can I tear you away for a bit?" she asked Harper, giving Henry a fond smile.

"Sure."

"Are you staying for dinner?" he asked. Despite his protests that he was feeling fine, he looked pale.

"Of course," Harper said. She kissed his cheek and followed Scarlett from the room.

"He looks better than I expected."

Scarlett linked her arm through Harper's and guided her toward the den. "You probably thought he'd be in bed."

"I did."

Inside the comfortable room, Violet, JT and Logan awaited her. Feeling very much like a fifth wheel, Harper sat down in a chair and waited until everyone else had been seated before she broke the silence.

"You all look so grim. What's going on?"

"How did your trip to South Africa turn out?" Violet began.

Sensing they were warming up to the difficult topic, Harper decided to play along. "It's a lovely country. I told Grandfather we should look at putting a hotel there."

"And what did he think of that?" Again Violet.

Scarlett rolled her eyes. "Stop dancing around what we want to know." Her tone was exasperated. "Did you meet your father?"

"Yes."

"How did it go?"

"No worse than you'd imagine. Being confronted by a twenty-nine-year-old daughter he never knew caught him by surprise."

"Was he courteous?" Violet asked.

"He invited Ashton and me to dinner."

Scarlet piped up. "Where is Ashton?"

"On his way to Las Vegas. The restaurant is opening in two days. I have no idea if it will go well."

"I'm sure it will be fine," Violet said. She glanced at Scarlett and then at JT, who nodded. "Logan was able to figure out who blackmailed your mother."

In the craziness of the past week, Harper had forgotten that little tidbit. "Who?"

JT spoke. "My father. He needed money for a top-notch defense lawyer."

"How did he come by the files?"

"It's my fault," Scarlett said. "If I hadn't brought them home, I wouldn't have lost them."

"You didn't lose them," Logan reminded her, a muscle popping in his jaw. "Someone broke into your suite, knocked you out and stole them."

"Technically," she countered, "I opened the door thinking it was you."

Violet stepped in. "I blame Tiberius. If he hadn't poked his nose in where it didn't belong there wouldn't have been any files in the first place."

"It was my father who went after the information my uncle had gathered on him and hired the guy who hurt Scarlett. He's the one who blackmailed Harper's mother," JT chimed in.

Harper shut her eyes and let the voices wash over her. She floated in darkness until someone touched her arm and brought her back.

Logan knelt before her, his dark brown gaze confident and reassuring. "We retrieved both the information and the money."

She sandwiched Logan's hand between hers, leaned forward and kissed him on the cheek. "Thank you."

"No need to thank me."

She gazed from him to her sisters and finally to JT. This was her family, she realized. Not some stranger in South Africa who wanted nothing to do with her.

"I'm so lucky to have all of you," she told them.

"So, now that your secret is safe," Violet began, "are you going to take the CEO job?"

This was important to all of them, she realized. It meant that Scarlett could continue pursuing her acting and Violet could stay in Las Vegas with JT. They expected her to do the job she was trained for.

"Whenever grandfather wants me to take over, I will."

Twelve

T wo hours before the restaurant opened for the first time, Batouri's kitchen was operating more smoothly than Ashton had a right to expect. After being gone during the week before their grand opening, he'd half feared he was coming back to absolute chaos. Thanks to Cole, this was not the case.

Without any major crisis to deal with, Ashton had too much space to think. He tried to focus on the food, but bits of conversations with Harper kept intruding. He second-guessed how he'd handled things when she'd told him she loved him. Had it been a mistake to question her sudden change of heart? He'd been on the verge of sweeping her into his arms and agreeing to make all her dreams come true when the message about her grandfather's stroke had come to her phone.

Carlo approached him. "Harper is here. She's asking for you."

Ashton followed Carlo from the kitchen, struggling to

keep from rushing past the restaurant manager in his excitement to see Harper. She stood by the hostess stand, tense and uncertain in a white dress that draped her slim form in wispy layers of lace. Her hair had been pulled back from her face and loosely clipped in a romantic style. The impact of her appearance stole his breath.

He crossed to her and gave her a kiss on the cheek. From her surprised expression, she'd obviously expected something different.

"I haven't heard from you," he said, making no attempt to hide his unhappiness. "How is your grandfather?"

"The stroke was minor and he's stubborn. Keeping him at home for the past few days has been a challenge when he already feels strong enough to go back to work."

"I'm glad to hear it. What did you tell him about South Africa?"

"That it's a lovely country."

Her answer disappointed him. "That's not what I meant. Did you tell your grandfather the truth about LeDay and your mother?"

"He's just had a stroke. It would be cruel of me to burden him with such a shock." She looked down at her hands. "And thanks to Logan, my mother's blackmailer has been stopped."

"You don't ever plan to tell him." He saw the truth in the way she was avoiding meeting his gaze. "You don't think he'll love you anymore if you're not his flesh and blood."

"Five years ago he went looking for Violet and Scarlett simply because they were his granddaughters. He loves them. What's to say he wouldn't stop loving me when he finds out we're not related?"

"You don't really believe he would do that."

"I don't." Her voice didn't rise above a whisper. "But I can't take the chance. And they're all counting on me."

"Who?"

"My sisters. JT and Logan. They're happy. Their lives

are perfect exactly as they are. If I don't take over as CEO either Scarlett or Violet will have to and neither one wants the job."

In a flash, he saw the future unfold. She would take the CEO job and live in New York City. He would move on to bigger and better things with the new show. The network was ready to get behind him and push him into superstar range. There would be more shows, more opportunities to expand his career. Most important, he and Harper could start a life together.

But was it the life either of them wanted?

"Can we talk about this later?" he asked.

"There's no need. I think you've told me everything you need to."

"Not by a long shot." But he could tell she wasn't listening. "Meet me after the restaurant closes tonight."

"I have too much hotel business to take care of before I fly back to New York tomorrow afternoon. I promised Grandfather that I would step into his shoes for a while. It was the only way I could get him to rest and not worry about the company."

"When will you be back?"

She shook her head. "I'm not sure. It might be a permanent move."

Ashton's heart sank. She would spend the rest of her life living a lie. He wanted what was best for her and this wasn't it. But there was a bright spot to her decision.

"Then I guess we'll be seeing a lot of each other. Lifestyle Network agreed to most of my demands."

"Not all?" Her half-smile was wry.

Ashton gave a one-shoulder shrug. "Those I didn't get aren't all that important."

"You're going to do the show?"

"It means we can be together in New York."

She avoided his gaze. "You know you'll hate being stuck in the city."

"I don't know that." Her lack of enthusiasm for their upcoming proximity left him questioning whether she wanted him in her life. "New York has a lot to offer in terms of culinary experiences."

"Did you agree to cut your hair?"

"It's part of the rebranding."

"Don't do it." She reached up and swept her fingers into his hair, tugging his head down. "Promise me."

"I can't. They're right. In order to appeal to a wider audience, I need a different look."

"You won't look like you."

"It's just hair."

"It's not. It's part of your image. You are the daring adventurer. The guy that charges into dangerous locales and bravely eats whatever exotic fare the population considers typical."

"I can't be that guy the rest of my life."

"Why not?" She stared at him intently. "That's the man I fell in love with."

Her words hit him square in the breastbone. Living without her these past few days had been hell. He couldn't face a future apart from her. But telling her that he loved her wasn't going to make the problem between them go away.

"Because I realized after meeting your father that the traveling I do keeps me apart from people I care about. I don't want to be alone the rest of my life. I want you."

"You can have me and all the adventures you could ever want."

"A part-time relationship with you isn't what I had in mind."

Then her lips were on his and his arms went around her slim body. The kiss was frantic and tasted like goodbye. Ashton's heart was a bowling ball in his chest by the time her lips peeled away from his.

"We're good together," she said.

"The key word is *together*." He cupped her face and

kissed her lightly on the lips. "Tell your grandfather the truth and we can go adventuring together."

"I thought you wanted the Lifestyle Network show."

"I'd rather have you happy and whole."

"Then you understand how I feel about you." She grabbed his hands and pulled them away from her face. "Do the show. It's what's right for your career."

"In the past few weeks I've decided I'm more than my career. What about you?"

She wouldn't meet his gaze. "It's getting late. Shouldn't you be in the kitchen inspiring your staff?"

Ashton eyed her set expression and wondered what would change her mind about permanently taking over as Fontaine's CEO. With a tight nod, he gently kissed her forehead.

"I'll see you in the restaurant later."

"Good luck tonight." With those parting words, she was gone.

With the opening of Batouri mere hours away, Ashton should have been completely consumed by what was happening in his kitchen. He wasn't. Reporters and food critics as well as celebrities and other assorted VIPs would be among the evening's guests. They were expecting a masterful culinary performance tonight. He needed to score big.

That would be easier if Harper hadn't shown up in his kitchen this afternoon. Telling himself that keeping her feet to the fire was for her own good didn't unravel the knot of misery in his chest.

It wasn't until service was well underway that he had a chance to step out of the kitchen and circulate through the room. Before he'd ever stepped in front of a camera, he'd been a successful executive chef and restaurant owner. He recognized a satisfied crowd when he saw one.

As he schmoozed those who could make or break Batouri with a single negative review, he tried not to make it obvious that there was only one table in the room that held his complete attention. And it was the last one he visited.

"Absolutely fabulous," Scarlett said, the first to speak up. The vivacious, stunningly beautiful brunette glanced away from Ashton and nudged Harper's arm. "My sister's idea to have you open a restaurant in her hotel was nothing short of brilliant."

"Wonderful," Violet agreed, a note of concern beneath her upbeat tone. "I think you two make a terrific team."

"That's nice of you to say, but I'm sure your sister would disagree." Ashton had no idea why he felt like baiting Harper on a night where he needed her complete support. Maybe it was the fact that she was looking through him rather than at him. "In fact, the success of the restaurant should be placed squarely at her feet. She smoothed every feather I ruffled in the construction process and probably had to stop the chefs I interviewed from adding arsenic to the food they served me."

Scarlett laughed in delight.

Violet looked appalled.

Harper glared at him. "It's your food everyone loves."

"You were the one who inspired me." The room fell away as he captured her gaze and held it. For a second he saw past her unhappiness and glimpsed the passion she'd demonstrated in Africa. His heart stopped. Maybe there was hope for them yet. He shifted his attention to her sisters and offered them a smile. "Thank you for coming to support Harper."

Not waiting for a response, he moved off.

Behind him, Scarlett spoke up. "Do whatever you have to, but don't let that man get away."

Harper said something in reply, but it was too faint for him to catch. Still, he was feeling better than he had in days as he reentered the kitchen. Nothing was a done deal. Persuading her to be true to herself would be a lot easier if he showed her how to do it.

* * *

At a little after six in the afternoon the day after Batouri's successful opening, Harper entered her grandfather's apartment and found him in the living room, his cell phone in one hand, a glass of Scotch in the other. This is how she imagined he'd go out: running his business while relaxing at home. Working was as much a part of him as breathing. Is this what she wanted for her own life?

Spotting her, he gestured her in. "Sam, I have to go. My granddaughter just arrived, and we're going to have dinner together."

As soon as he hung up, she came forward and hugged him. What she'd come here tonight to say wasn't going to be easy. The urge to blurt it out nearly overpowered her, but that sort of shock couldn't be good for a man who'd suffered a stroke a little over a week ago.

"I heard the opening of your restaurant was a resounding success," he said as they sat down at the large dining table.

Only two places had been set. To Harper's relief, they weren't at opposite ends of the twenty-foot table. Her mother would be horrified if she discovered that Harper had shouted the tale of her infidelity from one end of the dining room to the other.

"It went very well. The reviews had nothing but wonderful things to say. You were right to suggest I approach Ashton."

"I had a feeling you two would be good for each other."

Unexpectedly, Harper flashed back to their two nights at the tent camp and felt heat rise in her cheeks. "How come?"

"He's a hugely talented chef and the adventurous sort. You've always been an armchair globetrotter too focused on the future to have fun in the present. I thought he might benefit from your knack of focusing on the finish line and you might give him an opportunity to surprise you."

Her grandfather had nailed what had happened between her and Ashton. "How did you know?"

"You don't think I'm this successful in business because I'm a lucky devil, do you?" Her grandfather offered her a crafty smile. "Did you ever wonder why, after you worked so hard to learn the business, I still went ahead and created the contest between you, Violet and Scarlett?"

Since her grandfather was laying his cards on the table, she might as well play hers, as well. "Because you weren't sure I was the best choice?"

"I knew you were the best choice. I just wasn't sure you knew it."

Harper had little trouble following his logic. "I never really believed I was going to be CEO. I wanted it very badly and worked hard to make sure you approved of me."

"I more than approve of you, Harper. I want you to succeed me."

She had to state the obvious even though it exemplified the lack of confidence her grandfather had just criticized about her. "I'm the only one left standing as far as the contest goes. Scarlett has returned to acting part-time. Violet intends to stay in Las Vegas with JT."

"And what do you want?"

His question surprised her. "To be CEO." But she was not as confident as she'd been a month earlier.

"Do you?"

A better lead-in to what she had to confess wasn't going to present itself. "A week ago you asked me what I was doing in Africa." She gathered a steadying breath and tried to calm her agitated pulse. "The truth is, I went looking for my father. My biological father."

Now that she'd made her shocking revelation, she braced herself for her grandfather's outrage. When he continued to eat his steak without reacting, she frowned.

"Why aren't you asking me anything?"

"Did you find him?"

"Yes."

"And?"

"What do you mean, and?"

"I'm assuming you didn't travel that far without some idea of what you expected out of the encounter." He gave her more credit than was due. "Was he pleased to meet you?"

"Not really." She set her fork down and picked up her wine. "He had no idea I existed."

"Your mother never contacted him." A statement. Not a question.

"Why are you so calm about this?" And then it dawned on her. "You knew about my mother's affair and the fact that I wasn't your biological granddaughter."

"Yes."

"You never told me."

"Why should I? You're my granddaughter."

"Not by blood."

"I love you, Harper. You have been my joy for every single one of your twenty-nine years."

"I had no idea you'd feel that way. You went to such lengths to find Violet and Scarlett and make them part of the business. I worried that you didn't have faith in my ability to succeed you."

"Scarlett was unhappy in Los Angeles and her career was sinking fast. What she lacked in business experience she made up for in intelligence and people savvy. Violet deserved better than Tiberius Stone's small-time casino. She knows Las Vegas inside and out and it shows. Her hotel is the most profitable of all three." He grinned. "You're surprised."

She really wasn't. "Would you have picked her if she hadn't taken herself out of the running?"

"No. She might know Vegas, but you understand our entire organization. I need you as CEO." When she didn't immediately speak, he regarded her solemnly. "Unless you decide you no longer want the job."

"In truth, I'm not sure. One of the reasons I went to Africa was because when I learned I wasn't a Fontaine, a part of me was relieved."

"I can understand that. You've put a lot of pressure on yourself."

"Then I met Greg LeDay and I didn't have an aha moment. He wasn't happy to meet me. He had no interest in starting any sort of relationship. There are a whole bunch of people I'm related to that I'll never get to know."

"Give him some time to think about it. He may change his mind."

"I doubt it."

The epiphany she'd expected upon meeting her biological father hadn't happened. She'd been no closer to discovering who she really was. What had changed her was the time she'd spent with Ashton, seeing Africa through his eyes. Those days had given her a deeper understanding of what made her happy.

"All my life I've wanted you to be proud of me," she said. "It's why I worked so hard."

"And I am."

"From things my father said, I knew you wanted a Fontaine to be at the company's helm."

"Now you're thinking that if you take over one won't be?"

"Actually, I'm not sure I'm as ready to be in charge as I thought."

"You want to stay in Las Vegas?"

"No, I think Violet should take over Fontaine Ciel." That would surprise her very capable sister. "I'd like to spend several years consulting in the area of development."

"Let me guess. Traveling the world to determine the best places to expand?"

"Something like that."

"And you think I should stay on in the meantime?"

She smiled. "You and I both know you're not ready to

stop working. Maybe you could try slowing down a bit.
Let your staff handle more."

"You're asking a lot of an old man."

"I trust that you have it in you."

At eight in the morning, Batouri's kitchen was a peaceful place. Surrounded by stainless steel, alone with his
thoughts, Ashton did the one thing that had saved him for
the past twenty years. He cooked.

The five days since Batouri had opened had been hectic
ones. He'd been tweaking the menu daily, using the spe-
cials to experiment, finding the perfect blend of traditional
and unexpected.

He hadn't seen Harper since the night Batouri had
opened. She'd gone to New York City and hadn't yet returned. Each day Ashton grew less confident that he'd made
the right decision. He'd turned down the Lifestyle Network
show, deciding if he wanted to prove how committed he
was to her happiness, he'd have to demonstrate it in a big
way. Now his hopes that she'd choose traveling with him
over living a lie were dwindling.

Despite how things turned out, he was glad he hadn't
pressed her to join him. She'd wanted him to. But for him
to make such an important decision for her would have
brought her back full circle to her current dilemma. What
was it Harper wanted for herself?

Almost as if thinking about her had compelled her to
find him, Harper stepped into his kitchen.

"I thought I might find you here."

"Where else?"

She looked exactly the same as the first day he'd met
her. The unflappable executive with her hair smoothed back
into an elegant French roll. Expensive but understated jew-
elry adorned her slim neck and delicate earlobes. The hem
of her designer power suit sliced her kneecaps in half and
showed off her toned calves.

Polished. Professional. Perfect.

His heart sank. She'd obviously chosen her future.

"I spoke to my grandfather about taking over as CEO."

"You didn't tell him the truth then."

"No, I told him." She shook her head in bemusement. "Turns out he's known all along."

"Smart man, your grandfather. But I don't know why that surprises me. Look how you turned out."

"I hope you're going to be okay with my decision."

"I will get behind whatever you choose."

"You're going to take the job with the network then?" She looked disappointed.

He decided not to leave her feeling that way for long. "No. I turned them down."

She brightened. "You're going back to *The Culinary Wanderer.* That's wonderful."

"No to that, as well."

"What? I don't understand."

"You were determined to take the CEO job, which meant I couldn't continue traveling with *The Culinary Wanderer* if we were going to be together. But at the same time, you were right about going with the network. They wanted me to become something I'm not."

"What are you planning to do?"

"You suggested that I work on a cookbook. With the success of Batouri, I was considering opening another restaurant in New York, and Vince is exploring opportunities with other networks."

"You've given up your television career to be with me?" She regarded him in confusion. "But why?"

"I realized something these past few days. I no longer feel invincible. Before I met you I had nothing to lose. That's changed."

Harper stood perfectly still while her mind raced. "I don't understand. You had a great deal at stake. *The Culinary Wanderer.* A brand-new cooking show. Batouri."

"Television shows and restaurants will come and go. The only irreplaceable thing in my life is you."

"Me?"

"The woman I love."

"You love me?"

"Hadn't you guessed?"

"When it comes to love, I'm not too well versed on the ins and outs of romance."

"You haven't had much experience." He took her left hand and placed her palm over his heart. "Neither have I, so you'll have to excuse me if I've bungled a few things."

"I suppose it's something we could work on together."

"I'm glad you said that." He reached into his pocket. "Because I want to spend the rest of my life working on it with you. Marry me?"

His eyes were the most brilliant blue she'd ever seen as he gazed down at her. Harper's mouth went dry. Spinning through her head were all the reasons why it would never work between them.

Like her father, he wouldn't be able to stay put for long. He had restaurants in several countries. Traveling for business meant temptation would lurk around every corner. Would they end up like her parents?

Their opposite approaches to decisions—he would be rash and impulsive while she would study and plan—guaranteed they would fight endlessly.

Her tendency to work too much would cause him to get impatient and bored.

"Yes." Not one of her doubts could stand up against the love she felt for this man. "Oh, yes. Scarlett told me make sure you didn't get away and I wholeheartedly agree."

As metal touched her skin, she looked down. Ashton was sliding a large ring onto the third finger of her left hand. Two circles of diamonds, one white, one pale pink, surrounded a pink diamond. It was a unique take on a traditional halo style engagement ring and absolutely...

"Beautiful," she murmured.

"Not nearly as beautiful as the woman who will wear it." He kissed her long and deep. "I love you."

"I hope you still feel that way when I tell you that I'm not taking over as Fontaine's CEO."

"Why not?"

"Because I'm going to travel to cities that don't have a Fontaine hotel to scout locations. Good thing you're going to be free to travel with me because I don't much like the idea of leaving you home alone."

"Interesting that you should bring this up. Remember that idea you had for a travel series on romantic hotel destinations?"

"Did I say romantic?" she teased. "Actually, romantic is probably a great idea."

"Phillips Consolidated Networks agrees with you and they want us to come up with a list of hotels. The more exotic, the better."

"I thought you were done with them."

"Not completely."

"Were you going to run off and do another travel show without me?"

"Of course not. You don't seriously expect that the producers are going to send me to romantic destinations by myself, do you?"

Dismay made her frown. "If you think I'm going to stand by and let you travel to the world's most beautiful places with some gorgeous, charming female version of you…"

His mouth settled over hers, effectively cutting off her tirade. She wasn't quite done fighting and it took several minutes of kissing for her to become sufficiently limp in his arms. When he thought he could get a word in edgewise, he relinquished her lips.

"My darling, I know you perfectly well. There is no gorgeous, charming female version of me as my costar.

There is only the gorgeous, charming female better half of me that is you."

"Me? Starring on television?"

"What do you say?"

"I'm absolutely terrified." She paused, and a broad grin bloomed. "So yes."

"This is going to be a fantastic project." Sweeping her off her feet, he carried her out into the restaurant's dining area. "You. Me. Exotic destinations. Think of all the amazing places we'll make love."

She laughed. "It all sounds very exciting."

And perfect. Because with Ashton's help she'd discovered her passion and the best version of herself. Most days she might still work too hard, but Ashton would be there to remind her to play, as well. Together they would accomplish anything they set their minds to.

When it looked like Ashton intended to carry her out of the restaurant, Harper stopped him. "Wait, I need my *go* bag."

Ashton paused near the door. "You have a *go* bag?"

"Over there by our booth." She pointed over his shoulder.

"Why do you have it with you?"

"So I'll be ready to leave at a moment's notice."

With a disgusted noise, Ashton exited the restaurant, leaving her bag behind.

"Wait, I need that."

"Not right now." With long strides, he carried her past the casino floor and straight to the elevators. "Because the only place you're going is your suite. With me."

And that sounded just right because the biggest adventure of her life was being with the man she loved.

* * * * *

"City boy can't handle the heat?"

Grant laughed. "Actually I thought you might need a break."

"I don't take breaks," she told him, tilting her chin in defiance. "And a little heat never bothered me anyway."

Unable to stop himself, he stepped forward and slid a stray hair behind her ear.

"Good to know you can handle activities that work up a sweat," he murmured, mentally cursing himself for crossing into the carnal-thought territory.

Tessa reached up, put her hand in his and smiled. "You're going to have to do better than that, Slick. Clever innuendos won't work on me."

"Oh, I'm just getting warmed up, Country. Throwing you off your guard is my main goal here."

"I thought producing and directing this movie was your main goal."

He leaned in, close enough to smell her musky scent, feel her warm breath on his face. "I'm an expert at multitasking.."

* * *

When Opposites Attract…
is part of The Barrington Trilogy: Hollywood comes to horse country—and the Barrington family's secrets are at the center of it all!

WHEN OPPOSITES ATTRACT...

BY
JULES BENNETT

Published in Great Britain 2014
by Mills & Boon, an imprint of Harlequin (UK) Limited,
Eton House, 18-24 Paradise Road, Richmond, Surrey, TW9 1SR

© 2014 Jules Bennett

ISBN: 978-0-263-91473-3

51-0714

Harlequin (UK) Limited's policy is to use papers that are natural, renewable and recyclable products and made from wood grown in sustainable forests. The logging and manufacturing processes conform to the legal environmental regulations of the country of origin.

Printed and bound in Spain
by Blackprint CPI, Barcelona

National bestselling author **Jules Bennett**'s love of storytelling started when she would get in trouble as a child and would tell her parents her imaginary friends were to blame. Since then, her vivid imagination has taken her down a path she'd only dreamed of. And after twelve years of owning and working in salons, she hung up her shears to write full-time.

Jules doesn't just write Happily Ever After, she lives it. Married to her high school sweetheart, Jules and her hubby have two little girls who keep them smiling. She loves to hear from readers! Contact her at authorjules@gmail.com, visit her website, www.julesbennett.com, where you can sign up for her newsletter, or send her a letter at PO Box 396, Minford, OH 45653, USA. You can also follow her on Twitter and join her Facebook fan page.

This entire trilogy is for my amazing agent, Elaine Spencer, who, when I mentioned a horse series, said, "Horses? I'm more familiar with dogs, but go for it." From one animal lover to another, thanks for holding my hand during this journey.

Also, a special thank-you to F.J. Thomas, my Twitter buddy who answered many questions regarding the world of horses and racing.
Any mistakes are mine alone.

One

With a nice, round backside greeting him as he stepped over the threshold of the fancy stables, Grant Carter was more certain than ever that accepting this film project was not only a chance of a lifetime, it was a gift from God.

He might be looking to settle down and calm his ways, but to ignore the perfection displayed before him would be a sin. Besides, Grant knew his place, and he hadn't worked this hard in Hollywood to blow it just because temptation seemed to be glaring right in his face. Literally.

Temptation would have to wait, because producing a film revolving around horse-racing icon Damon Barrington was an opportunity he couldn't pass up…no matter the nightmares that followed him here.

The shapely woman in front of him might be a slight distraction, but that's all she could be. The new clause typed up in his contract had been reinforced before his arrival at Stony Ridge. Apparently, fraternizing with anyone involved in this film was a no-no. Shame, that.

Besides, even without the clause, nothing could cripple him more than being thrust back into the world of horses. But he could compartmentalize and he could be a professional on set. He simply couldn't let personal conflicts pass the barrier he'd built around his heart.

Grant eyed the round bottom hugged by tight black riding pants. *Damn clause and personal demons.*

The familiar smells of the straw, the feed, the leather saddles; the sight of beautiful Thoroughbreds... The combination brought back memories—memories that had no place in his life. Especially now.

Concentrate on the backside. A body like that could surely cure all ails. Even if she was off-limits, he had already taken a mental picture to fuel fantasies.

"Excuse me. Can you tell me where I can find Tessa Barrington?" he asked, carefully stepping farther into the stables, straw crunching beneath his new boots.

The petite, yet curvy woman stood up, turned and slid the vibrant red ponytail back over her shoulder. And he'd be a complete liar if he tried to deny the punch to the gut he felt when those sapphire eyes landed on him. In an instant, he wondered how many times she'd used those intriguing eyes to lure a man into her clutches.

Between the body and the face, she was a stunner, but he wouldn't be as clichéd as to say so. No doubt she had men falling all over her, and he refused to be so predictable.

"Are you the producer?" she asked, setting aside the brush she'd been using on the horse.

"One of them. Grant Carter." He closed the gap between them and extended his hand.

"I'm Tessa."

Surprise slid through him, but he prevented himself from dropping his jaw...just barely. So, he'd been admiring the beautiful jockey. Interesting.

When she propped her hands on her slender waist, just above her flared hips, he nearly swallowed his tongue. That sweet little package all wrapped in denim and plaid? Who knew he had a thing for country girls? Of course, Tessa Barrington was hardly just a country girl. This woman put the fear of God in most male jockeys, trainers and owners, if rumor served correctly.

"My father said you'd be arriving today." She gripped his hand, her gaze sliding down to his feet. "Pretty shiny boots you got there, Slick. We'll have to scuff those up a bit."

He couldn't help but smile at her piercing glare, her judgmental words. A woman who didn't hold back and wasn't throwing herself at him? He liked her already.

When she pulled her hand from his, Grant hated how such delicate features had calluses on them, but he knew this jockey took her lifestyle seriously. She didn't get to be the number-one contender in the country by sitting on the sidelines sipping mint juleps and wearing oversize hats.

"It's a pleasure to meet you," he told her, offering a smile. "I have to say, you're quite impressive."

A perfectly sculpted brow lifted as she crossed her arms beneath her breasts.

Grant laughed. "That didn't come out right."

Seriously? Was he in high school and suddenly unable to form an intelligent sentence?

"What I meant to say was I'm impressed with your talents."

Damn it. Nothing was working for him right now.

"I'm assuming you mean because of my racing," she replied, her brow still raised.

Relieved that she'd let him off the hook, he tilted his head. "I know you have a busy schedule—"

"It's beyond busy, Mr. Carter."

"Call me Grant," he told her, cutting off that curt tone. "We'll be spending a great deal of time together over the next couple of weeks."

Tessa turned, picked up the brush and stepped back into the stall with the stud. "Mr. Carter—"

"Grant," he reminded her with a grin.

Her eyes darted to his, then back to the horse she'd been brushing. "Mr. Carter, my schedule is pretty tight. I came up with a spreadsheet so you can see when I'm practicing, when I'm working in the stables and when I have time blocked off for you. Your area on the sheet is green. I would like to stick to this spreadsheet, but if you have other engagements during our time, I can attempt to rework it."

Grant tried his hardest not to burst out laughing. She was

starting to sound like his oh-so-organized twin sister...or at least how he remembered his sister before her accident.

Seeing as how Tessa still hadn't shown a hint of a smile, he assumed she was dead serious. Wow, this woman would be tough to crack. He loved a challenge, but something told him she wanted nothing to do with this movie. Most people would be thrilled to know Hollywood wanted to make a film around their life and on their property. The majority of the women he knew would give their entire shoe collection to be associated with a Bronson Dane movie with Max Ford as lead actor.

Grant watched as Tessa stroked the horse's mane with precision and care. This woman was obviously not impressed with him or this film. She seemed to be in her own world of details and structure, from the spreadsheet to her perfectly placed low ponytail. He had a feeling the beautiful Tessa Barrington rarely had her feathers ruffled.

And he'd so love to ruffle her. But beyond coproducing this film, he couldn't get swept back into the world that had ruined his family's life. He had to keep any personal emotions off this set. His next goal, of starting his own production company, was within reach, and he'd be damned if he'd let his guilt and fear hold him back.

"When is my first time slot, Tessa?" he asked, propping his hands on his hips as he took a step back from the open stall. "My team will be arriving in a month, and I plan on outlining the sites for the order of filming after I visit all the locations. But I'm flexible. I'll work around you."

With perfect ease, she turned, tapped the brush against her palm and tipped her head. "I know my father agreed to have me help you, but my racing has and always will come first. I should make it clear I'm not happy about this film and I don't endorse any part of it."

Grant couldn't help but grin. Apparently Tessa wasn't a fan of having her work disrupted. Actually, she was a refreshing change from the women who stumbled over themselves to get his attention because of his celebrity status and his bank account. Tessa was obviously impressed with neither, which only made her even more intriguing.

"I understand you're a busy woman," he repeated, hoping to use a little charm to get on her good side. "I'll try not to take up too much of your time."

"I only agreed to let you shadow me because I refuse for this film to be anything but accurate. I don't want my father's life spun into something ugly or devious."

Interesting. Clearly, Tessa had had an unpleasant experience somewhere along the way, and now Grant was in her path of anger. Lovely. Nothing like spending the next month working closely with a bitter woman.

"I will make sure this movie is done to everyone's satisfaction and is the best film we can produce," he promised.

"Looks like we'll both be getting our way, then," she said with a tight smile.

Both get their way? His eyes roamed over her delicate frame. Oh, the possibilities. Slipping that tight ponytail down would be the first. Unbuttoning her stiff shirt would be next.

And making use of that empty stall would be another.

Yeah, this would definitely be a long month.

Tessa knew when a man was attracted; she wasn't stupid. And in all honesty, she found this hotshot producer pretty sexy, but she'd built up an immunity to sexy, smooth talkers.

Besides, the last guy who'd captured her attention was a city boy through and through. His polished shoes, designer suits and perfectly coiffed hair hadn't bothered her. What bothered her was when he'd decided to use her name and finances to further his small-business venture.

There was no way Tessa would let herself get sidelined by some captivating, powerful stranger from Hollywood just because he made her heart beat a bit quicker with that one-sided smile and those heavy-lidded eyes.

Most twenty-five-year-old women were getting married and

having babies. Tessa opted to chase her own set of dreams—the Triple Crown.

There was no time for serious relationships when she lived in a stable, training most hours of the day. And she most definitely thought more of herself than to let go of her innocence for a quickie.

Besides, she'd learned the hard way how cruel relationships could be and how the word *trust* meant different things to different people.

"I need to take Oliver out for a ride," she told Grant, hoping he'd take those sultry eyes and be on his way for now. "I assumed when Dad said you'd arrive today, it would be later, so I had blocked out a two hour window for you after lunch."

He checked his watch. "I can come back, but it may help if I have that spreadsheet, so I know when not to disturb you."

Tessa sighed. He was mocking her. That was fine; she was used to it. But the last guy who'd decided to make a joke of her had found himself out one girlfriend and a whole lot of pride by the time she'd finished with him. Of course, his mocking had come on a whole other, more painful level.

She moved to the next stall, where Oliver, her beautiful Thoroughbred, waited for his warm-up. Oliver wasn't her racing horse. No, he was her baby, and she loved him as dearly as she would her own child. He was a bit finicky, a bit hyper some might say, but Tessa and he understood each other. And they pretty much both loathed outsiders.

"I'll bring that spreadsheet to our meeting," she told Grant as she slid open the stall. Oliver, restless as usual, started his bucking dance, his way of letting her know he was more than ready to go. "I can meet you back here in two hours—"

One second she was talking and the next she was in Grant's arms. She hadn't seen him move, but suddenly he was pulling her away from the opening in the stall.

"What are you doing?" she asked, looking up into the most impressive set of dark, near-black eyes.

Grant stood frozen, his arms wrapped around her, his eyes

now wide and focused on Oliver. With his attention not directly on her, she could take a moment to appreciate the strong jawline beneath the dark stubble, the tanned skin, his firm grip on her, giving her the opportunity to learn that he had fabulous muscle tone beneath that new gray flannel shirt.

And he smelled so damn good. Perhaps she was just glad to be inhaling something other than hay and horse poop, but Grant Carter's aftershave, cologne or the combination of both was masculine, strong and sexy…just like the man.

"Grant?" she asked, sliding from his grasp.

His gaze went from the stallion to her and held, before he shook his head as if to focus.

"He jumped when you started to step in," Grant told her, taking a step back and raking a hand through his short, messy hair. "I didn't want you to get hurt."

Still confused at his overreaction, but a little touched by his instant ride to the rescue, Tessa crossed her arms. "Hurt? I won't get hurt tending to the horses, Grant. Oliver is always like this. That's why I'm the only one who handles him."

Grant shrugged. "My apologies. I'm just not used to horses."

She tilted her head, still trying to get a feel for this newcomer into her world. "Are you going to be okay on this set?"

"I'm fine." He sent her another killer, knee-weakening smile. "I didn't want you hurt, that's all."

The way those dark eyes held hers, and the soft, yet firm tone of his voice washed over her like a warm, protective blanket. She didn't want to feel anything for this man. But that protective streak, and an underlying secret vulnerability, made him even more attractive in her eyes.

"I don't think that's all," she commented, calling him out on whatever seemed to cripple him. "I don't want to be rude, but you are working on a film about horses. Shouldn't you know something about them?"

That sexy smile spread wider across his face as Grant eased forward with a slow, easy stride any cowboy would envy.

But this man was from L.A., the city of sin and silicone. If it weren't for the newly purchased clothes, which were so fresh looking they might as well have the tags dangling, Tessa would swear he lived on a farm.

But he was in the film industry. He probably always looked the part. Appearances were everything to shallow people.

Grant stopped when the tips of their boots nearly touched, and she had to either stare at the way his dark gray flannel stretched across his firm pecs, or glance up and meet that dark gaze. Either body part would tempt a nun, and Tessa was finding it hard to remember what she was saying when he towered over her and looked straight down into her eyes as if he could see her deepest secrets.

She'd been tempted before in her twenty-five years, but never this fast, this hard. Tessa feared she might be in over her head with Grant Carter because they'd been in each other's presence for mere moments, which was barely a blip on the radar in the grand scheme of things.

"Learning all about horses is why I have you. I've waited years to get a project of this caliber." His eyes roamed over her face, from her eyes to her lips and back up. "And when I want something, I find a way to make it mine."

Why did those arrogant words hold such promise? And why did she delight in the way chills raced over her body?

Had she not learned her lesson? Pretty words and attractive men were all around her in this industry. She'd been naive enough to fall for a smooth talker, had nearly taken his ring while dreaming about their future. She wouldn't make that mistake twice.

And she certainly had no room for overeager hormones. She had races to win and titles to collect. Nothing could come between her and her goal...not even if it was wrapped in chiseled muscle and a white-knight attitude.

But she couldn't deny the man tempted her more in these few moments than her ex had in the months they'd been together.

Tessa was proud she still had her virginity. Some women

might be embarrassed by the fact, but she felt that was just another layer of her strong will. And a promise to her late mother.

But Grant did make her hyperaware of desires she'd never fully engaged in.

Good grief, why did she have sex on the brain? She'd just met this man, but those broad shoulders and mesmerizing eyes, combined with his protective streak, made all her lonely girlie parts perk up and wonder exactly what she was missing out on.

"I'm not interested in anything other than my racing and my horses," she told him, damning her voice when it didn't sound as strong as she'd wanted. "Don't waste your fancy charms on me."

One corner of Grant's mouth lifted in a mocking smile. "Oh, my fancy charms aren't going to waste, Tessa. You're just as attracted as I am. It's natural to see a beautiful person and allow your mind to wander into fantasy. There's no need to deny the facts."

Tessa laughed, took a step back and crossed her arms over her chest again. "If your ego is going to be the third wheel, we may have to adjust the spreadsheet to accommodate. But I'm afraid my time can't be stretched so thin, so check it at the door, Slick."

Grant laughed and, damn him, she just knew if she was going to lie around him, she'd have to be more convincing. There was no way she could let her guard down, or she'd find herself falling directly into his seductive, high-class world.

Two

The wide, curved staircase leading up to the second-story balcony overlooking the entryway would be the perfect place to shoot the opening scene. Grant wanted to begin the movie with the early years of Damon and Rose Barrington, and since this home was the focal point for their family, this would be where they began.

Taking mental notes as he walked through the main house at Stony Ridge Acres, Grant could already picture Max Ford, the lead in the film, leaning over the balcony, watching two little girls frolic in the open floor plan.

Of course, Max was playing the younger version of Damon Barrington, when he had first started making a name for himself on the racing scene.

Grant couldn't help but smile at the image of a young Tessa running through the house, which had been handed down to Damon from his own father. Even as a child, Tessa probably had had the whole family on a tight schedule, from lunch breaks to riding times.

"Grant."

Turning toward the wide side hallway, Grant smiled as he moved through the open foyer to greet Damon. The tall, thin man with silver hair had a presence about him that demanded attention and respect. Grant was more than happy to devote both, considering this film would take him to the next level of his career plan.

Directing had always been a passion. Grant loved the up

close and personal contact with the actors, loved the level of trust they built with each other.

But now he was ready to take that next step, and coproducing this film would only add another monumental layer onto what he'd already attained.

"I apologize for not being here when you arrived," Damon said, slapping him on the back. "I trust you found Tessa in the stables?"

Bent over, looking sexier than she had a right to.

"I did," Grant confirmed, keeping his carnal thoughts to himself. "I'm meeting her in a bit to go over a few preliminary questions. She has a schedule for me."

Damon's robust laughter filled the foyer. "That girl. If she's not on a horse, she's at her computer with color-coded schedules."

That woman needed to relax, and Grant fantasized about making that happen during his month-long stay here on the estate before his team arrived. Of course, he had to maintain his professional manner because of that clause he was growing to hate more and more.

Stupid "no fraternizing" section. He'd had one slipup a few years ago. Okay, so he and the makeup artist had drunk a bit too much and had made headlines, but that was in the past. Yet he was still paying for his sins.

And he refused to get in deeper than lust. Tessa was sexy as hell, but her world and his did not and could not mesh.

Besides, he wasn't ready to settle down. In the future he wanted to have a family, but right now he didn't have the time. No reason he couldn't get Tessa to relax a little and enjoy herself, however. They would have weeks together, and he didn't intend to spend them looking at his watch and checking some damn spreadsheet to see when he could take a bathroom break.

Flirting while he was here would help him keep his mind off his real issues.

"Apparently my allotted times are in green, but I've yet to see the schedule."

Damon sighed, raked a hand over his face. "She is her mother's daughter. My late wife had labels on everything, each day scheduled to the minute. Used to drive me insane."

"I'm hoping when Lily arrives for the filming, the two of you can talk," Grant said, referring to the A-list actress playing the role of Rose Barrington in the early years. "She's been studying your wife's biography and looking at the pictures you supplied, but I know it will help to have a firsthand account from you."

"I look forward to speaking with her." Damon beamed. "I still can't believe a movie is being made of my career and life."

"You're a remarkable man, Damon, and you can't deny you have an incredible dynasty here. Not only did you win the Triple Crown, you now have a famous daughter who is a jockey and another daughter who is a trainer. Everything in one perfect family. Some may say you're the luckiest man in the industry."

"Luck has nothing to do with it," Damon corrected with a slight grin. "Life is all skill and patience. Remember that and nothing can stop you."

Grant had a feeling there was so much more to this man than racing and owning a prestigious horse farm. While those elements were key, Grant got a true sense of family loyalty here. Besides the countless framed pictures hanging along the walls in each room, celebrating various family milestones, Grant had seen the pride in Damon's eyes when discussing his girls, and that same pride and protection in Tessa's eyes when she talked of her father.

Being part of this film thrilled Grant more than he'd originally thought. Family meant everything to him…which was why he could never face his sister again after ruining her life.

Shaking off the haunting memory, Grant focused on the film. When Anthony Price and Bronson Dane had first approached him, he couldn't say yes fast enough. The big break he'd been working for, fighting for, was finally here, and he wouldn't let anything stand in his way…even a beautiful, sexy jockey. She might be totally opposed to this film, but she really had no say over the matter.

Of course, she could make these next several weeks difficult, but he'd find a way to crack her outer shell. She might be immune to his charm, but she was attracted. He'd seen the way her eyes widened, the pulse at the base of her throat sped up, and more than once he'd seen her gaze dip to his lips.

Yeah, she was cracking already.

"Listen, I've got to head out and meet a man I'm thinking of hiring on as a groom. But I shouldn't be gone too long." Damon checked his phone, then slid it back into his pocket. "Please, make this your home. Look anywhere you like, and Tessa can show you around the grounds. I assume you got your stuff into the guesthouse?"

"I did," Grant replied. "I appreciate the use of it. Though I'd be perfectly content in a hotel until the on-site trailers arrive."

Damon waved a hand. "Nonsense. We have two extra guesthouses, other than the one my oldest daughter, Cassie, and her baby live in. They're a bit on the small side, but they're better than any hotel or trailer."

On that Grant would agree.

"I'll be back later if you need me, but I imagine Tessa will have everything under control."

Laughing, he nodded. "I have no doubt."

When the elderly man walked out the front door, Grant continued his stroll around the house. He'd been through it before, but now he was looking at even finer things and really thinking of each scene, each facet of Damon's life.

Several scenes would be shot at various horse parks before and during the races, but he would mainly stay here, directing the shots from the estate. Bronson and Anthony would be more on location, traveling with their wives and kids.

Bronson Dane and Anthony Price were half brothers and a force to be reckoned with in the film industry. And Grant was beyond thrilled they'd asked him to coproduce this movie about the Barrington dynasty.

Glancing at his watch, he noted he had about five minutes until his scheduled time, so he headed out the front door and toward the stables. Wouldn't want to be late and have to be rescheduled to—gasp—the yellow slot.

Grant smiled as he walked across the lawn, calculating all the ways he could throw off Ms. Spreadsheet. How could he not want to have a little fun with this? People who were that uptight missed out on all the joy in life.

He totally understood the need to be serious, when the time called for such actions, but wasn't life supposed to be fun and enjoyable? A spreadsheet for daily life? Who actually lived that way?

Tessa stepped from a stall just as he came to the entrance. Sliding her hands into the pockets of her very slim, hip-hugging, mouthwatering riding pants, she headed toward him.

"Punctual," she said, closing the gap between them. "I think we'll get along just fine."

Grant allowed his eyes to roam over her face. A fine mist of sweat covered her flushed skin, and damp tendrils of hair clung to her forehead where her riding helmet had rested.

"Why don't we go inside, get some water and talk?" he suggested.

Tessa crossed her arms over her chest and offered a smile that flashed a dimple just to the right of her full lips. "City boy can't handle the heat?"

He laughed. "Actually, I thought you may need a break."

"I don't take breaks," she told him, tilting her chin in defiance. "And a little heat never bothers me."

Unable to stop himself, he stepped forward and slid a stray lock of hair behind her ear, letting his hand linger a bit at the side of her face. Tessa's swift intake of breath pleased him. He had a feeling nothing much set her off her game.

"Good to know you can handle activities that work up a sweat," he murmured, mentally cursing himself for crossing into carnal-thought territory. Thoughts led to actions, and he didn't have the time or the authority for such shenanigans.

Tessa reached up, put her hand in his and smiled. "You're going to have to do better than that, Slick. Clever innuendos won't work on me."

Grant couldn't help but grin. "Oh, I'm just getting warmed up, Country. Throwing you off your guard is my main goal here."

Keeping her eyes on his, Tessa tilted her head. "I thought producing and directing this movie was your main goal."

He leaned in, close enough to smell her musky scent, feel her warm breath on his face. "I'm an expert at multitasking."

She patted his cheek as if he were a little kid, and laughed. "It's good to have goals, Slick. Now, what do you say about grabbing some lunch? Your two-hour time slot just narrowed down to an hour and fifty minutes."

She sauntered around him, while Grant stood there looking like a complete moron as he watched the sexy sway of her hips in those taut riding pants.

But from the heat he'd seen pass through her eyes, and that frantic pulse at the base of her throat, he knew she wasn't unaffected by him.

This project had just got a whole lot more interesting.

Three

Tessa let herself in the back door of her father's home and nearly wept at the refreshing, cool air that enveloped her.

She'd gotten overheated outside, though her rising body temperature had nothing to do with the unseasonably warm spring day and everything to do with the hotshot city slicker who thought he could get under her skin. And if she didn't get some distance, he just might.

A whole month? She'd spent only a few minutes with the potent man and he'd pretty much touched every single female nerve she had. How on earth could she survive a month of Mr. Tall, Dark and Tempting?

The last thing she wanted was to, well…want him. Wasn't he technically the enemy? At least in her world. Sexy, fast with the seductive words and lingering glances…

The thought of this movie, of being thrust into the media, made her stomach churn. And there was no way she could be blindsided by another charmer, who was probably used to women trailing after him, hoping for a sliver of his affection.

She dealt with enough media, being a female jockey and Damon Barrington's daughter to boot. But a movie was a whole new level of limelight she really didn't want to enter into.

And she'd had enough types like her smarmy ex to last several lifetimes.

As Tessa grabbed a bottle of water from the refrigerator, the door behind her opened and closed. She straightened and turned to see Grant leaning against the counter, arms crossed over his wide chest, his eyes on her. Those eyes visually sampled her, and Tessa refused to enjoy the shudder rippling through her.

"Water?" she asked, holding up the bottle.

"No, thanks. What hours do you put into riding?"

Horse talk. Much safer ground.

Uncapping the bottle, she took a hefty drink. "Waking hours. But right now, I also tend each horse and clean stalls, until Dad hires a new groom. There's always work to be done. I'm at the stables from morning till night. And on the nights I can't sleep, I come over and ride to relax. I've been known to sleep in the barn."

"You live close, then?" he asked.

Tessa nodded. "My property is the next one over, but it's not near as big a spread as this. All of my horses are here."

"Your dad mentioned your sister lives in a guesthouse."

"Cassie and her baby live here." Tessa rested her elbows on the granite island and squeezed her bottle. "She moved back onto the estate when her jerk husband left her, right after Emily was born."

A muscle in Grant's jaw ticked. "Not much of a man, leaving his wife and baby."

Tessa warmed at his matter-of-fact statement. "On that we can agree. And since her ex was the previous groom, we obviously need a new one."

"A female trainer and jockey," Grant murmured. He held her gaze and smiled. "Isn't that very unusual?"

This was a common question from people outside the racing world. "Yes, but we're both good at what we do. There was a time not too long ago when women weren't allowed to be trainers. My dad used to tell stories about how he'd sneak women into the stables early in the mornings, to help train his stock. He swore they were better for a horse's demeanor, because men tend to be harsher, more competitive."

Grant shifted his weight, leaning against the counter as if

processing all she threw at him. "I read that in his bio. That's quite intriguing, actually."

Intriguing? Tessa didn't want him using that word when he was staring at her with such intensity. Did the man ever blink? Or just mesmerize women with that heavy-lidded gaze?

"Cassie is the best trainer I've ever seen," she told him, circling the conversation back to the reason for this little meeting.

"She's older than you, right?" Grant asked.

"By three years."

"She never had the itch to become a jockey?"

Tessa nearly laughed. Cassie was so gentle, so nurturing. She was much better left in the stables, where she could tend to the horses...many of which needed her gentle touch.

"No. She's more a behind-the-scenes type." Tessa took another drink of her water before replacing the cap. "My dad taught us every aspect of the racing industry. I was practically raised in a saddle. Cassie is more delicate. She's perfect as a trainer. Me, on the other hand, I love the fast-paced adrenaline rush of the race."

Grant smirked as he moved closer, stopping and resting his elbow on the counter beside her. "I wouldn't think such a perfectionist, and someone who holds on to their control the way you do, would be such a fanatic about adrenaline rushes."

Tessa turned her head, cursing herself when those dark eyes shot a shiver of arousal through her. "I have several layers, Slick. Don't try to uncover too many at once."

A corner of his mouth lifted, and she found herself staring at his dark stubble. How would that feel beneath her hand... her lips? Why was she letting him get to her? There were so many things she needed to focus on right now, and the feel of a man's facial hair was nowhere on her list. Yet her skin still tingled, and she couldn't help but wonder what would happen if she actually touched that dark stubble.

"I'd like to uncover as many layers as possible," he murmured.

How did this man come onto the scene, literally hours ago, and already have such power over her heart rate?

"You sound hesitant," she told him, holding his stare, refusing to be intimidated. "Not that I'm complaining."

Grant laughed. "There's a small annoyance in my contract."

Tessa stood straighter, bothered that even with him leaning on the counter, she was shorter than him. Being petite was an advantage and requirement for a jockey, but right now she wished for a few more inches.

"Something in your contract?" she asked with a grin. "And what does it say? No flirting or charming while filming?"

"More like no seducing while filming," he corrected, a hint of amusement lacing his voice.

Tessa swallowed hard. She was quickly drowning in deep waters. "Seducing? Is that what you are trying to do?"

His eyes dropped to her mouth, then moved back up to meet her gaze. "Oh, if I was seducing you, you'd know. Flirting is harmless, isn't it?"

Was it? She wasn't so sure anything about Grant Carter was harmless. Not his dark eyes, not his naughty grin and certainly not his smooth words, which washed over her, through her, like a breeze on a warm summer day.

In no time he had sent shivers down her spine, made her smile, attempted a rescue and had her questioning why she was hanging on to her virginity. None of that had happened with the last guy she'd dated and considered marrying.

The timing couldn't be worse. Between the film and the upcoming races, she just didn't have time to wonder why Fate had decided to dangle this all too alluring man in front of her.

And why she had to be so attracted to someone with the exact qualities of the jerk she'd just dumped a few months ago? Had she not learned her lesson when he'd tried to exploit her and when that failed, he'd tried to ruin her career, just so she'd be forced to marry him and move to some overpopulated, confining city? Had he honestly thought she'd hand over money for him to get his newfound business off the ground?

If he had truly loved her, respected her career, she would've gladly supported him in any way. But he'd laid down ultimatums, and in the end Tessa had pointed him back to that city he loved so much.

She thanked God every day that she hadn't tumbled into bed with him. She'd assumed they were getting married, and she'd wanted to make their honeymoon special.

Thankfully, she'd made a promise to her mother to wait for real love and marriage.

"Do we need to add that to the spreadsheet?" he asked.

She shook off thoughts of her ex and met Grant's hard stare. "What's that?"

That wicked grin of his widened, deepening his dimples. "Flirting. Is that something you need to figure in, or should I add that into my two-hour time slot? I am a master at multitasking, you know."

"So you've mentioned before."

"I think I'll keep my two hours to work, and throw in a little flirting when you least expect it."

Had the heat kicked on in here? Tessa resisted the urge to undo a button on her shirt for some extra air. She also refused to rub her damp palms along her pants. She would not give Grant the satisfaction of knowing he was getting to her.

"So I need to be ready for you at any time?" she asked, forcing her eyes to remain locked on his.

"Ready? You could never be ready, Country."

She studied his tanned face, his chocolate eyes beneath thick brows. "Why is it I have a feeling you have a problem with controlling your hormones?"

"Oh, I can control them," he assured her. "Because if I couldn't, I would've already kissed you."

That simple declaration weakened her knees. She leaned back against the counter and took a deep breath. If she couldn't avoid the roller coaster of emotions, she may as well enjoy the ride.

"Then it's a good thing you have control, because kissing me would be a mistake."

Yeah, that was a gauntlet she knew he'd pick up. Why was she flirting, purposely provoking him? She did not have time for this. Beyond that, she didn't like him—or didn't want to like him—and she sure as hell didn't like this whole movie idea. But there was nothing she could do about it at this point.

Damn, she was attracted, and she hated every blasted nerve that sizzled for him.

"That so?" Holding that mesmerizing smile, he inched closer and whispered, "And why would kissing be a mistake?"

"For one thing, I'm not comfortable with this movie."

His lips turned up slightly. "Anything else?"

"I don't have time. In case you're unaware of how the season works, I'm gearing up for the first of many races, which I hope will lead me down the path to the coveted Triple Crown."

"I don't think a kiss would throw off your rigorous routine." He laughed, still continuing to invade her personal space. "And I'm more than aware of how the season works. I did thorough research for this film."

"You don't seem like the type of guy who would do thorough research on anything," she retorted. "You seem too laid-back."

In a flash, his hands came up, framed her face, and he had her all but bent over onto the island. The hard planes of his body molded against hers. Sweat trickled between her shoulder blades as she waited to see what he would do. And that wait only made her more aware of just how sexy, how powerful this man was. Her breath caught in her throat as his face hovered mere inches from hers.

"Baby, I'm thorough…with everything."

His mouth slid over hers, and Tessa was glad she was wedged between his hard body and the counter, or she would've withered to the floor. The full-on attack sent shivers through her entire being, affecting areas never touched.

And there it was. That click. A click of something so perfect sliding into place, but Tessa couldn't focus on it because Grant was consuming every bit of her thoughts, her body, with one single kiss.

He coaxed her lips apart with his tongue, leaving her no choice but to accept him. How could a kiss be felt in your entire body? Such a simple act sent tremors racing one after the other through her.

A slight groan escaped her as Tessa gripped his thick biceps.

Before she could revel in the sensations sweeping through her overheated body, Grant lifted his head, met her gaze and smiled.

"Sorry. Guess I can't control my hormones."

"What about that clause?" she asked, cursing her breathless tone.

That sultry grin spread across his face. "I didn't come close to violating the clause."

Grant walked out the back door, and it took Tessa a moment to realize that she still had over an hour left in the time she'd allotted for him. And she hadn't given him his copy of the spreadsheet.

With a sigh, she sank onto the nearest bar stool and came to a conclusion. Grant Carter had caught her off guard, and he'd been right. She would never be ready for him.

Four

Grant glanced at the spreadsheet on the kitchen counter in the guest cottage he was staying in. Although "cottage" was a loose term for the two thousand square foot home, complete with patio overlooking the stables and a massive walk-in shower in the master suite.

As he raked his eyes over the colorful paper, he took another sip of the strong coffee he'd just made. Little Miss Country Organizer would be pissed. He was already five minutes late…which may or may not have been on purpose.

Of course, she'd given him the spreadsheet a day late, so it wasn't as if she had a leg to stand on in her defense.

Yesterday, after he'd lost control and kissed her, he'd walked around on his own, and by the time he returned to his guest cottage, she'd taped the schedule to the front door.

But in defense of his tardiness today, he'd had an early-morning call from Bronson Dane regarding a hiccup in the crew's plans for arrival, and he'd had to deal with that. Grant took another sip of the coffee and placed the half-full cup back on the counter. No time to finish it, and he had a feeling Tessa wouldn't care about his excuse for being late.

Why did he feel as if he was heading to the principal's office? She was a grown woman, she had no control over him and he wasn't going to get suspended. So why get all wrapped up in the details of a color-coded piece of paper?

Grabbing the house key and shoving it into his jean's pocket, Grant headed out the door and made his way toward the massive two-story stables. The stone building, with its dark wood trim and weathered wooden doors, would make an impressive backdrop for many scenes. It suggested power and wealth, much like the great Barrington patriarch himself.

When Grant stepped over the threshold, he saw Tessa heading toward the opening of the stables atop a Thoroughbred. Without a word, he stood still and admired the scene, both as a producer and as a man.

She had her dark red hair pulled in that low ponytail again. The crimson strands slid back and forth as her body shifted in the saddle. Her simple white shirt was tucked into jeans that looked perfectly worn in all the right spots. Grant's palms literally ached to feel those slim hips beneath them. For someone so petite and delicate looking, she had curves that would make any man drop to his knees and beg for anything and everything she was willing to give.

"Are you just going to stand there or are you coming in?" she asked without turning around.

He couldn't help but smile. "I'm actually observing right now."

Throwing a glance over her shoulder, Tessa quirked a brow. "Observing the barn structure or my rear end?"

Unable to stop himself, Grant laughed. "I was taking in all the structures."

"Are you going to make an excuse as to why you're late?"

Grant shrugged as he moved along the side of the aisle and closed the gap between them. "Do you care about an excuse?"

"No."

"Then I won't offer one."

"Perfect." Taking the lead line, she moved the Thoroughbred toward the open door to the riding ring. "I assumed you weren't coming, and I was going to take Romeo out for a run. But if you want to talk, I'll put him up."

Grant didn't want to talk, didn't want to ask questions. He found himself wanting to watch her work, watch how she moved so gracefully and efficiently. The woman had a rare talent, and she was so damn beautiful. Stunning women were everywhere in L.A., but the majority in the circles he ran in were surgically enhanced. None had that porcelain skin, deep blue eyes, a cute little dimple and dark red hair. None of them wore cowboy boots with body-hugging jeans and Western shirts. And none challenged him the way Tessa did.

For once in his life, he was the pursuer.

"I'm ready to work if you are," he told her.

She turned the beautiful horse around, dismounted and led him back to his stall.

After her saddle was back on the wall, she took a brush and started grooming the animal in large, circular strokes. "Romeo is going to learn to race. His father was a winner, and I can't wait to see him fly."

There was love in her tone, Grant noted. "How long will he train before he can race?"

"Cassie'll have him ready to go next year. He's not quite there yet."

With ease and care, she moved around to the other side and repeated her motions. Her delicate hands were so gentle, and if he'd stop fantasizing about those hands on him, Grant might actually concentrate on the fact he was here to do a job.

The world of racing and horses was certainly glamorous to some, but not to him. Nothing about this sport appealed to him...except the sexy jockey in front of him.

If he didn't start compartmentalizing soon, Tessa would suck him under, and he honestly didn't think he was strong enough to climb back out.

"Do you have a favorite track?" he asked.

Her eyes met his over the back of the horse. With a wide grin she replied, "Yeah, the one where I win."

Grant stepped closer, but still remained outside the stall. "How old were you when you started racing?"

"Officially? Eighteen. But I've lived and breathed horses my entire life." With precise motions she swept the brush over the horse's side and toward its flank. "I didn't play sports, didn't even go to my prom. I much preferred to spend my time right here."

Hooking his thumbs through his belt loops, Grant shifted his stance. "I imagine there's not a place on this farm you haven't ridden."

"You'd be right. If I'm not training, I'm riding for fun."

Grant smiled. "Care to show me around?"

"I'd love to, but since you were late, your time is less now, so we won't be able to go over as much of the estate."

"When I got here you weren't ready, either."

"Because I thought you were a no-show."

He stepped even closer, still watching her over the side of the horse. "Not all of us can live by a schedule."

Tessa stared for a moment, then turned and put the brush away. Grant had a feeling he wasn't scoring any points with her, but it was fun to get under her skin, and especially fun when she had no comeback.

"Follow me," she told him as she stepped from the stall and headed toward the front of the stable.

Grant turned and gladly followed those swaying hips. "Which horses are we taking out?" he asked, dreading her response, but refusing to succumb to fear and let his vulnerabilities show.

"No horses," she called over her shoulder.

Grant released a deep breath. He couldn't let the fear cripple him, but he was relieved they were leaving the horses in the barn. He followed her into another large, two-story barn on the property and smiled.

"A four-wheeler?" he asked.

"Stick with me, Slick. I'll show you all the cool country toys."

Oh, the possibilities of comebacks with that statement. But Grant knew it was probably best to keep his mouth shut.

Tessa threw her leg around the seat and straddled the device, then sent him a saucy look. Damn woman. She was teasing him on purpose, and he was a sucker, falling for her antics.

Maybe separate horses would've been safer.

"You don't have a problem with me driving, do you?" she asked with a grin.

Mercy. With her legs stretched wide over the seat, her body leaning forward to grip the handles, Grant knew he needed to take control, and fast, before this vixen completely made a fool out of him. She was mocking him, taking his attraction and blatantly throwing it back in his face.

And he deserved it. But two could play at this game.

Grant slid on behind her, making sure to tuck in real tight from torso to hips, gripping her thighs with his own. His hands slid around her tiny waist and his mouth came in close to her ear. "I don't mind this one bit," he whispered, pleased when she trembled.

Tessa turned her head slightly, enough to meet his gaze, her lips nearly brushing his. "Don't make this weird, Slick."

Grant flattened his palms on her taut stomach. "*Weird* was not the word I was thinking."

She fired up the four-wheeler, turned her attention toward the opening of the barn and took off. Grant literally had to hold on to her because the force with which she exited nearly threw him off the back…which was probably what she wanted.

Oh, this little excursion was going to be fun.

Did he have to hold on so damn tight? He was practically wrapped around her, and instead of feeling trapped or confined, Tessa felt…aroused and anxious.

This man kept her on her toes, and she never knew what he'd say or do next. But she did know one thing: she refused to fall for charms or let her hormones control her. After all, what did her hormones know? She'd never fully used them before.

Another city boy who exuded power and intensity would not deter her from what mattered most—winning the upcoming races and making sure Slick didn't get any ideas about exploiting her family or spreading rumors. Nothing else mattered.

And she had to keep telling herself that, considering the way his hard chest pressed against her back, those strong thighs fit perfectly down the length of hers, and his size made her feel so delicate and protected. She didn't want to feel any of those things. Tessa was quite happy with the way life was right now, before Grant had stepped into her stable with those heavy-lidded eyes and that day-old stubble that she knew would tickle her palm.

As she headed out beyond the buildings and guesthouses, she frowned at her sister's cottage and the empty parking space in front. Cassie had texted earlier to say Emily was running a fever and she was running her to the urgent care facility. Hopefully, it was nothing serious.

Cassie had a full plate, being the trainer for Stony Ridge and now a single mother. All the more reason they needed to hire a new groom. The timing couldn't be worse for being one man short. They'd tried a replacement after Cassie's ex left, but that groom had ended up moving out of state, so here they were, waiting on their dad to find another.

Tessa sped up, moving down the edge of the property line toward the most beautiful place on the estate. She knew Grant would love it, and she had no doubt at least one part of the film would be shot at this location. So many memories were held here, and she figured he'd want to know the special history of her parents.

Even though her mom had been gone for a while, Tessa felt every day the indescribable void she'd left. There was always an ache, an emptiness in her chest that had settled deep when Rose had passed. Nothing and no one could ever fill that gaping hole.

She and her mother had shared so much. Rose had always stressed the importance of not giving away love or your body to just anyone. Both were too precious to throw around.

Tessa had always promised her mom she'd wait for the right man. He just hadn't come along yet.

She highly doubted the man molded to her back was "the

one," but he certainly was more tempting than any other guy she'd ever encountered.

Tessa cruised over the rise and came to a stop so Grant could take in the view.

"Oh…that's…wow. Tessa, that's beautiful."

Up ahead lay a valley with a large pond surrounded by evergreens. The water always seemed so vibrant and glistening. A part of her was thrilled that his reaction was all she'd hoped.

"I always ride out here to relax," she told him. "It's so peaceful."

Turning slightly to see his face, she watched as his eyes roamed over the land, as if he'd never seen a more beautiful sight. She wanted to study him, memorize everything about him, but what would be the point? He wasn't staying, and even if he were, she didn't have time for a relationship, didn't want a relationship and certainly didn't intend to start one.

They'd technically just met, so all either of them was feeling was pure lust. Lust would get her nowhere but on a road to heartache. She was totally out of her element here.

Added to that, she highly doubted she was Grant's type. He probably wasn't too keen on virgins. Kissing was her limit until she found someone she truly felt a deep connection with, and if Grant ever knew that… Well, he would never know that, because this whole train of thought was coming to a crashing halt.

Seriously, this whole string of ideas only led down a path to a dead end.

"Want me to take you down there?" she offered.

"Please."

She revved up the four-wheeler and took off down the slight slope toward the pond. Once at the water's edge, they couldn't be seen from the main house in the distance.

Grant slid off the seat first and offered a hand to help her. As much as she wanted to bat it away, she accepted it. Hey, if a sexy man was going to play gentleman, she was going to take full advantage of the situation.

He dropped her hand once she was on her feet, and Tessa smiled as his eyes roamed over the wide pond.

"My father used to bring my mother out here for picnics," she related. "I remember her telling me and Cassie about them."

Tessa glanced toward the water and sighed. "I never got tired of hearing about their romance. I think it's important for children to see their parents in love, to know what they should look forward to, and not settle for anything less."

Grant turned his attention to Tessa. The ends of her ponytail danced in the breeze, her eyes were focused off in the distance and her arms were crossed over her chest. He knew she was trying to visualize the moment her mother had told her about, knew Tessa was more than likely a romantic at heart.

"And is that why you're single?" he asked. "You're not going to settle?"

Glancing over to him, Tessa quirked a brow. "No, I'm not. I shouldn't have to. I'm not looking to marry right now, anyway. I'm a little busy. What about you, Slick?"

Grant laughed. "I'd love to settle down. My parents aren't much different from yours. And I agree it's important for parents to show their love. I plan on having kids and I want them to see how much I love their mother."

Tessa's eyes widened, her mouth dropped.

"What?" he asked, stepping closer so that he could see the navy specks in her eyes. "Didn't expect me to have goals in the marriage department?"

"Actually, no, I didn't." She stared at him for another moment before turning back to look at the lake. "I ride Oliver when I need to get away. I get on him and he just automatically comes down here. Recently..."

She shook her head, and Grant waited for her to continue, but she didn't. He didn't like the sadness that slid over her face as she gazed at the water.

"The racing getting stressful?"

"No more than usual. But it's something I love, so the stress is mostly self-induced."

Tessa eased down onto the ground, pulled her knees up and wrapped her arms around them. "Go ahead and have a seat, Slick. Unless you're afraid you'll get a grass stain on your new designer jeans."

He didn't tell her his jeans weren't designer or new, but he did plop right down next to her, a little closer than she was probably comfortable with. But she was trying to get under his skin, so he damn well would get beneath hers.

A smile spread across her face. "Spend much time in the country?" she asked.

He'd grown up in a modest home surrounded by fields and wildflowers in the heart of Kentucky, but she didn't need to know that. She already had an opinion of him, and he'd break it down by his actions, not his words.

"Enough," Grant told her. "Much more peaceful than the city. But there's a reason for both, and some people just aren't cut out for the other."

"What about you?" she asked. "You're all city boy. Are you going to be able to handle the next few weeks here with me?"

Unable to resist her jab, Grant reached up, slid a stray strand of her hair behind her ear and allowed his hand to gently roam back down her cheek in a featherlight touch. She trembled beneath his fingertips.

"I think I can handle it," he whispered, purposely staring at her mouth, waiting for that dimple to make another appearance.

Her eyes widened before she turned back to the pond. She might be all tough exterior, but Grant had a feeling the lovely, intriguing Tessa Barrington had layers upon layers to her complexity. He wanted to peel each one away and find what she truly had hidden inside.

"Do you have other special areas on the property?" he asked, circling back to the fact he was indeed here to do a job, and not to seduce.

"All of the estate is beautiful," she told him. "There's a wooded spot on the edge of the property that has this old cabin. It was the first home on this land, built long before my dad lived here. He never tore it down, and Cassie and I used to play there when we were kids. It's also where my dad proposed to my mom."

"Show it to me."

Grant hopped to his feet and extended his hand to help Tessa up. She resisted for all of a second before slipping her delicate hand into his. Before she could fully catch her balance, Grant tugged her against his chest, causing her to land right where he wanted her.

What the hell was he doing? He knew better than to play games like this, but damned if his hormones weren't trying to take over. That whole chat he'd had with himself about compartmentalizing had gone straight to hell.

But each time he was with Tessa something came over him, something he couldn't explain, and he was drowning in confusion and…her.

Tessa's breath caught, and those bright blue eyes held his. With her body molded against his, Grant had no clue what to do now. Well, he knew, but he was supposed to be a professional and not get tangled up in this world on a personal level. Mentally and emotionally, he couldn't afford to.

Besides, the last thing he needed was to get kicked off the set before filming even started.

Yet, as usual, lust controlled his actions.

"What about you, Tessa?" he asked, eyeing her lips. "Are you all country girl or could you handle the big city?"

Something cold flashed through her eyes before she pulled away and glanced at her watch. "You only have twenty minutes left, Slick. Better go see that cabin."

Whatever trigger he'd just hit on, Grant had a feeling he would annoy her even more before he figured out what he'd said that upset her. Because he knew their body contact hadn't gotten her so angry. No, he'd seen desire in her eyes, maybe even confusion—a glimpse of an internal battle, but not anger.

He followed her back to the four-wheeler and climbed on behind her. This time Grant held on to the back rack instead of Tessa. He was treading on thin ice as it was.

Five

She rode effortlessly, with captivating beauty. The way her body controlled the stallion, the strength she possessed, the determination on her flushed face... Grant could watch Tessa Barrington for hours, and was well on his way to doing just that.

Tessa turned the corner and headed toward him. With all the laps she'd made, there was no way she could've missed him standing here. They'd already spent the past two days together, and he had no time scheduled with her today. But that didn't stop him from wanting to see her, to learn more. And this sexual pull was dragging him into this damn world he'd worked so hard to put behind him.

"She's amazing, isn't she?"

Grant turned at the sound of a voice and found himself looking into another set of bright blue eyes. "Yes, she is. You must be Cassie." He glanced to the baby asleep on her shoulder. "And who is this?"

Cassie's smile widened. "This is Emily."

Grant took in the pale blond curls peeking beneath a bright green hat, and wondered if the little girl had those Barrington blue eyes.

"How old is she?"

"Just turned one last month."

Cassie turned to watch Tessa round another curve, and Grant studied the woman's profile. She was beautiful just like her sister, with her blue eyes and bright red hair. But there was something more fragile, almost sad about Cassie. He'd learned enough about this family to know Cassie's ex used to work in the stables but had left shortly after the baby was born. Anger bubbled within Grant at the thought of a deadbeat dad ignoring his kid.

But as he watched her, Grant realized there was another layer of emotions in Cassie's eyes as she focused on her sister. Concern.

"You worry about her," he said, not bothering to ask.

"I do." Cassie shifted the sleeping toddler to her other shoulder. "She pushes too hard at times. Strange coming from me, since I'm her trainer. We already practiced today, but she and Don Pedro are made for each other. They're happiest in the ring. Of course, that passion is what makes winners, but her biggest competitor is herself."

Grant could see that. In the few days he'd been here he'd seen Tessa out of the stables only during their "allotted" times.

"Does she do anything for fun?" he asked.

"You're looking at it. She lives for this."

On one hand Grant admired Tessa's drive and determination. He had more drive for career than anything himself. But on the other hand he found it sad that this was her whole life.

And from a purely personal level, the thought of her spending more time on her horse than off flat out terrified him.

Her career stirred up so many haunting emotions. Not that they weren't always there, but having the lifestyle thrust in his face all day only made the memories that much more hellish.

Yet the attraction was something he hadn't planned on... and couldn't ignore.

"She doesn't date?" he found himself asking before he could keep his mouth shut.

Cassie spared him a glance. "She just got out of a relationship, which is another reason she's pushing herself even more."

Bad breakup? While Cassie didn't say it, the message was implied. And there was a story there. Grant never turned away an intriguing story....

"So when will the rest of your crew arrive?" Cassie asked.

"A few weeks." He caught her smile and laughed. "You seem excited about this."

She shrugged her free shoulder. "What's not to be excited about? My father is an amazing man, a prestigious horse owner and winner. A movie about his life will be awesome."

"You forget you and Tessa are a huge part of his success, and in continuing the Barrington tradition." Grant glanced at the track as Tessa came flying by again. "I don't think your sister feels the same."

Cassie nodded. "Tessa and I don't always agree on things. Besides, she has her reasons for not being so thrilled about this film."

"And you aren't going to share those reasons, are you?"

Cassie laughed. "Nope."

Emily started to stir on her shoulder, and Cassie patted her back. "I better head back inside and get dinner started. It was nice to officially meet you, Grant."

"I'm sure you'll be seeing more of me."

She walked away, and Grant turned back to watch Tessa, but she was out of sight. He took his boot down from the rung of the fence and headed into the stable.

He found her in the last stall, pulling the saddle off Don Pedro's back and hanging it up. At some point he'd quiz her on the reason behind the horse's name, though he had a pretty good idea.

He knew enough Shakespeare to know Don Pedro was a prince in *Much Ado About Nothing,* and her recreational stallion's name, Oliver, stemmed from the villain, who later repented, in *As You Like It.*

Apparently Miss Barrington had a romantic streak. So why was she fighting this obvious attraction?

Straw shuffled beneath his boots as he made his way closer. Oliver shifted in his stall and Grant froze for a half second before he forced himself to keep walking.

He would not revisit that time in his life. Fear was only a state of mind, and he'd be damned if he'd let it overtake him.

"I just met your sister," he said as he moved in closer.

Tessa didn't stop her duties, didn't even spare him a glance as she picked up a brush and started her routine circular brushing.

"Emily is adorable, but she slept through our meeting." Grant tucked his hands into his pockets. "Cassie seems pretty excited about the film."

Maybe that comment warranted a grunt, but he wasn't sure the noise was directed at him or the fact that Tessa was reaching up to brush the horse's back.

"It's a beautiful day—"

"What are you doing here?" she asked, tossing the brush into the tack box with so much effort it bounced right back out.

Grant paused. "Working."

"No, here in the stable. Right now. What do you want?"

Her eyes were practically shooting daggers. Okay, something had pissed her off and he had a sinking feeling that "something" was him. How did women get so fired up, when a man was still left clueless?

"I was watching you train," he told her honestly. "I'm just amazed at your talent."

Tessa moved around Don Pedro, coming to stand in front of Grant. Propping her hands on her hips pulled her shirt tighter across her chest, and he had to really concentrate to keep his eyes level with hers and not on those tiny strained buttons.

"Don't you have a film to be working on instead of ogling my sister?"

For a second he was shocked, then shock quickly turned to a warmth spreading through his body. She was jealous. Best not to laugh or even crack a smile. But damn, he liked knowing he'd sparked some emotion from her other than disdain for his occupation.

He could have fun with this morsel of information, but he was never one to play games...especially with women. He may have dated his fair share of ladies over the years, but they always knew where he stood with their relationship. Besides, he was ready to start settling down, making a home and a family, after this film wrapped up.

For now, he wanted to get to know Tessa on a personal, intimate level, away from her racing lifestyle. He had interest in the woman, not the career.

"Actually, I was watching you *and* working." He crossed his arms and met her icy stare. "We'll be shooting here, and I was watching as the sun moved in the sky, to see where it is at certain times and how the shadows fall across the track. Your sister came up to me to introduce herself, since we hadn't been formally introduced yet."

A bit of heat left Tessa's expression, but Grant couldn't resist. He stepped closer and bent down until her eyes widened and her warm breath feathered across his face.

"And if you're not interested in me, Country, then it wouldn't matter if I was flirting with your sister or not, now would it?"

He turned, walked out of the barn and kept going until he was back in his guest cottage. Damn woman could make a man forget everything but the thought of kissing her senseless and finding a better use for that smart mouth.

Since she was raised a well-mannered lady, for the most part, Tessa found herself standing outside Grant's cottage. The sun had long since set, and she'd been in the stable, talking to herself and trying to find a way out of groveling and apologizing.

There was no way out.

After a gentle tap of her knuckles on the mission-style door, Tessa stepped back and waited. If he didn't hear her knock, she'd leave. At least she could say she'd tried.

A large part of her hoped he didn't hear.

But a second later the door was flung open and Grant stood there, wearing only a towel, chest hair and water droplets.

"Tessa." He hooked an arm on the half door, causing his muscles to flex and her mouth to go desert dry. "What are you doing here?"

"I...I came to apologize." She tried to focus on his face, but dear mercy, all those bare muscles were distracting her. "Um...for earlier."

Grant smiled and opened the door wider. "Come on in."

"Are you going to put clothes on?"

Laughing, he stepped back to let her pass. "You want me to?"

She came face-to-face with him and nodded. "I think it's best."

He closed the door behind her and went toward one of the two bedrooms. Tessa hadn't been in this cottage forever, but it had the same layout as her sister's. Open floor plan, with the kitchen and living area in front. Grant had thrown a shirt over the back of the sofa, running shoes sat by the door and the smell of a fresh, masculine shower permeated the air.

Between that clean scent and those muscles he'd had on display, Tessa was having a hard time remembering the reason for her visit.

Grant strolled back into the room, wearing knit shorts and pulling a T-shirt over his head. "Care for a drink?"

"No, thanks." She twisted her hands and remained in the doorway, because if she moved any farther into his temporary home, she feared she'd want to move further into the world she'd sworn off. "I just wanted to apologize for being rude earlier."

"Rude? I didn't think you were rude." He leaned a hip on the edge of the sofa and crossed his arms over his broad chest. "You were honest. I'm flattered that you were jealous."

Flattered? He might as well pat her on the head like a good little girl and send her off to play with her toys.

"I wasn't jealous." She would go to hell for lying. "I'm just protective of Cassie, and I know your type."

The corners of his mouth threatened to curve into a smile.

If he was mocking her she'd beat him with her whip. No, wait...he'd probably enjoy an aggressive woman.

He'd been so playful when they'd first met, so quick with his wit and his smiles. Her instant attraction had worried her, but now her feelings for him were growing.

Which begged the question, what did Grant like in a woman?

"What is my type, Country?"

"You think your city charm will win you any lady you want," she told him. "Cassie has her hands full. I realize she was introducing herself, but I just didn't want you getting any ideas."

He straightened, then slowly crossed the room until he stood directly in front of her. "Oh, I have ideas. None of them involve Cassie, though."

Tessa tried to ignore the shiver of excitement that crept over her...tried and failed. She didn't want to find him appealing, didn't want to spend any more time with him than necessary. She didn't trust him. He oozed charm, and in her experience, that led to lying and deceit.

Backing up, hoping to make an escape, she reached blindly for the handle on the door. But as she retreated, Grant stepped forward. His fresh-from-the-shower aroma enveloped her, and his damp hair, hanging in a tousled mess over his forehead, practically begged for her to run her fingers through it.

"You could've apologized when you saw me tomorrow," he murmured as he came within an inch of her face. "Why did you need to stop by now?"

Because she was a glutton for punishment. There was no other excuse.

"I wanted to clear the air before I saw you again. I didn't want anything to be uncomfortable."

One hand came up to rest on the door beside her head as a grin spread across his tanned, stubbled face. "I prefer to clear the air, too."

In one swift motion, his head dipped down to hers and his

free hand came up to cup the side of her face. Tessa's back was firmly against the door, and she had nowhere to go…not that she wanted to go anywhere, because Grant's mouth was so gentle, so amazingly perfect. Instead of pushing him away, she kept her arms at her sides and tried to remain in control of her emotions. But she did open her lips at his invitation, She was human and couldn't resist temptation, after all.

Slowly, his tongue danced with hers and chills spread from her head to her toes in a flash. Before she could get too wrapped up in the moment, Grant stepped back. Tessa lifted her eyelids, meeting his dark gaze.

"Since we don't want things to be uncomfortable," he told her, his hand still framing her face, "you should know I plan on doing that again."

Tessa couldn't speak, could barely think. How in the world did she end up with zero control here? She'd just wanted to apologize, and instead she'd gotten the most tender, yet toe-curling kiss of her life, and an amazing view of Grant's bare chest.

"What about—"

"The clause?" he asked, intercepting her thoughts. "Seeing as how you're attracted, too, I don't see why we can't pursue more. Behind closed doors, of course. No one would have to know, Tessa."

"I'm not interested," she told him, lying through her still tingling lips. "Save your attraction for another woman."

Grant dropped his hand. "Then it's my turn to apologize. I assumed by the way you look at me, the way your pulse beats at the base of your neck, the way you catch your breath when I touch you, that you were interested in me, too. And the way you participated in that kiss… But apparently, I was mistaken."

He leaned right next to her ear, so close his lips brushed against her lobe when he whispered, "Or you're lying."

Tessa tugged on the door and moved out of his grasp. "Good night, Grant."

Like the coward she was, she ran away. Nobody made her feel more out of control, more internally restless than this infuriating man.

Surely that didn't mean...

Tessa sighed as she climbed into her Jeep. She had a sinking feeling that Grant Carter was the man her mother had told her about. The man who would come along and make her question how she'd gotten along without him in her life.

The one man she'd been saving herself for.

Six

Tessa slid out of her worn boots and set them beside the back door. Then she hung her heavy cardigan on the peg and moved through her kitchen toward her bedroom. Spring had arrived early, but the nights were still pretty cool, and she wanted to relax in a nice hot bath after her late-night ride. She was a creature of habit, and her raspberry-scented bubble baths were a nightly ritual and the only way she allowed herself to be pampered.

As usual, she hadn't been able to fall asleep. But this time, instead of having horses and racing on her mind, her thoughts had been full of a certain Hollywood producer who had kissed her so gently, yet so thoroughly, she couldn't even remember what kissing another man was like. Not that she'd kissed a slew in her life, but enough to know that Grant Carter knew how to please a woman.

And that was the main thought that had kept her awake. If he could cause so much happiness within her body with just a kiss—and a tender one at that—then what would the man do when he decided to really take charge and not hold back?

Her antique clock in the living room chimed twelve times. Midnight. The same time every night she found herself getting back home from her ride on Oliver. He always stuck his head out of the stall when she returned to the stable late at night. It was almost as if he knew her schedule, knew she'd be back for one last ride to wind down her evening.

Tessa padded into her bedroom, undressing as she went, so

when she made it to the hamper she dumped in all her clothes. When she entered her bathroom, she paused.

Grant Carter was consuming way too much of her time, both in person and in her mind. She plucked the short cotton robe from the back of the bathroom door and went to the old desk in the corner of her bedroom to boot up her laptop.

For a man she'd met just two weeks ago, a man who'd kissed her like no one ever had, she really should learn more about him.

Of course, the internet gave only basics, but that was certainly more information than she had right now. He had a whole file on her life, her sister's and her father's. Grant and his crew knew way more about her childhood and the entire backstory of the Barringtons, so Tessa felt it only fair she level the playing field.

Clicking on a link, she quickly learned that Grant was a twin, but there was no other mention of this sibling.

She glanced at his birth date. A Christmas baby. Tessa's eyes widened as she stared at the screen, inching closer because there was no way she was seeing that number correctly.

He was ten years older than her? As if her virginity, his obvious experience, her country life and his city life weren't enough major blockers between them, he was ten freakin' years older.

With a groan Tessa moved to her bed with the laptop and sagged back against her plush pillows. Grant was out of her league. She could tell by the way he'd kissed her, by how he flirted and his laid-back mannerisms, that he was more experienced with life than she was. But ten years was a hell of a lot of time.

She ventured into the area of pictures. Image after image she clicked through showed a smiling, sometimes heavy-lidded Grant, and in most of the pictures he wasn't alone. Beautiful women were his accessory of choice, apparently. Surprise, surprise.

So, what? Was his kissing her just passing time while he

was here? Did he choose a woman on each set to keep him company? No, he had that clause that prohibited that. But she had a feeling Grant Carter was a rule breaker when it came to getting what he wanted.

Hollywood was a far cry from Dawkins, Virginia, and the fast-paced city life was something she just couldn't—and didn't want to—grasp.

Another man, another city charmer with smooth words, flooded her mind. But he'd had hidden agendas: marrying her for her family name.

The hurt of betrayal still cut deep. Hindsight helped, because she could admit that she'd never loved him…at least not the way she thought she'd love the man she would marry.

Tessa's eyes slid back to the screen, where Grant's dark gaze held hers. Stubble covered his jaw, and she knew from experience how that felt against her palm, her lips.

Now more than ever she was convinced she needed to keep her eye on him. He was a slick one, probably expecting her to turn to putty in his hands. She wouldn't be played, and she wouldn't fall for another man just because of physical attraction. He couldn't be the one for her. Tessa was merely confusing frustration for lust.

She honestly didn't think Grant would do anything underhanded like Aaron had done, but she had to be cautious. No way would she be blindsided again.

But she also had to be honest with herself and admit Grant pulled emotions from her that Aaron hadn't even touched on.

Groaning, she shut off the computer and returned to her spacious adjoining bathroom. Her bubble bath was calling to her. She had to be back in the stables by seven, so didn't have time to waste online…no matter how intriguing the subject.

After several days at the stables, today they were changing up the precious spreadsheet. Grant couldn't wait to spend the majority of the day with Tessa away from Stony Ridge. She was taking him around town to show him various locations, such as the old feed store and the church. Grant was banking on shooting a few scenes in the quaint, historic community.

The script already had several locales specified, but Grant wanted to get a good idea of lighting during different times of day, possible angles, and the atmosphere of each place.

Last night he'd been unable to sleep, so had emailed Bronson and Anthony all the notes he'd taken thus far. The grounds and main house were going to be the primary focus, as well as tracks to showcase the actual racing and practicing.

While drafting his email, he'd seen headlights cut through the darkness. When he'd peered out his window, he'd noted Tessa's Jeep parked next to the stables, and had smiled.

Every part of him had wanted to go to her, had wanted to get her alone in the night. He'd had to conjure up every bit of his strength not to go see her, kiss her and discover just how far they could take this attraction.

But he'd refrained, because he had work to do and only a narrow window of time to get it all done. Besides, he wanted to keep her guessing about his motives, because in all honesty, he had no clue what the hell he was going to do about Tessa. She held too much control over him, and he didn't like it. Never had a woman posed so much of a challenge and appealed to him all at the same time.

There were moments when she seemed so sultry and sassy, and other moments when his words or actions seemed to take her by surprise in almost an innocent way.

Added to that convoluted mess, that damn clause was going to come back and bite him in the butt if he wasn't careful.

Was Tessa Barrington worth all this flirting, seducing and sneaking? Seriously, was he willing to risk this film on a roll in the sack with her?

Hell no. But he hadn't bedded her, and if he did...well, he'd have to make sure no one ever knew.

And bedding her was all he could do. He was already treading a thin line, emotionally, where the beautiful jockey was concerned. Her life revolved around horses, and his...well, it was in the city, far away from the risk of horses and the life he'd once known in a small country house in Kentucky.

Some might say he'd run to one of the biggest cities in America to get away—and they'd be absolutely correct.

Grant left his cottage and made the short walk to the stables. He'd purposely left thirty minutes early to throw Tessa off even more. Damn spreadsheets. He had his lying on the kitchen table, but hadn't looked at it since he got it. He was always allotted the same time bracket each day: two hours after lunch.

Except for today, when his green column was wider and took the slots from nine to three. Six hours, and he was going to make the most of them...both professionally and personally.

Tessa was heading from the stable to her Jeep as Grant neared. Once again she had her hair tied back in that ponytail—he had yet to see it any other way—and she had on a long-sleeved plaid shirt tucked into well-worn jeans and battered knee boots.

She might be prim and proper, but her wardrobe was nothing new. Tessa wasn't a spoiled princess who just looked the part of a jockey. She was all jockey, and her appearance proved it. He'd never seen her fuss with her hair or worry about her appearance. Hell, he'd never seen her with makeup on.

And yet she still stole his breath each time he saw her... which just proved his point of how fine an emotional line he was treading.

"Let's get going, Slick," she said, not missing a step as she got to the Jeep and hopped in.

Grant bit back a smile at her abrupt tone. She was something. Most people, women especially, would be tripping over themselves to please him because of his celebrity status. Yet somehow, with Tessa, he felt as if he had to work to gain approval.

And that was just another layer of her complexity. She couldn't care less about his status, and that suited him just fine. Caused more work to get her attention, but still suited him. At least this way he could keep his feelings separated and not go any deeper beneath Tessa's very arousing surface.

Grant hopped in the passenger's side and barely got his seat belt clicked in place before Tessa was speeding down the driveway.

Her white-knuckle grip on the steering wheel and her clenched jaw were telltale signs she was agitated. And being angry only made her sexier.

"Want to tell me what's wrong?"

She spared him a glance before gripping the wheel even tighter and turning onto the two-lane country road taking them toward town.

"That kiss," she muttered. "It won't happen again."

Um…okay. She'd seemed to be a key player in the exchange the other day, but something had ticked her off, and apparently she'd spent a lot of time thinking about this because she'd worked up a nice case of mad. One step forward, two steps back.

"You didn't enjoy it?" he asked, knowing he was on shaky ground.

"My enjoyment doesn't matter," she countered, eyes focused on the road. "I won't be the one you use to pass the time while you're working here. I'm too busy, and I'm not into flings."

Confused, and working up a good bit of irritation himself, Grant shifted in the seat to look at her fully. "I don't use women to pass the time," he informed her. "I'm attracted to you, and I acted on it. I wasn't in that kiss alone, Tessa."

"You're ten years older than me."

Why did that sound like an accusation?

"And?" he asked.

"I'm…you're…"

She let out an unladylike growl, and Grant again had to bite back a smile. "What does age have to do with attraction, Country?"

"When I started kindergarten you were getting your driver's license!"

This time he did laugh. "I believe we're all grown up now."

"It's just not right. Your life experiences, they're levels above mine, and I won't be played for a fool."

The word *again* hovered in the air, and Grant wanted to know what bastard had left her full of doubts and insecurities. But he refused to let himself cross into anything too personal.

Tessa's shoulders tensed up as silence settled between them. Grant didn't want her angry. He wasn't even sure what had spawned this, but he was here to work and there was usually enough drama on sets. He didn't need this on top of it.

"I read you have a twin," she told him, breaking the silence. "But I never saw anything else."

Tension knotted in his belly. "My family isn't up for discussion."

"Seriously? You know everything about mine and you—"

"Not. Up. For. Discussion."

Tessa shook her head and sighed. "Looks like we're at a stalemate then."

Stalemate? No. He refused to discuss his family—his sister—but he also refused to let this attraction fizzle because of a past nightmare that threatened to consume him at any moment.

"Pull over."

She jerked her gaze to his briefly. "What?"

"Pull over."

Once she'd eased to the side of the road, Grant waited until she'd thrown the Jeep into Park before he reached across the narrow space, grabbed her shoulders and pulled her to meet him in the middle.

A second later his mouth was on hers, and she all but melted. Grant indulged in the strength of the kiss for long moments before he let her go.

"Don't throw stumbling blocks at me, Country. I'll jump them," he told her. "Don't lump me with whatever jerk broke your heart. And do not downgrade yourself by thinking I'm using you simply to pass the time."

She lowered her lids and sighed. She was exhausted. Physically and emotionally. No wonder Cassie was worried. Guilt tugged at Grant's heart. Damn it. His heart had no place in this.

She didn't want this movie made, didn't want him here and was fighting this attraction. He wanted the movie and he wanted Tessa.

Grant hated to tell her, but she was fighting a losing battle.

"What's really bothering you?" he asked. "I realize you're uncomfortable with...whatever we're doing, but that wouldn't have you this angry."

When she met his eyes, she shook her head. "I'm not sure. It may be nothing, but I'm just so paranoid lately."

"Tell me what it is, and I can help you decide if it's nothing. That way you won't drive yourself insane with your internal battle."

"Too late," she said with a smile. "My dad hired this new groom a couple days ago. We needed to fill the slot, but this guy...I can't put my finger on it. He almost looks familiar. It's his eyes, but I can't place him. He's really quiet and keeps to himself."

Squeezing her shoulder in reassurance, Grant said, "I fail to see an issue."

"It just seems like every time I turn around he's there. I don't know if he's spying on me or what." She paused, bit her lip and went on. "I know this sounds silly, but what if he's out to harm the horses or sabotage my training? We don't know this man and the timing..."

Grant didn't think this was a big deal, but if Tessa was concerned, he'd definitely look into it. Because she was right, the timing was perfect if someone wanted to ruin her racing season. Better to be safe than sorry. And he sure didn't want anyone to screw up this film before it got started. This was his big shot at producing with the biggest names in the industry. No way in hell was someone going to come in and ruin everything.

"He passed the background check, and from what I can tell he's a very hard worker." Tessa blew out a sigh. "Maybe I'm just paranoid because of Cassie's ex. We thought we could trust him, too."

Grant cupped Tessa's cheek, stroking her soft, delicate skin. "I'll keep an eye out for the guy and do a little digging of my own."

"Really?" she asked, her eyes widening.

"Yeah. I mean, I can't have some random guy wreaking havoc on the set. Best to get to the bottom of this now before my crew arrives."

Tessa nodded and pulled from his grasp. Putting the car back in gear, she drove back out onto the highway.

Grant realized his words may have hurt her, but he wasn't quite ready to admit he was falling for her a little more each day. So there was no way he could tell her that he'd be watching this stranger like a hawk to make sure he wasn't out to take advantage of Tessa or any of the other Barringtons.

He may have told her it was all about the movie, but that was a lie. A good portion of it was because he refused to see Tessa hurt.

Damn. There went that heart of his, trying to get involved. But a little voice whispered that his heart was already involved.

Seven

The feed store showed promise. Maybe not for an entire scene, but most definitely for a backdrop or even during the opening credits.

But the little white church, complete with bell in the steeple and a picturesque cemetery amid a grove of trees, would without a doubt be in at least one pivotal scene.

"This is where my parents were married," Tessa told Grant as she pulled her Jeep to the side of the gravel road. "It's small, but my mom wanted an intimate wedding. She was very private."

"Sounds like someone else I know," Grant said, throwing Tessa a smile before stepping out of the vehicle.

She came around and joined him as he stared up at the simple structure. Tall, narrow stained glass windows adorned either side of the arched double doors. A narrow set of steps led up the embankment toward the church, and Grant could easily see Damon Barrington and his young bride marrying here.

With a director's eye, he could see a smiling, maybe tearful couple exiting the church, while rice sprayed them and lined the path to an awaiting car.

Key to the start of the movie was the whirlwind romance of Tessa's parents. They'd known each other for only six weeks, but according to Damon, he didn't need to know Rose a moment longer to be sure she was the woman he wanted to spend his life with.

Unfortunately, she'd passed all too soon.

Grant's eyes drifted to the cemetery, then back to Tessa, who was also looking toward the graves…and he knew.

"You want to go see her?" he asked softly.

A brief smile spread across Tessa's face as she nodded. "You don't have to come, but I can't drive out here and not go visit."

Without a word, Grant slid his hand into hers and headed up the slope. He let her take the lead and found himself standing in the shade of a large oak tree. The sunny spring day had a bit of chill to the air, so he slipped his arm around Tessa's shoulders.

Or that's what he told himself. Honestly, he wanted her to know she wasn't alone, wanted her to know he was here. He couldn't fathom the heartache of losing his mother. Nearly losing his sister had crushed him, leaving him in a world he couldn't even describe.

"This never seems real," Tessa whispered. "I should be used to not having her, but I always feel… I don't know. I guess I feel something is missing."

Grant stared down at the polished black stone with a single rose emblem beside the name Rose Barrington.

"I can't imagine the void that slips into your life," he told her. "Nothing replaces that."

The hole in his heart for his sister had never been filled… never would be unless he faced her.

"You just learn to cope," Tessa said softly. "There's no other choice."

Grant let the gentle breeze envelop them, allowing the silence to take over. He had no idea what to say, so he said nothing. There was no need to try to fill the moment with useless words.

Tessa bent down, rested her hand over her mother's name and whispered something. He took a step back to allow her more privacy. Other than his sister, his heart had never ached for another woman until now.

Even though her mother had been gone fifteen years, Tessa

was obviously very torn up. More than likely coming here for her was both comforting and crushing. And seeing Tessa so vulnerable wasn't something he'd planned on.

At one time Grant's family had been close, had had a bond that he'd thought nothing could destroy. But he'd murdered that when—

"You okay?"

Grant shook off his thoughts and realized Tessa had come to her feet and was studying him.

"Fine," he told her, refusing to let past demons haunt him. "I wanted to give you some privacy."

She moved on through the cemetery, and he followed, taking in strangers' names and various dates. Some stones were obviously decades old, and others were fairly new.

"This area holds a lot of meaning to your family," he commented as Tessa moved in behind the church.

Large trees shaded the entire area, providing a canopy over the stones. Grant could hardly wait to show Bronson and Anthony the stunning scene.

"I hope to marry here someday," Tessa said. "I still have my mother's wedding dress. It's old, but it's so simple and classy, I want to wear it."

Grant could see her with her auburn hair pulled back in a timeless style, and wearing a vintage gown. She'd make the most alluring of brides.

He wasn't too happy thinking of another man waiting for her at the end of the aisle, but it was hardly his place to worry about such things. After all, in a few months he'd be out of her life.

"I bet you have everything all planned out in a color-coded spreadsheet," he teased as he stopped and turned to look down at her. "I'd guess you have each detail, down to the shade of each flower."

Tessa narrowed her eyes, tilted her chin. "Maybe I do."

Grant laughed. "Nothing to get defensive about, Country. Some people are just wired to never relax."

"I relax," she countered, crossing her arms over her chest. "I'm relaxing right now."

He took a step forward; she took a step back. They danced that way for a few moments until Tessa's back was up against an old weeping willow.

Grant rested an arm on the trunk above her head and smiled when she had to tip her head to look up at him.

"You're relaxed?" he asked. "The only time you've fully relaxed with me was when my mouth was on yours. You never take downtime, and you work yourself too hard."

"That's not true," she said, her words coming out almost a whisper.

Grant took his free hand and traced a line up her neck, right over her pounding pulse. "Really?"

Tessa continued to hold his gaze, never wavering. And he wanted to keep her guessing what he'd do next.

"Then in that case—" he leaned down, coming within a breath of her lips "—have dinner with me."

Her eyes widened. "I don't think that's a good idea, Slick."

"Sure it is." Grant eased back, just enough to give her room to breathe. "You pick the day and time. I can work around you, but I want to have dinner with you, and I want you to take one evening to do absolutely nothing."

"I'm training," she insisted. "I have way too much to do and…"

"And what?"

"And I can't think when I'm with you," she whispered. "I want things, things I shouldn't. I can't get involved, Grant."

"With me or with anybody?" he asked, resisting the urge to kiss her until she lost her train of thought. But she was torn, and emotional right now.

That made two of them.

"Anybody." She placed her hands on his chest and eased him farther away as she straightened from the tree. "Besides, we couldn't be more different, and when the film is over, you'll be gone. I already said I won't be the one to help you pass your time here."

Grant shoved his hands into the pockets of his jacket. "I asked you to dinner. I'm not asking you to have a wild, torrid affair worthy of headlines."

Not yet, anyway. Damn that clause. He had to get creative here, to protect not only his career but his peace of mind. Sex was all he could afford, all that he wanted.

Yeah, keep telling yourself that.

"Dinner only?" she asked.

"Unless you find me irresistible and can't keep your hands off me," he countered, offering her a smile, hoping to lighten the mood. "In that case, we'll have to keep it a secret so I don't get fired."

"I'm pretty sure I can keep my hands off you, as long as you keep those lips off me."

Grant winced. "Ouch, you really know how to drive a hard bargain. But I want you to relax, so I'll keep my lips to myself."

She raised a brow and twisted her lips as she contemplated. "Fine. Dinner. One evening and nothing more."

"What night and time?"

She slid her phone from her pocket and searched. No doubt she had her spreadsheet on that damn thing, too.

"Tomorrow at seven."

"Perfect. Don't wear anything too fancy, and come by my cottage."

"You're not going to pick me up?" she asked.

He shrugged. "I don't want you thinking this is a real date. It's just dinner, remember?"

"As long as you remember, that's what matters."

Grant suddenly felt as if he'd won the lottery. Of course, a miracle had been performed. Tessa had not only agreed to spending downtime with him, she'd agreed to relax.

And he might have to keep his lips off of her, but she'd said absolutely nothing about his hands.

Eight

Don't wear anything too fancy.

Tessa nearly laughed. Oh, she had fancy clothes for uppity events she was forced to attend, but those gowns and dresses lived in the back of her closet, more than likely collecting dust on the shoulder seams that were molded around the hangers.

After working in the stables, helping Cassie clean stalls, Tessa did shower and throw on fresh jeans and a white shirt, rolling up the sleeves. She shoved on her nicer black boots and grabbed a simple green jacket to top off her "not a date" outfit.

The air outside had been a bit chilly, and she knew she'd be cold when she came home later.

She groaned as she grabbed her keys from the peg by the back door. How the hell had she let him talk her into this? Intriguing as he was, she simply couldn't allow herself to sink deeper into his world…a world of class and glamour. A world she'd narrowly escaped a few months ago, along with a man who'd claimed to care for her.

But something about Grant seemed to pull her. He had no qualms about the fact that he found her attractive, but he also seemed genuine, and at the cemetery he'd been supportive and caring.

He also guarded his family…that had been evident when she'd brought up the topic of his twin. And while his instant raised shield intrigued her, leaving her wanting to know more, Tessa could appreciate the value of privacy. Ironic, considering she loathed the idea of this movie, of virtual strangers invading her space, her life.

But Grant seemed to be truly concerned about her feelings. He'd gone out of his way to assure her he'd portray her family in the best light.

He understood family. And, she had to admit, was starting to understand her. He was a Hollywood hotshot, used to elegance and beauty surrounding him. Yet he was blending just fine here in her world.

She didn't want him to have so many layers, because each one threw her off and made her wonder about the possibilities beyond those kisses.

No. Tessa shook off her thoughts as they started down a path she wasn't ready to visit.

If Grant knew she was a virgin, he'd probably give up his quest...or he'd see her as a challenge he needed to meet.

Dinner. He'd only said dinner. Added to that, he'd promised to keep those talented lips to himself. A part of her was disappointed that she wouldn't feel them, but the logical side of her knew this was for the best.

Each kiss made her yearn for...well, everything he was willing to offer, which scared the hell out of her. She'd never desired so much from one man, never considered giving in before.

But somewhere along the way, she felt as if they'd crossed some sort of friendship line. She found him easy to talk to, and as much as she hated to admit it, she wanted to spend more time with him. She really didn't have friends outside her racing world, and Grant was refreshing...kisses and all.

That friendship line they'd crossed held a lot of sexual tension, and Tessa worried one day all that built-up pressure would explode.

Which was why she had to stop this roller coaster of hormones before it got too far out of control. The two different worlds they lived in would never mesh, so why even add something else to her list of worries?

Besides the upcoming season, as if that weren't enough stress, she really wasn't comfortable with the new groom. When she'd mentioned this to her father, he'd waved a hand and told her she was imagining things and was probably just still skeptical because of Cassie's ex.

Yet the stranger had made a point not to get too far away from her and Cassie as they were cleaning stalls earlier. He'd been working hard, but still, Tessa had a gut feeling he'd been trying to listen to their conversation.

But that was a worry for another day. Right now, she had to be on her guard for her dinner "not date."

Tessa hopped in her Jeep and made the short trip back to Stony Ridge Acres, her heart beating a bit faster. Why was she getting so worked up? This was dinner. They had to eat, and were just doing it together.

When she pulled up in front of his cottage, he'd turned on the porch lights. The sun was at the horizon, but in no time it would be dark.

Before she could knock on the door, Grant swung it open and...

Tessa laughed. "What are you wearing?"

Grant wiped his hand on a dishrag and glanced down. "An apron. Don't you wear one when you cook?"

"I thought we were going out," she said, trying her hardest not to stare at him in that ridiculous apron, which looked like a woman wearing a grass skirt and coconut bra.

"I never said that," he countered, taking her hand and pulling her inside. "I said we were going to have dinner together. And I'm cooking. Besides, how can you relax if we're in public?"

Would've been a hell of a lot easier than in the lion's den.

Something tangy permeated the air, and Tessa's gaze drifted toward the open kitchen. "If you're cooking anything associated with that smell, I'm impressed."

Grant headed back to the kitchen, leaving her standing at the door. "It's just barbecue chicken, but it's my mother's sauce recipe. I also have some baked potatoes and salad. Hope all of that is okay."

"My mouth is watering already."

He threw her a glance, his dark eyes traveling down her body. "Mine, too."

Tingles slid all over her, through her, and Tessa had no clue how to reply to that, so she took off her jacket and hung it on the hook beside the door. After dropping her keys in the jacket pocket, she headed to the kitchen.

"Want me to set the table or anything?"

"It's done and so is the food," he said, removing the ridiculous apron.

Apparently, he'd taken full advantage of the very well-stocked cottage.

In no time he'd set the food on the small round table, covered with a simple red cloth. Thankfully, he hadn't gone to the trouble of romantic flowers or a candle. This she could handle. The sultry looks and kisses...well, she could handle them, but they left her confused and, okay, aroused.

Tessa concentrated on her food and prayed he had no clue where her mind had wandered, though she feared her face had turned a lovely shade of red.

Small talk during dinner eased her a bit more, and she nearly laughed at herself. Had she expected him to pounce on her when she arrived?

Tessa picked up her empty plate and stood.

"Leave the dishes," he told her, reaching across to place his hand on her wrist. "I'll get them later."

"I can help with them now. You cooked, so at least I can help clean up."

"You're my guest. I'll get them."

Because she never backed down from a fight, she carried her plate to the sink. "Technically, you're our guest, since you're on Barrington grounds."

She'd just turned on the water and was rinsing the dish

when Grant's hands encircled her waist. His lips caressed her ear.

"You're not relaxing," he whispered, his breath warm on her cheek, her neck, sending shivers down the entire length of her body.

The dish slipped from her wet hands and into the sink. "I'm relaxed." Any more and she'd be a puddle at his feet. "I just wanted to help."

Strong fingers slid beneath the hem of her shirt, gliding over goose bumps.

"And I promised you a night of relaxation."

Did he have to whisper everything in her ear? Could the man back up a tad and let her breathe? Because if he didn't, she feared she'd turn in his arms and take that mouth she'd promised herself never to have again.

"Grant..."

"Tessa," he murmured, his lips barely brushing against her neck.

"You promised not to kiss me."

Soft laughter vibrated against her back from his strong chest. "I'm not kissing you. I'm enjoying how you feel. There's a big difference."

"I can't... We can't..." She couldn't even think with the way his fingertips kept inching around her abdomen. "Wh-what are you doing?"

The bottom button of her shirt came undone, and then the next. Grant splayed his hand across her taut stomach and eased her back against him. "Relaxing with you."

Unable to resist, Tessa allowed her head to fall back against his shoulder, her eyelids closed. Reaching behind her, she raked a hand over his stubbled jaw. The roughness beneath her palm aroused her even more. Grant was all male, all powerful, and yet so tender.

When had a man held her in such a caring, yet passionate way? When had she allowed herself to enjoy the simple pleasures of being wanted?

Tessa wasn't naive. Well, physically she was, but mentally she knew Grant wanted her body. He'd told her as much, and she knew he wasn't asking for her hand in marriage or even a committed relationship. But right now, she could be open to this moment and relish it. They were both still fully clothed, both just enjoying the other.

As his hand inched higher, her shirt traveled up, as well. The edge of his thumb caressed the underside of her silk bra and her nipples quickly responded to the thrilling touch.

Tessa's breath quickened as she turned her mouth to his.

When he didn't respond to her kiss, she pulled back.

"I promised," he murmured.

"I'm letting you out of that verbal contract."

Grant's mouth slammed down onto hers, and Tessa lost track of everything else around her. His touch consumed her, making her ache in a way she'd never thought possible.

Grant's hand slid from beneath her shirt and she turned around, pressing her chest against his as one hand held on to the nape of her neck and the other gripped her bottom through her jeans.

Being wedged between the hard planes of Grant's body and the edge of the counter was a very wonderful place to be.

Tessa wrapped her arms around his neck and opened her mouth wider, silently inviting him to take more.

What was she doing? This wasn't why she'd come here. But now that she was in the moment, she didn't want to stop to rationalize all the reasons this was wrong. Because her tingling lips, aching body and curling toes told her this kiss was very, very right.

Grant's mouth traveled from her lips to her chin and across her jawline. Everywhere he touched, everything he did to her had her wanting more. The man certainly knew exactly how to kiss and where to touch. Everything to pleasure a woman.

And that revelation was the equivalent of throwing cold water on her.

Tessa wriggled her hands between them and eased him

back. Those heavy-lidded eyes landed on hers while his lips, moist and swollen from kissing, begged for more. But she had to stop. This kissing and groping was as far as she'd ever gone…so anything beyond this point would be a disappointment to him.

Tessa met his gaze, refusing to be embarrassed for who she was, the values and promise to her mother she desperately tried to cling to.

When she'd been with Aaron, she'd been tempted, but she'd assumed they would marry, and she'd wanted to wait.

But the level to which Aaron had tempted her didn't come close to the fire of arousal she felt right now with Grant.

Her eyes held his, and as she opened her mouth, he held up a hand.

"Don't say you're sorry," he told her.

Tessa shook her head. "No. I'm not sorry, but we can't do this."

"We can and we were," he countered. "What happened? Something scared you."

Yeah, the big city playboy and the country virgin. Could they be any more clichéd? Why couldn't she be this attracted to someone in her league, or at least in her town?

Moving around him, because she needed distance from his touch, his gaze and his masculine aroma, Tessa walked over to the sliding glass doors and looked out into the darkness. Mostly all she could see was her own reflection, and that was worse than looking at Grant. What she saw was a coward.

"Talk to me," he urged as he stepped closer, but didn't touch. "I'm not going to push you into anything, Tessa. But I want to know what happened."

He stood behind her, their eyes locked in the reflective glass. Tessa sighed and turned, crossing her arms over her chest.

"When I told you I wouldn't be the one to help you pass the time on set, I meant it." He opened his mouth, but she held up a hand. "And I didn't say that initially, or now, to offend you. I said it because you need to know where I stand, where we stand. The differences between us, Grant...they're huge."

"Is this the age thing again?" he asked, stepping forward to brace his hands on her shoulders.

"That's one reason," she confirmed, hating how vulnerable and defensive she felt. "I've never been with a man before, Grant. Ever."

She waited for the words to sink in, waited for him to drop his hands and take a giant step back, as if she'd just drawn a line in the sand and on her side was the plague.

"Tessa, you're not a virgin."

"Yes, I am." She tilted her chin, refusing to be ashamed of what she was just because society felt she should be another way. "I promised my mother I'd wait for love. My body is something I value, Grant. I want my first time to be with someone I truly care about, who I know cares for me.

"I won't lie," she went on, when he remained silent. "I've never before been kissed in a way that made me forget everything and want to give in to all my desires." She took a deep, steadying breath, bringing her hands up to grasp his wrists. "But with you, I want more."

"I value your morals," he answered. "I probably respect you more for them. But you know there's something here. This is more than just lust, more than just sex. You need to let yourself live."

Shifting his hands, causing hers to fall away, he slid the pads of his thumbs over her bottom lip. "A woman with as much passion as you have, as much desire lurking in those eyes, has never fully committed to another man?"

Tessa shook her head, not knowing what to say next. This was the part when a man turned totally weird or ran out the door...not that there had been many men to begin with. Her ex had certainly thought he could persuade her. Now she was even more thankful Aaron hadn't convinced her.

Since Tessa was at Grant's house, she figured this was her cue to go. Shoulders back and pride intact, she stepped around him and went toward the door. She'd barely pulled her jacket from the hook before a hand closed over hers, another at her waist.

"Don't leave."

With his strong body surrounding her, and those two simple words that held so much meaning, Grant engulfed her.

"I can't stay, Grant. I'm not ready to give myself, and even if I did, you'd be disappointed."

"Look at me."

Forgoing the jacket, she dropped her arm and turned. But instead of seeing confusion or disappointment in his eyes, she saw tenderness, plus a heavy dose of desire. And determination.

"First of all, no matter what you did to or with me would ever be disappointing," he told her, framing her face between his hands so she had no choice but to face him head-on. "Second, the fact that you're a virgin doesn't scare me away, if that's what you were waiting on. And if it scared other guys before, then they're jerks and don't deserve you. Whether we sleep together or not is completely your call, Tessa. I enjoy you, I enjoy talking with you, learning from you and, yes, kissing you. But the ball is in your court. If you don't want to take the next step with me, I totally respect your decision. But don't expect me to stop kissing you at every chance I get."

At his warm smile, Tessa found herself grinning. "I wouldn't mind you kissing me whenever you want. I can't promise I'll ever be ready for more with you. Not that I don't want it, I just can't give myself, knowing it would only be a fling."

Grant's lips touched hers briefly before he pulled back and looked into her eyes. "You're the strongest woman I know."

"I'm not feeling strong," she retorted with a laugh. "I'm feeling like I want to forget the fact you're not staying, and throw aside all rationale."

"Country, you know where to find me." He stroked her lips

once more. "But I'm not giving up. You're so passionate and I want to be the one to uncover that hunger you've kept hidden."

Well, that declaration certainly wasn't helping matters. Besides the fact she'd be seeing him every single day, he'd been so understanding, so comfortable with the news that she was a virgin. Which would make him even harder to resist.

But on the flip side, he would try harder, be even more charming and irresistible. Her mother had always told her the right one would accept and understand her values, and try not to push her.

And without hesitation, Grant had accepted her. Which made him all the more tempting, and quite possibly...the one she'd been waiting for?

Nine

How the hell did he cope with this bombshell? He'd never been in this situation before and honestly had no idea how to react, let alone what to say.

Had he said the right thing?

Running a hand down his face, Grant stared out his patio door toward the pasture, where a few horses grazed off in the distance.

For the sake of his career, here he was, in a world he'd sworn off, finding himself drowning in a woman he wanted just sex from, only to find out she was a virgin.

Grant laughed at the irony that was now his life. The damn film hadn't even started yet, and he was sinking deeper and deeper into worlds that threatened to leave him weak and vulnerable. Way to stay in control of the game.

He glanced at his watch, noted it was time to head to the stables, and sighed. No matter his personal feelings—and he couldn't deny there were very personal feelings involved now—he had to remain on task and get the job done. This was still his livelihood, still his reputation on the line if he wanted to move on up in the movie industry.

As he headed out the door, his cell phone rang. After shutting the door behind him, Grant stepped off the narrow porch.

"Hey, Bronson," he said.

"I hope you're sitting down, man. I've got news for you."

Freezing in his tracks, Grant gripped the phone. "Good news or bad news?"

"Beyond good. Marty Russo has been in contact with me and Anthony. He's willing to back your production company if this film takes off like we think it will."

"Are you kidding me?" Grant asked, suddenly seeing his dream spiraling closer toward reality.

On the other end of the connection, Bronson Dane laughed. "Not at all. If this movie is a hit like we all believe it will be, Russo Entertainment wants you to come on board and branch out with your own company."

Grant could hardly believe this. He'd been a director for years, had worked his ass off to get to the point of producing, and now, before his production debut, he might already have a chance at starting his own company?

He'd been fortunate in the past several years to have some major deals, which set his name on the film map. But his own company would take his career to a whole new level.

"Man, that's great," Grant said. "I don't even know what to say."

"You deserve it," Bronson replied. "Marty was going to call, but I wanted to be the one to tell you. I'm sure he'll be calling you later today."

Grant had worked with the man several times. Being the CEO of Russo Entertainment, Marty often had a direct hand in the company's films, and was a very hands-on guy. Grant respected the hell out of him and had every intention of not letting him down.

"Anthony and I are wrapping up at Churchill Downs today. Between there, New York and Maryland, we've covered the main tracks and have some amazing areas for scenes. We should be arriving at the end of next week."

Grant continued walking his path again as he and Bronson discussed the church, cemetery and other local places that had meaningful ties to Damon Barrington's past.

By the time he disconnected the call, he was beaming. The sun had risen, the spring day was beautiful and promised to be warm, and he had the chance of a lifetime right within his reach.

But his smile faded and fear set in when he saw Cassie running alongside the fence and Tessa on a horse, barreling faster than he'd ever seen seen her go.

Fear flooded him, and he had to force himself not to over-react. Another time, another woman flashed in his mind and nausea threatened to overtake him.

Especially when Tessa kept pulling back on the reins and yelling, alarm lacing her voice.

Grant ran to the fence, having no clue how he could help or even what the hell had happened.

The horse seemed to reduce his speed, barely, but then reared up, after which everything seemed to happen in slow motion. Tessa screamed, slicing a new layer of dread straight through Grant. When she fell off the back of the horse, he leaped over the fence, not giving a damn about anything but getting to her.

He crouched down beside her as she was rolling onto her back, gasping—whether in pain or because the wind had been knocked out of her, he didn't know.

"Tessa, honey." He ran his hands gently over her, praying for no broken bones, no broken skin. "Talk to me. Are you hurt?"

She groaned and tried to sit up, but he placed a hand on her shoulder. "Just lie here for a minute," he told her.

"Macduff…where…" Tessa continued to try to catch her breath as she searched the track. "Is he okay?"

Fury bubbled within Grant. Was she seriously more worried about this horse than her own welfare?

Because she wasn't going to relax until she knew about the animal, Grant glanced back and saw Cassie managing just fine, along with the new groom. They'd taken control of the horse and were leading him into the stables.

"He's fine," Grant told her. "Cassie has him."

Tessa's shoulders relaxed into the dirt and her eyes closed

as she exhaled a shallow breath. The color had left her face and her arm was draped across her ribs.

"I need to know what hurts, so I can tell the squad." He pulled out his phone and barely hit the 9 before she put her hand over his.

"No, I'm fine." Her eyes locked on to his. "Don't fuss with calling anyone."

"Like hell I'm not, Tessa."

Bad memories played through his mind like a horror movie...only it had been real life. Internal injuries were by far even more terrifying. He'd done a somewhat good job of keeping these two worlds—caring for Tessa, and her lifestyle—apart. But the two had just collided and blown up in his face.

"You're white as a ghost, Grant. Are you okay?"

He ran a hand down his face and nodded. "I'm fine. But you're going to get checked out. Internal injuries may not make their appearance known until it's too late."

"Grant—"

"You can either ride in an ambulance or I'm taking you, but this is not up for debate."

Tessa flinched at his raised voice.

"Is she okay?" Cassie asked, squatting down next to them.

"She's stubborn," Grant hissed, coming to his feet. "Talk some sense into her while I call for the medics."

While he did so, he at least heard Cassie taking his side. No way in hell would he allow Tessa to ignore what had just happened. And knowing her, she'd probably get right back on the damn horse and go another round.

After his call was placed, he returned to Tessa, who was now sitting up with Cassie's arm supporting her.

"They're on their way," he told them.

"I hate to leave her, but I need to tell Nash she's going to the hospital, and I need to go find Dad."

"Who's Nash?" Grant asked.

"The new groom," Tessa told him. "Go, Cass, I'm fine."

Cassie shot Grant a look, but he nodded, giving her the

silent go-ahead. There was no way he would be leaving Tessa's side.

"I'm sure Dad will be at the hospital as soon as I let him know," Cassie said.

"That's fine. I've got my cell, so he can call me, too."

As soon as the squad arrived and loaded Tessa—carefully, as per Grant's demands—he went to get his rental car to follow. As much as he wanted to ride with her, he needed his vehicle, because when they left, he sure as hell would be the one bringing her back.

"This is all really silly," Tessa complained as Grant eased his car into the drive, passing beneath the arched sign for the estate. "I can stay at my house just fine, Slick."

"We already went over this. You can stay at your house with me or at my house with me. Since you only huffed when I gave you your options, I decided we'd stay here so your dad and sister are closer."

Tessa rolled her eyes as he parked in front of the cottage. "I only live one property over."

He turned, offered her that killer smile complete with dimples and said, "Yes, but there are several acres separating the two. Your father and I agreed this was best."

"My father probably has no clue you have the hots for his daughter, either," she mumbled.

Grant barked a laugh and came around to help her out. She wasn't some invalid. She'd fallen off Macduff because she'd not been paying attention, and the once-abused horse was still skittish.

Cassie had bought the horse from an auction, and they all knew he'd been mistreated. But Cassie was a softy for any animal, especially ones not properly cared for. Tessa was confident she could keep him under control...and she had, until she'd seen Grant walking toward the stables, phone to his ear and wearing the most brilliant smile. He'd stolen her breath,

and she'd lost her concentration. Macduff was nervous, anyway, but the accident was totally her fault.

Grant slid his arm around her as she started to climb from
the car. "Really, I can walk," she protested. "I won't fall over."

"The doctor said you had a concussion, and you admitted you were dizzy." He tightened his grip. "You're not going
down on my watch."

Okay, so a bit of her was thrilled at the fact he wanted to
care for her, but she seriously could've taken care of herself.
Did he think she was sharing his bed tonight? Surely that
wasn't a reason behind his insistence to keep her at his place.

Once inside the cottage, Grant gave her no option but to sit
on the sofa with her feet propped up. Her protests were completely ignored as he removed her boots.

"Now, what can I get you to eat? You haven't had dinner."

Tessa hadn't given food a thought. "What do you have?
Just something light. I'm still queasy."

"I'm pretty sure there are some cans of soup in the cabinet."

Laying her head against the back of the sofa, she nodded.
"That will be fine. Any flavor, I'm not too picky."

Even as tired as she was, she couldn't close her eyes. Watching Grant bustle around the kitchen, getting her dinner ready,
really hit her hard. Aaron had never taken this much care of
her. He'd never tried to put her needs first. Of course, hindsight was a real eye-opener, because the man had been only
out for himself to begin with.

But there was something special about Grant. He obviously loved his family, which was a huge indicator that he
was a nurturer. The fact he was so easy to talk to also proved
to her that he wasn't the self-centered city slicker she'd first
thought him to be.

When he brought her dinner on a tray, Tessa smiled.
"You're so good to me, Slick. I could get used to this."

He took a seat on the coffee table across from her and
smiled. "I could get used to you lying on my couch watching me."

After taking a few mouthfuls of chicken soup, she glanced back over at him and sighed. His eyelids were heavy, his hair all messed from running his fingers through it. Normally he looked so polished, the picture of perfection. Now he looked... exhausted.

"I'm sorry, Grant."

"What for?"

"This. Being a burden, scaring you."

He blinked and eased forward, cupping her face with one strong, warm hand. "You could never be a burden to me, Tessa. If I didn't want you here I could've taken you to the main house, to Cassie's or back to your own home. I want you here so I can watch over you, and I want you here because something is building between us and I refuse to ignore it."

Inching forward, Grant placed his lips softly on hers. "As for scaring me, if you ever do that again I'm going to hack into your computer and delete all your saved spreadsheets."

Tessa laughed, reaching over to smack his shoulder. "You wouldn't dare."

He eased back with a half grin. "Maybe not, but when you fell...there are no words, but I'll never forget that feeling."

He glanced aside, almost as if he was trying to compose himself. Had he truly been that scared, that worried for her? This wasn't the first time she'd seen the stark fear in his eyes when it came to horses. That first day they'd met he'd acted concerned for her safety.

"Hey," she said, waiting for him to turn back to her. "I've been riding since I got out of diapers, Slick. That wasn't my first fall and it won't be my last. Yes, it sucks, but sometimes it just happens."

Raking a hand down his face, Grant sighed and came to his feet. "Why don't you finish your dinner, and I'll go find you some more comfortable clothes to sleep in."

"What about you?" she asked. "You haven't had dinner."

"Honestly, my nerves are shot. I couldn't eat if I wanted to."

With that revelation, he walked away. Obviously, her fall

had torn him up in ways she never would've imagined. When she'd been lying on the ground and he'd been at her side, his face had been so pale, his eyes so wide as he'd tried to take in her entire body at once, assessing the damage.

At the E.R., he'd been forceful and matter-of-fact with the staff, almost demanding that she stay overnight for observation. The doctor had assured Grant that since she'd never lost consciousness, she would be fine to go home as long as someone watched her.

So here she was, being watched by a man who made her tingle with a simple touch, who kissed her as if she was the only desirable woman in the world, and who had her rethinking her reasons for remaining innocent.

This should be an interesting night.

Ten

"*Melanie!*"

Fear consumed him, bile rose in his throat as the scene before him unfolded.

Screams filled the evening, the thundering of hooves seemed to be in surround sound, and all Grant could do was look on as his twin sister held on to the out-of-control mare.

Their parents and the trainer all shouted commands, running after them, but Grant, still atop his own horse, could only stare from behind.

He'd done this. All in the name of a joke and a dare, he'd put Melanie in danger.

The shrill sound coming from his sister jolted him out of his horrified, frozen state, and he kicked his mount into gear and charged after them. He had to do something, had to rectify this somehow. Fear fueled him, while adrenaline blocked out all the possibilities of what might happen if that animal threw her.

He leaned into his horse, kicking his flank once again to move faster.

But it was too late. Melanie's mare saw Grant's coming in fast, and bucked, sending Melanie off the back. She landed with a jarring, sickening thud.

As he jumped off his horse and his parents and the trainer gathered around, Grant knew things had gone from bad to worse and hell was opening up to swallow him.

His beautiful, talented, always smiling twin sister wasn't moving....

Grant jerked up in bed, the sheet twisted around his waist, sweat dampening his forehead, his chest.

Damn. That nightmare hadn't made an appearance in so long, and he could've gone the rest of his life without having that dream.

There wasn't a day that went by when he didn't relive that life-altering moment. But the dreams...they were all too real and obviously the penance for his sin.

Grant swung his feet over the side of the bed, yanking the sheet off. He needed fresh air, some water, and he should probably check on Tessa.

Tessa. No doubt the events of today had brought on the nightmare. Because he'd been just as terrified seeing Tessa on the out-of-control stallion and then her fall...

Raking a hand over his face, Grant came to his feet and padded to the kitchen, careful to be quiet as he crept past Tessa's door. He'd insisted she keep it open in case she needed to call him for anything. She'd fought him a little on the matter, but Grant had refused to back down.

After he grabbed a bottle of water from the fridge and took a long drink, he set it on the counter, walked toward the patio and opened the door, welcoming the crisp night air. The refreshing breeze cooled his heated skin and calmed him, but that damn nightmare and images of today still rolled over and over in his mind.

Nothing was as nauseating, as horrifying or as crippling as watching someone you cared for caught in a helpless situation, and knowing there wasn't a damn thing you could do about it.

But unlike Tessa's situation, Grant had caused his twin's. His beautiful sister could've been killed. Sometimes he wondered if death would've been better than being a paraplegic.

"You okay?"

He turned, finding Tessa standing in the shadows. His T-shirt hit her midthigh, leaving beautifully toned legs revealed.

"I'm fine," he answered, turning back to the starry night, silently willing her to go away.

He couldn't keep looking at her, not when his emotions were so high and his heart was still in his throat.

And not when he'd just admitted to himself he was starting to care for her more than he thought he would. There was no way he could keep all his emotions separated now. More penance for his sins.

"Sorry if I woke you," he told her. "I was going to check on you in a minute."

Bare feet padded along the hardwood floors, and Grant clenched his fists as Tessa came to stand beside him. Her sweet jasmine scent mixed with the cool night air and surrounded him.

He hated how vulnerable he was. Hated how his need for her consumed him.

Turn back. Turn back before I take what I want.

"Want to talk about it?" she asked, her soft voice washing over him.

Sparing her a glance, he shook his head. "You should be in bed."

"I feel fine," she insisted, reaching out a delicate hand to grip his bare biceps. "What's keeping you up?"

Songs of crickets flooded the night, and Grant couldn't find the words. Right now he couldn't even think, given his vortex of emotions. Her fall, her nearness…her virginity.

"I guess I'm just still keyed up after today's excitement."

"Is that why I heard you cry out in your sleep a few minutes ago?"

Grant jerked around, causing her hand to drop. When she said nothing more, only crossed her arms over her chest, he muttered a curse and raked his fingers through his hair.

"I used to have nightmares," he admitted, not going into further detail. "I had one tonight. It's no big deal."

Bright blue eyes studied him for a moment before she

spoke. "They must be a big deal if this is an ongoing thing, Grant. Have you talked to anybody about them?"

"Like a shrink?" He laughed. "No. I'm fine."

Her gaze slid over his bare chest, then back up. She might as well have touched him with her soft fingertips because the effect was the same. His body responded, and there was nothing he could do to stop the heavy dose of arousal that kicked into high gear...as if he needed his hormones to bump up a notch.

"You should get back to bed," he told her, silently begging her to get her barely covered butt out of here before he forgot how delicate and innocent she truly was.

If she only knew the control she held over him...

"I want to help you." Stepping forward, she slid that delicate hand back up his arm and over the curve of his bare shoulder. "You may not want to talk about the dream, but I can stay up with you so you're not alone."

Grant's control snapped as he grabbed Tessa's slender shoulders and backed her up two steps to the frame of the patio door. Her eyes widened as she peered up at him.

"It's best I'm alone right now," he growled. "I want things I shouldn't, and my mood isn't the best. Go to your room, Tessa."

Her eyes filled with tears as she brought up her hands to cup his face. "You don't scare me, Grant. Whatever you're dealing with, I can help."

"I may not scare you, but right now I sure as hell scare myself."

Closing the slim gap between them, Grant crushed her lips to his. Her soft hands slipped around to grip the back of his neck, her fingers threading through his hair.

Why didn't she listen? He wanted her, more than any other woman before. If she'd just gone back to her room... Granted, he'd given her about a minute's warning, but damn, she was here in his house and barely dressed in the middle of the night. And he had all these emotions whirling around. This was so much more than lust, and it was so much more than sex that he wanted from her.

But damn it, he couldn't let himself get too personally involved.

Grant tried to deepen the kiss, but she beat him to it. He wanted to apply more pressure, but again she was ahead of him.

Obviously, she wasn't scared of the desperation in his touch, and she sure as hell wasn't scared of the warning he'd issued to her.

On one hand he was thrilled she hadn't gone back to her room, but on the other he worried he wouldn't be able to stop. The need for her clawed at him, consumed him.

Tearing his mouth from hers, he kissed a path down her throat. Her body arched into his as she groaned, giving him another reason to progress. When his fingers found the hem of the T-shirt, he slid his hands up beneath the cotton, finding soft, smooth skin and satiny panties.

He dipped one fingertip inside the snug elastic, needing more, silently questioning where the boundaries were.

A soft cry came from her lips as Grant lifted his mouth away. Resting his forehead against hers, he ran his fingers over her, nearly falling to his knees when her hips bumped against his hand.

With that silent invitation, he eased into her warmth, taking every bit of passion she was allowing. The fine line of control had snapped the moment she'd come to him, wanting to save him from himself. He couldn't be saved, but he could give pleasure, and right now that's all he had in him.

"Grant."

Her whispered plea had him claiming her mouth once again as his hand continued to pleasure her. She gripped his shoulders and her body jerked.

"Let go, Tessa," he all but growled against her lips.

And as if she'd been holding on to that same thin line of

control, her body stilled against his and she cried out, her fingernails biting into the bare flesh of his shoulders.

With her head thrown back against the door frame, her
eyes squeezed tight and her mouth parted, she looked every
bit the vixen he knew he could uncover.

When he removed his hand and stepped closer to slide his
arms around her, he felt Tessa's entire body tremble, out of
arousal or fear, he wasn't sure. She was an innocent, and he
had her backed against a door frame like a horny teen who
couldn't control himself. And he'd just taken a portion of her
passion and used it, technically, to make himself feel better.
She'd gotten too close to his hidden shame, and he'd opted to
turn the tables, so to speak, and take what he wanted. Okay,
not all he wanted, but enough that he knew he was a jerk.

So he stepped back.

Panting, her lips still moist and swollen from his touch,
Tessa didn't look like a virgin, and he wanted her even more.
Wanted her in his bed, spread all around him, so he could
show her just how good they'd be together. But he also had
to be realistic and not just a selfish ass.

"Go back to bed."

"Grant." She started to reach for him and he stepped back
again, ignoring the flash of hurt in her eyes.

"Go, Tessa, before I ignore your innocence and take what
I truly want."

A lone tear slid down her cheek as she blinked, then turned
and walked quietly back to the guest room. Grant groaned and
leaned against the door frame.

That damn tear was like a knife straight to his heart. He
hadn't meant to hurt her, but if he'd taken what she was offering, she'd be even more hurt in the long run.

A woman like Tessa wanted more out of a man than just a
fling. She wanted marriage, a family. And he wanted those
things, too, but not in this world she lived in.

He'd kept the hurt and guilt in a separate compartment in

his heart for so long, but being around Tessa allowed each and every emotion to flood to the surface.

He truly thought he could keep his mind focused on work, had convinced himself he was ready to take on a film that would make him face his demons.

But after today's events, he knew he'd only been lying to himself.

In a few months he'd be leaving, and as much as he wanted Tessa, he knew even if they came to mean more to each other, neither of them would give up the life they so loved.

So he needed to keep his damn hands and lips off her, because she was getting harder and harder to resist. No matter how much he was coming to care for her, giving up what he'd worked for wasn't an option. He wouldn't give up his life in L.A. He'd worked too hard for his career.

Besides, he had run fast and far from the world of horses years ago.

Filming that world was one thing, but living in it would be pure hell. Especially now that he knew exactly what it felt like to have Tessa come apart.

Grant clenched his hand and slammed it against the doorjamb. How the hell did he undo that mental image? How did he expect to work with her and not want her even more?

When Grant woke the next morning, Tessa was gone and there was no sign she'd ever been there. Nothing less than what he deserved after his adolescent behavior.

He walked by her room, noting the perfectly made bed. Everything was back to the way it had been before she'd spent the night.

Grant walked into the room and spotted the T-shirt she'd slept in. It was neatly folded and lying atop the antique trunk at the end of the bed.

And because he was all alone, he lifted the garment to his face and inhaled her sweet scent.

He'd had his hands on her last night, had her trembling beneath him. She could've been his in every way.

But at what cost?

That damn clause prevented him from getting too involved, though he'd probably already crossed that line when he'd been feeling her bare chest and had slipped his hand inside her damp panties. But he knew Tessa would keep their secret rendezvous to herself.

Clause aside, if he'd slept with her, she would've regretted it, and the last thing he wanted her to see when she looked at him was regret. Hurt he could handle, regret...not so much.

He was still going to be leaving, and she deserved so much more than sex from a man who was only passing through.

Today he'd be talking with Damon and Cassie. Thankfully, he could avoid Tessa, and they both could take time to figure out what the hell was going on between them.

Lust, yes. Desire, most definitely. But was there more, only he couldn't put a definite name on it? The thought worried him, because he had a feeling he could want more with her, but couldn't let himself face all the pain and regret he'd fought so hard to keep away. And he couldn't risk getting back into a lifestyle he'd run so fast and far from.

There was a reason he hadn't visited his sister and saw his parents only when they came to him. He just couldn't tackle all the crippling emotions that always seemed to chase him.

Grant made his way to the main house and entered through the back door. After he'd been here for over a week, Damon had insisted Grant quit knocking and just walk in.

When he stepped into the kitchen, the sweet aroma of cinnamon rolls assaulted him. A beautiful, middle-aged woman with a cap of short silver hair was bustling around the room and humming. Grant cleared his throat so he didn't scare her.

She turned and smiled. "Good morning, Mr. Carter."

"Morning," he replied. "I'm supposed to meet Damon."

"Oh, he'll be down shortly." She picked up the plate of

gooey rolls and extended it toward him over top the granite island. "Fresh rolls from the oven. Would you like one?"

"I can't turn down anything that smells this good," he told her, reaching for a warm pastry.

"I'm Linda, by the way." She pulled out a small saucer and set it in front of him, along with a napkin. "Coffee?"

"Please. Black."

Soon he was in breakfast heaven. Homemade cinnamon rolls and coffee. He could so get used to this film set. Some he'd worked on had been out in the desert; a few had been in a jungle with no indoor plumbing. But this estate? Yeah, Grant could get used to these amenities...and he wasn't just thinking of the food.

"I'm happy to see someone sit and actually enjoy my cooking while it's hot," Linda told him. "Cassie rarely shows up because she's busy with Emily, and Tessa is too worried about keeping her weight as a jockey. Damon usually eats, but it's grabbing and heading out the door."

"And do you cook every morning, anyway?" Grant asked, sipping the steaming coffee.

"Every morning without fail. One of these days the family may decide to all come in and actually use that dining room." She smiled. "They're just too busy, if you ask me."

"Well, I have good news. Next week more of my crew will be arriving. You're in luck. They like to eat."

Linda laughed. "Well, then. Looks like I need to make a trip to the store and throw together some menus."

Grant polished off the roll and eased back in his chair, in no hurry to leave his present company. He had a feeling this woman might know things about this family that many others didn't.

"How long have you worked here?" he asked.

Linda placed her palms on the edge of the island. "This summer will be fifteen years."

Perfect.

"So you knew the late Mrs. Barrington?"

Linda nodded. "I did. She was a beautiful woman. Her girls most definitely take after her. That vibrant red hair, those bright blue eyes. A rare mix, but the Barrington women have a special mark of beauty."

"Was there ever any rivalry between Tessa and Cassie? Cassie seems very content to stay behind the scenes and be the trainer. Has that always been the case?"

"Cassie has always been a bit shy, but she'd do anything for anyone and sacrifice her own happiness to make others happy." Linda paused before going on. "I dare to say that's how she ended up with Emily's father, that arrogant prick. Pardon my language."

Grant smiled. "I'm getting a vibe that Cassie's ex-husband isn't liked around here very much."

"He's not liked at all. How could you leave a woman when she's just delivered your child? I ask you. He's no man, he's a selfish coward."

"I completely agree," Grant replied. "What about Tessa? What can you tell me about her?"

Linda smiled again, her eyes softening. "Sweet Tessa. She wants to be the best at everything, and she'll push herself until she becomes that way. I've never seen anyone more in competition with themselves than she is. To be honest, after her mama died, she completely submersed herself in the horses. She loved them before and competed heavily, but she had a life. Now she's in those stables all day and sometimes all night."

Not last night. Last night she'd been trembling beneath his hands, silently begging for things she couldn't possibly be ready for.

"I've heard her ex isn't too popular around here, either," Grant said, mentally moving on from last night's interludes.

Linda rolled her eyes and grabbed a pot holder as she made her way to the stove built into the wall. "That man wanted Tessa for two reasons—her name and her money. And then..."

Grant waited while she pulled another pan from the oven,

but when she didn't continue he rested his elbows on the counter and asked, "Then what?"

Shaking her head, Linda turned back toward him. "I'd best not say. You'll have to talk to Tessa."

"Did she love him?"

The woman smiled, cocked her head to the side. "I'm thinking I like where this line of questioning is going."

"It's all pertinent to the film."

She laughed. "That may be, but it's also important to you on a personal level, yes?"

"I'm not here for personal reasons," he replied.

No matter what was or wasn't happening between him and Tessa, he couldn't let anything slip. That clause hung over his head, and if he and Tessa decided to…whatever, then that would be in private and kept between them. Period. He had no other option if he wanted to take his career to the next level. And he needed this film and Russo Entertainment to get him there.

Some might say advancing his career was just another leg of this race he ran to stay as far away from his family and past life as possible. Grant liked to believe he was just securing his future.

"Grant."

He turned and came to his feet when Tessa's father stepped into the room. "Morning, Damon."

"Hope you weren't waiting too long."

"Not at all," Grant replied. "A cinnamon roll, coffee and wonderful company is never a bad thing."

Damon smiled and reached for a roll. "Linda's specialty. She's a whiz in the kitchen."

"Not that anyone in this family sticks around long enough to really enjoy my talents," she muttered with a slight grin.

"Are you ready to get started?" Damon asked. "I've arranged a tee time for ten o'clock."

"We're golfing?" Grant asked.

"I am. You can play caddie if you want."

Grant laughed. "I suck at golf, but let me run to the cottage and change, and I'll be back."

"I'll be here."

Grant rushed back to his house, barely glancing toward the stables, because he feared he'd see Tessa and that hurt in her eyes again. Female laughter rippled from the open doors and his heart flipped. She was in there with her sister, and they were fine. She probably hadn't given him another thought.

So while he was on the golf course with her father today, Grant would try his damnedest to not let her consume his every single thought.

Eleven

Tessa ignored the buzzing of her phone and pulled Don Pedro out of his stall. No way in hell was she answering, or even acknowledging another text from Aaron. What the hell was he thinking, texting her? He'd also called, but thankfully, she'd missed that and he hadn't left a voice mail.

Stupid jerk. Did he honestly think she'd want to have any contact with him after what he'd put her through?

She had the Arkansas Derby in a few days, and she had to qualify to move on to Kentucky. And she would qualify, as soon as she got distractions out of her life. Aaron would not be a distraction because she refused to allow him the mind space.

But there was another man, a more dangerous man, consuming her thoughts. Even though she'd tried all morning, she couldn't exorcise him from her mind.

Unfortunately she could still feel Grant's hands on her body, his lips on hers, the strength of him pressing her against the door. The way he'd forced her to relinquish control and completely come apart.

She had so many emotions swirling around in her, she didn't know where to put them all. On one hand she wanted more. She wanted to know how else Grant and she could pleasure each other, because she had a feeling she'd gotten only a meager sampling.

On the other hand she was embarrassed for her actions. She'd come to console him, and ended up practically clawing him and writhing in his arms.

And she was still tingling from the experience.

Now he wasn't just in all her thoughts, he was nowhere near her and still causing goose bumps to pop up.

"Everything okay?" Cassie asked, stepping into the stable from the ring. "You seem distracted."

"Aaron has been texting me."

No way could Tessa explain what she'd experienced last night...or hadn't experienced, since Grant put on the brakes. She'd wanted him, would've probably given in to her desires, but he'd given her an orgasm and sent her back to bed. What was that? The adult equivalent to milk and cookies? Why did he call the shots?

"What does he want?" Cassie asked, sliding her hands into her pockets.

Pulling herself back to the present, Tessa shrugged. "I have no idea. He's just asked if we can talk. I refuse to answer him."

"Jerk," Cassie muttered. "Well, we need to get going, because I'm supposed to meet with Grant this afternoon."

Tessa stilled. "What for?"

"He wanted to interview me and ask questions about my perspective regarding the movie. He's meeting with Dad this morning."

Tessa's grip on the reins tightened. She wondered what he thought about discovering her gone this morning. There was no way she could wake up and see his face, not after their raw emotional—and physical—connection last night.

"Well, this is interesting," her sister said, a smile spreading across her face. "Has a certain producer caught your eye?"

Tessa laughed. "More like I've caught his."

"Even better," Cassie squealed, clasping her hands together. "You can't keep things like this from me."

Leading Don Pedro toward the ring, Tessa fell into step beside her. "I don't even know what there is to tell," she began. "He's made it clear he's attracted to me, but I don't have time for this, and we're so different.... I can't even name all the reasons."

"What's the main one?"

Tessa squinted against the bright spring sun. "His life is in the city. He's not a dirt-and-boots type of man."

"So? A sexy guy like Grant can be anything he wants. What else bothers you?"

"Our age. He's ten years older than me."

Cassie sighed. "You mean he's experienced?"

"Well, there's that, but he's just… I don't know. Out of my league."

Cassie gripped her arm and shook her. "Don't ever say things like that. Nobody is out of your league. If Grant is interested, why not see what happens? Age won't matter, and as far as him being a city boy, that's just geography. Unless you're not interested in him."

"I'd have to be dead not to notice him on a physical level, but when he kisses me—"

"Wait," Cassie interrupted, holding up her hand. "Kisses? As in plural? Why didn't you start there when I asked about him? Why start with all that's wrong instead of what's putting that dreamy smile on your face?"

"Because I'm scared," Tessa said honestly. "I want him too much and I just… I'm afraid to give in."

"Mama made us promise to hold out for love. I truly loved Em's dad, even though he didn't love me. I still do in some ways, even though he's gone." Cassie shook her head and smiled. "I've never seen you even question putting aside your fears for a man. That should tell you something, Tess."

Nodding, she returned her sister's grin. "I know. But I need time to think, and I can't do that and work on qualifying, too. So, let's get our day started."

"Fine, but this conversation is far from over."

Tessa laughed. "I had a feeling you'd say that."

Grant's meeting with Damon was insightful. They'd talked quite a bit already, but today Grant was able to get more personal, detailed information from the man. They'd gone over the script with a finer lens, as well.

He wanted Damon to have a hands-on experience. As co-producer, Grant wished to showcase not only the racing legend, but the man behind the Barrington dynasty.

And now Grant was headed to Cassie's cottage to talk to the shiest Barrington sister. He was very interested in getting her angle on being not only Damon's daughter and growing up with a famous father, but also as a trainer for the mogul.

Grant had barely knocked on Cassie's door before she answered it. "Hey, come on in."

He stepped over the threshold, taking in the spacious cottage that mimicked his. Of course, his wasn't littered with a Pack 'N Play, a high chair and various kid toys.

"Emily is lying down for her afternoon nap," she told him, closing the door behind him. "We should have a few uninterrupted hours."

She gestured for him to have a seat on the floral sofa. "Can I get you a drink?"

"I'm good, thanks."

Cassie took a seat at the other end of the couch. With a sigh, she propped her feet on the coffee table and offered him a smile. "I'm really excited about this film, Grant."

Easing into the cushions, he nodded. "I'm pretty anxious to get things going. Once my crew arrives, this place won't be the same for a few months."

Cassie shrugged. "It's the busiest time of the year for us, but we'll be here and gone with the upcoming races. So at times we'll all be tripping over each other and other times you'll have the place to yourself."

"I promise we will all work around your and Tessa's training. It was written into the contract, but I wanted you to hear it from me as well, so you didn't worry."

"I appreciate that." She eased an arm along the back of the couch and pinned him with her blue eyes. "Should we talk about you and my sister now or after you interview me for the film?"

Grant paused for a second, because not many things in this life surprised him, but then he laughed. "And what is it you'd like to know that she hasn't already told you?"

"I'd like to know if you're toying with her or if you're genuinely interested."

"Anything we have going on is really between Tessa and myself," he told her.

"Of course it is, but you need to understand who you're dealing with." Cassie slid her hair behind her ear and paused, as if to choose the right words. "Tessa has never made time for herself for anything. Dating especially. She's gone on dates, don't get me wrong, but she never dates for any length of time because the guys normally can't handle her love and dedication to her career."

Love and dedication to a career? She was speaking his language.

"She's had one very serious relationship and that ended recently," Cassie went on. "I won't get into details, because she'd kill me, but he used her. He'd put a ring on her finger and taken that as his green light to make her his mat to walk on."

Grant wouldn't mind meeting this jerk. Perhaps meeting him with a swift punch to the face.

"She's got major trust issues," Cassie told him. "Not only that, he was a big-time city slicker. So if you're seriously pursuing her, you have your work cut out for you."

"There's a clause in my contract that prevents me from fraternizing with crew members on location," he informed her. "And technically, Tessa would fall into that category, since we're working with her. So everything you think you know needs to be kept to yourself."

Cassie nodded. "Understood. But keep in mind, my sister doesn't deserve to be kept a secret, or only brought out when it's convenient for you."

"Are you warning me away?" he asked, knowing every

word she said was true. He just hated how she painted the accurate picture.

She tilted her head. "Not at all. I actually think Tessa needs a little distraction in her life. She needs to have fun, especially with this being the most stressful time for her. I just wanted you to be aware of how fragile she is, even though she tries to put up this tough persona."

He had a quick flash of Tessa being thrown from the horse, of trembling beneath his touch....

"I'm aware of how fragile she is," he said. "And I'm not backing down."

Cassie's smile widened. "Good. Now, what do you want to ask me about my childhood and my father?"

Twelve

"You can do this, baby girl."

Tessa stared down at her father, who patted her leg. The Arkansas Derby was about to start, and this intensity just beforehand was the moment she loved. That feeling before every race. The thrill of nerves swirling through her belly, the cheering crowd, the anticipation of thundering hooves against the hard dirt.

God, she loved her job.

"This is a cakewalk for you, Tess," her sister said. "You ready?"

Tessa nodded. "Let's do this."

Cassie led Don Pedro, and Damon walked by her side. Tessa knew Grant was around, but thankfully, he'd made himself scarce since the incident in the guesthouse a few days ago.

Perhaps he'd decided she wasn't worth the trouble. If that was the case, fine. At least she knew up front and not after her heart got too involved. But she had a feeling he was giving her room to come to grips with what had happened...or he was battling his own issues. Either way, Tessa was pleased with the space he'd given her.

The sun was bright in the sky, promising a beautiful day, and Tessa couldn't wait to celebrate. That attitude wasn't cocky, just positive thinking, which she'd learned to do long ago in this business.

A trail of riders made their way to the starting gate. A variety of colors from the jockeys' shirts and horse blankets added another layer of beauty to the sport. There wasn't one aspect of racing that Tessa didn't love, didn't embrace.

Her own light blue shirt with a bright green star and a diagonal white stripe across her torso and one sleeve had been her mother's design, and Tessa wore the jersey proudly with each race, feeling as if her mother was right there with her every time.

Once she and Don Pedro were in position, Damon and Cassie left her and Tessa took in a deep breath. All the training, all the countless hours always came down to just a few precious minutes.

She leaned down, patting her Thoroughbred's neck, and whispered, "We've got this, don't we, Don Pedro?"

In no time the signal was issued and Tessa readied herself for the gate to move, allowing her the freedom she needed to take a qualifying position.

Adrenaline pumped through her veins, and she gripped the reins, ready to take the first step in making her mark as another Barrington champion.

Grant couldn't help but cheer when the official results came in and Tessa qualified. She not only qualified, she came in first. Damn, but she was impressive to watch on that track.

He'd never been so nervous in all his life as he was in those moments before the gate lifted. Now he wanted to go to her, wanted to congratulate her. But he wouldn't be able to resist hugging her, kissing her.

He had to keep himself in check, though. Congratulations were one thing, but anything else in public could cost him everything.

Grant made his way to the stable, only to find Tessa surrounded by reporters and family. Slipping out his notepad and pen, he started scribbling. He'd been taking notes the entire day, on everything from the camaraderie of the jockeys to the excitement in the stands.

Tessa pulled off her matching blue helmet and wiped her

forehead as she smiled for one of the cameras. She was stunning. Her beauty radiated through her smile, and her love of the horses, of the sport, came shining through in ways words never could express.

Grant moved away, knowing anything he wanted to say to Tessa could wait until they were alone. As he turned to make his way back through the crowd, his phone rang.

Moving over to the far side, where there was less commotion, or as little as he could get, considering he was near the grandstands, he pulled his cell from his dress pants and glanced at the caller ID before answering.

"Hey, Dad."

"Grant," his father's voice boomed. "Haven't heard from you for a few weeks. How are things going?"

"Really well." He continued to move away from the crowd, heading toward the end of the stands. "I'm actually at a race right now."

"Oh, damn. I'm sorry, son. I never know when it's a good time to call."

"No problem. If I can't talk, I just won't answer. Is everything okay?"

"Fine." His father sighed. "To be honest, your mother is worried about you."

Grant turned his back to the sun and slid his free hand into his pants pocket. "Dad—"

"Now just listen," he interrupted. "I know you're going to say you're fine. I know you'll tell me there's nothing to worry about, but that's why I'm calling and not your mother. I'll tell her anything to give her peace of mind, but I want you to be truthful with me. Is this project harder than you thought?"

"The film itself won't start for another two weeks, so it's been pretty easy so far."

"You know I'm not talking about the actual film, son. How are you holding up working around the horses?"

Yeah, unfortunately Grant knew exactly what his father

had been referring to, but he'd tried to dodge it…just as he'd been dodging this topic for years.

"Honestly, it's hard, but not unbearable."

"Do you think you'll be able to stick it out?"

For the chance at starting his own production company? Hell yeah, he'd stick it out. Besides, this was the biggest film he'd ever worked on, and there was no way he'd let some minor insecurity form a roadblock on his path to being even more successful.

He'd originally taken on this film because so many key players were involved, and he wanted every layer of career achievement possible.

But he hadn't planned on Tessa. Hadn't expected to be blindsided by a feisty, yet innocent vixen who made him face his fears…and his feelings.

"I'll be fine," he told his dad. "So now you can tell Mom I am doing great and you won't be lying."

"When do you think we'll be able to see you?"

Grant smiled at an elderly couple that walked by. "I'm not sure. I'll be on location for a couple of months at least. I may be able to take a brief break right after that."

"Well, there's another reason for my call."

Grant knew it. He'd been waiting on this "other reason." Spotting a bench along a stone retaining wall, he made his way over and took a seat. He had a sinking feeling he'd need to be sitting when his father asked the next question.

"Since you're moving on and making progress," his dad continued, "your mother and I would like it if you would come visit when you're done filming. Melanie would like to see you."

Grant closed his eyes, waiting for that stab of guilt and angst that always accompanied his sister's name. He knew Melanie had asked to see him over the years, but he just couldn't. And he wouldn't put her through trying to be kind to him. How the hell could she even stand to say his name, let alone be in the same room with him? He'd nearly killed her…

and from the way she was living, he might as well have. He'd murdered her dreams, her promising future.

"I don't think that's a good idea, Dad."

His father sighed. "You can't avoid her forever, and you can't avoid the issue."

Oh, he could, and he had been for several years. Grant believed he was doing the best thing, letting his sister live without seeing him and being reminded of how he'd stolen the life she'd so loved.

In all honesty he wanted to see her. As twins, they shared a special bond. But he worried that she'd only be reminded of how he'd physically destroyed her.

Even though he hadn't seen her, he always asked about her, and never missed sending her a Christmas or birthday present.

Wow. What a coward's way out.

But in some ironic, twisted way, he was making this film as a tribute to her. A small gesture, considering, but he couldn't turn back time and reverse the damage he'd done.

"When I'm done filming, I'll fly you and Mom out to see me," he offered.

"We always come to you," his father said. "And not that we don't love seeing where you live and work, but you need to come home, son. It's been long enough."

No, it hadn't. Because Grant knew if he went back home and saw the stables, saw the old farmhouse, saw Melanie, he'd be imprisoned by that damn nightmare he'd worked like hell to stay out of.

He'd actually hoped taking on this film would help him conquer those demons once and for all. Conquer them so much that he could return home on his own terms, without the begging and pleading from his parents.

"Listen, Dad, I'll call you in a few days. Tell Mom I'm fine and I'd love to see you in L.A. when I'm done filming."

He extended his love and disconnected before his father's stern tone could kick in. Even though Grant was an adult, he still respected his parents and didn't want to disappoint them, but he couldn't go home.

It had taken him a good amount of time to be able to face even them, let alone his twin sister.

He'd left home only months after the accident and hadn't looked back since. He'd needed the polar opposite of that small farm community he'd grown up in. L.A. was as far away and as opposite as he could get.

So, no, when this film wrapped up, he would not be returning to Kentucky to his hometown.

Late that evening, when Grant knew everyone was either asleep or in for the night, he sneaked down the hall of the hotel to Tessa's room and tapped lightly.

He hadn't seen her alone since the night at his cottage. He missed her, missed talking to her.

How had something as common as sexual attraction turned into so much more?

The hotel door cracked slightly as she peered out, but when she recognized him, she pulled it open farther.

"Grant. What are you doing here?"

He took in her hair, slicked back into a low bun, but it was wet, so he knew she'd showered. The leggings and long-sleeved T-shirt she'd donned fit her petite, curvy body beautifully. The woman was never rumpled or disheveled. Ever.

"Can I come in?"

Without a word, she stepped back. To torture himself or to give her something to think about, he brushed against her on his way through the door, and appreciated the swift intake of breath she rewarded him with.

He'd been wandering around for most of the evening. He'd had dinner alone, looking over fresh notes about the race, the atmosphere, comparing them to old ones, emailing Bronson and Anthony. And then he'd been stewing over his father's call.

But he hadn't seen Tessa for...too long.

"You did amazing today," he told her, raking his eyes over her.

She closed the door, leaned back against it and smiled. "Thank you. It's a relief to have today over with, but now the work and pressure really begin. But this is the part I love. The buildup, the anticipation."

"Take this win and leave the rest for tomorrow," he told her.

He glanced around the neat space, noting the perfectly made king-size bed, the single suitcase on the stand.

"I didn't want to interrupt after the race. You had quite the press surrounding you." Her fresh-from-the-shower scent and those hip-hugging leggings were killing him. "I had to tell you congratulations."

Tessa's smile widened. "Thanks. That means a lot to me."

Pushing away from the door, she moved through an open doorway to a small living area. When she sank onto the floral sofa, she gestured toward the other end. "Have a seat."

He sat down on the edge of the couch, rested his elbows on his knees and leaned forward. "So, we go back to Stony Ridge tomorrow?"

"Yeah. More training awaits," she told him, tucking a bare foot up onto the couch. "Did you get more useful information today?"

"I did. I've touched base with Bronson and Anthony, and we're excited for next week, when they arrive."

Tessa stared at him, her gaze never wavering from his. "Want to tell me what's wrong? I know you came to congratulate me, but there's more."

How did she know? She barely knew him, and here she was, so in tune with his emotions, his body language. They were all alone, yet instead of any seducing or flirting, she'd picked up on his emotional state. What was he, a damn woman?

She'd gotten so far beneath his skin, he couldn't hide anything from her. Especially after she'd witnessed his raw emotions the other night.

"Long day," he told her. "I didn't mean to interrupt you

if you were getting ready for bed. I just didn't want to come by earlier when you were busy, and then I was sidetracked."

By the haunting words of my father's call, and so many damn emotions.

"You've avoided me," she told him. "For two days, you've talked to everyone but me."

"I'm working," he retorted, even though he knew where she was going with this. So he beat her to it. "Besides, you were gone the other morning when I got up, so I assumed you were uncomfortable. I wanted to give you space."

"You were angry." Tessa traced her finger over a small pink flower on the cushion and shrugged. "Seemed like you were hiding."

Angry, no. Fighting to earn her trust before taking things to the next level, yes. He'd never worried about getting to know a woman, learning all about her and actually caring for her before taking her to bed. Tessa had woken something in him, something even more primal.

"I don't hide from anything," he protested. "Especially a woman."

Her eyes came up and met his. "No? You've made a point to be in my business every day for five days, and the last two you vanish."

Grant gritted his teeth. "I was working."

"Me, too. So, do you want to talk about it?"

"What?"

She flattened her hand, smacking the cushion between them. "You have nightmares you refuse to face. Or we could discuss the fact that had you not stopped the other night, I would've given myself to you."

Silence settled between them, joining the already crackling sexual tension.

Her eyes narrowed. "Pick one."

Grant came to his feet, resting his hands on his hips. "Fine. Why were you ready to throw away your virginity on me the other night? You've held on to it this long, why not wait for someone who might actually stick around? Someone who is more compatible with you? Because, as you've established, we're too different."

For the first time since he'd stepped foot inside her room, he saw doubt flash across her face. Good. He wanted to make her think, make her really want him. Because he wanted her with a force he could barely control.

"We are different, Slick." Her blue eyes traveled up the length of him as she tilted her head and smirked. "And maybe you were right, stopping the other night."

"I was." Hard as it had been to put the brakes on, he'd known the decision was the right one, and he was the only one who'd been thinking beyond that point. But they would get there...when they were both ready.

Tessa came to her feet, crossed her arms over her chest and sighed. "I know we're different. I know all the reasons we shouldn't be together intimately, but there's a part of me that doesn't care. A part of me that just wants to let you do anything you want."

Grant had to really fight himself to stand still, to let her speak. But her words—her honest, raw words—were killing him.

"You do things to me," she went on. "The way I feel when I'm with you is...different. That may only be one-sided, but I'm finding the attraction harder and harder to fight."

No, this spark of something beyond physical was most definitely not one-sided. He'd found it harder than hell to stay away from her for two days, while trying to focus on the job.

"Why are you fighting it?" he asked.

"Because...well, what if I'm a disappointment to you? What if I'm disappointed myself in all of it? I mean, I've gone this long, and if I give in, what if I'm let down?"

Grant's control snapped as he snaked an arm around her waist and pulled her flush against his chest. Her hands came up to his shoulders as she caught herself.

With his lips a breath away from hers, he whispered, "I

guarantee when I get you in my bed, nobody will be disappointed, Tessa."

Her eyes widened. "When? You mean, you don't plan on stopping again?"

"I'm not taking you here," he told her. "I want you to be trembling with want. I want you to think about me, about us, when you're training, and I want your fantasies to override anything else."

"Why?" she whispered.

He nipped at her lips. "Because you're so self-contained, and I can't wait to see you out of control and knowing I caused it."

Her fingertips curled into his shoulders as he slid his mouth over hers. The brief, powerful kiss nearly had him dropping to his knees before her. But he had to remain in control here, because he was damn determined to get her to loosen up.

He tore his mouth from hers and stepped back. "Lock that door behind me, Country, and I'll see you back at Stony Ridge."

Once again, he left her when they both were nearly shaking with desire. But he wanted more than lust, more than just sex. And damned if that didn't scare the hell out of him.

Thirteen

Things were starting to progress at Stony Ridge. Trailers were set up for the actors and other producers and directors, who should be arriving in just a few days. This film was about to get under way, and for once Tessa was glad.

Now maybe Grant would have other things to do besides tempt her, tease her, then walk away. How dare he do that to her twice? What game was he playing?

She might be a virgin, but she wasn't that naive. He wanted her, yet he kept denying himself. Did he think he was being gallant? Chivalrous? Well, in her opinion he was being a player, and she would put a stop to that as soon as her training for the day was over.

She'd had enough of being pulled around. And honestly, she cared for him and knew he cared for her, or he would've already taken her or moved on. Grant had self-control, and he was holding on to every last shred for her.

Well, enough was enough. Tessa wanted him, and she would be the one to decide what was best for her body…not him.

She leaned down, patted Don Pedro and set out at a trot. Today she'd keep it easy, especially since Cassie had to take Emily to the doctor for shots.

"Care if I ride with you?"

Tessa turned to see her father coming from the stables, leading Cassie's newest problem child, Macduff.

"Not at all. You sure you want to get on him?"

Damon shrugged. "He'll be fine. I'm bigger than you, so you were easier to buck. And Cassie's been working with him."

Tessa nodded. "Then saddle up and let's go."

She waited, actually finding herself eager to ride with her father. So much in life got in the way of their time together. Between her training and preparing for the movie, Tessa figured this would be the last time for quite a while that they would have alone, with no added pressure.

She gripped the reins and fell in behind her dad. When he set out toward the back of the estate, she kicked her horse into gear and eased up beside him. She knew exactly where he was heading.

The early-morning sun beat down, promising another beautiful, yet unpredictable spring day. As always, she'd checked the forecast when she'd woken, and seen possible thunderstorms later in the afternoon.

"Won't be long, this place will be overrun with famous actors and the threat of paparazzi," her dad told her as he took in the new on-site trailers.

"I hope whatever security they have will be able to keep the crazies away." Tessa hated the thought of strangers around her horses. "I just hope they respect my privacy."

Damon laughed. "You may find you like the behind-the-scenes view. If not, you can always hide over at your house. No one will come there."

"Not unless it's reporters or crazed fans," she muttered as they passed the last of the trailers.

Damon laughed. "We have security for your property, too."

Tessa smiled, but her eyes were on the man talking to some workers who'd brought the trailers. Grant had on well-worn jeans, aviator sunglasses and a black shirt with the sleeves rolled up his muscular forearms. He might be trying to look as if he belonged in the country, but the man was still polished, still citified and damn sexy. Even his sporty rental car stood out next to the full-size trucks on the estate.

"Your producer is working hard to make sure everything is perfect for his crew," her father commented as they neared the pond.

"He's not my producer," she retorted.

Damon pulled back on his reins at the edge of the water and glanced over. "Honey, I know I'm an old man, and your father to boot, but anyone can see the way you look at him. And, more importantly, the way he looks at you."

Tessa groaned. She did not want to be discussing this with her dad. Cassie was about the only person Tessa ever confided her secrets to. Maybe if their mother had lived...

"I miss her, too," he told her in a low voice. "I know you miss her, especially now. I can tell you're confused, but if you want advice, I'd be happy to give it."

Tessa laughed. "I'm not discussing the birds and the bees with you."

Damon's own robust laughter rippled through the air. "Please, I don't plan on getting that in-depth here. I was talking more about your heart, Tessa."

When she glanced over to him, she saw he was serious. He wanted to offer his thoughts from a parenting standpoint. Considering he was the only parent she had, she valued his opinion and the special bond they had.

"What about it?" she asked, almost afraid of his response.

"Risks have to happen. If you want anything out of life, you have to take a risk. Standing on the sideline, watching as chances go by, will only leave you with regrets."

She swallowed and looked back out onto the glistening pond.

"You take a risk every time you compete," he went on. "You take a risk of getting hurt, of hurting someone else or your horse."

Tessa whipped her head back around. "I never even consider that a possibility."

His smiled warmed her. "Because you've learned to take the risk and lead by faith. You let your heart guide you each time you get on that horse and head toward the finish line. Love is no different."

"I never said anything about love." Even to her, the defense sounded weak. "He just…he confuses me."

"Your mother used to confuse the hell out of me," Damon said with a soft chuckle. "I started asking her out when she was sixteen, and she didn't say yes until she was eighteen. I knew she was the one, but I was older than her, and to be honest, I think that scared her. In some crazy way, she worried she wouldn't measure up to standards I'd set for the woman I wanted."

Tessa swallowed, unable to admit that was one of her main fears. Was it that easy to just let go?

"What worries you about Grant?"

With a shrug, she pulled on the reins when Don Pedro started to shift. "We're so different, Dad. He's not a country boy, but practically drips big city."

"And?"

"What do you mean, and? I hate the city. That was one of the reasons I broke it off with Aaron."

Her father's face turned to stone. "That man isn't even worthy of mentioning, and he is nothing like Grant. Aaron didn't care about you. If he'd looked at you even remotely the way Grant does, then things may have been different. But Aaron was using you and trying to steer you away from your career. Has Grant done any of those things?"

Tessa shook her head and sighed. "He's amazing."

"Well, you're an adult and you make your own decisions, but please, don't get so caught up in racing and this image of a perfect world you've built for yourself that you don't stop to take a risk…and enjoy the benefits."

Tessa closed her eyes, relishing the soft breeze, wondering what risk she should be taking. Maybe admit to Grant that she had developed feelings for him? Go to his cottage tonight and seduce him?

She nearly laughed. She wouldn't know the first thing about seducing a man, and certainly not one as sexy as Grant Carter.

But one thing was for sure. She was done waiting and playing his game.

Grant was completely worn-out. There had been a mix-up with the number of trailers and they were still one short, but after some calls he'd gotten everything straightened out.

He'd sent a text to his coproducers, informing them they were good to go whenever they wanted to come. He figured they'd arrive earlier than stars Max Ford and Lily Beaumont.

The two headliners of the film were going to help him catapult to a whole new level, and Grant could hardly contain himself at the thought of his own production company. Marty had sent an email outlining the prospect, and Grant was glad no one had been around to see him read it, because he'd been smiling like a kid with a new puppy. And he may have read it through twice. Okay, three times.

He had just unbuttoned his shirt and pulled it from his jeans when someone knocked on his door.

Please, don't let it be another issue with the trailers.

When he jerked open the door, Tessa stood there, her hair flying loose around her shoulders. A fitted tank, with a long-sleeved plaid shirt over top, unbuttoned, showcased her flat stomach. Her jeans hugged her hips, and the punch of lust to his gut nearly made his knees give out.

She'd never looked this...relaxed. Seeing that massive amount of red hair dancing about in the wind, he nearly groaned, because he could practically feel it sliding along his bare body.

Which meant she couldn't come inside. The emotional impact she kept hitting him with was targeting closer and closer to his heart.

Grant stepped out onto the porch, pulling the door shut behind him.

"I'm sorry," she told him. "Is this a bad time?"

Her eyes raked over his bare chest and Grant clenched his fists. "No."

Those bright blue eyes darted around, as if she was suddenly insecure about something…or was reconsidering coming here.

"Everything okay?" he asked.

With a sigh, she shook her head. "Actually, no. I can't handle this tension between us anymore."

Damn. She was about to get aggressive, and he wasn't sure he could turn her down if she started showing signs of power and control. He'd witnessed this only in her schedules, never with attraction. And damn if that wasn't a whole new level of sexy. He was already turned on as it was, and his zipper was growing exceedingly tighter.

Taking her hand, he led her off the porch.

"Where are we going?" she asked.

He kept walking, heading toward the back of the estate, away from his cottage and the closest bed. Although he was about to his breaking point, so even the grass was looking pretty inviting right about now.

"Let's go for a walk," he told her. "Things are about to get crazy around here, and maybe I want to just do nothing. Not work and not talk about us. Maybe I just want to walk and hold your hand."

Tessa groaned. "It's going to storm soon," she told him. "And I need to talk about us. I need to know where I stand with you."

Grant kept walking, knowing his silence was driving her insane. But honestly, he had no clue what to say to her. He wanted her, plain and simple, but he really didn't think she was ready, and the last thing he wanted for her was regrets. He wanted so, so much more. But since he couldn't identify those wants, how could he express them to her? Life had been much simpler when this was only sexual attraction.

Tessa's delicate hand remained in his as they walked through the pasture. In the near distance, frogs croaked from the pond. Grant was starting to really settle in here, but he knew in his heart he couldn't get too attached to this place... this woman.

But that didn't stop him from wanting her, from aching for her and waking every night fantasizing about her.

"If you've decided I'm not worth your time, I get that," she finally said.

Grant smiled. He'd known she wouldn't be able to just relax and take a walk. He remained silent, because he also knew she wasn't finished saying whatever was on her mind that had caused her to show up at his cottage.

"I mean, you've had enough time to think about this, and knowing how different we are and how...inexperienced I am, I can totally see why you would want to keep your distance. But what I don't understand is why you kiss me, why you say you want me, yet do nothing about it."

The first fat drops of rain started and he jerked her to a halt, turning her to face him.

"I do nothing about it, Tessa, because I'm filled with nothing but lust. That's not what you need. You need gentle, and I can't guarantee that, either. I want you on a level I've never known. You drive me crazy with an ache that threatens to overtake me."

The skies cut lose as he thrust his hands into her hair and captured her lips. His tongue invaded her mouth, taking her, pleading for her to take him. She gripped his shoulders as the cool drops soaked them. But nothing could make him pull away from her. He'd come to the point where he craved her taste, needed her touch. What the hell would happen if he got her naked, lying against his body?

When she pulled back, glancing up at him with droplets dripping from her lashes, he groaned and took her mouth again. His hands traveled down to her abdomen and gripped the hem of her tank, tugging it up. He needed more...needed whatever she was willing to give. And when this was over, he'd have to be satisfied with what he got.

Tessa's body arched into his, her hips grinding against his erection. He encircled her bare waist with his hands, allowing his pinky fingers to dip below the edge of her jeans.

Never in his life had he craved a woman as he did Tessa. And seeing as how this was new ground for him, he was terrified he'd hurt her.

A clap of thunder tore them apart as lightning lit up the darkening sky. Tessa grabbed his hand, pulling him toward the pond. She was running and laughing as the rain continued to drench them. Even with her hair and clothing plastered to her body, she was stunning as she guided him through the storm.

They circled the pond, and Grant knew exactly where they were seeking shelter: the old cabin nestled in a grove of trees. Tessa led him onto the porch as another thunder and lightning combination filled the evening.

Panting, she leaned against the post and smiled up at him. But as he moved closer, her eyes widened, her smiled faded. He was losing control, and he wondered if he'd ever had it where she was concerned.

"Tessa—"

She covered his lips with one slender fingertip. "Please. Don't stop this again, Grant. I need you. I need this."

He was lost. No way could he say no to her.

This beautiful, precious woman was offering something so rare and special. He wanted to be the one to show her all about passion and desire. He wanted to be everything to her... but all he could be was her lover. No more.

"I can't deny you," he told her, pushing strands of clingy red hair away from her face. "I don't know why I tried. But I admit...I'm scared."

"Of what?"

"This. You. Your first time shouldn't be in a shack in a thunderstorm."

"This shack holds special memories for me. I used to dream here as a little girl. I would daydream about horses and Prince Charming." Tessa reached up, sliding her body against his as she circled his neck with her arms. "My first time can be any-where, as long as it's with you."

He dropped his forehead to hers and whispered, "This may as well be my first time, as nervous as I am right now."

Tessa nipped at his lips. "Then let's get inside and fumble through this together."

Fourteen

Tessa couldn't believe she was doing this.

The old key was hidden above the door frame just like always, and as soon as she opened the door and replaced the key, she reached back for Grant's hand and led him inside.

He closed the door and she turned to him, nearly laughing at the pained expression on his face. He was so utterly beautiful and he was worried...for her. Her heart tripped in her chest and fell. That was it. She'd gone and fallen in love with this man she'd sworn to stay away from, the city slicker who'd invaded her privacy with not much more than a wink and a smile.

"Don't worry about me," she told him. "Do whatever you like."

Grant shook his head. "Funny thing. I don't know what I like anymore. This is all new with you and I want...I want this to be good. But I'm barely hanging on here, Tess."

She smiled, loving that she had this control over such a powerful man. Obviously, she was going to have to take the initiative or they'd be dancing around this sexual tension come Christmas.

With her eyes locked on to his, she peeled off her plaid shirt and let it fall to the ground with a noisy, wet smack. She toed off her boots and tried as gracefully as possible to shimmy out of her wet jeans. Although *shimmy* wasn't the right word— she more or less hopped and grunted until she was finally free. Not the sex appeal she'd been hoping for, but when she glanced at him again, his eyes were on her legs, her nearly transparent tank and her erect nipples. His gaze consumed her, burning her skin.

Praying for courage, Tessa reached for the hem and pulled the tank over her head, tossing it aside and leaving her in her very wet, lacy white thong and matching bra.

"I may have planned a little seduction at your cottage," she admitted, resisting the urge to cross her arms over her chest. "But when you opened the door, I kind of chickened out."

Grant continued to give her a visual sampling, and she wished he'd say something, do something. Her body was trembling with need and an ache she'd never known.

She'd been aroused before, plenty of times, but this time was so different. She feared she'd explode before he ever got his clothes off.

"Slick, if you don't say something, I'm going to have to wrestle myself back into those wet jeans."

He swallowed and took a step forward. "You're beautiful, Tessa. I wish I could go slow, but I'm afraid the second I get my hands on you I'm going to snap."

Feeling suddenly even more powerful, she propped her hands on her hips, proud of the way her chest jutted out. "I'm not glass, Slick. Let's see what you've got."

With a smirk, Grant started undressing at lightning speed, and it was Tessa's turn to stare. Thunder and lightning continued outside, and she had never been more excited to be stranded in the middle of a thunderstorm.

Once he was completely naked, Tessa couldn't keep from gaping. Of course she'd seen a naked man, but had never been with one.

"I'm not sure if I should feel self-conscious or if my ego just got boosted," he told her. "But the way you're looking at me isn't helping my control."

"Maybe I don't want you controlled," she whispered. "Maybe I want you not to hold back, but just take me."

She was playing with fire, and she totally knew it. But she'd waited her whole life for this moment, and she didn't want it to be perfect, to be slow and sensual. She didn't want him to think or analyze. She wanted action, wanted him without worry or rules or restrictions.

Tessa had nothing to compare this moment to, but if she was letting her emotions guide her? Yeah, they were out of control, and there was nothing more she wanted than to be... taken.

Grant moved forward, like a stalker to his prey. Shivers raced one after another through her body. Anticipation and arousal consumed her.

"Last chance, Country. You sure you want me...reckless?"

Tessa couldn't stand not having contact another second. She slid her hands up his damp, bare chest. "I wouldn't have you any other way."

Grant's arms wrapped around her waist, pulled her flush against his taut body, until every single point from her knees to her chest was touching him.

And then his lips were on her. Not on her mouth, but on her neck, trailing down to her breasts. He arched her backward, causing her to grip tight to his bare shoulders.

His assault wasn't unexpected; he'd warned her, after all. But what she hadn't anticipated was how she'd feel, how her body would respond...how the thrill of being taken, consumed, would override any euphoria she'd ever experienced.

Grant cupped her bottom, lifting her against him. He walked toward the old, sheet-covered chaise in the corner of the room and laid her there, his body coming down to cover hers.

The weight of him, the strength of him was so new, yet so welcoming. Instinct had her spreading her legs, allowing him to settle between them.

Grant's hands roamed down the dip in her waist and over her hips. "I want to touch you everywhere, Tessa. But right now, I can hardly wait to be inside you."

Reaching up to stroke the wet hair falling across his forehead, she smiled. "We both want the same thing, then."

"As much as I'm barely holding on here, I have to make sure you're ready."

Her skin tingled, her body ached and she was damn near quivering. If she was any more ready, she could finish this job alone.

Grant eased back, sliding a hand between them to find where she ached most for him. Just that one, simple touch had her hips lifting, her hands gripping his biceps.

"You're so beautiful," he murmured as he stroked her. "So responsive."

Tessa closed her eyes, allowing him to take over, and relishing the moment. As much as she wanted to move faster, she didn't want him to stop whatever his talented hands were doing.

Grant wanted to slide into her, but he couldn't stop pleasuring her with his hand. He wanted this to be solely about her. Her head thrown back, her eyes closed and her panting all brought pleasure to him.

And that right there told him just how special she was. He'd never been a selfish lover, but he'd also never taken the time to pleasure a woman and just watch her, ignoring his own wants, needs.

"Grant, please..."

Yeah, he couldn't deny her, not when she was already begging.

Grant eased back farther as realization dawned on him. "I don't have protection, Tess."

A sweet smile spread across her face. "You're lucky I was coming to seduce you. I have a condom in my jeans."

He shot off her and went in search of her wet jeans.

"Front pocket," she said, laughing.

Grant searched there, pulled it out and ripped it open. Once he was covered, he settled back over her.

When he leaned down to take her lips, Tessa wrapped her legs around his waist. Thunder rumbled so hard, so loud, the windows in the cabin rattled.

As she opened her body, her mouth to him, Grant tried to ignore that tug on his heart. He couldn't get too immersed in this, couldn't invest his emotions. Tessa had come to him, so he wasn't taking anything she wasn't willing to give. They both knew where the other stood. But right now, he didn't care about tomorrow, the film or what was going to happen after the project wrapped up.

All he cared about was Tessa.

With as much ease as he could manage, Grant slid into her, pausing when she gasped for breath.

He tore his mouth from hers. "You okay?"

She nodded, tilting her hips. "Don't stop."

Gritting his teeth, Grant complied. Never before had he been in this position, and he wasn't sure what to do, how to make this perfect for her.

But when Tessa ran her hands over his shoulders, threaded her fingers through his damp hair and started moving those hips, he knew she was needing more than him fumbling his way through this. Who was the virgin here? He was so damn nervous, but Tessa's sweet sighs and pants told him she was more than aroused.

Resting on his forearms, Grant leaned down, capturing her lips as their pace picked up a rhythm that was going to have him out of control in no time.

When her body quickened, he tore his mouth from hers, needing to watch her face. He wasn't disappointed as her muscles clenched, her mouth dropped open, her eyes squeezed shut and she let out the sweetest moan he'd ever heard.

All that wild, red hair spread out around her as she came undone, bowing her back. And that's all it took for Grant to follow her over the edge.

* * *

Tessa was…well…speechless.

How had she missed this experience all these years? She'd put her career, her horses and organized lifestyle all before her own needs. And now that those needs had been met, she would never let them go neglected again.

"I can practically hear you thinking," Grant told her, stroking his hand over her bare arm.

He lay on the chaise, Tessa atop him, their arms and legs tangled, and she had zero desire for this storm to pass. This moment in time was one of the few she wanted to freeze. She wanted to lock this moment in her heart, to hold it tight, because right now, in Grant's strong arms, she felt everything in the entire world was absolutely perfect.

"You're not having regrets, are you?"

Tessa smiled against his chest. "Never. Just enjoying us."

Those stroking fingertips sent shivers over her body. Every touch from this man reached something so deep within her, she feared she'd be ruined for anyone else.

"I've never appreciated being stranded in a thunderstorm," he told her. "But I have to say, this definitely has its perks."

Tessa laughed, making a fist on his chest and propping her chin on top. "I never thought of storms as romantic before, but now I won't see them as any other way."

"I've worked on scenes set in thunderstorms. They're not near as fun as this."

The sun had set, so only occasional flashes of lightning illuminated the cabin, allowing her to get brief glimpses of Grant's killer smile amid dark stubble.

"We can try to make it back," she offered. "I mean, I don't want you to feel like you're stuck."

"I have a beautiful naked woman on top of me. I assure you, even if the weather was sunny and perfect, I'd be in no hurry to leave." He gripped her hips, turning them to align with his. "I don't feel stuck. Lucky, satisfied and relaxed, but not stuck."

Tessa flattened her palm against his strong chest. "I'm glad I waited. I'm glad we met, even if I wasn't a fan of this film."

Grant chuckled. "And how do you feel about the film now?"

"I believe you'll do the best job portraying my family in a positive light. That's what I was most worried about."

When she rested her head against his chest again, Grant's hands slid through her hair, moving it off her back so he could stroke those fingertips up and down again.

"What else worries you?" he asked.

She laughed. "About the film or life in general?"

"You have that many worries, huh?" He kissed her forehead and nudged her legs apart until she straddled him again. "Maybe I should just take your mind off all of them for a while."

She jerked up. "Again? I mean, already? Aren't you...you know, done?"

Grant's rich laughter made her feel like an idiot.

"Hey, cut me some slack, Slick. I'm new here."

His hands encircled her waist. "Oh, you're not new anymore. You're experienced, and now I want you to take complete control. Do what you want."

Her mind raced. Other than what she'd read in books, she really had no idea what to do, because she'd never experienced anything firsthand.

"I only brought one condom," she told him as another bolt of lightning lit up the sky, slashing through the windows. "I wasn't expecting..."

"I've never had sex without protection," he told her. "My last physical was only a couple months ago and I was clean. But it's your call. I'll only do what you're comfortable with."

Tessa bit her lip, wondering what she should do. Her body told her one thing, her mind told her another.

"Well, I know I'm clean, and I've been on birth control for other health reasons."

He tipped his hips slightly and slid his hands up to cup her breasts.

"You're not playing fair," she told him.

"Oh, baby. I'm not playing. I'm taking this very, very seriously."

He wanted her to take control? Fine.

Tessa sank down on him in one slow, easy glide. She smiled as he groaned. More than likely he thought she was being torturous, but in all honesty she wanted to make sure she wasn't too sore. But, hey, if he thought that was sexy…

"Tessa," he all but growled. "Honey, you're killing me."

The endearments he tossed about warmed her. She kept telling herself not to read anything into them, but keeping an emotional distance was downright impossible.

Tessa blocked out any negative thoughts, because right now, she intended to show this city slicker just how country girls liked to be in control.

Fifteen

Tessa jerked with a start, wondering what had actually woken her up. Beneath her, spread out on the chaise, Grant groaned and twitched.

Arms and legs tangled, Tessa tried to sit up, but Grant's hands gripped her shoulders.

"Melanie, stop!" he yelled.

Tessa froze. Melanie? Whoever this woman was, she was causing him nightmares. *Please, don't be a girlfriend. Or worse...a wife.*

"Grant." Tessa tried to break from his hold as she patted the side of his face. "Grant, wake up."

The storm wasn't as violent as earlier, but growls of thunder still filled the night. The occasional lightning was the only thing cutting through the darkness of the cabin.

"I'm so sorry," he cried.

Tessa couldn't stand the anguish ripping from him. So she did the only thing she could think of: she slapped him, hard.

Grant stilled and his eyes flew open. For a moment she couldn't tell if he was truly awake, angry or still living the nightmare.

"Tessa?"

Still naked from lovemaking, she crossed her arms over her chest and eased back. "I'm sorry. I didn't mean to hurt you, but you were having a bad dream."

Grant ran a hand over his face and sighed. "Sorry I woke you."

"Seeing as how this is the second time you've woken me with a nightmare, and this time you yelled out another woman's name, care to tell me what's going on?" she asked, trying to remain calm.

Just because he'd done so didn't mean anything. He was obviously hurting, and Tessa wasn't naive enough to believe he hadn't been with other women before her.

But the fact he'd shouted it out while lying beneath her naked did warrant an explanation, in her opinion.

"Who's Melanie?" she asked, when he still didn't answer.

Grant shifted, obviously trying to get up, so Tessa came to her feet. Apparently the sexy moment was over. In the dark, broken by random flashes of lightning, she scrambled to find her clothes and get into them while Grant did the same.

"Melanie is my sister," he told her after several minutes of silence. "She's my twin."

A wave of relief washed over Tessa. Okay, so she wasn't dealing with the proverbial "other woman."

"Why do you have nightmares about her?"

Grant finished putting on his clothes and walked over to the door, opening it to look out onto the dark night. "Just something that happened in my past. Nothing that has to do with you."

She'd be lying if she didn't admit, at least to herself, that his comment hurt. Why wouldn't he open up to her? Was he that protective of his sister? Something had happened, and from the way his nightmares seemed to consume him, Tessa had a feeling whatever had gone on in his past was extremely traumatic.

"It's pretty dark out," she said, trying to change the subject and not be a clingy woman demanding to know what he was thinking. "We can try to go back, but I don't have a flashlight."

When she stepped up beside him, he wrapped his arm around her waist, tucking her against his side. "You're in such a hurry to leave. I'm going to start thinking you don't like my company."

"Oh, I thoroughly enjoyed your company," she said with a laugh, trying to lighten the intense moment. "I'm just not sure how comfortable either of us will be with nowhere to sleep tonight."

"I was fine with you lying on me. Of course, I'd recommend you lose those clothes you just put on."

Tessa swatted his flat abs. "You have a one-track mind now that I've let you have your wicked way with me."

"Oh, I had a one-track mind all along. I can just be more vocal about it now without offending you."

They listened to the rain, watching as the storm rolled through the night. Tessa would never look at this cabin the same again. This place had a special new meaning to her now. And a whole new meaning to her dreams.

"I hate to bring this up, but no one can find us here," he told her. "I can't let it out that we're sleeping together."

And if the secret nightmares hadn't caused enough hurt, this cold realistic fact sure did. She'd known there was a clause in his contract; he'd mentioned it before. But she hadn't thought it would be an issue. And now that they'd been intimate, she hadn't thought about lying or hiding it.

"I don't mean to make you upset," he added, obviously picking up on her thoughts. "I just can't afford to risk my career."

Wrapping her arm around his waist, she squeezed him tight. "I wouldn't do anything to damage your career. Besides, I don't expect you to keep sneaking out to sleep with me."

Grant turned, taking her by the shoulders and pinning her against the edge of the door. "Well, I expect more than just this, Tessa. Because I can't see you in public doesn't mean I can't come to your house every night, slide into your bed and pleasure you over and over. I've not even begun to explore you, and I'll be damned if another man is going to show you all there is to intimacy."

His matter-of-fact tone thrilled her.

"What if you get caught?" she asked. "Your crew will be

arriving in two days, and security will be tight around my premises and Stony Ridge. Do you plan on teleporting into my bedroom?"

He tipped his hips against hers. "Baby, I'll make it happen, if that's what you want."

Grant nipped at her lips, slid his hands through her hair to tilt her head, allowing him better access.

"Tell me that's what you want," he murmured against her lips. "Say it, Tessa."

God help her, she was drowning, and she had no one to blame but herself. She'd gotten this ball rolling when she'd set out to seduce him earlier, and now she was paying the price.

"Yes," she told him, gripping his hard biceps as his mouth traveled down her neck. "I want you no matter how we have to sneak."

This whole sneaking, lying and hiding scenario went against everything she knew. Her life consisted of schedules, organization and training, but she had a feeling she was going to love this new Tessa that Grant had uncovered.

The idea of sneaking around added an element of excitement and power. She would still have control over the when and where.

The only problem? What would this new Tessa do when the time came for Grant to leave? Because he'd still never said anything about staying.

"Looks like everything is ready to go," said Anthony Price as he admired the trailers and the equipment set up outside the stables. "I'm impressed there were no glitches. There's always a setback."

Bronson laughed. "There's a setback when *you're* in charge. I completely trusted Grant to take care of things."

Grant knew these half brothers felt a sibling rivalry. Of course, it wasn't that long ago that the two had been heated enemies. Then the secret, decades old, revealed the two were indeed both sons of Hollywood's most recognized icon, Olivia Dane.

"I had a few very minor hiccups, but managed to smooth them over before you both arrived," Grant admitted. "I would like to try to get the stable scenes shot either first or last. With Tessa and Cassie training for the Kentucky Derby, we really can't be in their way."

"I agree. We can shoot those first." Bronson looked through the folder he held, shuffling papers. "I'm intrigued about that cabin that's back on the property. I'd like to see it. Not that I don't trust your judgment, I just want to get a feel for it."

Grant smiled. Oh, he'd gotten his own feel for the cottage. And he wouldn't be able to keep a straight face while they were filming any scenes down there.

Not only had he violated the contract by getting involved with someone on the set, he had done the deed on the set itself.

"Max should be arriving tomorrow," Bronson said. "I'd like to get his take on things, as well. We just wrapped up a film together a few months ago, and he added some great insight."

"I worked with Max a few times," Grant replied. "He's one of the best actors I've ever been involved with, and Lily is such a sweetheart, I know this is going to be a major success."

"I agree," Anthony interjected. "I'd like to check out the grounds before everyone arrives, though."

Grant motioned toward the expansive stables. "Right this way."

As the three headed across the wide drive, Tessa flew by on Don Pedro and rounded the corner in the track. Grant couldn't help that his eyes followed, couldn't help his gut clenching at the sight of her as memories of a few nights ago stirred. Memories of a wild thunderstorm, when she'd abandoned everything she'd known. Every fear, every worry and every part of her she'd handed over to him with a trust that still made his knees weak.

"Damn."

Grant turned at the soft curse from Bronson, and found the brothers staring back at him.

"Tell me you didn't," Anthony said.

Grant shrugged. "What?"

"The beauty that just went by on the track," Bronson chimed in. "And I'm not talking about the Thoroughbred."

Grant took another step, hoping the guys would follow and he could face forward without looking them in the eye. "We've spent a good bit of time together. She's my go-to girl for questions and the tours."

"As long as you don't go to her for anything else," Bronson muttered as they neared the open door of the stable. "Marty will have your butt if you pull another stunt like you did with the makeup artist."

Grant laughed. Yeah, he'd never live down the whole makeup artist debacle. "I assure you, I'm not revisiting that time," he stated.

As they passed through the stalls, Grant noted Nash cleaning out Don Pedro's stall, and wondered if Tessa was still having reservations about the scruffy-looking man. To Grant he just seemed like a hard worker. Maybe a bit mysterious, with that long hair and scruffy beard, but he wasn't dirty, he kept to himself and worked harder than anyone else Grant had seen here.

So far Grant's investigator had turned up nothing. Apparently the new groom was just quiet.

He didn't even lift his head when the three men passed by. No, Grant didn't believe the stranger was out to sabotage the Barringtons or the upcoming race.

When Tessa sped by once more, visible through the stable doorway, Grant made a point to keep walking, keep his mouth shut and show no emotion. Damn, this fling might be harder to keep secret than he'd thought.

When they stepped out into the afternoon sunshine, Cassie greeted them.

"Hi, guys." She walked over, all smiles, and extended her

hand. "I'm Cassie Barrington. You must be Bronson and Anthony. We're so excited to have you here."

The brothers shook her hand and offered pleasantries.

"Tessa is just about finished," Cassie commented. "She's been pushing herself today, so I'm making her stop after this set."

Grant grunted. "Is today different from any other day with her self-discipline?"

Cassie laughed, holding her hand up to shield the sun from her eyes. "Not really, but something has been up with her the past two days. Can't figure out what."

Grant knew exactly what had been up with her the past two days. But he totally ignored the questioning looks from Bronson and Anthony. No way in hell was he even mentioning Tessa's name in anything other than a professional way.

The slightest slipup could cost him not only this film, but a future with his own production company.

After being intimate with Tessa, he couldn't help but look at everything from a whole new perspective.

No, he didn't want to lose this film or his credibility. But, more importantly, he didn't want to lose his family. Tessa had helped him see that.

And at some point, he'd have to tackle that heavy burden he'd carried for so long.

"Cassie, if you don't mind introducing Tessa to Anthony and Bronson, I'd appreciate it." God, he was a coward. "I have a phone call I just remembered. Also, your dad wasn't home, so when he gets here could you do those introductions, as well?"

"I'd love to," Cassie replied, oblivious to any turmoil within him. "Do what you need to. Tessa and I can take things from here."

As Grant walked away, he heard Anthony mention the pond and the old cabin. Yeah, Grant couldn't be part of that. One step near that old shack with Tessa around and everyone on set would know. He had never had a problem holding his emotions in check before, but something had stirred in his heart when he'd taken Tessa to bed. Something deep within him had awakened, and he worried that whatever it was would get him into trouble before all was said and done.

Sixteen

Tessa hated that she stared at the clock. Hated that her ex had left two more voice mails today pleading for her to call.

But most of all she hated that she was angry when each hour ticked by and Grant didn't show.

In the past two days, he'd barely been a blip on her radar. Today Anthony and Bronson had arrived, and Cassie had been the one to introduce them.

Her father had immediately swept the young Hollywood hotshots away, and Tessa had no doubt Damon had filled their heads with stories of the past. Stories from the family, from the racing seasons and his victories. The man was proud of all he'd accomplished, as well he should be. He'd not only won the Triple Crown, he'd raised two daughters and kept the family business close. No outside trainers, no outside jockeys. Stony Ridge was definitely a family affair, and definitely unique. Which was what made the Barrington legacy so special and film-worthy.

Tessa had just gotten into her cami and panty set and pulled her comforter back when something pecked on her second-story bedroom window. She crossed the room and eased the curtain aside to see Grant below, tossing pieces of mulch from her landscaping.

Tessa unlocked the window and slid it up. "What are you doing? I have a front and back door, you know."

"Well, I thought you would think this was romantic," he called up to her. "I needed pebbles, but all you had was bark.

Had to make do. But at least it all fell back to where it belongs. You should appreciate that, seeing as how you like organization."

Tessa laughed, rolling her eyes. "I'll go unlock the back door."

A shiver of excitement swept through her. Even though he'd seen every inch of her, she still snagged the short cotton robe off the end of her bed. Belting it as she bounded down the steps, she couldn't help but grin. Grant was nothing if not original.

When she unlocked the door and eased it open, he stepped right in and looked down at her with a wide smile. Only a small accent light in the corner of her kitchen lit up the space.

Tessa didn't usually have men in her house, so the overpowering presence of Grant excited her.

"It's late," she told him. "I was just about to go to bed."

"Sounds like perfect timing on my part."

When she started to turn away, he snagged her wrist, pulled her up against his broad chest and tipped her face back so that she looked him in the eye. "I've missed you," he murmured, a second before his mouth came down to claim hers.

His hands plunged into her hair as he tilted her head. Tessa had no choice but to wrap her arms around his neck and give back. She'd known him only a month, but she already knew the way he tasted, the way he held her so tightly, the way he kissed with passion and power. And she knew that, in those few days she hadn't been with him, she'd missed him.

How the hell would she cope when he left for good?

Grant eased back. "You have no idea how hard it's been for me to keep my distance."

Tessa pulled from his arms and headed out of the kitchen. "Not too hard. You've managed to not even speak to me. Pretty sneaky, having my sister do the introductions."

Footsteps hurried behind her and an arm snaked around her waist, lifting her off the ground. Not that she'd complain about the hard chest she'd fallen back into.

"I couldn't be near you," he all but growled in her ear. "It would take only one look and Bronson and Anthony would know. I can't hide how I feel about you, Tessa. I'm not the actor here."

Smiling into the dark, she clasped her hands over his. "Why don't you come upstairs and show me how you feel? There's no hiding in this house."

Grant swept her up and hooked an arm beneath her knees as he started for the staircase. "I've always wanted to carry a woman up the stairs and into her bed."

Tessa nibbled on his neck, inhaling the fresh aftershave she'd come to crave. "I'm glad I'm your first in something. Levels the playing field somewhat."

He stopped at the landing and looked into her eyes. "Honey, you're a first for me in so many ways."

Tessa wished there was better light, because she wanted to read his expression more clearly. Unfortunately, her bedroom was at the end of the hall and the glow spilling into the hallway a faint one.

"I hope you know I plan on staying awhile," he told her as he strode toward the room.

"I'd like to see you leave," she joked. "I admit I feel a little naughty being so secretive. I only hope no one noticed you sneaking over here."

"Glad I could bring out your inner vixen," he said with a loud smack on her lips. "And I doubt anyone saw me. I dressed in black and I walked."

Tessa jerked back. "You walked?"

Setting her feet on the floor, Grant aligned her body with his. "Yeah. I didn't want to risk anyone seeing my rental car pull in here, and walking makes it easier to dodge security, even though they're not that thick right now, and I actually think there's only one guard on duty tonight."

Tessa framed his stubbled face with her hands. God, she loved the feel of those whiskers beneath her palms. And dressed all in black? This man was the epitome of sexy.

"You went to a lot of trouble to be here," she told him, placing a quick kiss on his lips, then easing back. "I better make it worth your while."

Grant's eyes widened and his nostrils flared as she loosened the belt on her robe and sent the garment fluttering to the floor. She didn't have on the sexiest of pajamas, but this was Tessa. Cotton, simple, natural.

Of course, she'd be naked in seconds anyway, so what did it matter?

"You going to stare all night or start peeling out of your burglar gear?"

His lips tipped in a grin. "You have a smart mouth."

"Of course I do. That's one of my most redeeming qualities."

Grant pulled his long-sleeved T-shirt over his head and tossed it aside. Those glorious muscles, a sprinkling of chest hair and 100 percent raw male stared back at her. And as much as Tessa would love to stand and stare at him all night, she wanted to touch him even more. Wanted to explore him and take her time now that they were on her turf.

She already knew each time being with Grant would make it harder to let him go in the end...and harder to hide her feelings when they were in public.

But he'd shown her a new side of love, without using the words. And for now, she'd embrace the moment.

Tessa put Oliver in the stall and was surprised to see Max Ford already on the set so early. He must've really wanted to be here at the start of the day.

In the two weeks Grant had been sneaking into her bed, they'd gotten closer and developed a routine. But he always crept back out before sunup. She knew he would; he'd told her as much up front. But that didn't stop the thread of hurt that went through her each day she woke up alone.

Somehow the fact that he came and went during the night lessened their relationship. Tessa knew they had something special, but after the past two weeks she felt she was nothing more than a booty call.

At first the sneaking had been fun and flirty, but as the days went on she felt it only cheapened the moments they shared.

After brushing down Oliver, she went to get some feed, but as she turned a corner she hit the hard chest of Nash.

"Excuse me," he said, his voice low.

Tessa stepped back, still leery of the quiet man. "It's okay. I should look where I'm going."

"My fault." He made no motion to move, but propped his hands on his hips. "Lots of action going on today already."

"Yes," she agreed, surprised he'd said more than two words to her. "I imagine it will only get crazier in the coming days. Max is here now, and Lily is due to arrive tomorrow."

"Max Ford is playing your father, right?" the groom asked.

Tessa nodded as she studied him. His beard didn't seem to fit the man. His eyes were bright blue, almost as bright as hers. His hair was a bit long, falling over his ears and collar, but his hands looked very well groomed. Odd how some parts of him appeared flawless and other parts downright unkempt.

"Lily will be playing my mother," Tessa told him.

He seemed to process that as he shifted his feet on the straw-covered floor. "And will this film start before your parents were married?"

"I think so."

"They're covering your dad's personal life as well as his career?"

Tessa had no clue what this line of questioning had to do with anything, but she replied, "Yes. It's all pretty much set around my dad. The rest of the family will be secondary characters, I suppose. We're not nearly as exciting as him, anyway," she said, trying to joke. Only Nash wasn't smiling.

"I need to get some feed," she told him as she maneuvered around him. "Sorry I ran into you."

Before he could ask another bizarre question about the film, she headed down the aisle. At first she'd been skeptical, but Grant hadn't uncovered anything, and Nash's background check had been spotless. So far he'd been a hard worker. Quiet, mysterious, today a bit nosy, but he'd been gentle when caring for the animals and he'd never given any reason to believe he was out to harm anybody.

But Tessa still had that uneasy feeling.

After she'd fed all the horses, her own stomach growled. A few days ago she could've asked Grant to join her for some lunch, but not today. Their time for being out in the open was over…at least until the film wrapped up. But what then? Once the movie was done Grant would return to L.A. and Tessa would remain right here.

This path they'd started down was not going to lead them to a happy place, and she really wished she'd listened to herself in the beginning. But in all honesty, she would've still taken this road with Grant. There was something unique and different about him. He made her feel special, hadn't made her feel as if her morals and her choices were ridiculous. He'd actually respected her more for her decisions in life.

And that's how she knew this was the man her mother had told her to look for. One who didn't laugh at her for her thoughts, dreams or goals. One who encouraged her, cherished her and lifted her up. Who cared for her even after she'd shared her morals and her reasoning.

Tessa stopped just outside the stables and watched as four beautiful males stood in a serious-looking meeting. Grant drew her gaze, but Bronson, Anthony and Max were very nice to look at, as well. They were all happily married, and Tessa wondered how they made that work, as all three men had demanding jobs. From what Tessa had heard, Max was a newlywed and his wife was from the East Coast.

Tessa rolled her eyes. What on earth was she doing, thinking about marriage and long-distance relationships? She and Grant had never discussed anything beyond the filming.

Added to that, she had a race to prepare for. She didn't have time to choose monogrammed towels for nuptials that were taking place only in her head.

When she marched in the back door, Linda was pouring a glass of sweet tea. With a smile, she slid it across the island to Tessa.

"I saw you coming," the elderly woman said. "You looked like you could cool off. I know just from standing in here, looking at the fine man scenery, how heated I was getting."

Tessa laughed. "You're rotten, Linda."

"I'm old, honey. Not dead. And those four men out there are going to have all the women in town begging to be extras on the set."

Tessa took a long, refreshing drink. "Good thing we have added security. Besides, three of those four are married."

"Might as well be all of them," Linda muttered.

Tessa's glass clunked back down on the smooth granite surface. "Don't be shy now. Say what's on your mind."

With a shrug, Linda rested her hands on the edge of the counter. "Just saying the way that man looks at you, he won't care about no other woman sniffing around."

The nerves in Tessa's belly fluttered. How did he look at her? Was it just lustful or was there more? She wanted to know, wanted to sit and gossip, but where would that get her? If she was destined for heartache at the end of this film, there was no point in getting her hopes up now.

"Don't frown, Tessa," Linda told her with a smile. "I know you well enough to know you're already calculating how much time you have left with your man. But trust me, love works in its own way. People don't trust that sometimes. Just step back and let your hearts figure out what's best."

Tessa shook her head. "Oh, there's no love. We just..."

Linda's brows rose as her grin spread. "I know what you're just doing, and I'm so happy for you. Your mama would love Mr. Carter."

Sliding her fingertip over the condensation on her glass, Tessa tried not to let the burn in her eyes turn into full-fledged tears. There wasn't a doubt in her mind that her mother would love Grant. What wasn't to love?

"You borrow trouble," Linda went on. "Enjoy yourself. You're only young once, honey. Trust me when I say this will all work out."

Tessa reached across the counter and squeezed Linda's hand. "I'm so glad I have you."

"The feeling is mutual. I love you and Cassie like you're my own girls. I'm always here anytime you need me."

"I know you are. That means so much to me." She paused, then added, "But you need to know that whatever you think about Grant and me, you can't repeat it. He could lose this film if anyone finds out."

Linda straightened. "I've seen things, heard things in my years here that would curl the hair on your head. I've kept secrets and will take them to my grave. I won't utter a word about your man."

Tessa wondered what secrets the woman held on to. Secrets made Tessa nervous, but she knew there was no way Linda would budge.

One good thing, at least no one would discover Tessa and Grant's affair. She hoped.

Seventeen

"I hate her already."

Cassie laughed. "That's because she's stunning, rich and nice. Let's tie her up by her perfectly polished toes."

Tessa eyed Lily Beaumont, Southern beauty and female lead, as Bronson and Anthony showed her around the property and pointed out her trailer.

Cassie and Tessa had been trying to work, but they were just as starstruck as everyone else. The film star's beauty and that Southern accent had all the men at Stony Acres ogling the Hollywood sweetheart.

"It's hard to hate someone when they're beautiful and sweet," Tessa sighed. "I really want to, though. I mean, she's not even fat. Is she perfect everywhere?"

"Maybe she has a third nipple."

Cassie laughed at her own joke as Tessa slung her arms over a fence post. If she was honest with herself, it wasn't Lily's beauty that bothered her so much...it was how Grant would react to it.

The man lived in the land of perfection, worked with gorgeous women all the time. And Tessa had seen Lily in movies before, but in person...she was beyond stunning.

"Regardless of our green-eyed monster rearing its ugly head," Cassie said, leaning in next to her on the fence, "Lily is the perfect person to play the younger version of Mom."

Tessa smiled. "She really is. Mom's beauty was flawless,

she had that accent and such delicate mannerisms. Lily may not have to do much acting at all."

"We better get back to work." Her sister patted her arm. "Once our jealousy for her perfect figure and her ability to look beautiful after flying across the country subsides, we'll go introduce ourselves."

Tessa started to turn when she spotted her father coming from the house. "Looks like Dad is already beating us. I wonder what he thinks of her playing Mom."

"He okayed it. That was one stipulation for him agreeing to the film," Cassie informed her. "He wanted to have final say so over who portrayed him and Mom."

Tessa turned her gaze to her sister. "I didn't know that. I'm glad. I think Max and Lily will be perfect."

While Tessa had hated the thought of this film in the beginning, now she was growing more and more anxious to see the finished product. After getting to know Grant, seeing how much care he was taking with her family's legacy and portraying everything just so, she realized this film would be a beautiful tribute to her parents.

Cassie's arm came around to settle on Tessa's shoulders. "This is going to be hard for us. Seeing how Mom and Dad fell in love, married, raised a family…"

"…and when she died," Tessa finished, around the lump in her throat. "Yeah, it will be hard, but I'm sure Dad will need us to be strong. This film is a good thing. Our family has worked hard for where we are, and I'm glad Hollywood took notice of it."

"Speaking of working hard, let's get to it, sis."

Tessa looped her arm around her sister's waist and they turned from the fence, heading back to the stable. As they held on to each other, Tessa knew they'd be doing a lot of leaning on the other for support during this time. As exciting as it was to have Hollywood's hottest actors and producers making this film, the reality was that their family had real emotions and would forever have that void that only Rose Barrington had filled.

Grant hadn't seen Tessa in two days. He'd barely seen her flash by in the ring. He'd put in long nights, sometimes all night, as some scenes needed to be shot late and the lighting with the moon and such had to be exactly right.

He worried that she'd been in her house, in her spacious bed, waiting for him. And as much as he ached to sneak back over there, he hadn't been able to catch a break.

On the mornings when she'd come over to the estate, he'd been heading into the cottage to catch a few hours' sleep before going at it again.

She hadn't approached him, hadn't even glanced his way.

So, being the smart man that he was, he knew she was either trying to hide their relationship, was pissed or was worried about training. He'd venture to say all of the above.

Lily had told him how wonderful the Barrington ladies were and how much Tessa looked like her mother. Grant had merely nodded, because he seriously feared if he opened his mouth and started discussing Tessa with anyone on the set, all his emotions would show.

But a second day of not seeing Tessa was killing him. In two more days the crew was taking a three-day break. It had been scheduled in advance, and Grant knew exactly what he would do with that time off.

He needed to be with Tessa for more than just sex. He needed to show her how important she was to him.

After he made a few calls, he headed back to the pond, where today's sequence would be filmed. A simple picnic with Max and Lily...aka Damon and Rose.

Watching them fall in love through the camera was magical. Everything about this film so far gave him goose bumps, and that rarely happened on the set. Perhaps he was so emotionally involved with the family, he automatically felt a strong bond with the backstory of the characters.

But as he watched on the screen for the first kiss, Grant didn't see Max and Lily, or even Damon and Rose. He saw himself and Tessa.

Had he fallen for her? How the hell did that happen? He'd warned himself not to get in too deep with her, but now that he'd admitted to himself how he felt, he knew more than ever he had a past he needed to face. If he didn't, there would be no chance of a future.

Grant had every intention of settling down, of falling in love. He wanted a marriage like his parents had, like the Barringtons had.

And Tessa might have a list of reasons as to why they didn't belong together, but he was about to show her all the reasons they did.

If Grant wanted to catch Tessa, he knew he'd have to beat her to the stables and talk to her before she started her training. Thankfully, he'd gotten to bed around one in the morning, as opposed to being up all night. After a few hours of sleep, he was ready to talk to her and drop a hint of his surprise.

Grant pulled his barn jacket tighter around his chest as the cool early-morning air sliced through him. As soon as the low-hanging fog wore off, however, the day promised to be beautiful.

The fresh smell of straw and horses hit him before he entered the stable. While he was getting more used to the atmosphere, he still wasn't fully comfortable.

Oliver bobbed his head over the door of his stall, almost as if looking for him. "Hey, buddy," Grant said.

There, talking to the horse was a major step. Touching and, heaven forbid, riding were still off-limits.

He moved farther into the stables, nearly jumping out of his skin when Macduff started causing a ruckus, stamping his hooves and bucking.

That one would need a lot of work and loving care, but he had confidence in Cassie. From what he'd seen of her as a sister, daughter and mother, she was gentle and nurturing. Just what that hellion needed.

As he passed by Macduff, very cautiously, Grant eased over to the other side of the aisle...and tripped. Once he'd regained his footing, he turned back to see what he'd fallen over.

And saw a foot sticking out of the open stall.

Tessa was lying amid the hay, a plaid blanket wrapped around her, straw in her hair and the most peaceful look on her face.

Moving into the stall, Grant squatted down beside the sleeping beauty and pushed a strand of crimson hair from her silky cheek. She stirred, but remained asleep, a small smile lighting up her face.

Even in sleep she stole his breath. Given this reckless manner in which he'd found her, Grant couldn't help but smile himself. Miss In Control At All Times looked as if she'd spent the night rolling around in the stall.

Which conjured up another image, of both of them in the stall. A bit itchy and uncomfortable, but he'd take Tessa any way and anywhere he could. His attraction and need for her knew no bounds.

"Hey, Country." He cupped her shoulder and squeezed. "You're sleeping the day away."

Watching her lids flutter as she came awake only added to that zing in his heart. Damn it. Zing? He was totally gone where she was concerned, if he was thinking of words like *zing*.

But there was nothing about her he didn't find appealing. Now what would she have to say about that, once he decided to tell her how he truly felt?

"Grant." She sat up, smiled and wiped straw and hair from her face. "What are you doing here? Did you work all night again?"

"We wrapped up around one or so." Because he wanted,

needed to touch her, he plucked straw from her flannel shirt. "What are you doing, sleeping with the horses?"

"Keeping an eye on them."

She came to her feet and promptly started folding her blanket. Grant stood as well, crossing his arms over his chest.

"What on earth are you watching them for?" he asked.

"Macduff wasn't acting right, and Nash offered to stay, but I sent him on home."

"Is Macduff okay?"

She stacked the blanket on a tack box in the corner and turned back to offer a smile. "I think he's still adjusting. If he keeps acting off, not eating and being pouty, I'll have Cassie call the vet."

With her hair in disarray, her shirt untucked and rumpled, Grant found himself liking this morning Tessa.

"Oh, no," she said, holding her hands up. "You've got that look."

He stepped forward. "What look is that?"

"You know."

Grant smiled, closing the gap between them. "I do know, but you don't seem to be putting up much of a fight."

Her eyes darted around as she backed into the corner.

"Nowhere to go," he whispered as he reached her. "And we're all alone."

He placed a hand on either side of her face, caging her in between his body and the wall. Her eyes widened and arousal shot through them as she stared back. That unpainted mouth beckoned him…and who was he to refuse.

Softly, slowly, Grant claimed her lips. Tessa's body arched into his as she opened for him. He could completely drown in her love. That may be his ego, and his hope, talking, but Grant had a gut feeling that what they'd formed here was indeed love. He knew she felt it as well, but saying the words aloud needed to come at the right time.

And he couldn't fully give himself until he confronted his family and his past.

He nipped at her lips and lifted his head, pleased to see he swollen mouth and closed lids.

"I had a reason for coming in here," he murmured. "Bu you make me lose my train of thought."

Tessa looked up at him. "You mean preying on a sleepin woman wasn't your goal?"

"No, just an added perk." He rested his hands on her shoul ders, loving the feel of her delicate body beneath them. "I hav a three-day break coming up."

"Really? And I suppose you have plans in mind?"

Did he ever. "We have plans," he corrected. "I've even dis cussed things with Cassie, and she thinks it's a great idea fo you to take some time off."

Tessa broke free of his hold and stepped around him. "Wai a minute. I can't take three days off. I'm training."

He turned to face her, ready to defend his case, because he knew this argument was coming. "You've been training and living in the stables your entire life, Tessa. Let's be honest, all you've done is work. You deserve a break."

With jerky, frantic motions she started pulling her hair back into a low ponytail, then tugged a band from her wrist to secure it.

"I can't just leave. I have a schedule, Slick. I need to stick to it. My horses need to be exercised daily."

"And Cassie has already said she'd be more than happy to do that."

Tessa crossed her arms, chewed on her lip, and Grant knew she was thinking of another reason. Was she worried about spending so much time alone with him? The getaway certainly added a whole new layer to their relationship.

He merely kept his mouth shut and waited, because for every argument she had, he had a response. He would be tak ing her away from here even if he had to throw her over his shoulder and manhandle her out.

"I'm not comfortable leaving Nash, with him being so new."

Grant laughed. "He's your father's employee. I'm sure your

dad has control over his own worker. Besides, he's been here long enough to know what to do for a couple days."

"What about the clause? Now Cassie knows we're..."

Still smiling, Grant shrugged. "She's your sister. I was aware she already knew, and I know she won't tell anybody. I trust her, and I needed someone to help me get all this arranged, anyway."

Tessa sighed, glancing up to the ceiling and shaking her head. "Why am I even considering this?"

Grant eased forward, knowing he had her, but going in for the kill, anyway. "Because you want to." He slipped his arms around her waist and pulled her flush against him. "Because you know you need the break and because you want my body."

"Well, that's a little TMI for this early in the morning."

Both Grant and Tessa turned to see Cassie smiling at them.

"Sorry to interrupt," she said. "Just thought I was coming to work."

Tessa laughed. "Don't mind him. He's got a one-track mind."

Grant's cell chimed from his pocket. Stepping back from Tessa, he pulled it out and sighed. "I have to take this," he told her. "We'll talk later."

As much as he hated leaving without her definite answer, even though he knew she'd go, he had to take the call. Max Ford's agent was on the phone and the man was not known for his patience, so keeping him waiting was not smart.

After Grant stepped outside and took the call, he sent off some texts to Tessa, letting her know when to be ready, when he'd pick her up and what to pack. The packing thing was easy, considering he had that detail planned, as well.

He could hardly wait to wrap up today's shoot, because for the next three glorious days, Tessa Barrington would be his, and she was going to find out just how important she'd become to him.

Eighteen

Seriously?

Tessa eyed the private jet as she stepped from Grant's rental car. "You've got to be kidding me," she said, glaring at him over her shoulder.

"What?" He closed his car door and rounded the hood to take hold of her arm. "We're getting away. How else do you think we'll get there?"

"I assumed we'd drive somewhere, but seeing as how I don't even know where you're taking me, I really hadn't thought about a plane."

Grant chuckled. "If it takes more than a couple hours by car, I always fly."

And in her world she flew as little as possible, seeing as how she loved the open road, loved seeing new places, meeting new people. Most often when she traveled, though, it was with horses and not a powerful, sexy man.

Just another difference between them. His jet practically screamed business mogul. Being showered with luxurious gifts was new...and another reminder of how different they were. Not that her family couldn't afford such things; they just didn't focus on flashy trips or material objects.

Of course, her father had a jet, but Tessa rarely used it. When did she have time to travel other than going from race to race?

"So where are we heading?" she asked as Grant led her toward the steps of the plane.

"I believe you mentioned something about never having a prom."

Tessa halted in her tracks. "I'm almost afraid to ask what you're talking about."

Squeezing her arm, Grant urged her on up. "Consider this the limo to pick you up."

Glancing back over her shoulder as she climbed the steps, Tessa smiled. "I only have this small bag, no room for a formal."

"I've taken care of everything, as any good prom date would."

Tessa's belly did a flip. The man literally thought of everything. But she wondered just what would be waiting for her once they got to…wherever it was they were going.

"Good evening, Miss Barrington," the pilot said as she stepped on board.

She smiled. "Good evening."

Tessa moved inside the luxurious cabin. Behind her, Grant chatted with his pilot for a bit before he joined her. Tessa was still standing in amazement, studying the openness of the plane.

In the far back was an L-shaped sofa, while off to the other side were two club-style chairs and a flat-screen television. Another small seating area was directly in front of her, and there was a door in the back, no doubt leading to a bedroom.

"Wow, this is impressive, Slick." She moved over to the sofa and sank onto the corner cushions. "Now I know why you fly everywhere."

Grant laughed and took a seat in a club chair. "You'll have to come over here to buckle up, babe."

Tessa moved to the other seat and fastened her belt. In no time they were taxiing down the runway and soaring into the sky. She loved watching out the window, loved seeing just how small everything got in seconds.

"How can you drive everywhere, when it's clear from the way your face lights up, looking out the window, that you love to fly?" he asked beside her.

Tessa shrugged, keeping her gaze on the ground below. "I love the adventure of a road trip. In a plane it's all over so fast. Besides, I like to travel with my horse."

Grant reached out, taking her hand in his and stroking his thumb along her palm. Part of her wanted to read more into this trip, but the other part, the realistic part, kept her grounded.

He was just taking her off somewhere so they didn't have to sneak. Being away from the film, away from where the paparazzi were camping out, would be easier. She actually appreciated how much he'd gone through to get them out. He'd talked to Cassie to clear the schedule.

The old Tessa would've been angry at him for going behind her back. But the new Tessa, the one who had fallen for this Hollywood hotshot, was flattered.

"When will you tell me where we're going?" she asked.

Grant shrugged. "It's nothing too exciting. Just a little cabin in the woods in Colorado. I own a good portion of the area, so we'll have complete privacy."

She eyed him, quirking a brow. "Define 'a good portion.'"

"The mountain. I own the entire mountain."

Of course he did. Why buy the house when you can buy the mountain? Silly of her to think differently. Granted, she and her family had money, but they didn't think in terms of mountain buying.

Right now all she wanted to do was enjoy these next three days. Anything that came after that would just have to wait.

For once in her life she wasn't looking at a spreadsheet, wasn't going by a schedule and wasn't worried about training.

Whatever Grant had planned was fine with her, because he'd shown her he was more than capable of making her forget her surroundings. Now she couldn't wait until he showed her again.

And she fully intended to enjoy this little fantasy while it lasted.

* * *

Little cabin?

Tessa laughed as they parked in front of the "cabin."

"I believe you referred to this as little."

Grant nodded. "It is, compared to the home I have in L.A."

She rolled her eyes and exited the car. The two-story log home was built in a rustic style, but with a wide porch stretching across the front and a rather large second-floor balcony with three sets of double doors leading out onto it, Tessa had a feeling this home was easily five thousand square feet.

"Did you have this built?" she asked.

He pulled their two pieces of luggage from the trunk and headed toward the front door. "Yes. I wanted someplace I could escape to between films. I have a condo in Hawaii, but I've always loved the mountains. There's something so peaceful about being up here with the fresh air, the quietness. I rarely get up here, but it's so worth it when I do."

So he liked the country. Okay. Maybe they weren't so different, after all.

Grant unlocked the door and gestured for her to enter ahead of him. If she thought the outside was impressive, the inside was spectacular. The floor plan was completely open, with a large sunken living area. Windows covered the entire back wall and overlooked the city below. *Breathtaking* wasn't the right word to describe it.

"I'd live here if I were you," she told him, making her way to the picturesque windows. "How do you ever leave?"

"Well, when work calls, I have no choice."

Tessa turned back to him and raised a brow. "I'm ready to sell my house and live here. Do you rent rooms out?"

Laughing, Grant crossed the spacious living area and came to stand beside her. "You should see this in the fall when all the leaves have turned. Or in the winter with all the snow. It's almost magical."

Tessa wanted nothing more than to still be around during those seasons, yet realistically, that probably wasn't going to happen. But her imagination was pretty good, and she could practically see the assortment of colors on the trees in September, the pristine white branches in January.

This cabin wasn't just magical, it was romantic.

Tessa turned, slid her arms around Grant's waist and rested her head against his chest. "Thank you so much for bringing me here. Had I known how amazing this was, I wouldn't have argued."

He wrapped his arms around her, stroking her back. "It's okay. I knew you'd see the error of your ways once you arrived."

Tessa swatted his shoulder and laughed.

"You haven't even seen the best part yet," he told her, easing back to look into her eyes. "There's a surprise in the master suite for you."

Tessa couldn't stop her eyes from roaming over his body.

"Not that," he told her with a smile. "I have something for you. You can go look now or later."

"Well, considering it's about nine o'clock, I have a feeling that we'll be otherwise occupied, later...."

He nipped at her jawline, traveled toward her ear. "You do have the best ideas," he whispered against her skin. "But I assure you, there's plenty of time for you to have your way with me."

Tessa couldn't help but laugh again. "You're always so eager to offer your services. But I'm selfish, and I want my surprise."

Grant's cell rang, cutting into the moment. When he groaned, Tessa stepped back, disappointment spreading through her. Of course these three days wouldn't go uninterrupted. He hadn't said he'd stop working, just that they were going to get away.

Well, they were away...with phones.

Could anybody truly get away anymore? There were far too many ways to access someone, and unless there was an emergency, Tessa honestly didn't want to be bothered. Once she'd warmed up to the idea of going away, she'd wanted Grant all to herself with no outside matters interrupting them.

Silly of her to assume that's what he'd want.

Perhaps he wasn't as emotionally invested as she'd first thought.

"Sorry about that," he told her, pulling his phone from his pocket. When he glanced at the screen, he sighed. "I have to take this. The master suite is upstairs, at the end of the hall."

While Tessa was excited to see her present, she would rather do so with him and not have to share his attention with callers.

God, that sounded whiny. He'd taken her away on a private jet, to a cabin and mountain that he freakin' owned, and she was throwing a pity party in her head. Yeah, that was wrong. But she'd truly thought they were on the same page. Truly thought this trip was about taking their relationship to another level.

Apparently, she shouldn't assume.

After her mental lecture, Tessa headed upstairs. The wide hallway led straight toward a giant bed. The entire second floor was a giant master suite.

Seriously, she really wanted to live here. Could all her horses come? A stable would have to be built and...

Tessa shook her head. This was fantasy. She wasn't living here, she was briefly vacationing. After three days she'd be back to reality and Grant would resume his grueling schedule and traveling, as well. They were shooting at the estate, but they also planned on being at the main race, to capture the pure essence of the industry and her father's legacy.

Her cell vibrated in her pocket, but when she pulled it out and saw a text from Aaron, she cringed.

Stop avoiding me. I said I was sorry. I need to see you.

Tessa shoved the phone back into her pocket. As always, she didn't reply, and she certainly wasn't going to start now, when she was ready to enjoy a few days with Grant. No way was Aaron and his persistent texts ruining her weekend. She refused to allow anything to interrupt her and Grant's special getaway.

As she stepped into the massive bedroom, all done up in creams and soft earth tones, she turned, taking in the natural beauty of the exposed beams in the ceiling and on the walls, the wide windows offering more spectacular views of the mountains.

And there, hanging on the closet door, was a large white garment bag with a paper pinned to the front, with her name on it.

As she crossed the room, Tessa's mind ran wild. What on earth could he possibly be thinking?

She unzipped the bag, exposing the most exquisite gown she'd ever seen. Long, strapless, sapphire-blue, of flowing chiffon material... Tessa slid her fingertips over the delicate fabric before taking it from the bag. Did he intend for her to wear this? Obviously, but now?

Why not? The dress was beautiful and the thought of playing dress-up totally appealed to her. When did she ever get out of her riding boots and flannel? Dressing up to her was wearing her riding attire during races, because of the silky material and the bright colors.

Quickly, Tessa shed her clothes, folded them and laid them on the old trunk at the foot of the bed, then donned the gown. The side zipper went up perfectly, almost as if this dress was tailor-made for her.

As she looked in the mirror, she saw that the dress matched her eyes. And with her red hair spilling over her shoulders, for once in her life Tessa felt beautiful.

She swallowed the sting of tears as she reminded herself this was still a fantasy. But she would live it happily these next three days...which would have to last her a lifetime.

Nineteen

Grant had changed into his black dress pants and a black shirt. That was as far as he was willing to go for this prom. Besides, the attire didn't matter, it was the memories.

He'd finished his phone call with his mother and had changed as fast as he could in the downstairs bedroom. His clothes had been packed. He'd called in favors all over the place to get deliveries made to the house on short notice, and he'd paid a hefty price.

Tessa stood at the top of the stairs with her crimson hair floating around her shoulders. The strapless blue dress flowed over her petite frame and made her eyes even more vibrant.

And suddenly the amount he'd spent meant absolutely nothing. He'd double it in a heartbeat to see Tessa looking so stunning, so sexy and so his for the next three days.

"I have no idea what you've got planned," she said as she started her descent. "But I'm in love with this dress."

Grant laughed, holding out his hand to take hers as she reached the base of the steps. "I'm loving how you look in that dress. You can thank Victoria Dane Alexander for that dress."

Tessa's eyes widened. "The famous designer?"

"She's the sister of Anthony Price and Bronson Dane. I called in a favor, and she happened to have several designs on hand for last-minute calls such as mine. She was more than happy to ship this once Cassie informed me of your size."

Tessa's eyes watered. "You must've had this planned, but you asked me just this morning."

Grant shrugged. "I knew I'd get you away from that stable one way or another, even if I had to drag you."

"You're amazing, Grant. I can't believe you just snap your fingers and people do what you want."

He laughed, escorting her toward the patio doors. "It's not quite that easy, but it does help to know the right people, have money and an ambition."

Turning to face her before he led her outside, Grant smoothed his palms over her bare shoulders, down her arms, and grabbed hold of her hands. "Are you ready for prom night?" he asked.

Tessa blinked, her mouth wide, then she smiled. "You're kidding."

"Not at all. It's a shame you never had one, so I re-created it...in a way."

She laughed. "This is by far a step above a high school prom, Slick. You flew me here in a private jet, and we're on a mountain you own. Oh, and you provided a dress from one of the top designers in the world, who happens to be married to a prince. Did I leave anything out?"

He pushed the glass double doors open and led her out onto the wide balcony. "Actually, yes." Thank God the flowers were in place—that hefty tab was worth it, as well. Grant picked up a small bundle of red roses from one of the stone posts. "Your flowers."

"Great, now my mascara is going to run," she said, dabbing at her eyes. "This is why I never wear makeup."

Grant swiped his thumb beneath one leaky eye. "You're beautiful with or without, Tessa."

She held the bundle to her face, closed her eyes and inhaled. When she focused back on him, a radiant smile lit up her entire face.

"Is it pathetic to admit a man has never gotten me flowers before?" she asked. "I mean, I've had flowers presented to me at races, but from a man who..."

He slid his thumb along her jawline. "Who what? Cares for you? Finds you intriguing, mesmerizing, sexy?"

"Yes," she whispered.

Grant cupped her face and nipped at her glossy lips. "You don't know how glad I am to be your first...again."

Tessa's body trembled against his. "You're spoiling me, Slick. I'm not sure I'll be able to let you go once the film is done. I'm loving this fantasy getaway."

He wasn't ready to think that far ahead, wasn't ready to discuss the future and certainly wasn't ready to let her go.

Yes, he wanted her for longer than the filming, but he could make no promises...yet. First he had to fully seduce her. He'd already seduced her body; now it was time to seduce her heart. He also had to return home...soon. Which was what the call from his mom had been about.

"I'm sorry," Tessa told him, shaking her head. "I didn't mean to make you uncomfortable when I said that."

Had she taken his silence as an indicator that he was uncomfortable? She couldn't be further from the truth. But right now was all about her, and he wanted Tessa to see just how much he cared for her. Just how far he'd go to see her smile, to take a break and enjoy life...with him.

Grant stepped away, went over to the outdoor entertainment area and turned on the music. When he glanced back at Tessa, she burst out laughing.

"You're kidding, right?" she asked.

"All the music from tonight is from your senior year," he told her, as a familiar tune filled the night. "What else would play for your prom?"

"Well, at least it's not oldies from *your* prom," she joked.

Grant plucked the flowers from her hands, set them aside on the table and jerked her into his arms. "Now you're fighting dirty. You calling me old?"

She shrugged, sliding her hands up his chest, over his shoulders and into his hair. "Not if you think you can keep up with me."

Grant's body heated as he pulled her flush against him. "Oh, baby, why don't you try to keep up with me?"

"With pleasure."

She pressed closer and opened her mouth to his. Grant splayed his hands across her back, loving the bare skin he encountered, but loving how she shivered in his arms even more. He caused that. He knew just how to hold her, how to kiss her, how to make love to her. There was no other man on earth who could say that.

Grant might have power, but this petite sprite held all the control where he was concerned...and that was even more of a turn-on.

Tessa's breasts pressed against his chest as the upbeat song ended and a slower one began. Still gliding his mouth over hers, he began to sway. Dancing with Tessa wasn't something he'd ever thought of doing before she'd mentioned the prom, but he was so glad he'd come up with this somewhat silly plan.

Any reason to have her in his arms was good enough for him, and if they had to fly a few hours to get away, to make her feel special, it was all worth it.

He was merely laying the groundwork for his future—hopefully, with her.

Tessa eased back, her hands playing with the ends of his hair, her body still pressed against his. "I can't believe you went through all of this for me."

"Why can't you believe it?" he asked.

She shrugged. "Dinner and a movie is one thing. Flying to a private mountain to dance under the stars is another."

"You deserve this and so much more," he told her.

"I hate sneaking because of the film," she told him, going for honesty. "But if this is your idea of being sneaky, I'm completely behind it."

"Stick with me, babe. No one will catch us, and you'll have the time of your life."

"I just..."

Looking into those bright blue eyes, Grant waited, but she

shook her head and rested it against his shoulder. He wanted to know what was on her mind—not just now, but all the time. Hadn't they passed the point of keeping things locked inside? Not that he had any room to judge.

When Tessa shivered against him, he looked down. "I guess I was too busy planning the prom to take into consideration the weather with that dress."

She wrapped her arms around his waist and moved her head to rest against his chest. "You'll have to get creative to keep me warm."

She was killing him. In that dress, with her sexy words and her somewhat still innocent ways, Tessa Barrington was surely going to be the death of him.

But this trip was about laying it all on the line. Coming clean about where he stood with his feelings, what he wanted from her, and finding out what she was willing to sacrifice to be with him.

Could the man be more perfect? How in the world would she ever be able to say goodbye to him, let alone date anyone else?

But she wanted to concentrate on now. Her whole life she'd planned ahead, unable to truly enjoy the moment.

And if there was ever a moment to enjoy, this was it. Standing in Grant's arms, dancing beneath a starry sky while he did his best to re-create an event in her life she'd missed.

Yeah, a little chilly air wasn't going to ruin things for her.

But a part of her knew they were still sneaking—now just on a grander scale.

Obviously, this level of sneaking was meant to impress her...and it did. But it also drove home the point that he was not taking their relationship beyond intimacy of the body—forget intimacy of the heart.

"I'm having a hard time keeping my hands off you," he whispered in her ear. "With your body against mine, the way you look in that dress. I've had you, but I can't stop wanting you."

Tessa smiled into his chest. His raw words shot straight to her heart. She loved this man. Loved him for his passion for life, loved him for the reckless way he made quick decisions, and loved him for the way he maneuvered so much to give her a few days of absolute bliss and peace.

The man was completely unselfish, and right now she held all the power.

No matter what the future held for them—whether as a couple or apart—they were together now. And this was a fantasy night he'd staged just for her.

Mustering up a bit of courage, Tessa took a step back from his arms, reached for the hidden side zipper and eased it down until the dress fell to a puddle at her feet.

Grant's eyes slid down her body, sending even more chills racing over her bare skin.

"I do like an aggressive woman."

That was good, because she liked that look in his eyes. "I always feel beautiful around you. Like I'm the only woman in the world."

Grant reached for her, sliding his hands around her waist and pulling her against him. "You're the only woman in my world."

Before she could question exactly what he meant by that, Tessa was swept into a fantasy come to life as Grant laid her down on the cushioned chaise and made love to her beneath the stars.

Twenty

Tessa rolled over in bed, finding the other side completely empty. Darkness enveloped the room, and she glanced at the clock on the nightstand. Nearly one in the morning.

Where was Grant?

Grabbing the throw that was folded at the bottom of the bed, Tessa wrapped it around herself and padded carefully through the spacious master suite. The double doors on the far wall were cracked, and when she peeked through, she saw Grant standing against the railing, the full moon casting him in a soft glow.

Easing one of the doors open, she made her way out into the cool night, then stopped. What if he wanted to be alone? Maybe he'd come out here to think? Just because they shared a bed didn't mean she had the right to invade his privacy.

She'd barely turned to go back inside when his voice cut through the night.

"Stay."

Tessa froze. When he didn't turn, didn't say anything else, she adjusted the throw around her and walked toward him. Pressing her back to the rail, she settled next to him. But when she looked up at him and saw anguish in those once-sultry eyes, worry consumed her.

"You had another nightmare?" she asked.

Grant's eyes remained fixed on something in the distance, almost as if he was watching whatever nightmare that plagued him unfold. Tessa didn't say another word. He'd told her to stay. Maybe he didn't want to talk, but he obviously didn't want to be alone. That in and of itself was a huge step up from his last nightmare.

"My sister is paralyzed from the waist down because of me."

That statement, in his rough, throaty tone, had Tessa locking her eyes on his, waiting for him to elaborate.

"We used to take riding lessons," he went on, still staring out into the night, as if he was talking to himself. "Melanie loved horses. As a little girl she would wear cowgirl boots with everything, even her nightgown. She loved everything about horses.

"We took lessons, and we were pretty damn good. I ended up quitting because of sports and girls, but Melanie kept at it. I supported her, and she always came to all my games. We were just…there for each other, you know?"

From Tessa's angle she could see moisture gathering in his eyes. Her heart ached for him, for the battle he'd fought with himself and for the demons he'd carried for so long.

"One day I went with her to the barn. We lived in Kentucky and had several acres. Nothing major, but enough for a barn and a couple horses. We'd just graduated the week before, and she would be off to college in the fall for equine studies. I was ready to move to L.A. and hit film school."

Grant gripped the rail, dropped his head forward and sighed. "I ruined her life, Tessa. I made her race me, knowing the horse she was on was new, knowing it was skittish and rebellious.

"My horse spooked hers when I came up behind them, and the thing took off. Melanie started screaming, calling out commands, but the stallion kept going. I can't…I can't get that image out of my brain."

He lifted his head, turned his face toward hers, and Tessa couldn't help but reach for him. She rested a hand on his bare arm and waited for him to go on.

"When I kicked my horse to go faster, that scared hers even more and he bucked. She fell off the back and…"

His eyes closed, as if he was trying to block out the memory. A moment later he drew in a deep breath and focused his gaze back on hers.

"I don't know what I thought I could do, but I just wanted to get up beside her, to help somehow. But I ended up doing so much more harm than good.

"Now you know why I'm so leery at the stables, why I freaked out when you fell. I couldn't live through that again, Tessa."

"What does your sister think of you working on this film?" she asked.

Grant shrugged. "I haven't talked to her since I left for film school. After the accident, she had surgeries and therapy, but the doctors told us the chance of her walking or using her legs again were slim to none. After a couple months, I couldn't handle it anymore. I couldn't look at her because guilt would eat at me. She should hate me, should curse me every day of her life. I stole everything from her, Tessa."

Tessa's heart broke for this man. "Don't you think you hurt her even more by shutting her out? She's your twin, right? I'm sure you two shared a special bond before the accident. You think because she is in a wheelchair that she doesn't love you?"

"She shouldn't."

Grant stepped away and turned his back on Tessa. Oh, hell no. He wasn't shutting her out, too. Not after this revelation. Not when his hurt was threatening to become a wedge between them.

"You're not a one-man show, Grant. You don't need to tackle everything alone. Talk to me. You opened up to me for a reason. Let me help."

He whirled on her, arms flying. "Help? What can you help do, Tessa? I ruined her life. And I'm telling you because I want you to know the real me. The uglier side, the damaged side. I want you to see that I have issues, I have fears, and they all stem from the world you live in. I've been able to keep my distance for the most part, but the more involved with you I get, the more immersed in that world I find myself. I'm terrified. The more I'm with you, the harder it is to keep my emotions under control."

His last two words were whispered, and the weight of his statement crushed her. He was right. Horses, racing, fast speeds were all part of her world...the only world she knew and a world he wanted no part of. And another reason he'd chosen to be so secretive. Coming out in the open about his feelings would only make him force things he just didn't know if he could face.

"Accidents happen, Grant," she assured him. "People can be injured anytime, anywhere. I could be put in a wheelchair by falling down steps or being in a car accident. Don't let that fear control you. Don't you think it's held on to your life long enough?"

"But I caused this accident and the result is crippling." His eyes sought hers as he raked a hand over his messed hair. "I needed you to know. I couldn't keep this inside anymore... not with you."

"Why now? Why let me in now?"

He closed the space between them, lifting his palms against her cheeks and framing her face. "Because I'm falling in love with you, Tessa."

Her heart caught in her throat. "You're... Are you serious?"

A ghost of a smile danced across his face. "I am. But I need you to know why I worry. Your world revolves around this lifestyle that threatens to consume me at times."

"I don't think you'd be as stressed and controlled by this fear if you'd talk to your sister," Tessa told him, reaching up to hold on to his wrists. "What do your parents say?"

"They're always trying to get me to come home. I've been able to avoid it over the years by flying them out to see me. I just don't know that I can face Melanie."

"Maybe we could face her together?"

Grant's eyes widened. "No. I'm not putting this on you."

"You didn't put this on me," she countered with a smile. "Maybe I want to help, because I've fallen in love with you, too."

He nipped at her lips once more. "I know. I knew when you came to my cottage, ready to seduce me. I knew you'd never give yourself to someone you didn't love."

"I did love you then," she admitted. "I had barely admitted it to myself. I actually kept trying to deny it, but there's no fighting such a strong emotion. I never had a clue love could be so all-encompassing."

Worry lines settled between his brows. "How will this work? I mean, I still can't publicly be with you until this film is over. I live in L.A. and you live in Virginia."

Tessa nodded. "There's a lot against us. We'll just have to find a way."

Grant wrapped his arms around her, pulled her close. Inhaling his warm, masculine scent, Tessa tried to relax. They had to make this work. She'd given up too much of herself to accept anything less.

"Don't worry, Tessa," he whispered. "No matter what I have to do, we will find a way."

She clung to the man, the promise, and the hope for their future. Because she'd never fully loved like this before, and this unchartered territory scared her to death.

As much as Tessa hated to have the magical weekend come to an end, she knew it was time for them both to get back to work. After all, the sooner Grant wrapped up the film, the sooner they could go public with their relationship.

She loved that term in regards to what she and Grant had. For the first time in her life, she truly felt she was on the right path with the right man. And she couldn't help but think her mother was smiling down on her with approval. Tessa only wished her mom was here in person to share in their happiness.

"Will we be able to visit your mountain again?" Tessa asked as Grant escorted her to the awaiting car, driven by their one and only accomplice, Cassie.

Tessa had simply told her father she was taking a couple days off to go visit a friend. Damon Barrington was a smart man and more than likely knew what was up, but he didn't say a word.

"Anytime, babe."

"Well, looks like the getaway agreed with you two," Cassie told them. "I'm glad you're back, though."

"Something wrong?" Tessa asked, as Grant put their bags in the trunk.

Her sister's eyes were shielded by her sunglasses, so Tessa couldn't get a feel for what was going on. The wind on the tarmac whipped Cassie's red hair about her shoulders.

"Aaron called me while you were gone."

Tessa froze.

"The ex?" Grant asked, placing his hand on the small of Tessa's back as if to stake his claim.

Cassie nodded, reaching back to control her hair in the strong breeze. "He informed me you've been ignoring his calls. I told him you were busy working, and I may have..."

"What?" Tessa asked.

"I may have said you were seeing someone."

Grant swore, and Tessa groaned. "Oh, Cass."

"Wait," Grant said after a moment. "Did you tell him my name?"

Cassie shook her head. "No. I've not told anybody. I just said that so he'd know you've moved on."

Grant rubbed his hand along Tessa's back. "It's okay, then. As long as he doesn't know who, I'm safe, and hopefully, he'll see she's not available."

Tessa jerked on the car handle. "I wasn't available to that jerk even before you came along, Slick. He had his chance and forgiveness is not an option."

Grant smacked a kiss on her lips. "Hopefully, he's done calling."

While Cassie got into the driver's seat, Tessa settled in the back next to Grant. These were their last few moments of freedom before he headed back to working on the film. He'd still come to her house, but she absolutely couldn't wait to be his, in public, without the sneaking around. Although sneaking did have a certain naughty appeal.

"I want to be able to see all hands at all times back there," Cassie called back as she pulled out onto the main road. "I don't play chauffeur to just anybody."

"We appreciate all you've done," Grant said, draping an arm around Tessa's shoulders.

"I'm just glad my sister is happy."

They chatted about the upcoming race in Louisville and strategy. Tessa couldn't wait to get to the race, couldn't wait to see that blanket of roses draped across Don Pedro. He deserved the win for all his hard work, too.

"I love the Shakespearean names, by the way," Grant interjected at one point.

She caught her sister's eye in the rearview mirror. "Well, we have a little difference of opinion when it comes to their names," Tessa stated. "She's more pessimistic than I am. Mine are Don Pedro and Oliver, but Cassie's newest rescue is Macduff."

From the front seat Cassie laughed. "He may be the hero in *Macbeth,* but he's a killer in the end."

Grant chuckled. "So Tessa is the romantic and you're the more…cynical sister?"

"I prefer to think realistic," Cassie said, throwing a smile over her shoulder.

Tessa knew Cass had had a bad time after her ex left, so she could hardly fault her for being so bitter. Poor Macduff, he'd just have to live with the name.

Cassie dropped Tessa off first, so Grant could properly kiss her goodbye without prying eyes.

"See you in my room tonight," she murmured against his lips.

"Leave the back door unlocked for me," he told her as he pulled her bag from the trunk.

After grabbing the suitcase and waving them off, Tessa drew her keys from her purse and let herself into her house, smiling as she closed the door behind her.

"When you move on, you really move on."

She jerked around, heart pounding, to find Aaron comfortable as you please in her living room, sprawled out on her sofa.

"What are you doing here?" she exclaimed, remaining by the door, trying to order her heart rate to calm. The unexpected visitor had scared her to death.

Rising to his feet, Aaron crossed the floor and narrowed the gap between them. At one time she would've been excited to see him. At one time she'd thought herself in love and ready to accept his ring.

Right now all she felt was anger and a sense of being violated. He'd already tried to use her, and spread rumors of cheating and using illegal drugs for her horses, a fact that was quickly disputed. Did he honestly believe she'd invite him into her home?

"How did you get in here?" she asked.

"I came to see you," he told her, as if this was a perfectly normal visit. "You wouldn't return my texts or calls. Cassie was of no help when I talked to her the other day, and I wasn't able to get away from the city until now. She told me you'd moved on, but I knew once I came back and explained how wrong I was, and how sorry I am for hurting you, you'd see that we belong together."

Tessa laughed, crossing her arms over her chest. "Seeing you only makes me hate you more for how you treated me. How the hell did you get in?"

"The spare key you have hidden outside."

She made a mental note to move the thing the second he

was gone. Never in her wildest dreams would she have thought he'd use it.

"Get out, Aaron," she told him with a sigh. "You wasted your time coming here."

"Because you were locking lips with the famous Grant Carter?"

Damn it. He couldn't know that. Of all people, he would use that against her, for no other reason than spite.

"Anything in my life, personal or otherwise, is absolutely none of your business. Now get out or I'll call the cops and have you arrested for trespassing."

His hand came up and caressed her cheek. Tessa stepped back and swatted it away. "Don't," she told him in her lowest tone.

"I made a mistake, Tessa. I know I used you, I know I hurt you, but I want to make this work."

Resisting the urge to roll her eyes, she shook her head and jerked her front door open. "There is no 'this' to work on. You treated me badly, I dumped you, it's over. Now, I have work to do."

Before she could react, Aaron reached out, wrapped his hand around her arm and jerked her toward his chest.

"You seriously think I'll just walk out of here? We belong together, Tessa."

She was too angry to be scared of his strong grip, of his harsh tone. "Get your hand off me."

"Was I not good enough for the almighty Barrington princess? You claimed you hated city life when I tried to get you to move. What do you think that hotshot will do, huh? Do you think he'll move here and settle in the country with you?"

Tessa said nothing as she tried to break his strong grasp.

"He has a reputation, you know," Aaron went on. "He's a player, Tessa."

"At least he doesn't manhandle me."

Aaron gave her arm a good squeeze as he shoved her away. "You'll regret leaving me. That's a promise."

When he walked out the door, Tessa's level of fear spiked. She didn't take well to threats, especially just before her biggest season.

What had he wanted from her? Did he not get the message the first time, when she'd told him she never wanted to see him again?

He'd been with her for her family's name, for their wealth. She'd been gullible once, and she sure as hell wasn't going to be that way again.

No matter what Grant's reputation was in the past, Tessa knew better now. He'd told her he loved her, and she fully believed him.

Rubbing the tender skin on her arm, where bruises were already forming, Tessa closed the front door and locked it. A car flashed by the side window and sped down her driveway. Obviously, he'd parked behind the garage, where she couldn't see it. Jerk.

Nothing could get in the way of her racing season or her new relationship with Grant.

But he needed to know about this unexpected visit. If Aaron let this secret slip, it could destroy Grant's future, damage his career.

She needed to focus solely on the race, but right now she had to shift focus to Grant and keeping him safe.

Twenty-One

Grant turned the knob on the back door, surprised to find it locked. He knew it was later than usual, but he'd promised he'd come over. Had she gone to bed? Surely she wouldn't just forget.

Just as he was pulling his cell phone out to call her, Tessa flipped on the kitchen light and came rushing to the door to unlock it.

"Sorry. I was trying to watch for you, but with your black ninja gear it was kind of hard to see."

"I assumed it would be unlocked," he told her as he came in and shut the door behind him.

"I prefer it to stay locked while the movie is being filmed. Never know what crazies will go traipsing around."

When she crossed her arms over her chest and glanced around the room, Grant stepped forward. "Hey, what's wrong?"

Meeting his gaze and attempting—and failing—to smile, she shrugged. "Just trying to stay cautious."

He rested his hands on her slender shoulders. "I live in a land where people get paid to lie. You, my darling, are terrible at it. Now, what's going on?"

"Aaron was inside my house when Cassie dropped me off."

"What? Why didn't you call me right then?"

Tessa shrugged. "Honestly, I was trying to figure out how to protect you. I didn't want you rushing over here. What if he stayed behind? What if he was waiting for you? He could've snapped pictures and held them over you for blackmail, or he could've started an altercation. I couldn't chance it."

"I don't give a damn about me, Tessa. You're obviously shaken up. I should've been here." Rage boiled within Grant a some bastard who thought it was okay to toy with her. "Wha the hell was he doing in your house?"

"He apparently used the hidden key, which I have sinc removed."

She stepped away from Grant and started toward the livin room. After turning on the lamp on the end table, she too a seat in the corner of the floral sofa. When she crossed he arms around her waist and stared up at him, Grant settled di rectly in front of her on the squat coffee table.

"What did he say?" he asked, trying to keep his ange under control, when in reality he was ready to punch thi Aaron jerk in the face.

"Just that he wanted me back, that he made a mistake." Tessa's eyes met his. "He also saw us kissing."

Grant cursed, raking a hand over his head. "Well, we can' change that now. If he says anything we can just call him jealous ex who didn't like a Hollywood type staying here."

"I'm sorry," she told him. "I don't want to come betwee you and this film. I just wanted to make sure he was gone and I knew you'd be discreet coming out tonight."

Grant reached for her hands. "Nothing will come betwee me and the film...or me and you."

He would go to Bronson and Anthony and just explain he decided. At this point, he needed to tell them, because h was falling deeper and deeper in love with Tessa and couldn' avoid the truth any longer.

Besides, he wanted to stop hiding. It wasn't fair to the re lationship they'd developed, and it wasn't fair to her. Wha they had was special and couldn't be kept behind closed doors

Glancing down at their joined hands, Grant zeroed in o the bruises on her forearm.

"What the hell is this?" he asked, gently stroking her skin. His eyes came back up to hers. "Tessa?"

"Aaron was pretty upset when I refused him and demanded he leave. Nothing I couldn't take care of."

Grant came to his feet. "He assaulted you."

Tessa leaned her head back on the sofa and laughed. Actually laughed, while he was fuming with rage.

"He didn't assault me," she corrected. "He grabbed me, I threatened to call the cops, he left. End of story."

"This is not something to blow off." Grant sank onto the cushion next to her. With a sigh, he reached up to stroke her cheek. "Why do I find your independence so appealing?"

Shrugging, she smiled and nestled her face against his palm. "Same reason I find your arrogance and white knight routine appealing."

"I wish you would've called me. I'd gladly accept an altercation and an opportunity to punch him in his face."

"I was fine. Besides, you'd just been here and I knew you needed to talk to Bronson and Anthony about the film. You coming right back would only confirm Aaron's allegations. Right now he has no proof and just sounds like a jealous ex."

"Nothing is more important than you, Tessa." Grant cupped his other hand over her cheek and forced her to look him in the eye. "Nothing."

"I'm fine," she repeated.

"I hate seeing you hurt, knowing some bastard put his hands on you."

"He's not coming back, and if he tries to blackmail me, we'll face this together."

Grant shook his head. "Yes, we will. But I worry—"

She placed a fingertip over his lips as her gaze held his. Their conversation from a few nights ago kept replaying in his mind, and she knew exactly what he was thinking.

"Slick, you can't keep me down. I know you are scared of the horses, I know me riding them bothers you, but it's who I am. I might get hurt, but I'll get over it and move on. And I

hope I do all of that with you." Her other hand slid up his chest
and around his neck. "Now are we going to talk all night or
are you going to take me to bed?"

Grant laughed. "I've created a monster."

"And you love every minute of it."

True. He did. But if he ever got a hold of this Aaron jerk
he'd pummel his face for the marks he'd put on Tessa. No
man should ever lay his hands on a woman in such a manner.

And Grant might just have to look the guy up to remind
him of that.

The Kentucky Derby was the most prestigious horse race
known to man—and there was so much more to it than oversize hats and mint juleps. The buildup, the anticipation, the
glamour all centered around a few short moments on the track
and a lifetime of praise for one lucky winner.

And Tessa was going to be that winner. She'd trained her
whole life for this. Waited to follow in her father's footsteps,
knowing she'd be the first female jockey to win.

Nerves danced in her belly. She knew Grant and his crew
were here taping, but she didn't have time to worry about their
job...she had her own job to do.

Once the race was over, she'd see Grant—hopefully in the
winner's circle. So far Aaron had kept away, and hopefully
he would stay that way. Right now, she didn't have space in
her mind for him.

"You've got this," Cassie said, holding on to the lead line
and taking Don Pedro toward the gates. "It's a beautiful day
for a race."

Tessa glanced over to the beautiful women in their delicate, colorful hats, the men in pale suits. The laughter, the
drinking, the betting—she loved the whole ambience. There
was something magical about the Derby and she wanted to
take a piece of that magic home with her—the same way her
father had done.

"I'm proud of my girls." Damon walked on the other side

of the horse and escorted them to the gate. "Both of you have done me proud no matter how today turns out. Your mother would be proud, too."

Tessa didn't want to get choked up, didn't want to even think of the fact that her mother wasn't here to share in this monumental moment.

Eyes straight ahead, Tessa focused on the beauty of the sunshine, the soft gentle breeze. Seriously, the day couldn't be more perfect.

As she lined up amid the other jockeys, she didn't speak and barely threw a smile to those on either side of her. While the horse racing industry was a close-knit community, Tessa had never been one to be too chummy just before a race. Everyone had their own little quirks, and hers was that she got into the zone by focusing and having chitchats with herself in peace and quiet.

The crowd cheered, creating a roar over the entire track. Nothing mattered but the end.

Tessa gripped the reins with one hand and reached down to pat Don Pedro with the other. It was showtime.

Tessa and Don Pedro were immediately swallowed up by press, cameras and family in the winner's circle. Grant wanted to go to her, tell her that he'd decided to come clean with Bronson and Anthony. He wanted her to know that she came first in his life.

But he remained where he was near the grandstands. He wanted to talk to her in private, wanted to be able to have her undivided attention and let her know that she was the most important part of his life.

He also wanted to get to Bronson and Anthony soon, because he didn't want them hearing it from an outside source.

No way in hell would he let Aaron get any pleasure from grade-school-level tattling.

Grant hated lying, and he thought for sure Anthony and Bronson would understand. But they'd have to tell Marty, and he wasn't so understanding.

Hours later, when Tessa was back in her Louisville home, because most jockeys and owners kept a place in the area, Grant knocked on her door, ready to come clean, to tell her what he'd decided. Excitement and nervousness flooded him.

When she opened her door, her red hair was down, free from the tight bun she'd had it in while racing. Her face was void of any makeup and she'd put on an oversize denim shirt and black leggings.

"Grant." She crossed her arms over her chest. "I thought I would've seen you after the race."

Yeah, he knew she'd be upset about that, but he honestly couldn't go to her just then. He'd needed to be alone with her, to tell her what had transpired while she'd been fulfilling her dreams. He had some dreams of his own...and every single one of them included her.

"I couldn't get down to you." Mentally, he hadn't been able to, he added silently as he stepped over the threshold. "We need to talk."

Her eyes widened, but she nodded as she moved toward the open living room. When she picked up a large bag of ice and eased down onto the sofa, Grant eyed her.

"What happened?"

She lifted her shirt and shifted the ice pack beneath it, wincing as she did. "I was careless."

That sliver of fear slid through him, gliding right over the excitement he'd felt only seconds ago.

"What happened?" he repeated.

Settling back against the cushions, Tessa closed her eyes and sighed. "We were in the barns, and Nash was brushing Don Pedro. I stepped behind another horse and got kicked. Rookie mistake, but my mind was elsewhere."

Grant rested his hip on the edge of the couch and started unbuttoning her shirt from the bottom. "Let me see."

"It's not a big deal, Grant."

Ignoring her protest, he got four buttons undone and slid the material aside before removing the ice pack.

The giant bruise covered her entire side, and it sickened him to see her delicate skin so marred. But so much more could've happened to her. There was no guarantee that because she was a professional she was exempt from injuries.

"Tell me you went to the hospital to have this checked out," he exclaimed, eyeing her.

"Gee, thanks for the congratulations on my win, Slick."

He met her gaze, knowing her victory was the most important moment of her life so far. "I've never been more proud. We got some good shots of you, by the way."

"Really?" she asked, her smile beaming. "That's awesome."

"Now, please tell me you had this looked at."

Rolling her eyes, she nodded. "The on-site doctor actually had a portable X-ray machine. I have two cracked ribs, but I'm fine."

Cracked ribs? The countless possibilities of what could've happened filled his mind and made his stomach clench.

"Fine?" Grant sighed, gently replacing the ice and leaving her shirt undone. "This isn't fine, Tessa. That careless mistake could've cost you more than just a few cracked ribs."

Brows drawn together, she stared up at him. "What is wrong with you? I said I'm fine. They will heal."

He got to his feet, paced the spacious living area, trying to find the words. He'd had his mind made up when he'd come. He was ready to drop the film for her, ready to give this a try, but how could he when she reminded him of that painful time in his past? How could he be with her knowing she lived the life that had crippled his sister and held a choke hold on him, as well?

Damn it. He hated how quickly he could be reduced to

being so vulnerable where Tessa was concerned. Tears burned his eyes and he gave himself a minute before he spoke.

"I can't do this anymore," he whispered as he turned back to look at her. "*We* can't do this anymore."

She tried to straighten up, but cried out in pain and held her side. "Don't do this to me."

When he started to step forward to help her, she shot daggers at him with her eyes, so he stopped. "Don't...not if you're ending things."

"I can't handle this, seeing you hurt, knowing at any time you could be paralyzed, too."

"We've been over this," she cried. "I thought we'd moved past all of this fear you had. Did you even call your sister like I asked you to?"

Grant shook his head, cursing the tears still threatening to consume him. "I will. I swear. I'm just... I can't go all-in yet with you. I love you, but..."

With careful movements, Tessa rose to her feet and clutched her shirt around her torso. "You're a coward, Grant Carter. You can't take on a relationship with me until you tackle the relationship with your sister. And I don't want a man in my life who can't live with me the way I am."

Grant didn't blame her for being angry, Hell, he was angry with himself. This wasn't what he'd planned to tell her when he arrived, but once he'd seen her hurt, that torrent of fear had rushed through him again and he realized he couldn't live his life always worried.

Tears gathered in Tessa's eyes, but she lifted her chin and narrowed her gaze. "You have no idea what I would give up for you. I'd give up everything this second if I knew you were ready, because I believe in us. I believe in you. But you have to face Melanie."

Grant stepped forward, stopping when she held up her hand. "No. I don't want to hear it. You obviously already made your choice."

Swallowing back emotions, he shoved his hands into his

pockets. "I can't be anything to you with how my life is right now, Tessa."

"You can't be anything to me until you decide that what we have is more powerful than your fear."

She turned to walk from the room, throwing a glance over her shoulder. "Lock the door on your way out."

And she was gone. The hurt in her voice, the unshed tears… he'd caused all that.

It was time to talk to Melanie, put this nightmare from his past to rest one way or another.

He'd lost his sister years ago, and now he'd lost the woman he loved and wanted to spend his life with.

Tessa was right. He'd been a coward, but no more. It was time to face those demons that had chased away everything good in his life.

Twenty-Two

He'd come too far to back out now. And after years of avoiding this confrontation, Grant knew there was nowhere else to hide. He'd tried traveling, he'd tried drowning himself in work and he'd tried avoiding the topic altogether.

But the fact of the matter remained that years of fear and nightmares had led him right back to where he'd begun, in a small town in Kentucky. And now he stood on the stoop of his sister's small, one-story cottage.

His parents knew he was in town, but he'd assured them he wanted to talk to Melanie alone. God, how he wished Tessa were with him now. She was so courageous, so strong. He needed to draw from that strength. But she was in his heart, and she'd made him face this moment, made him realize that nothing in his life would truly be right, and that he couldn't move on without finally letting go of the guilt.

And there was only one way to do that. First, he'd settle his past, then he'd try to win back his future.

Before he could press his finger to the bell, the wide front door opened and Grant's whole world stilled.

"Were you going to knock or had you changed your mind?"

Melanie sat in her wheelchair, her long dark hair spilling over one shoulder, her legs so thin. But it was her face that shocked him the most. She was smiling…at him.

"Grant?" Her eyes sought his. "Are you coming in?"

Swallowing, he merely nodded. God, what an idiot. He

couldn't even speak as he stepped over the threshold. She'd eased back, and once he was in she closed the door.

He took in the open floor plan, the spacious layout and sparse furniture. Perfect for getting around in a wheelchair.

"Dad told me you were coming," she said, her voice sounding just as unsure as he felt. "Do you want to come into the living room?"

When he turned to look at her, damned if his whole heart didn't clench. That questioning expression on her face only added to the guilt he felt, the shame he was here to finally admit.

"If my being here is too hard, I'll go." He shoved his hands into his pockets, waiting to follow her lead. The last thing he wanted was to make her even more uncomfortable. "I just... God, Mel..."

She bit her lower lip and nodded. "I want you to stay. I miss my baby brother."

The childhood joke had him smiling. "You're only older by twelve minutes."

Shrugging, she wheeled past him and into the living room. Following her, he ran through his head all he wanted to say. As if years of torment and grief could be summed up in a few moments. As if any words would rectify this situation he'd caused.

When she stopped next to the couch, he took a seat beside her. He'd barely settled when she reached over and grasped his hand.

And just like that, something inside him burst. Emotions over a decade old poured out of him, and he wasn't the least bit ashamed that he sat there crying like a baby.

"Mel, I can't even begin..."

He held her hand to his mouth, pressed a kiss on her knuckles. Tears streamed from his eyes as she brought her other hand up and cupped his cheek.

"Grant, it's okay. I'm fine."

She was coming to his defense, trying to minimize the severity of this situation, this life he'd caused her. Hell no.

"Don't," he told her, gripping both her hands in his as he wiped his damp face on his shoulder. "Don't defend me. I deserve nothing but anger from you. I honestly can't take it if you're going to pretend life is just fine. I stole everything from you, Mel. I robbed your life of all the dreams you had."

She shook her head and offered him that sweet smile he'd sworn he'd never see again. "You stole absolutely nothing. I had a rough time at first, obviously adjusting, but I love my life, Grant. Do I wish I could walk? Of course, but I'm doing so much with my life, I can't be sorry I'm in this wheelchair."

Grant slid off the couch, crouched down at her feet, still clutching her hands. "I want to fix this. I'm used to getting what I want, used to having all I wish for. But I can't undo this, Mel. It eats at me. I've struggled with what I've done, struggled with losing you. But every time I think of all that, I realize what you lost."

Tears welled up in her eyes. "Being in a wheelchair is nothing compared to losing my brother. Nothing, Grant. I never blamed you. I ached for you, for the guilt I knew you'd taken upon yourself, for the fear that made you run."

He dropped his head to their joined hands. "I'm done running, Mel. I don't deserve to be asking to be part of your life again, but I want to be. Is there any way we can try? Is there anything I can do?

He closed his eyes, silently pleading for her to love him, though he deserved to be kicked out of her home, her life.

Instead of harsh words, she kissed the top of his head. "I've waited years for you to come back to me."

Lifting his gaze to hers, Grant felt the weight of guilt and crippling fear ease from his body. "I love you, Melanie."

"I know you do," she told him with that sweet smile. "And if you ever run from me again, I'll hunt you down."

Laughing, Grant came to his feet, kissed her hands and sat back on the couch.

"Now, tell me about this film you're working on." She held up a palm before he could say anything. "But first, tell me about the woman. I know there's a woman involved, or you wouldn't have stayed on the set this long, with all the horses there."

Laughing, Grant began to explain Tessa, explain how he'd messed things up with her, but planned on making them right.

"Sounds like someone I'd love to meet."

"I can't wait for you to meet her," he told his twin. "You'll love her."

As he started to explain the film, Melanie's eyes welled up with tears, but she smiled the entire time. And Grant knew he'd won back a place in his sister's heart. Of course, he had a feeling she'd been holding his spot for a long time.

In the days since coming back to Stony Ridge, Tessa hadn't seen Grant. Hadn't seen movement around his cottage, hadn't seen that flashy sports car…nothing.

She should've known when he hadn't come down to the winner's circle after the biggest race of her life that his priorities were film first, her second.

The hurt sliced deep, but there wasn't much she could do about it. No way could she fight against the heavy weight that lived inside Grant's heart.

Trying to focus on her life without him, she shoved her hair over her shoulders and headed toward the main house.

The scene today would be shot in the living room, so Tessa made a point to get there early so she could talk to Bronson or Anthony. Not that she cared where Grant was; she was just curious. That's all.

As she entered the back door, Linda was taking freshly baked bread from the oven. Tessa inhaled the tantalizing aroma. "You could tempt a saint with your baking," she told her.

"I keep thinking that man of yours will come in, but I haven't seen him since before you all left for the derby."

Tessa shrugged. No way was she commenting on the "mar of yours" part, or the fact that he'd been absent around here.

"Has Bronson or Anthony come through yet?"

"I believe Damon was talking with Bronson in the living room. They've arranged all the furniture and even brought in some new pieces for the shoot today."

Tessa had to admit this was pretty cool. As much as she'd hated the film at the beginning of the process, she kind of liked the crew that had been here.

"Care for some bread? Better get it before the guys come in," Linda told her, setting the bread on the cooling rack. "I swear, this bunch likes to eat. Makes me so happy."

Tessa laughed. "Maybe later. I really need to speak to someone first."

Sure enough, Bronson was in the living room, but her father was nowhere in sight. Perfect. She certainly didn't want to discuss Grant around her dad.

"Bronson," she said, stepping over the lighting cords. "Do you have a minute?"

He turned from setting up a camera and offered her a killer smile. "Of course. What can I do for you?"

"Is Grant going to be on set today?"

Yeah, just come out and ask. No leading into that. She may as well stamp Pathetic on her forehead.

Bronson's brows drew together. "You hadn't heard?"

"What?" she asked, fearful of what was coming next.

"I assumed everyone knew, but Grant quit."

Tessa's breath caught in her throat. "Quit? How can he quit?"

With a sigh, Bronson rested his hands on his hips. "I really hate getting in the middle of things, but I work with celebrities, so that's virtually impossible. Grant resigned his position because of the clause he violated."

Tessa's mind ran all over the place. They knew about her and Grant? Was he forced to quit?

"I can't say that I blame him," Bronson went on. "He's in ove with you, you know."

Tessa nodded. "I know, but we aren't together anymore. n Louisville we…"

"That's strange." Bronson rested a hip on the edge of the new prop sofa. "He came back the day after the race, spoke with me and Anthony, got Marty Russo on the phone and re-signed, stating he'd violated the conduct code."

"You mean, you didn't hear it from someone else?" she asked.

"Actually, I already had an idea something was going on between the two of you. Someone named Aaron Souders left a message with my assistant, stating he had some news about Grant he was going to take to the press, but Grant is the one who told me."

Tessa rested her hand on the end table, trying to take in Grant's actions. What was he doing, giving up all his dreams like this? How could he just drop the one movie he'd been waiting to make?

"Marty was pretty disappointed, especially with Grant so close to getting his own production company."

Tessa jerked her attention to Bronson. "His own company?"

The producer's dark eyes widened. "I see you didn't know about that. Grant was offered his own company under Russo Entertainment once this film wrapped up. I'm not sure if Marty will still offer that to him now that he's quit."

Tessa wrapped her arms around her waist. Questions, nerves, confusion all consumed her.

"Where's Grant now?"

Bronson shrugged. "He mentioned going home, said he had a past to face. After that I don't know where's he's going. I do know that Anthony and I are meeting with Marty, though. There's no way we can't stand up for Grant, when he's the best guy we've ever worked with on set and we need him."

Facing his past? Her heart clenched. Could he truly be ready to work through the nightmares and move forward?

"But what about the clause?" she asked.

Bronson smiled. "I'm pretty sure that was for the old, care free Grant. The new Grant has eyes for only one woman now."

Tessa had an idea, but she needed help, and Bronson was just the man for the job. If Grant was strong enough to put his heart on the line and go home, then she was certainly strong enough to put her own heart on the line and go after her future

"Call Grant," she told him.

Grant couldn't believe he was back on the set. So much had happened in the past two weeks. He'd spent a good portion of that time with his sister and his parents, falling back into old patterns and reconnecting those bonds he'd thought for sure he'd severed. But they'd welcomed him with open arms and he promised to bring Tessa once racing season was over

But then he was doubly shocked when Marty called and asked him to return to the set. Apparently, Bronson and An thony had come to his defense and informed Marty that Grant was in love with the woman he "broke the clause" with, and now Grant was needed back at Stony Ridge.

But being there was hard. Everywhere he looked he saw Tessa. Glancing at the stables, he could practically see her stalking through with her tattered boots and hip-hugging jeans. At his cottage he saw her when she'd spent the night all virginal in his T-shirt, her hair spilling over her shoulders

Today, though, would be a true test of his will. They were shooting at the cabin on the back of the property, and Bronson had asked Grant to get there early to help set up the lighting

Sure. No problem.

He'd planned on going to her now that he was back, but he'd wanted to do it in his own time. He had hoped for something more romantic than a scene with everyone standing around as spectators to the life he'd derailed, and was desperately trying to get back on track.

Grant headed out there on foot, needing the time to think Of course, during his walk he thought back to the thunderstorm, when he and Tessa had come here…and she'd given herself to him for the first time.

Man, he missed her. He had to figure out a damn good way to let her know just how much he truly loved her, because he'd totally botched things up back in Louisville.

He remembered that the key was hidden above the lintel, but when he glanced up, he found the door already open a tad. Easing the creaking panel wider, Grant stopped in the doorway and stared at the most beautiful sight.

"I was hoping you'd show."

Tessa sat on the chaise where they'd made love. She was wearing the gown he'd purchased for her when they'd gone to Colorado, and she had the most beautiful smile on her face.

Realization dawned on him. "We're not filming here today."

"No, you're not."

Grant eased on in, closing the door behind him.

"I was going to make you grovel," she stated as she crossed one slender leg, shifting the side split of the dress to reveal skin all the way up to her hip. "But then I realized you'd already been through a lot, and so have I, and I'm done playing games."

He laughed. "And you're taking charge again."

"Of course. First, I know you went to see Melanie. How did that go?"

Grant slid his hands into his pockets, resisting the urge to cross the room, rip that dress off her and worry about talking later.

"Better than I'd ever hoped. She's amazing, and I cannot wait for you to meet her. She's come so far and actually works on a horse farm for handicapped children."

Tessa's smile widened. "I'm so happy you went to see her. I'm really proud of you. But now I want to move on to the nonsense of you quitting over the clause."

Grant shrugged. "I figured Aaron would no doubt tattle, so I beat him to the punch. I'm man enough to stand up for what I want, and admit when I do something wrong."

"And what do you want?" she asked, coming to her feet.

His heart picked up its pace as she crossed the small room. "I want everything."

"This film?"

"Yes."

She ran her hand up over his chest. "The production company you didn't tell me about?"

He swallowed. "Yes."

Her lips hovered just under his. "Me?" she whispered.

"God, yes."

No more playing around. Grant snaked his arm around her waist and closed the narrow gap between them as he slammed his mouth down onto hers.

That taste, that touch, the soft sighs...he'd missed them all. He'd ached for them while he and Tessa had been apart.

She wound her arms around his shoulders and flattened her chest against his. All too soon she lifted her head.

"Bronson claims if we marry the clause is void."

Grant smiled. "Is that so? And here I'd planned on asking you to marry me without even knowing about that little loophole."

Tessa stepped back, went over to the old end table and picked up a sheet of paper. "Actually, I have everything spelled out right here."

Looking down at all the colors and bold lettering, Grant laughed. "Another spreadsheet?"

"This one is much more enjoyable than the last one I gave you."

His eyes scanned the days, the hours. "You have me in all the slots, Country."

"That's right, Slick. You're all mine. So don't ever, ever think of leaving me again, because you know how I hate to redo my spreadsheets."

He tossed the paper aside, sending it fluttering to the floor. "You know what I hate? That fact that you have on too many clothes."

Yanking the side zipper, Grant helped her peel out of the dress, leaving her clad in absolutely nothing but a smile.

"So it looks like we need to marry so I can keep my job," he told her as he ran his hands up over her curves.

"I'll do anything to keep your reputation and career intact."

Smiling, he picked her up and laid her on the chaise. "I may also need to marry you because these last two weeks were pure hell, and I love you more than any film or any production company."

Delicate fingertips came up to trace his cheek. "I'm glad you were miserable, because you deserved it. Now you deserve to be rewarded for your good behavior."

Grant laughed as he started shedding his clothes. "I do love a woman in charge."

* * * * *

A sneaky peek at next month...

Desire™

PASSIONATE AND DRAMATIC LOVE STORIES

My wish list for next month's titles...

In stores from 18th July 2014:

2 stories in each book - only £5.49!

☐ The Fiancée Caper – Maureen Child

& Matched to a Prince – Kat Cantrell

☐ Taming the Takeover Tycoon – Robyn Grady

& Redeeming the CEO Cowboy – Charlene Sands

☐ The Nanny Proposition – Rachel Bailey

& A Bride's Tangled Vows – Dani Wade

Available at WHSmith, Tesco, Asda, Eason, Amazon and Apple

Just can't wait?

Visit us Online

You can buy our books online a month before they hit the shops! **www.millsandboon.co.uk**

Special Offers

Every month we put together collections and longer reads written by your favourite authors.

Here are some of next month's highlights— and don't miss our fabulous discount online!

On sale 18th July

On sale 18th July

On sale 18th July

Save 20%
on all Special Releases

The World of Mills & Boon

There's a Mills & Boon® series that's perfect for you! There are ten different series to choose from and new titles every month, so whether you're looking for glamorous seduction, Regency rakes, homespun heroes or sizzling erotica, we'll give you plenty of inspiration for your next read.

By Request
Relive the romance with the best of the best
12 stories every month

Cherish™
Experience the ultimate rush of falling in love.
12 new stories every month

INTRIGUE...
A seductive combination of danger and desire...
7 new stories every month

Desire™
Passionate and dramatic love stories
6 new stories every month

nocturne™
An exhilarating underworld of dark desires
3 new stories every month

For exclusive member offers go to
millsandboon.co.uk/subscribe